MARKING TIME

Also by E.A. Markham

POETRY
Human Rites (Anvil, 1984)
Lambchops in Papua New Guinea (IPNGS, 1985)
Living in Disguise (Anvil, 1986)
Towards the End of a Century (Anvil, 1989)
Letter from Ulster & The Hugo Poems (Littlewood Arc, 1993)
Misapprehensions (Anvil, 1995)

STORIES
Something Unusual (Ambit Books, 1986)
Ten Stories (Pavic, 1994)

TRAVEL
A Papua New Guinea Sojourn (Carcanet, 1998)

EDITOR
Merely a Matter of Colour
with Arnold Kingston (Q Books, 1973)
Hugo Versus Montserrat
with Howard A. Fergus (Linda Lee Books, 1989)
Hinterland: The Bloodaxe Book of West Indian Poetry
(Bloodaxe, 1989)
The Penguin Book of Caribbean Short Stories
(Penguin, 1996)

MARKING TIME

E.A. MARKHAM

PEEPAL TREE

First published in Great Britain in 1999
Peepal Tree Press Ltd
17 King's Avenue
Leeds LS6 1QS
England

ISBN 1 900715 29 5

This book is dedicated to friends, some of whose portraits appear without, I hope, discourtesy. It's dedicated particularly to Don and Christiane Runghen in whose house in Vacoas, Mauritius, the first complete revision, in 1996, took place. Grateful thanks to Don, who made facilities at St. Andrew's School, Rose-Hill – of which he is Rector – available; and thanks to Meena Ah-Fo and especially Michèle Veerapen of the school, who put *Marking Time* on disc.

Grateful appreciation to the colleagues at Sheffield Hallam University who have read the manuscript and, tactfully, chosen not to recognise themselves in this work of fiction.

PART ONE

1

1996. Early in January. Tuesday

Percentages out of 100. The % is God. I cross out 61 and pencil in 59, question mark: this, I tell them, is how I empathise with Maurice whom I saw being taken away by strange-looking men in white coats. OK, that was a play, but it's based on someone. Let's start again: *Fifty-nine* or *Sixty-one*, fine-tuning the machine, like listening to the cricket commentary from Australia on, what is it now? long wave, making sure not to miss the fall of an England wicket because of the static; you get my meaning. I'm marking papers, the students can't see me; there's some distraction (off), on the radio; it's in the next room, but somehow you can always tell, something discordant, change of tone or pitch or something, so I drift in — it's in the kitchen — and hover. Yes, it's a murder. Young boy, old woman. Near here, too. A combination that vaguely drives you into the fascist camp. Ah well, back to work.

I had a friend who used to enjoy this job, the marking, the sense of power; a sad man but no sadder than anyone else. He's thriving now in the Arts industry somewhere. Quite early on he changed his name to that of a district in London, gaining gravitas, the sort of weight that comes with traffic-lights and zip-codes and late-night disturbance on the streets. He never lived, as far as I know, in the district whose name he bore, so we must mark him up for style, if nothing else. Like me he worked in Cultural Studies in a new university and that's why, in a sense, he is my enemy: that's one reason I like to think I mark *differently* from him.

It's cold and damp here in Sheffield; my friend Balham's well out of it. Back to work. Problem with teaching creative writing is that you've got to *mark* the stuff: attempts at wit in that first story seem somehow not to warrant the benefit of the doubt; it was always a bit strenuous, trying too hard to be cool, to be on top of it; a sort of knowingness that you'd slam for being male. Only, this is a woman, and one who'd kept so quiet during the seminars – or perhaps hadn't turned up much – that I don't remember her. So you

get my guilt vote for my not remembering you. But that was last
night. Last night, with the world asleep, I thought: Good for you.
Claim your space; spit it out, wrap your mouth round the bad pun
(What sort of mouth is it, anyway?); sing out of tune if you like. But
now, well now it's daylight, it's morning, and the sort of energy
which impressed me earlier doesn't seem quite so attractive now
I'm fresh. (This is a debate with myself, sorry; it might sound odd
said out loud, as I ponder, as I quibble whether fake energy is
better than no energy. There's a character in a 17th century play
for you: Quibble. A Marston play, perhaps. Quibble or Ramble.
More Marston than Middleton. But back to Natalie: the point is,
is fake energy better than no energy. *A Male thing, My Masters*.
Young boys killing old ladies on the radio. But for a woman who
isn't visible in seminar, who seems to vanish as I speak: is she
young? One of the mature ones coming back?) And really, it's a
sketch, not a story. In the course guide we ask for stories not
sketches; in the seminars we show you the difference; but you
don't show up. Tough titties. Like turning in a thirteen-line sonnet.
This sketch, though, isn't bad, nearly a story; wrong side of the 60
barrier, certainly. Unless 59 is a little high, too, a bit close to the
border.

  Borders should be easy things to cross, but in real life (and what
other form of life is there?) borders are more dangerous. A student
who is cavalier about these matters must understand that for the
marker, the assessor, the tin god sitting here, a border is a
dangerous thing to negotiate: who's watching your back as you
cross? If some sort of barrier is lifted – as between this little
Montenegro and that little Albania – and you come through, do you
pull the other 59s along with you, even though some are clearly on
the wrong edge of 59? How could you be sure about your judgement that one *fiftyninish* matches another *fiftyninish*. Rereading
the lot is out of the question. *Enter Second Marker in White Coat*,
call him Dave, poor bastard. When I saw that lot from the other
university, their mugshots, *The Sheffield Nineteen*, stuck up on a
board just inside the entrance to the English Department, and
heard about violence in the city, I thought: clever bastards to
escape the academy when no one was looking, congenital Second
Markers no more. By now the scholarly strain would have fallen

away from their faces; no longer stranded in the demilitarised zone of an old English Department (we're stuck here in between the Koreas, don't you know) or tiptoeing through land-mines (Is that still Angola: will it ever end?) of MPLA and Savimbi the Ugly, the weak smiles attesting to bravery under fire. When you think of all this – and our own *City Eight* is no improvement (there are 16 of us, but the *City Eight* sounds better, more beleaguered – and you probably wouldn't want to keep company with some of the other eight) – you want to ease up on the second marker, on Dave, and get it right first time.

So why is this student, this woman – I'm going to call her Natalie – causing me grief? (There's an interesting story in Borges. Or it might be a play by Carrington: when in doubt it's safe to cite a Borges story or a play by Carrington, and you won't go far wrong. Anyway, there's this story or play where in order to preserve the character's anonymity, she's given a new name by the author. Only, it turns out later that the new, made-up name is exactly the same as the woman's real name. And the reader, the audience has to play a minor ethics game to see whether fiction is taking unacceptable liberties with life. This comes to mind now only because I've called this student Natalie to protect her identity; and how can I be certain that I'm not thinking of some persistent Natalie who wrote this story for me in the past! That's probably not what I think, but the fact that I'm busily re-imagining this story, making it into something else, even stretching it to a Carrington play, makes me retreat a mark further from the 59. So, a provisional 58.)

Do I look forward to Natalie's two other stories trapped in this folder? There's a world created here, certainly, but a small one, narrow, not large enough to live in (we might have read Beckett together, with profit): trapped in this space you become a strange shape. Or you must break out. My prejudice... Maybe. I admit to prejudice; I say to them, the students, I tell them: I'm prejudiced in favour of good writing, imagination and risk. And they look at me and think: poor bastard; silly old fart; wanker, can he still get it up? Wonder if he has to take his teeth out to clean them? And I say to them (I'm a mind-reader, see!) I say, over-enunciating to show that dentures work – I might even spit a little in their direction – I say: we (royal we) here at City, believe in good writing, believe in imagination and *risk*. Don't think it's enough to elimi-nate the old cliché; we want you to go further (farther, higher). Imagination is good but not enough. Not enough to be cliché-free and stormy with imagination: what do we want? We want clear diction, good syntax and the thing to be well-spelt. (*Fascist*, from their OK milk-whipped faces.)

What? What's that? (Don't you think it costs me as well, to come in here, free of BO; no hint of garlic, no beer-breath; clean shirt, clean pants – you've got on clean pants? – and all that shit...)

Fascist; free-ranged, new-bodied, mouth full of raw teeth, mouth not for kissing. And I sit there thinking: I'm still earning marks for restraint. I mark my own paper and I'm marking me *up* for restraint. See, I'm not even going to shave that bit of wispy, waspy, what-you-call-it-nonsense off that boy/girl-clearly-never-been-kissed-by-a-good-woman-over-40 apology for a face: in the old days I could send you to the Albanian border where there was a barber hanging out. Now, yes, it's all utterly changed, students are loosed upon the world.

But the old loyalty thing comes into play. At dinner in London a few months ago a fellow said to me, a sort of carpenter/joiner, son of a friend, he said: you know when you mark your papers, remember you have a responsibility to me, to those of us not at your university, not at any university. And I take that on board; he's right, it's Natalie against him; so I feel like saying to Natalie: when you give me a sketch instead of a story, it's like being a carpenter, you know, making a table for my dining-room, a table to seat, say, six. You deliver the table and it seats only four. So I say: what am I going to do with my other two guests? And she says: imagine it's a pull-out job (she's cheeky, a tease); imagine that it's got two flaps, and that's where you seat your extra guests. So I say: that's very interesting, Natalie, but where are these flaps, then? And she says don't be so bloody literal; Calvino, whom you love so much, doesn't put flaps on his tables. And I'm pleased she remembers Calvino. And I say, Calvino doesn't have to put flaps on his tables because they're built into his flexi-structure, call it wit. That's why his three-page, French-polish jobs can seat up to a thousand if you put your mind to it and you've got that many friends. Now, this

Calvino, *he's a carpenter*. And she says, well, I'm no bloody good at carpentry; they didn't teach it at my school. And knowing the state of the schools, I'm about to hug her and say *there there*, never mind, darling, don't worry about it. But I catch myself in time and realise you can't be *physical* with a student, or all hell could break loose and before you know what's what friends and *stage* defenders of Natalie, two dimensional and unconvincing, will begin to stride out of their early drafts to molest you. So to protect myself I say in a distant sort of way: well, Natalie, you should have read the course guide, you know. And that would have told you your table needed flaps. At which point she either starts to cry or complains of harassment. (More worryingly, she might call you a control freak.)

Maybe I still have my arm, metaphorically, round Natalie (sentimental old fart, she thinks, winking at a friend her age), and I say: let's go back (to my place?) and prepare a bit; let's go back and read, oh, I don't know, something by Mrs Woolf, *To the Lighthouse*, maybe (calmer than *The Waves*, ha). Or we can go up to Leeds, to the West Yorkshire Playhouse where my friend Jude Kelly is putting on a new Soyinka. If we're still together after that we might try to hunt down a *Macbeth* in the region – that sort of thing. If it's all too stressful, well, just take down something off the shelf, starting from the wrong end of the alphabet to make it interesting. Yeats, perhaps; or some name beginning with X or Z. (Something Chinese, there's a good girl.) Go on, we're consenting adults, after all. Oh yes, and read a little Plato.

And now for a cup of tea.

With the cup of tea, a pause to peruse my list of things to do.

~~MONDAY~~   TUESDAY
(1)   RR. Money for studio?
(2)   Bank/Upton Park?
(3)   Laundrette/story

Must tidy up a little. Audrey's coming tomorrow: why am I uneasy about having Audrey coming to clean. I'm not uneasy about having Audrey coming to clean. And why should cleaning up before the cleaner still make you feel a bit of a fraud? So the

cleaner isn't coming to clean, just to keep you on your toes, to
prevent you, unsupervised, descending to piggery. If you were
turning into something suspect, something socially suspect, vot-
ing the wrong way, sort of thing, you wouldn't go to the laundrette,
would you? You'd go to the laundry. Better still, *you'd ask Audrey
to take your stuff to the laundry*. Anyway, must get on, must get on.
And really, much of this stuff isn't urgent: *Might well be Middleton
rather than Marston. Enter QUIBBLE at an English course committee meeting.*

QUIBBLE: Quibble quibble......Quibble, quibble quibble
CHAIR: Ah, I see what you mean.

Unless Quibble appears somewhere in Shakespeare. With Mis-
tress Quickly and that lot.

(1)   RR. Money for studio?
(2)   Bank/Upton Park?
(3)   Laundrette/story
(4)   RR. Timetable
(5)   Smythe. *Review. Omeros*
(6)   Write reference (Blower/Bower?)
(7)   Carrington Carrington
(8)   London Library £120
(9)   Additional dialogue for SM?
(10)   Read e-mail
(11)   Methuen/*Symposium*
(12)   Bradford Central Library
(13)   Drawing room scene – to Edinburgh?
(14)   RAE details to Julie
(15)   Avril
(16)   Halterbush play (BBC?)
(17)   Camoens/*Omeros*
(18)   RR/Payment for DTP (Lit Ed.)
(19)   St James Press
(20)   Little Book/Big Bk
(21)   Ring Lee
(22)   *Symposium*?

I keep doing it, making my little lists, things to do each day. Parcelling up the time, what? At the end of the day, nothing done, I cross out MONDAY and write in TUESDAY. And so on. I'm surprised, though, glancing down my list that, given the pressure of marking, I'm able to get *anything* done; I've accomplished four things, even though one might be just crossing out MONDAY for TUESDAY. Must have done that last night to set up today. Now I must cross out TUESDAY for WEDNESDAY – and add DENTIST: 10 a.m. Oddly enough the marking, which is the big thing at the moment, doesn't figure. Maybe that's how it is; when there's something so all-consuming you don't think to register it; registering it reduces it to something manageable; its own detail. A couple having a bad time take a few seconds off to make up the shopping list: *Milk, bread, chops questionmark, rice or potatoes, seven hours talk, fruit & veg, bank, post office,* etc. They're not going to write down *seven hours talk*, are they? They're going to emphasise that with *would you like to empty the bin?* Or *have you thought any more about it?* while adding *olive oil* and *salad.* Though I will say the shopping list is part of the plan, if not to prepare yourself for marking, at least to make sure you're not distracted while on the job. (On the job.)

I did go to the bank and I did leave messages for Royce (the unacceptable face of RR) to see if we could have use of the drama studio next year, and to find out why the fellow who did the desk top publishing for my literary editing students still hasn't been paid. (Royce's real name is Richard but there are two Richards in the Department so we call one Rolls and the other Royce. Rolls is the academic, someone we quite like, Royce the accountant is enemy territory. The naming is arbitrary, of course, like Creon in the Antigone play, not caring which of the brothers is the nice guy.) Stuff to write crowding in. I find I'm at my most productive when the pressure of marking builds up: suddenly all the fragments start expanding, connecting. Editing ideas start to make sense; it's a good time, it's a…

Meanwhile my cup of tea's gone cold; better make another one.

Towards evening I swallow my pride and make a threatening phone call. It's to Northern Ireland and I put on an Irish accent.

The joke went stale well before the cease fire, but we're creatures of habit. I call my principal tormentor, Carrington, to tell him we've kidnapped his wife and daughters and the ransom would be that he immediately stop writing plays; any relapse within X months necessarily incurring kneecapping and being forced to sit through his own version of the Shakespeare play. Ignore these warnings and we're talking death. And Carrington is supposed to play along and say: Ah, beJeysus, thank you for giving me fair warning, and wouldn't you be doing us all a great favour to turn me away from such childishness and me a grown man all these years struggling with this rogue gene that is within me, inherited from the Bishop who for my sins (and maybe his, too) I have to call the Dad when there isn't too many around to hear. But as men of the world, Pewter, who've been blessed to know the joys of woman, and more than one woman at that – and did you hear about the good widow of Limavady who wouldn't be denied? But that's another... So meanwhile we're here being massaged by the soft rain, insult to call it Christ's tears, because then there'll be no language left for storms and tempests. And they say, truly, all this wet is something left over from an Abbey stage-set, not when they doused the rising from the Lady Gregory play but just to remind us of family recently up from the sea and did you hear that unfunny English joke...? Of course the fellow has moved on now, to better things. To Maryland. But he's back in Ulster, apparently, to research a play. And I'm supposed to play the hard man of comedy and start the torturing over the phone to concentrate his mind, because even a travelled writer has a time limit on his answers, and there's something obscene in a man burbling on as if he were a book when wife and daughters are threatened with the torture.

But Carrington's away, away in Vilnius this weekend (Vilnius!), so I get cold feet and change the script; and although I'm frustrated that Carrington is in Vilnius becoming famous (and I am in Sheffield marking scripts), I commiserate with the wife, Minap, in Portrush; I commiserate with her for having to share a life with Carrington and to bear his children. But she doesn't know the code, she thinks I'm simply asking about her and the children, and thanking her for having put me up in Portrush that time, and she tells me about the new accomplishments of Susu, her elder daughter whom I remember well – the second one is named after Plato – and I am impressed.

I mustn't feel guilty about Minap, this is my purifying-myself-for-marking-scripts routine; getting rid of baggage, not acquiring more; this wasn't really an anti-Carrington call. I called him, really, because Dave at work was hassling me about the second marking, and my literary editing scripts weren't ready to hand over for second marking, so I had to pretend to be doing something more important and Carrington was involved in a book I was editing, indeed, was the subject of the book I was editing. And since there was heavy pressure in the department to publish (to publish and to do the research thing), people would tolerate your lateness with things, if you were researching, rather than self-indulgently *writing*.

In all this I was trying to deal with my own schizophrenia of damning Carrington and all his (many) works and at the same time using him, hopefully, to further my career. I was editing a collection of his plays for Methuen and this, obviously, changed the relationship between us. To edit someone's work is to acknowledge that person as primary and yourself as secondary. Unpalatable, but there it is. Of course, I had my quarrels with Carrington (it's in the family; we're from the same country, practically): didn't he really cut off avenues to better (greater) things?

But the man delivered; he wrote so many plays that we called him Lope, after da Vega, the seventeenth-century Spanish parody of the Renaissance who was reputed to have put together between 1,500 and 5,000 pieces for the theatre. Even if you settled for the lower figure, that's a lot of *play*. And I'm sure he didn't have armies of research students blocking them out. And here was Carrington, a man our age, just the wrong side of 50, claiming the sort of output you'd associate with a cricket score when your team's had a good day. A parody of a parody! We called him Lope, as I say, when we had a mind to be charitable; at other times, we settled for Barbara, after Madame Cartland, the novelist.

So he wouldn't be back from Vilnius (that's in Lithuania) for a week. Yet, I miss the man; we worked together in the past and he wasn't ungenerous, though when the partnership is unequal it's easy for *one* member to be generous; he cited me as co-author of a couple of the plays. That was when I was with a company in

Shepherds Bush and he was flitting backwards and forwards (like the young David Frost?) across the Atlantic. But those weren't the prize plays.

He was a scavenger turning everything into a play – from Lumumba in the Congo to my grandmother's drawing room in St Caesare. He wasn't shy about writing about his friends. (His Congo play was rather better than Conor Cruise O'Brian's.) So the best you could hope for was that you didn't come out looking too stupid. He made me look rather good in New Guinea, a place I never visited. I had been planning to go out to New Guinea to do a job for the World Bank, a media job. And it fell through. But Carrington got a play out of it (*Severus of Enga*, a good play produced by Yvonne Brewster with Talawa and of course published in the Methuen collection). I'd been reading up on New Guinea for months, going on induction courses, hoping to free myself from part-time teaching. Carrington was around then; he was writer-in-residence at a polytechnic in London, Kingston, and decided we should write the New Guinea play together, I supplying the 'local colour', he dramatising it from here. Carrington accompanied me to the Papua New Guinea High Commission in Victoria to get a feel of the place, then he went to an induction centre in Hertfordshire where we met the experts, and they showed us films of colourful men in war-paint and women with naked breasts, and they threw in lots of facts and figures, and warned us against riding motorbikes, and gave us a taste for Melanesian Pidgin; *Lukim yu* (see you) and *em bagarap* (it is broken) and names for the Queen and her son and heir (*Missis Kwin* and *Pikinini belong Missis Kwin*). Well, I didn't get to New Guinea, but Carrington got his play, and the scenes set in Kundiawa and Wapanamanda certainly convinced me. The power of art.

Maybe I should break off now and have a little drink; maybe something a bit stronger than tea.

I like to think that the act of marking makes me less mean, less malicious (I'm a malicious guy, I wish I wasn't). That's how far I've moved in this cleansing ritual in preparation for serious marking – three weeks of it. That's why this little tussle with Carrington, still striking a note that's – what's the word? – discordant, has to be wound up, wound down. It persists as the suggestion of a signal from a suspect tooth, which isn't quite an ache, but I'm well on the way to stilling that, then I'll be ready, intellectually and emotionally, for serious marking. Intellectually, I'm probably still a little bit too coiled-up to catch the students out. Emotionally? Well, that's too complicated. So let's start again (like the killers rehearsing the job in the Pinter play, McCann and whatever his name is, Goldstone, Goldberg, Goldstein – *Goldberg* in *The Birthday Party*). So, try harder: see some good theatre (check on the Soyinka at the West Yorkshire Playhouse); read some short stories (read the new Alice Munro collection); read some poetry (read Hopkins and think of Rupert Smythe, our poet-in-residence). That's the literary stuff. And for *balance* (we're children of the BBC, remember?) – for balance, I find myself preparing to browse through *Index on Censorship* – a rather nice woman runs *Index on Censorship*. For balance prepare to scan the newspapers to see how many house-owners have been repossessed this quarter, etc. The point is to come to the work able to respond with your fullest, most adult self. Of course, some people achieve that through sport (football, swimming; there's a woman at the university who fences). *Rigour with fairness, folks: Here at City...*

So, when I'm marking seriously even Carrington must be seen in a new light, even Carrington must be *revised*: I have to think something *good* of Carrington. The fact that he has pushed me into raiding his territory for material (he never stopped raiding mine) is, I suppose, a sort of credit in the bank (*must go to the bank*) for Carrington. That happened on his patch in Ireland when he was there ten years ago, on what I call, to confuse the reader, The Second Stockholm Connection. The 'connection' lasted about an hour and a quarter – however long it took the train to get from Antrim station to Coleraine. Then we disconnected at Coleraine, my Swedish partner staying there, me going on to Portrush, chez Carrington. (*Ah, Stockholm!*)

I can't now remember the woman's name, though I remember thinking at the time that it wasn't very Swedish sounding. I remember being embarrassed in the way you are when Christmas comes and you want to give the college cleaners a card and a bit of a present, and you realise then that you don't know their names, and you think if you were a woman you would know their names. Though I might perhaps be forgiven for not knowing Stockholm's name as that connection, in its length of tenure was too brief, too brief. Enter cleaner, call her Audrey.

It was all quite adventurous, really, looking back. This was my second trip to Ulster (or, the North of Ireland, to play it safe). On the first occasion Carrington had driven down to the airport to pick me up. So, second time round, an old hand, I followed instructions; taxi from Aldergrove to Antrim, then train to Coleraine; change trains at Coleraine, on to Portrush, *voila*. At the airport, this lady I didn't know was heading in the same direction, and it seemed silly not to share a taxi. Most of the other passengers on the flight were being picked up in private cars which, I suppose, added to our mutual feeling of being unloved; so we decided to share. £5.00. (If on of us gave the other £2.50, that would play well with the ethnologists and we could make jokes about who was buying whom.)

But no, the taxi-driver was having none of it; he wanted £5.00 each. That was a bit steep; both our respective contacts in the Province had told us that the taxi to Antrim would cost less than £5.00. And here was this man, this – I have to say it – stage Irishman whom we were disposed to liking because we found his accent so hard to understand, wanting to charge us, yes, £10.00. Why? Because you're not together, he seemed to be saying, you're not a couple. *How did he know that*? Was there a little bit of racism operating here? I glanced at my partner with new eyes, as they say; she looked very partnerable to me, in a Swedish sort of way, younger than me, perhaps, but not by much – not the sort of obscene age gap that you used to get in the old Westerns, between John Wayne, say, and the girl at the end of the film. And certainly, this Swede had spirit, she took the fight to the enemy; she pointed out to the driver the lack of logic in discriminating between people who slept together and people who did not. I thought she was exposing herself a bit there; the driver could have come back at her and pointed out that sleeping together wasn't necessarily the hurdle, because he might well have been prepared to carry a brother and sister travelling together as one package, for £5.00, whether they were sleeping together or not. The same if they were backpackers on holiday, whatever. Whatever little plan I had to negotiate, so that our

man would get something out of it and *we* wouldn't miss our
connection at Antrim, seemed a bit tepid after this.

For Stockholm it was a moral argument; we would see this
neanderthal off and approach our next taxi as a couple, even if it
meant missing the Antrim connection; she had only one piece of
luggage, but it was expensive-looking, in an unshowy sort of way,
and the coat, too, wasn't that of someone trying to save a few pence;
so it wasn't financial need that was driving this: it was a Swedish
we-won't-lose-out-on-our-rights-to-people-who-couldn't-name-
our-Nobel-prize-winners sort of thing. She put her arm through
mine, determinedly, and we prepared for the next taxi; I kissed her
on the cheek, thinking that I could get used to this, and we
snuggled up slightly in the soft rain. When the taxi drew up I kissed
Helga on the mouth, which tasted vaguely of tobacco. She said
something in Swedish which obviously meant that the heavens
were smiling on us as we sailed down her Sunday morning fjord;
and I agreed. And we got our ride to Antrim for just £5.00.

I should develop this. Think Carrington. Think Lope.

*

At some point – Ballymeana? Ballymoney? – we shared a drink
(drinking from the same carton, a tomato juice) and at Coleraine
said goodbye to our life together, conspicuously not exchanging
addresses. I started to write it up (novel, play, film, Radio Three
talk). But when I found it impossible to remember her name I
realised I'd lost it. For if you couldn't retain the sharpness of a
name – and it wasn't one of those Swedish names you'd make up
– you just couldn't take it further.

It bothered me that though I could imagine this woman in
circumstances other than being at the airport arguing with a taxi
driver it was that scene that fascinated me, and I didn't want to turn
my life into farce. I mentioned it casually to Carrington. We agreed
that there were strange, awkward nuances to this one, so we circled
round it, as if challenging the other to display bad taste. If we were
to write it up, it suggested one of those delicate, elusive Turgenev-
like tales that men our age, this late in the century (and particularly when you were talking about mixed-race stuff) weren't sure

we wanted to do. So he gave me a year to write it or he would. (I managed it as a short story; it's been published in a magazine called *Ambit*.)

*

Anyway, the point is, here we are – here I am – as if employing seasonal adjustment to the employment figures, feeling virtuous enough to take on the second year short-story folders for marking. (Forget about Balham, he never went through this sort of house-training process. Give television a miss tonight. Sorry, Bosnia. Attack another literary editing folder and then come back to Natalie.)

So, you see, I'm OK now. *Now, Pewter is himself again.* You must imagine this in a Laurence Olivier voice, camp and tongue-clipped, the perpetual send-up which used to pass as acting on the English stage. *But, soft, enough of bitchiness.* Welcome home everyone. Welcome the more talented, the more successful. Welcome home, younger men with beautiful wives. Welcome home, Carrington. Drink my wine, eat my food, *don't* sleep with my wife, daughter or dog; but drink up; eat. Brothers. Sisters. (Someone said about Carrington, after seeing one of his plays, that it wasn't bad for a man from a small island. Not in the first rank, of course, but not bad, not bad: if this were a West Indies cricket team, the man would have to be taken along at least as scorer. And that, I thought then, I think now, that's a bit harsh. I would certainly take Carrington along *at least* as the umpire. Fair's fair, as they say. Ours, you know, wasn't a cricketing island – in cricketing terms we sometimes spelt it Ireland – so we had to do our Latin homework instead. Ah, don't talk to me about underprivilege).

I'm told there are some people in Middle America who went mad some time ago without anyone noticing. Whole towns. Towns of towns. There must be a collective noun for towns of towns: *an outback of towns, a badland of towns, a hinterland of towns, an enemy of towns, a cabbage of towns... a mittelamerica of towns.* An adverb of towns. What was I thinking about? Oh yes, to cure these people you had to move them closer to a border: it was a hinterland experience, the security of geography that was driving them mad. So they rejected the cure and elected to stay mad.

What I was really thinking about, what brought this on, was the slight unease that a feeling of generosity (as towards my colleagues whose names I could never remember, as towards Carrington, but not, perhaps, towards Balham) mustn't lull you into being naive; that could be dangerous. I have to remember, when I pick up again that paper of Natalie's that's causing me grief, the one I've abandoned to the easier territory of literary editing, that when Natalie uses a cliché in portraying a relationship, she's lying about that relationship . (If only when you lied, you got a harelip, as in the Bible, as in Shakespeare.) Natalie's undermining, dishonouring those people: I must demand the subtext from her that I expect from self-advertising farts like Carrington and Balham. Last night when I was marking I was thinking not of those two but of myself with *let's call her X* in our little village in the *Alpes Maritimes*, sitting on the terrace, surrounded by oliviers, sun, wine, etc. French sex. And I thought of Natalie somewhere on the Abbeydale Road among other students and barking dogs and Sheffield accents and... and I relented. *Sentimental old fart*.

But let's stay generous and get on with the job ahead and be ready for The Second Marker, call him Dave, to whom I've promised to hand over the folders first thing tomorrow morning. Nine o'clock. So I check my WEDNESDAY list again, and add:

(23) Dave. (But I'm at the dentist's at 10)

This is the last thing I'll say about marking. But it's late and I'm tired and I'm not for some reason going to bed. I mean, I don't think you need to be fanatical about this, but surely it must matter, your state of dress, when you mark a young woman's script. (I would say any woman's script, but I'm not into this PC nonsense.) I'm not saying that it affects the *mark*, but the mark, for Christ's sake, is only part of the marking; this isn't a degree-factory; you come to university for the total experience, a small part of which (and who's to know how small? *Oh that's really small*) is the relationship between marker and marked, the *markee*, and part of the aesthetic relationship between them, surely, is the marker's state of cleanliness, mental stability and dress. (Julius Caesar was a better-dressed man than the Vercingetorix, remember?) There are exceptions, of course: if you were at Nsukka in the '60s, during the Nigerian Civil War, and you were taught by Christopher Okigbo and his team, and they took time off to write poetry and defend the university with hand grenades and Kalashnikovs (for in beating back the enemy they were defending the idea of the university), surely, you're not going to say to the man: I won't come to your seminar on O'Casey and Brecht and the young Soyinka until you change your bushjacket and unload the Kalashnikov. He, poor man, died in the act. Here in Sheffield no one is shooting at us, except the government, and the school management – but that's Smythe's script. Smythe is our poet-in-residence.

Back to my point: to be dressing-gowned and silken or, God forbid, naked, during the intimate act of marking is to take an unfair advantage, unfair because ungranted – it might even be violating a human right – and it's a request you couldn't properly make because to grant it isn't part of the student's contract, it would have to be labelled as extra-curricula; dodgy. Now, it's perfectly possible for an alert and adventurous student to say: OK, son, you're on: if you're going to be in a state of partial undress when you mark me, then I have the right to do the same when I'm being marked. (But then what if the student's in the pub, working nights; the onus would be on you, then, to mark at a time convenient to the student so that she (or he) is not exposed to embarrassment. To go further down that road is to get into Channel Four stuff.) Of course, the student might go the other way, suit of armour (amour?) and all that – and who are we to complicate a student's life in that way? I imagine Natalie might say: hang on a minute while I hang a few curtains, a few lace curtains across these gaps between words. Then maybe she'll put on the dark glasses – over her I's, get it? – so they don't distract. Now, she must decide whether to grant permission to enter her brackets. But there's her parentheses, you see; well, those are definitely out of bounds. At some point you look up to find she's wearing an overcoat, and a veil. You couldn't put a student through all that – you couldn't put her through the expense of all those curtains, to start with – just for the luxury of feeling yourself naked between the sheets while marking. (Though, I will say, a colleague at work swears by it.)

A thought: it's possible that Natalie's over-writing in that first story is an attempt to protect herself against my marking her script in bed. So I'll have to look at it again from a different position, sitting at my desk, dressed, sipping a small cognac. Now who can object to that.

A Diversion

It's a rush of blood and I don't need this, and I'll pay for it with the marking piling up, but earlier I found myself dropping off and unwilling to summon up the effort to get to bed: this is how you become slobbish, this is how you sink into OMS – Old Man Syndrome (this is an argument for partnership). A woman wouldn't let you get away with it. I have my responsibilities to real-life partners, to ex-partners, to Lee in London, to Lindsay, the Lady, as I call her, Henryjames-like, in Boston. I can't have them, wherever they are now, whoever they're with, thinking of me as something growing old and slobbish and shabby. A daughter, sharp and intolerant, is what you need at times like this, to slap you into presentability. Alas, no daughter.

Anyway, failing all that, I thought, with Carrington out of reach (Vilnius!) why should the plays stop; why should the Lope production line dry up? The little plays of his that I'm editing could be written in a morning. Indeed, some of them were. It's only pride that stops me producing similar stuff. So I thought, now at my most tired, warmed by a third cognac, I'll toss off a Carrington in the few seconds before going to bed: Carringtons come in groups, like buses, or tourists – maybe that's part of their claim to being contemporary. There are the Caribbean Carringtons; the adaptations (also Caribbean, some of them, fairly obscure, from the Dutch); the Canadian Carringtons (he went to university in Toronto); Carringtons colonising other bits of the known universe and Carrington's London plays, which would constitute my main selection. (A friend insists that I'm influenced in selection by the *titles*, not the plays, but that's what friends are for, to undermine you.) Carrington, having put us all in his plays, I savour the opportunity to reciprocate.

A Diversion (A Carrington Play) 12:15 a.m.

*I thought of setting it in Vilnius. Carrington in the lecture room, ready. There's a little group of people, seriously old; huddled in overcoats, etc.: the room is cold. People bearded, reading. Everyone silently reading. Men more heavily-bearded than the women; they're reading – reading Tolstoy & Akhmatova & Chekhov & Pushkin &...any Lithuanian writer I can dig up. Carrington forces them to put away their reading-matter and introduces a lecture on John Osborne & Caryl Churchill & Martin Amis &...*who would the poets be? *Carol Ann Duffy and Simon Armitage*: this is a British Council tour!

No, I couldn't do that, even to Carrington, so I start again.

A Diversion   (A Carrington Play) 12:17 a.m.

(Carrington is in his study. Parrot in cage UL, asleep. Night. Carrington working. Wife & daughters have left him; he doesn't notice; he's writing a play, one of his "English" plays. Scene: Crouch End (or Shepherds Bush). Enter two armed men accusing him of unspecified crimes. (Switch Sc. to Nuremberg?) Naturally, being Carrington, he sees this as part of his own mental process and starts to write the armed men into the play)

Act One

CARRINGTON:	*(looking up from typewriter)* I thought you'd come
1st ARMED MAN:	"Microfilms and microfiches" *(shoots CARRINGTON dead)*
2nd ARMED MAN:	Eh eh! *(angry at being made redundant, shoots CARRINGTON repeatedly.*

PARROT *awakes and recites the whole of Hermann Hesse's* Das Glas Glasperlenspiel, *which takes about 26 hours.)*

End of Act One

Act Two

(Scene, the same as end of Act One.)

PARROT: *(PARROT recites* The Glass Bead Game *in Richard and Clara Winston's English Translation of* Das Glasperlenspiel)

Applause *(off)*

End of play.   12:22 a.m.

Though it's late I start to prepare the den for marking. It's the awkward space in the flat that for a couple of years I didn't know what to do with, just using it as a book dump. The bizarre conversion by the landlords (not that I'm criticising the housing association, the rents are low) – the conversion left it railed off, like two sides of a giant crib defining a space the size of an old-fashioned box room. This is situated just as you come up the second run of the stairs as you enter the flat, on the right hand side, facing the kitchen. I quite like the fact that there's no easy way to get into it, that you've got to climb over the rail (leg over; *enjambement.* Lee does it backwards, curious); it's a manageable hurdle for anyone moderately fit, and really – although you don't want to press the point – shows at least that the person sitting in judgement over you, marking your paper, isn't a physical cripple (football, fencing, circus knives?) – a notion that might not go without challenge by the PC brigade: I'm not, as it happens, hostile to them, but there it is. Anyway, this little leg-over into the marking den is less strenuous than playing squash and goes some way to restoring, I think, the balance between marker and markee.

I'd spent three days furnishing the den with bookcase, arm-chair and reading lamp. The bookcase, two bookcases, eventually, were acquired after three trips to the Abbeydale Road (one large at £35.00, one small at £10.00). Then the armchair, a bit of luck after a lot of prowling about: Edwardian, reupholstered, £75.00 (in the sale) at *Cobwebs* at Broomhill – and the lamp, what's it called? *Endon*, elegant, Giacomettish, in black: £15.00 with lead). Add to this endless taxi fares. But getting there.

I shift books from floor to bookcases, from one part of the flat
to the den, making it relevant; lots of poetry, some general but
politically sexy stuff – Edward Said and Faludi (not Paglia, too
Balhamite); then runs of a couple of magazines (*Ambit*, associated
with Smythe, and *Bete Noire*, edited by one of our Externals); all
my Shakespeare, etc. Still, I'm not happy that this is the ideal
marking environment; I feel a bit exposed, self-conscious. And
there's something else, a whiff of cigarette smoke seeping up from
the flat below: surely, people get killed for less than that. You can't
be expected to *mark* in an atmosphere of cigarette smoke. (The
Americans would understand that.) I feel guilty about Lee, my ex-
partner, a smoker. In an effort to block it all out I pile the top of the
bookcases high with philosophy and history. That's better.

Now, to test the system; Endon light blazing; I'm sitting in my
Edwardian armchair, thinking that a little table might be added to the
suite (another visit to the Abbeydale Road?). But, we can still test the
system: how about writing another Carrington play, a quickie?

A Diversion (A Carrington Play)

(CARRINGTON *in his study. Night. Working.* PARROT *in cage UPL,
asleep. Wife & Daughters have left him. Scene: Holland Park or
Highgate. Ground floor.* CARRINGTON *writing play*)

CARRINGTON: *(Looks up, listens. Back to typewriter. Pause.
                       Gunshot (Off). CARRINGTON leaps up,
                       stunned. Quiet. He pats himself to see if he's
                       been shot. Doorbell. He looks at his wrist to
                       check the time. No watch. After a moment's
                       indecision, he strides to the door (Off).
                       Barrage of sound. A guitar.)*

MALE VOICES (Off): *(singing)* Happy birthday to you
                       Happy birthday to you
                       Happy birthday dear Daddy
                       Happy birthday to you

(CARRINGTON *edges backwards into view, while two young men in* *dreadlocks, one with a guitar, one with a home-made instrument,* *serenade him, but with a degree of menace*)

Happy birthday to you, etc.

(*Slight pause. They smile. CARRINGTON is about to say some-* *thing; but singing starts up again*)

For he's a jolly good fellow, etc.

....

And so say all of us

(*During this, the* MAN *with the home-made instrument moves to* *typewriter, glances at CARRINGTON's work, removes sheet of paper* *from typewriter and slowly crunches it up. He proceeds to do this to* *more work. The singing continues. They gesture to CARRINGTON to* *join in. But he stands on his dignity*).

DUET: And so say all of us
                  And so say all of us, etc.

(MAN *2 flicks a lighter, puts it to pile of paper; paper burns*)

DUET: Why was he born so beautiful, etc.

(*Choking & spluttering. PARROT wakes. Fade*)

END OF PLAY

This takes two or three seconds before I think better of it. The play I actually start working on is about the volcano in St Caesare. My sister in London tells me there are still about 1,500 people on the island. For a tiny island that still seems *populated*. I'd written a version of the play last year when the volcano struck; and nothing came of it. Now with new eruptions and evacuation, I'm stung into action. The reason why the play *must* be revised now is not unrelated to the fact that I'm up to my neck marking with all sorts of other deadlines. Overkill. Neurotic, I know, but there it is. In the play I reduce the number of characters to about half a dozen, chief among them my old headmaster Professeur Croissant and his side-kick, Horace, my mad cousin. They are holding out, in a sub-Shavian way, against attempts to get them to head for Antigua and further afield. What have you got to offer me, sort of thing? They have both travelled. Croissant's two wives and children are abroad (though a grandchild visits for the purposes of the play). Horace, mad but functioning, has a wife (and children, if he is to be believed) in England or Germany or France: he's the Casanova who can't dress himself properly, can't fix his teeth; but his random information on the classics is impressive. The Professeur is your classic control freak, putting pressure on everyone by staying put on the volcano island. Together, they do their tours of duty, they *appropriate* the living presence on the island; they are interviewed by visiting TV crews; they are snowed under by international aid. They are, of course, a comic turn, which probably won't please people from the island, including my own family.

Having made a start I can see a play emerging. I keep the old title: *Between a Rock and a Hard Place*...

Now I've got my hand in, now I've initiated the den with a play of my own, I can get on with the marking.

2

1988. Return to London

I came back from France with a play. It might have been better to
come back from France with the woman. But then you can't have
everything; and I did manage to put the woman in the play; and
give her the best part (she was the American, I was the Writer, and
the jaded and cynical will say that I sent us both up. Fuck them).

Maybe I sent it up a bit. If I did, I'd say I did it for Lee, the new
woman; (New Woman?) the non-American. Though I'm forever
committed to those scenes on the terrace in Spéracèdes, not *our*
terrace, alas. After work, after a hard day on the *chantier*, my
building kit somehow transformed beyond class by the coming-
home scene on a spacious terrace, high on the hills above Cannes,
feeling rather superior to the tourists down there! Lindsay sitting
here, summery, reading her book. Henry James, maybe. All very
writerly. I put down my lunch-box, etc., go inside the cabin to say
hello to our hosts, (Ralph would already be cooking, have a quick
wash, and come out to relax with Lindsay, her book abandoned,
while we sit like characters in a stage set recalling the day's jokes
(of Pierrot in the village, or Joseph or Rene on the site, of our hosts'
tolerance for a home-made wine going off, while we maintain our
writerly standards (Hemingway, Scott, Zelda, what?) by sipping a
rather good (bought at the shop) red wine. Before supper.

I would, in a play I will write, apologise to Lindsay, for bringing
her this late to France. I'm despondent at who will play us on the
stage.

I was back home now camping out in Carrington's place in
Crouch End, having difficulty contacting anyone. I rang Carrington
in Ulster, where he was writer-in-residence at the university, but
he was touring that weekend. I didn't call Lee immediately; I was
summoning up the energy to call Lee. Should ring the family, my
sister, but that could wait a day or two; yet, you wanted to make
contact so, in the end, I rang Balham – Balham, the man, not the
place: it wasn't quite as straightforward as that but I'm through
with justifying these things to myself. Balham's ansaphone said he
was out, and asked to state the time and *day* of the call. That seemed

funny, not funny that Balham now ran to an ansaphone, but the nature of the message on it, the explicitness of there being no one at home: what had suddenly made people in England so laid back? I remembered some years ago coming back from America (I was the traveller in the family), in the late-'70s it must have been, and ringing up my landlord in London about the rent; and the wife came to the phone and said: sorry, but her husband was away for the weekend, out of the country; she was alone in the house.

And I thought, coming back from America: how trusting, how innocent, how English. I told the story to friends, and chanced to mention it in the presence of Balham, a man I didn't see that often. Anyway, characteristically, he pulled rank and accused me of being naive, chided me for being overly receptive to the regulation, modulated, cream-and-strawberry voice: he was convinced that the husband in question had put the wife up to it, that he had clearly been at home at the time of my call: couldn't you just see him crouching with his buddies behind the door, or lounging in the passageway or on the stairs, armed to the teeth to confront the wife's lover, lured by the information that the coast was clear, house and wife untended.

Balham was someone you took in small doses. His radicalism had always been suspect. Back then, in our GCE days, Balham – tall and awkward, left-footed – like the rest of us had no particular objection to the 'well-modulated-girl-who'd-been-to-a-good-school' voice. His hostility to it (fake) came with a radical French girlfriend whose way with English – and with the English – was uncompromising. That was what had turned him off the 'Roedean and Bedales' set. So now, relieved to hear the ansaphone rather than the man himself, I declined to leave a message; a message would demand too much stamina. With a real friend you'd hesitate not to leave something on the machine, however brief, if only to allay anxiety; but Balham could take that. It's not even that I couldn't think of anything to say. (I had rung him as a bit of a joke: on the train home from Heathrow I fancied I saw a picture of him plastered on the underground station. Childishly, I was going to congratulate him on having 'made it'. But it wasn't that funny. With someone else, with Lee or... Carrington, even, I would have risked being playful, slipped into Confucius or Lao Tze mode: *have you eaten rice today*? sort of thing.)

Carrington's Crouch End flat looked both lived-in and abandoned. His books were all here, not in Ulster: how could he afford
to keep on this flat unless to demonstrate to the rest of us how well
he was doing for himself. But, it had its uses. (I still had, to the
dismay of my family, no house, no home – people tended to see a
ruin in the south of France as an eccentricity – my possessions
locked in a spare room in someone's house in Finchley.) I had rung
Carrington to say that I was installed, to thank him and what was
her name? the wife, for the hospitality. His wife (ah Minap!)
answered the phone in very precise English, and said how much she
was looking forward to meeting me; and I promised to come over to
Coleraine to meet her and the girls. I promised to ring back.

I was somewhat conscious of being part of this triumvirate, this
boys' own triangle refusing new shape, this male wedge – Carrington,
Balham, Stapleton (we tended to sport surnames) – inserted between every new relationship, resisting new shape, though Carrington,
late in life, seemed to have managed all right with his Minap, rescuer
from the Cook Islands: now Man & Wife & Daughters.

Balham and I went back a long way, as we say, doing GCEs
together in Kilburn, at the Polytechnic – this was late-'50s. We
were proud of ourselves that we, unlike our contemporaries from
the Caribbean, didn't run exclusively with the island pack.
Balham was Jamaican, not from St Caesare or Montserrat like the
rest of us. He had already discovered Africa, appropriated it, was
into boycotts of South Africa, blackness. I was a slow learner:
coming from a political condominium governed by Britain and
France, I bought the myth of St Caesarians being heir to two
cultures. (The ruin in Spéracèdes was to show me how wrong I
was.) Through Balham I discovered Africa. More recently, we'd
been trying to upstage each other in claiming an interest in things
Amerindian. That was really Carrington's territory. He went to
university in Canada and naturally laid claim to the Americas.

Lee refused to play my little games here. She didn't trust
Balham and she didn't know Carrington. She said we sounded like
a backing group, only that we lacked the musical instruments, etc..

That's why I'm putting off the call to Lee; somehow I didn't want
to ring her from this flat. She'd called me 'sporadic' and that hurt.
And of course that had made me more sporadic. Sporadic in my

interests, in my *interest*. It was too late now to apologise for being
sporadic. Too late or too soon back. None of the old questions was
answered: wasn't I still distracted by, yes, the vague sense of being
in the wrong place, of pursuing the wrong skill (would the 'French'
play do any better than other plays which flopped despite being
superior to the bulk of Carrington's output – ah, you couldn't help
being distracted into thinking yourself hard done by: *Enter beautiful
woman, Lee*. But I'm a puritan. I say; you have to earn these things).

Of course it was the play, the French play, that made it difficult
for me to ring Lee. For the Lady at the heart of the play wasn't Lee.
But Lee would be the Princess in the next play, which would be
written in verse. Although there was now no attachment to the
Lady, the fact that I'd spent four months writing her up, drawing
a line under the experience, really, but near to the place where we
might have lived, had things worked out – it all still seemed
disloyal to Lee. Lee's memory was recent, the Lady's long enough
ago to be literary. Though it wouldn't be seen that way. And what
was the prospect of a new scene (Oh, why weren't these women
revisable!) with Lee?

I could still ring her and remind her that I'd done no renovation
to the house in Spéracèdes as she wouldn't be living there

that... I'd honoured our agreement not to put her in my play

that, furthermore, it would be Sunday tomorrow; and if I didn't
come to the Club in Muswell Hill and watch her play tennis – what
colour shorts would she be wearing? – Sunday wouldn't be Sunday
but another dreary day of the week in England; and really, one
would have no option but to head straight back to the South of
France, to the ruin in Spéracèdes, and sulk. I would come to watch
her play tennis, pretend to read the newspapers and be cheerful;
buy the drinks.

I would promise her... But I didn't want to call her from
Carrington's flat; it felt tacky.

*

I woke with a start, the central heating had put me to sleep; it
was barely evening; I was in the sitting-room on the couch, a room
groaning with books: I remembered what someone had said about

writers' or scholars' rooms, that they were like fearful presences stacked with dead bodies. I was panic-stricken. I woke up from a dream of revolution. I was in Red Square, high up in a flat looking down; and Gorbachev was in the square below, looking up, thanking me (I was, clearly, in his apartment). The revolution was, it seemed, clearly one of many he'd survived, so he'd soon be coming up the stairs to shake my hand, to reclaim his own place. Meanwhile, other supporters started drifting into the square. A smart, small car pulled up and parked and someone, said to be Zhivkov, though I must have misheard, it must have been Zhukov, back from the dead, but a supporter of Gorbachev, got out; and a few people applauded.

The curtains in the Moscow apartment were closed, my head was poking out through the slit. This embarrassed me so I tried to open them, conscious that the room was a mess. It was a huge window facing the square, about six or eight panels with one set of curtains, brown velvet, meeting in the middle; and they snagged as I tried to open them; but in the end they gave a bit. I removed an empty beer can from the window sill and hoped, for some reason, that the TV set inside wouldn't be seen from the square below. The room reeked of smoke (though I don't smoke, and I was alone). The doorbell was ringing, a continuous ring. I went to open it to find, not Gorbachev but an old friend, a musician, someone who played the violin professionally with the regulation ravenous rash on the side of his neck. He had a hamper of food, and that reminded me that it wasn't a Russian revolution that was happening but Lee's birthday, and her children's birthday, which all fell within a few days of one another; and we were celebrating.

I woke up in a small panic wondering if it was Lee's birthday and I had missed it again. It wasn't. I was about to dismiss the dream when I noticed that Carrington's curtains were of brown velvet, the same as in Gorbachev's flat. Ah, but there was no television near the window, no revolution outside: I decided to ring Lee immediately.

*

Later, when there was an attempt to overthrow Gorbachev in Russia, I was too embarrassed to tell friends that I had dreamt it all.

*

Funny how disorientated you become. The first few seconds
waking up in a strange bed; or waking up abroad. I woke with a
sense of uneasiness palpably different from the sort of mild
irritation that had preceded my drifting off in my clothes. The flat
was warm – Carrington's central heating worked; I'd got some food
in, shopping at the Indian corner shop at the top of the road. The
wife at the check-out seemed to remember me: who did she think
I was? I didn't look like Carrington, who was surprisingly smooth-
skinned for a man of our age and, if the truth be told, a more
handsome man than I am. Though I remembered her, in her sari,
her midriff showing. I'd been in the shop a couple of times, once
when Carrington had a party and another occasion when I happened
to find myself at John La Rose's bookshop in Finsbury Park, which
was really just round the corner; and a couple of us had come down
to Crouch End to eat, to sample one of the numerous Indian
restaurants (we had ended up eating Italian) and we decided on the
spur of the moment to drop in on Carrington, who wasn't, of course,
at home. I'd gone into that same corner shop, and the woman behind
the till was pregnant, heavily so: where was the three-year old, four-
year old who would join the ranks of the black-English, the brown-
English complaining that people of my generation hadn't *achieved*
in this country, hadn't provided role-models? I had to watch myself
and not invent enemies – certainly not enemies this young.

Carrington didn't have a television in the flat (was he doing
these things for effect, consciously, for his memoirs?) and this
niggled because I was looking forward to a bit of English television. There was a natural space where the television had been, in
the corner, indentations in the carpet – brown, plush carpet:
Carrington must, indeed, be doing well, to be able not to let this
place. Had someone broken in and stolen the set. (We were on the
first floor, and the place hadn't been turned over; it was tidy but
casually so, books and papers and *objets d'art* suggesting someone
who hadn't really moved out, an unneat bachelor flat.) Lots of
boxes – books maybe. When would Minap, young wife from the
Cook Islands and baby daughters, begin to have an impact on all
this? Didn't she resent this frozen bit of Carrington's past? Was

that why Carrington insisted on putting up his old friends now, because in a couple of years' time it would all have to change?

*

Cookie Cookson Cookup Cooksky – we played these games. First, we had to make sure of each other again, two against the world, sort of thing. Then we would know when the games were drifting into something false. Lee was busy tonight. So tonight I would accept my punishment and go down to the Cook's Travel Agents near the clock tower in Crouch End and sign up on a private Cook's Tour to West Hampstead, on which Lee would be explored. There was, tonight, nothing cooking.

Maybe I'd been wrong to be guarded about Lee; she was pleasant, welcoming and played the game up to a certain point. She hadn't met Carrington's Cook Islands' wife, so we weren't making fun of a real person, though Lee would charge me later with doing just this with my Cookpuns. Lee wanted to see me, of course; but she was tied up tonight (Tied up? I hope with something silken and definitely not England-made.) She had a prior engagement, she was going to the South Bank Centre with a friend; she could do lunch tomorrow. Tomorrow after tennis?

How about lunch tonight after the South Bank?

After the South Bank it might be a little late for lunch.

A late lunch?

It might be a little tiring so late, for lunch.

Point taken.

She was playing tennis in the morning: how about lunch, tomorrow, after tennis?

Lunch hated waiting till tomorrow. Lunch hated being up-staged by tennis; lunch was threatening to be a five-letter word about to come out resentful and un-gay; but lunch tomorrow was fine. I declined to ask the identity of the South Bank friend, and she insisted that lunch be joke-free. So it was lunch tomorrow, minus Cook Islands aids.

(I had wounded myself in Lee's service, in-between waking up and phoning her. I was still luxuriating in the pain of it, and had every intention of using it to capture her sympathy. I'd gone to the kitchen to make myself a cup of tea, taking my own mug with me. It was the mug with a Cornish piskie on it that Lee had bought me when we had holidayed in Cornwall together a couple of years ago. It had been with me on a solitary journey to the South of France and had survived, unchipped, the handle intact. Tonight I'd dug it out of my case and thought I'd use it, not just to reinstate Lee, but to show some little sign of not having been completely taken over by Carrington in Carrington's well-appointed flat. And, naturally, I'd dropped the mug.

The instinctive sticking out of a foot to break the fall was something that pleased me, particularly as it caught me on the instep, just on that point of the instep where you couldn't be sure if you'd broken something, perhaps until the next day. I was going to charge Lee for having been wounded in her defence, *piskielated*.)

So I offered to make Lee lunch the next day. Awkward: she'd already done the shopping, so it made sense to have lunch at her place; and that would be more relaxing after tennis, without having to change, to go out. I couldn't work out if this meant lunch alone, lunch with children, lunch with the children and the South Bank friend... A general cookoff.

'Or, we could go out,' I persisted.

'That would be lovely, darling.' I hadn't quite meant it, I would have preferred lunch in her flat. But the 'darling' meant a lot. I asked about the children.

The children were doing their own thing, as boys did, into computers, into martial arts; the children were fine. They were growing up to resemble their father, but yes, they were fine. I liked that; the little alliance between us and against the father (poor man, Peter) was still in place; now, I could defend the father, I could 'understand' Peter's problems, in the mild, unconvincing defence you mounted for rivals who weren't really threatening. Peter was a pleasant man who worked for Oxfam and was often out of the country. In the service of international justice he had made himself virtually stateless and wifeless. We used, privately, to refer to him as the *Guardian*, as in the newspaper.

Lee and I had to edge back to the old, high ground; we had promised ourselves to correct that hint of imbalance that had prevented us gelling, except for short periods: we promised

ourselves lots of things, including, bizarrely, a daughter, late in the
day, to correct the tendency of boys; a daughter who would be
young enough, unlikely enough to turn us into sentimental fools,
someone so unlikely that even the boys (who were not natural
bullies except, emotionally, with their mother) wouldn't want to
bully. They would adopt her as a miniature mother, a little Lee; be
protective. At three years old Little Lee would be running the
show. She'd have an open expression and fat, little legs (that's how
I dreamt of her in France) wearing one of those loose-fitting
dresses that child-tyrants wear, something light and flowery, like
spring or autumn, with a low fun-making waistline, the long skirt
shifting her centre of gravity – like those joke footballers you get
on the replays: Keegan. Maradona. I had to pretend to give up this
fantasy because (a) it hadn't come about, though we took no
particular precaution to prevent it and (b) Lee was beginning to find
it suspect. Though I privately hung on to the image of those fat, little
legs in shoes without heels, stiff-soled, so that she'd have to clomp
in them like clogs: she'd come in clomp clomp from the garden
offering you a present, a feather, held out in her left hand, offering
you her sweater in a carrier bag. We never did agree on her name.

'Hrothvitha?' No no, too bad a dramatist; too *Christian*: we'd
find more adult uses for Hrothvitha.

I thought of Lee bounding round the Sunday morning tennis
courts. She was the right shape. She was the right size. She was the
right weight, she was the right colour. She was at the right stage of
ripeness; she was your Proust if he could be enjoyed all at once;
she was clothes hung fresh on the line to dry at our place in
Spéracèdes: she was the perfect *translator* of your favourite poet.
There was the right strain of sex imprisoned, but not cruelly, in that
valiant strip of cloth on the tennis courts – in her shorts. Did I have
a right to these feelings? Lee had dimples in the backs of her
knees, which embarrassed her, which she denied (both the
dimples and the embarrassment). At times like this I stop myself
thinking about Lee in case the vibes are picked up – by someone
out there, some pervert, lurking. Tomorrow, I'll go and watch her
play tennis; I'll take the Sunday papers and indulge in chit chat,
and then have lunch.

Over lunch we'll talk about the boys. Or about work.

*

The woman who owned the flat downstairs, who had handed
over the key to Carrington's flat, seemed pleasant – was he going
soft? – well-spoken, well-brought-up. Reminded him of those
girls he went to school with. GCE days. Kilburn. Girls from Mill
Hill and Golders Green and... Or maybe he was thinking of those
wonderful women wandering round Europe teaching English.
Convent-educated and radical women from Australia and New
Zealand and... All so well-spoken. That used to be a euphemism
for wearing the right woman on your arm: *how can such a well-
spoken girl be seen with the likes of Balham!* (Slightly unsettling,
back in England, at a loose end (dangling?). Loose end. No
television. No Lee: she'd been warm on the phone, but firm. *Warm
phone firm*. He imagined downstairs pronouncing those words:
warm phone firm: yes, you'll do.) Why is it, why was it that hours
back in the country you found yourself, what, regressing, yes,
settling into Balham mode. Balham mind-set.

Balham connected us to a sort of shadow world some of us tried
to ignore, to avoid. At school, bored with Jane Austen – though
secretly titillated by all that talk of young women in lots of skirts
trying to find themselves husbands – bored with the elementary
Supply & Demand yawn which passed for A-level Economics, we
would withdraw and march along Kilburn High Road talking about
this and that – the black bus-driver who *didn't* crash his rush-hour
bus; and we would applaud the man's restraint. We would talk
about the immigrant, the non-student, the woman from Barbados
or St. Lucia working at J. Lyons, who somehow didn't poison the
food and leave dozens of strangers dead or dying: restraint, etc. We
would end up occasionally, at a little Cypriot cafe, Casino-cafe,
near the bridge before Kilburn station and drink a glass of wine to
those paragons of restraint. We eschewed the pub; the pub was
plebeian, English. Now, all these decades later, some malcontents
are reminding us of those GCE fantasies. It's too crude to think that
Balham is still stuck in that place. Though someone has to be down
there, watching our back, so to speak.

We were welded to the notion that you had to prepare more fully
than others around you, for the opportunities would come (a Cook

Islands bride?) and you couldn't disqualify yourself beforehand
by accepting second best for lack of knowing what was best.
Whenever we got together – we two or three or whatever the in-
grouping was – it was to show off the level of our preparedness: if we
chanced even now to see a Carrington play together, as last time at
the *Tricycle*, the author could be relied on to do the expected thing
and damn it. Carrington would apologise for bringing us out on a
perfectly good night to something so like a tart, a good thing tackled
in haste, a 'fuck-up' rather than real yeast-rising child-bearing
floozy. Balham's tack seemed to be to confuse us with suits and
styles, including hairstyles, from Burton and short back and sides,
to dashiki and rasta, to Mandela shirts, whatever, not forgetting
women whose skin-colour matched the mood of the time.

No, I can't answer Lee's question about what, emotionally, I'm
running away from. Nothing, I say, hotly, casually, shamefaced:
Nothing. (*Nothing will come of nothing*.) I was not abused as a
child (except, I suppose by being brought up in St Caesare); I
wasn't traumatised on coming to this country as a schoolboy (Oh,
so many white faces!). I'm not gay. (You're hardly a barrel of laughs,
mate). But it's true, relationships are a hassle; a hassle I can't
sustain. *Yes*, I am a sporadic man. No, I don't expect any self-
respecting woman to put up with that. No, I'm not smug about it. Yes,
I am smug about it. Well, I am and I'm not. There are some questions
that shouldn't be answered too fully, I say, and head for the Travel
Agents. Enough about me. No one's going to call my bluff tonight.

*

At lunch with Lee, I told my 'eschew' joke. I'm losing my faculty
for jokes, my facility to tell jokes. So I attempted the latest
cricketing joke doing the rounds. West Indies had recently beaten
Australia in Australia. Hence the joke. The Prime Minister of
Australia, Bob Hawke, is a cricket fan. (And not a bad cricketer,
too!) So here goes. You need good teeth to say the word 'eschew',
which, come to think of it, rhymes with *a chew*. Lee is dutiful and
smiles; it's as she expects. Mark, Lee's younger son, is mildly
amused. He isn't particularly into cricket and isn't impressed by
jokes against Prime Ministers. So this is the joke. West Indies has
swept Australia aside in the first three Tests, to be frustrated in the

Fourth by Lloyd's tactical error in not declaring on the fourth afternoon, and – would you believe it! – giving Australia another lifeline next day by batting on for much of the first session, allowing Australia to get away with a draw.

Australia, like everyone else, had failed to come to terms with West Indies fast bowling; but unlike other teams – India, for instance, in Barbados the year before – they refused to give in, and decided on some sort of desperate counter-attack, hooking blindly at Marshall & Co. And, of course, the result was obvious; they got themselves out, hooking. So, enter Bob Hawke, Prime Minister of Australia and cricket enthusiast. He gathers his defeated team around him, gives them a pep talk and warns them to 'eschew' the hook. The result, in the very next match, the Australians get themselves out hooking. Word then circulates that Australian cricketers don't know what the word 'eschew' means.

Now, this wasn't really the joke; as a joke it was low-grade stuff, mildly amusing, mildly racist. The joke, perhaps, is that Hawke, a scholar, should want to use the word in that context, a word that he, himself, finds hard to pronounce. And as I say, 'eschew' isn't the easiest word in the world to get your mouth round: so, is the joke against cricket-commentators, Australian Prime Ministers, the English language...? Clearly, at lunch in West Hampstead, the joke was against me.

Peter, Lee's (ex) husband (there was no divorce) didn't stay to lunch. They still had good relations and he sometimes stayed over when he was in town, which wasn't often these days. He was off to the Sudan later that evening, having come in from somewhere yesterday, and was spending a few hours with his family. He had always maintained a presence in the flat in terms of old clothes, unsuited to the tropics, and other bits and pieces; from time to time Lee had threatened to pack up Peter's old clothes and deposit them all at Oxfam but she desisted on the grounds of taste: if you'd lost your husband to an Aid Agency, you didn't just turn around and take his clothes home, so to speak. It was with Peter that Lee had gone to the South Bank the night before, something I hadn't imagined. I watched him closely for signs of resentment, but there seemed to be none. *The Guardian*; I saw him cutting a Conrad-type figure in the tropics. In the end I relented and told him I had made a mistake not doing VSO or something similar when, on our first meeting I had talked of wanting, perhaps, to spend a bit of time abroad. Pride, you see. A humbler man, now.

And yet, the tone had been surprisingly upbeat. Music. Song. Before his going off to save the world, before lunch, Lee & Peter played the piano, sang. I had started preparing lunch, perhaps in an obvious attempt to lay claim to territory while Peter showered, packed; and Lee, hot and salty from tennis, sat on the piano stool in her shorts, looking good in her green shorts, hammered out a few bars, accompanying herself. Soon, we were getting out the song-book, the Golden Oldies – the Beatles Book abandoned for Cole Porter. This drew Peter from his shower; and as Lee played he accompanied her in a passable tenor, word-perfect. Then they changed places while he played something she couldn't manage, and she sang. Sang beautifully. These are old rituals, I thought, not minding it, as I shuffled between sitting-room and kitchen, stressing my kitchen responsibilities, to cover my lack of knowledge of the words to songs that everyone else seemed to know by heart.

Before Lee went off for her shower – and I put it down as a minor victory to me that in this case she chose to treat her husband as a guest, each having the bathroom to himself, herself, we reassembled downstairs and admired the garden. She had a wonderful 'Persian' garden at the back – her mother was Persian, her father had been a young diplomat there in the '40s, with Anthony Parsons – complete with a little square fountain, an arch of creepers leading to the fountain. Peter seemed to know the name of every little flower, plant and weed in the garden – the English name, the Latin name, the alternative name; he seemed to know who had introduced this or that cutting first to Kew, when, and from which continent. But he claimed to have no time now for gardening. Lee's garden, he said, made his work on the other side of the world, seem worthwhile. I was rather sad when he left.

Mark was with us at lunch. (Peter? Mark? (We made the old joke about the Synoptic Gospels: at least the elder lad, who was away, somewhere in Wales, climbing, was called Alex. The names seemed to belie the cosmopolitanism of this family.) Mark was a frail-seeming lad of eleven, very calm, whom I suspected of having a lurid private life, an internal life, to make up for his outward sensibleness, his tolerance of adults. Why was he so thin-faced when Lee, beautifully, wasn't? Even Peter, thinnish, had a strong face, rigour and Africa making him look a bit like those Swedes and other Scandinavian types whom you expect to wilt in the heat, but who out-patrol the blackman every time. It was as if Mark were quietly tugging against all that was Lee, without appearing to try, without effort. He buttered his bread as if this was the oldest ritual in the world, and, at the same time (so slowly and deliberately) as if he had invented it. I remember once when we were in the house alone together (Lee had gone off to a writing conference, and Alex was on a school trip and I did the fatherly thing), Mark had cooked lunch. It was pieces of chicken from the supermarket, and we did it in the oven. To save time, we started it off on the grill and then finished it in the oven. And as we ate our chicken – even then he had that manner, unrushed: no one was going to take away his chicken – he observed, as we were getting to know each other, that the bigger the piece of chicken cooked, the better the taste. Better, therefore, to cook the chicken whole, and then cut it up, than to buy the bits separately. Of course, he was right. And I could see how these truisms, these unhurried discoveries would gradually be absorbed and added to, and emerge in winning combinations; in GCEs, in success with women (and men), in PhDs.

Today, at lunch I thought back to that scene, and imagined the difference, say, of being a lad from war-torn Sudan: there, you couldn't assume that no one was going to take away your chicken. First of all you grabbed what was available; you operated not so much in a context of poverty but of uncertainty; you weren't necessarily made aware of the source of supply, so you couldn't be confident that it would keep coming: whether it was imported rice and tinned fish – you just had to grab whatever was there just in case it wasn't available tomorrow.

Peter, who had to leave early, said it was worse than that. Today, at lunch, the talk was, pleasantly, about videos and music, then Mark let slip that there were some lads at school who were a bit rough, and had beaten up one of his friends in the cinema. (He was vaguely amused at Lee's concern – imperfectly disguised by dramatising it – at the beating up. Apparently, beatings-up were strategic: you didn't often break bones.)

'So what do you do, avoid the cinema?' Lee had got everything under control. I was grateful for that. I didn't want to have to offer to go and sort them out.

'We're not going to avoid the cinema,' he said simply, without threat. But there was iron in the thin frame (The father's son?), a little smile on his face.

'I'm sure they're just like all bullies...' I started to say.

'Next time we knew they were going to the cinema, we took some friends along,' Mark cut through my bluster. Now, which one of us, Lee or I, would make a fool of ourselves?

Lee volunteered: 'What, to show you weren't scared?'

'Well, there were more of us than them... So we beat them up.'

Lee, relieved, distressed, proud, amused, then asked if anyone had got hurt.

'Not really; the odd scratch. The odd cut. Think someone got a sprained foot.'

'A sprained *foot*!'

All I could think of, looking at this thin asking-for-protection face were surreal images of old and lame Prime Ministers and Presidents ordering armies into battle. And that was ridiculous; it didn't fit. Later, in bed, Lee brought up the subject, that after all that mothering, here was her son and his rent-a-crowd mob already seeking to prove they were men getting ready to run the world.

It was my role to defend the son as I'd sometimes defended the father, merely to show my large-mindedness, hoping not to be taken too seriously. Then, to distract Lee with other matters, replaying images of watching her on the tennis court earlier, of what she might do to her opponents, and, reaching further back, to our own private tournament.

*

The problem was really with the re-emergence of Peter, and although she wouldn't admit it, it had thrown Lee slightly. Or was it *my* emergence from France? I like to think it was Peter. He was a non-husband, and non-husbands have no rights. For that matter, a husband had no rights, in the old-fashioned sense; but a non-husband who, however misguidedly, went off to save humanity, deserved some... consideration. (I thought of this as the 'Casablanca Syndrome,' Lee playing Ingrid Bergman to the funny fellow who had stood up to the fascists.) Lee resented having to explain herself to me. We talked instead of other things; not the refuge behind Kings Cross that she sometimes visited, a refuge for battered women. That was a no-go area. She had tried in the past, she claimed, to engage her men friends in this, but they had all abused it; they either appropriated the information, or sentimentalised the condition, or abused the statistics: they couldn't bring themselves to treat it with emotional honesty; and I was, apparently, among the worst of them. So today we talked of her magazine and the problems she was having. Lee edited *Rainbow*, the only decent black arts magazine in London and of course got no end of hassle because she wasn't black enough. I, of course, defended her right to edit the magazine and to reject rather bad poems about Mandela and put in their place excellent translations from Rumi, the 13th century Persian poet. She was desperate to give up the magazine, but we encouraged her to hang on so as not to give the nationalists a victory – the sorts of people who hinted that she was using me to gain creditability. There was some suggestion that we should edit the magazine together to take some of the strain off her. But I wasn't sure I had the strength to take that on.

But beneath all this, somewhere, was the real conversation: how can a man as insubstantial as Peter leave a shadow? Lee had once said of him: The Devil you know... *I* could be a more convincing devil. Did she sleep with Peter last night? The question upset her. She was losing control of her life and that upset her. Men moving backwards and forwards expecting her to be there upset her. Men self-obsessed and wanting to change the world upset her. Peter and I were the same man, she said, however much we tried to undermine each other, and that upset her. But at least Peter knew the old songs.

I agreed, disagreed, I agreed; but in the meantime how were we going to Morgan Forster – how were we going to connect?

This was not the reunion I had had in mind: maybe it was the fact that I wasn't held, hugged in youth, as a child, that was wrong. But Lee refused to let me pass this off as a joke. She felt that my solitary upbringing in St. Caesare, in a big house with my grandmother, wasn't the privilege I'd always claimed. Seeing your real family only at weekends just made you grow up thinking that that was what families did. Paid visits home. She called it neurotic of me not to admit that this is how I acted. No, I couldn't go on sheltering in St. Caesare, blaming its smallness and lack of hinterland for my predatoriness and wanting to take over the universe. All the while insisting the opposite to be the case. Even by my own sophistry, this posture of international refugee merely drew attention to myself, and made it impossible to empathise with the real refugee. She called me, in domestic matters, the Prime Minister.

As Prime Minister I was in Germany when my mother had died – representing what government? I had a homing instinct to be far away when emotional engagement beckoned. I suspected that Lee knew me too well for us to use language to communicate. Fortunately, I was a man, she was a woman.

Lee relented and said we should get up and make something to eat, and perhaps see if Mark wanted to do something, go to the cinema, perhaps. I spanked myself that the suggestion hadn't come from me.

*

As Prime Minister I was clearly responsible for Peter having died two months later in the Sudan.

*

3

Wednesday. Early Morning. Sheffield.

Thinking vaguely about a 61 year old man from Bristol, I realise
I'm playing with figures; I collect the rubbish, the dustmen
come on a Wednesday. My friends who are poets would make
some sort of poem out of this: 61-year-old man in the news.
Rubbish. Bristol, even. Why not note the time of day – after
Farming Today. Also, the fact that I'm undressed. Oh yes, there'd
be a stanza somewhere on the illness (Latin name) and the
breakdown in the Health Service which brings our man to the
attention of *The Today Programme*. Easy to be a poet. If I'd gone
down that route I'd be posturing on the circuit now with my three
or four slim volumes and, like Smythe, our resident poet, I'd
even be collecting my 'live introductions' at poetry readings
into a book. Don't talk to me about poets. (With the exception
of Lee, of course.)

Though the fascination lingers, of the Bristol man's age: 61.
Let's say that's the end of his active life; why should you think
him as young, unfortunate? Shakespeare went at 56 – *don't
think about it*. Why shouldn't he simply be *marked* out of 61
instead of some notional span of 100? Or is this relativism gone
mad. Someone was talking the other day about the breaking of
slogans. The role of the philosopher, the role of the writer,
whatever. Is 100% a slogan? Break it, break it; why not mark
out of a maximum of 61; out of a maximum of *three*! (*Three's*
excellent. Quality. *Two?* Well, two's satisfactory, but 2½ is
better: with 2½ you get the girl, or if you're the girl you get to
meet the gigolo, all tight pants and Verdi, on a southern beach.
Less than *two*, well, it's transportation for you, son; this is a
small country, etc. Or the cheaper alternative would be to send
you to university. I can't remember how far down the road I
followed this except to say that on the scale of 100, I reserved
the right to go up to 103. 105. (If not 61, then 105: *if... then*: What
an elegant construction! Do all languages have it? Are those
deprived who don't have it. Mind as scale (scales). Poised to weigh
possibility. Superior machine this, well-oiled. Good nick – to be

located by a PhD student in some strange place like Derby: that's
a university, see!) So if this scale of marking causes problems with
the Second Marker (Yer wot, 103?) and with the moderator and the
External – wonderful scene at the Exam Board – you might have
to compromise and convert the student into a different form of life,
a tree, say, longer living than a man, than a woman. So these
Second Yearers are potential oak (in some country, some part of
the country where there's no tree disease); that boy from Doncaster
with the ring in his ear promises, despite appearances to be
greenheart, durable, his feet deep into Guyana clay for the next few
centuries. But look at this, this failed creature – how did it get here,
who was on admissions that day? – this is a *fly*. But I'm beginning
to lose it.

Downstairs I'm trapped; trapped in my overcoat, nothing on
underneath, but shoes, laces not done up, and a bag of rubbish
in my hand. The dustmen come early and I'm feeling virtuous
in beating them to it. But my neighbour is waiting, fully dressed
for outdoors, raincoat neatly buckled, to interrogate me. I don't
know her name though on the letter-box she's Mrs something or
other (how could so many people have been married?). All the
names are on the letter boxes in front of us, and we've
exchanged Christmas cards the past two years; but I still mix
them up, my neighbours. They don't *look* alike but they are
alike, these 61ers (71ers? I'm the young man on the block, a
vigorous 50, their security, I like to think). Their independence
must make them see *difference* rather than similarities among
themselves (one's a couple and that helps): I don't want to praise
them for being able to do their own shopping and to climb stairs
and beat the wheelchair brigade. Though I suppose if they were a
different – dare I say it? – class, they would be in some shabby-
genteel guest house off the Brompton Road in London. Or in some
similar Brompton Road in Harrogate or York. (There's a play here
– there's a play everywhere – upgrading Rattigan, maybe *Separate
Tables* if you could be bothered. *But this woman is old*.
     She's dressed for going out – is it for her early-morning walk;
is that what keeps her going? – and wants to ask me about gas
fumes supposedly killing us. This is an old story, and I do

suspect that we're all a bit less healthy now than when I first moved into this house. I have fumes seeping through to my flat, she has fumes in her flat; we've called out the landlord; we've called up the Gas Board; they've come three or four times over the past eighteen months or so, but their instruments record nothing. Most times, as you'd expect, the fumes retreat just as the men to sort them out arrive. So no amount of sophisticated equipment (it wasn't that sophisticated, actually) has been able to detect a gas leak or any malfunctioning of the boiler. It's in the imagination, they hint to the over-61s (over-71s) some of whom half-suspect it might be true. It's from the drains, they say to me, cautious, unsettled by the weight of my books. They do their thing, then put up a card with a painted, yellow sun over the boiler in the kitchen, while we stand to see if the sun turns black. Give it a few weeks, months. And after some time – maybe a couple of months – the yellow circle does go brownish; but that's a slow poison, safe enough to live with. Then the fumes seem to go away. When they come back, and strongly, is when you've been away for a week or so, with the windows shut. (So is it only ventilation that saves you?) Or, as everyone points out, it strikes when the weather is cold, pointing a finger at the boiler. Though I seem to notice it at other times, after a bad phone-call, or sudden wakefulness in the middle of the night. And here am I at the front door, naked under my coat, rubbish in hand, being asked what to do about the gas leak. (*What's that Sophie Tucker line about pees and leaks?*)

Any thought of making something out of the 61-year-old man in Bristol fades, so I'm puzzled at the time of day – *where's she really going, fully dressed; where's the northern dressing-gown?* – the cold, icing you from the open front door – and I'm conscious of breathing in stale cigarette smoke. I'm thinking of something Chekhov said, that if you have a gun hanging on the wall in the first act, it should be fired before the final curtain. (*What would the poor man do if he lived in modern America?*) I think of that house in Dickens that blows up at the end, brought down by the *weight* of evil. Do I want to go out in this company? Someone must have made a note of our numerous warnings; the gas board must have a record of when they've been called out, unless their efficiency savings runs to tearing up records to do with customer anxiety. But someone, some rogue or mole (educated by us, a City graduate?) must have made a note of when they've been called out. So when our little housing association house blows up on the news – and again with greater detail on LOOK NORTH – someone will pay for it. God. Allah. Mother T. Why not that lady at No 36 Grasmore Road, Higher Openshaw, Manchester (which is a town in England). Some smartarse northern playwright will home in and write the play portraying us as casualties of capitalist greed and third-world incompetence. Come to think of it we might even do better at the hands of Carrington: he might have the imagination to attribute it all to the internal combustion of my books – all those dodgy ideas rubbing slowly up against one another; the thing fed by literary anthologies where enemies, placed on facing pages, repeatedly strike sparks, whatever: that might make us interesting to the viewer.

This lipless woman neighbour is enjoying my discomfort, she's tougher than I think; her children, grandchildren occupy more space in this country than I imagine; her eyes flick from my left hand, holding together the coat, to the untied laces, no socks; and she keeps talking. (I'm on the defensive thinking I must find time to go to the dry-cleaners and get some buttons put back on the coat – a lovely, long coat, inherited from Lee.) She says – they take risks during these conversations – that she's pleased that I, too, can smell the gas; her son came round the other day and pretended it was only the cat (*she whispers this*). We must keep representing the case to the landlords, though she's thinking of leaving, moving out. (This, too, is in confidence.) To be cruel I complain about the cigarette smoke here in the stairwell and on the top landing seeping through my door upstairs. She's a smoker, she says, but not a *heavy* one. I'm thinking of this light woman and whether she'd be heavy smoking 40 a day. (Linguistic Pragmatism, my friends in Linguistics call this.) There are two doors between her smoke and me, she says. I like that; I like the conceit of that, the two doors between her smoking and me. So I retract and say it's the other lot, the couple (I think of them as Herr and Frau Halterbush – a private joke) who are the culprits. Then she whispers more confidences and by the time I'm released to put the rubbish in the bin outside I have a vague sense of disorientation and feelings of displace-

ment. But somehow this makes me want to get on with it, even to
attack some marking. (*On attaque*, my friends in Spéracèdes say,
when they pick up a brush and dustpan.)

Back in the flat, sans rubbish, I start running the bath – don't
forget the dentist – and lining up literary editing for marking.

A good three hours: the marking is so elegant it's almost a
modernist poem; I like it. My processes of getting there are
sheer epic poem; I want to tell someone about it. Ah, but these
are *university* types, they're not writerly people; the real writers
only come in part time and work on the MA. Except for Smythe.
But I don't have this sort of relationship with Smythe – despite
the fact that we both love 'writerly' PASSWORDS for our computers: his is GOWER, mine BOYLE after the short-story writer and
novelist amputee, T. Coraghessan. So I'll have to talk to my
extra-curricular muse (muses) later. But for now I've got some
Firsts for Dave, the second marker, to look at.

*(A note about Dave: Dave is actually a person. But at City
you're never sure who's who. I get them mixed up, anyway.
There's Dave and Chris and Steve; then there's Joe and Ian and
Keif. They're all youngish, whitish; it's too strenuous trying to
distinguish between them. They don't help: no one's got one leg
missing; I see them all having the same mother who, agewise,
would be my wife whom I beat, for producing those sons: they are
my children, dear God. At least Smythe is different, he's got a real
name, Rupert, that can't be shortened to Rup. or Pete (which is
probably why he avoids going to America); can't be shortened,
either, into something new-universityish [see above]; maybe that
gives him the confidence to be our writer-in-residence. The
women are a little better. There is Fiona and Debby, Sara, Julie,
Linda. Names for middlebrow fiction. But then to lift it all there's
La Gardner, our Renaissance person, our – in academic terms –
marriage to old money. The Debbies etc. might have a sort of
bottom-spanking appeal but we like to think that the three who
stood out were La Gardner, Rupert Smythe and, well, Pewter
Stapleton. Oh, yes, and I forget, Rolls (real name Richard). Good
man. Head of Department. We liked him because of his wife, Liz.
She was a short-story writer. Canadian. And Rolls was gradually*

beginning to take on her accent. One day I'll write a play about him
turning into her: already I see his hips broadening. But Dave:
Dave's the man who'd be second marking my Literary Editing.)

Mid-morning

The good feeling of having delivered some scripts to Dave
vanishes as I cross the campus and encounter two men cutting
down our trees. I know them, they work here, in their uniforms,
which make them look stage-handy. I often stop to have a chat,
exchanging a word about their trimming and sweeping up of
leaves; about the weather, time, life. (Why write plays when
they mount themselves here, everywhere, sort of thing?) The
men seem to spend a lot of time tending the tennis courts; last
week they were clearing snow; they were miffed, then, because
in that very heavy fall, some official (an accountant) insisted on
parking his car in the usual place, so the men had to get out their
shovels, not just to clear a space for the car but a path to the side
of the building. The explanation was that the path had to be
cleared anyway, for students. At the time I'd been chatting to
them it was snowing again so we had the usual exchange about
Little Six Letters in power, and all that. I had urged them to go
slow. But that was bad advice because it was cold, they were
outside, it was snowing: to avoid being frozen stiff they had to
speed up the work. *Nature, it seemed, had no interest in learning*
about the march of history.

Today was different; they were cutting down trees, the
wonderful squirrel-inhabited hedge between the tennis courts
and Education. Why? What's going on? But I tune down my
response flicking, absurdly, through my mind the things I have
to get through this morning (I remember it's Wednesday and
there's some sort of English Department meeting this afternoon, but I won't go to it). But for now: the dentist, a couple of
paragraphs for Dave on the literary editing course because he
wasn't in the office when I dropped off the folders. So (I have to say
something to these men) why cut down the trees?

'Flashers.'

'What?'
'We've got flashers.'
(In this weather!)
I don't want, really, to hear any more of this.

*

It's a race against time: *what an odd thing to say, to think?* (Once, an optician said to me, 'You're short sighted,' and I thought: my life in a sentence.) But now I have an image of old men, lined up, some sort of race. Geriatric Olympians awaiting the starting pistol – will he lower the pistol, aim at the line? – wheelchairs and crutches straining, ready to knock the hell out of emphysema and cancer hopefuls. And the odd born-again leper. Their middle-aged children who stand to inherit egging them on. *Egging them on?* No no, give it a rest. I remember, though, teaching EFL in the old days: EFL, ESP, what have you – sounds like a Mozambiquan guerilla movement – and writing an entire play in idioms – though I'd be hard-pressed now to manage one of acronyms – for my Greek Cypriots, back in the Kilburn Poly days my first teaching job; got them to perform it, too. Abuse of power, I suppose. Resurrected it at Southgate for my Italians, Italians from Bari; Summer School, all those beautiful Alessandras and Francescas ('Juan Carlo, andiamo,' on our way to Shakespeare in the Park). But this won't do, I'm losing it (is my mind going?): where's all that logic (Logic) that used to locate you in that little room next to Russell and Wittgenstein? At least, as a young man it gave you something you might offer to superior women. Why so little impact on the life lived: mightn't it have been better, then, to be an *Accountant* and end up running the university? This, at least, concentrates the mind and, very quickly, I write the note for Dave.

LITERARY EDITING. Yr.3 10 points: A NOTE

This unit is a bugger to mark. There seems to be no way of reducing the workload of marking the three main elements – LOG, ESSAY and PROJECT – separately, before taking an aggregate. Though *some* sense of overview must be maintained, particularly in cases where the *feel* of a marginal First or Fail might warrant adjustment to the component marks.

One idea informing this unit is that aspects of the *academic* programme might be a little over-directed (the terrorists will deny this) encouraging a mind-set of dependency in the student. Have we gone too far the other way? Perhaps. I'll bring a little more focus to proceedings next year. But the aim will continue to be to encourage Yr. 3 students to take more responsibility for an area of study; as well as introducing them to elements of research.

Marks are likely to be suspiciously high this year as the course, in its scope and workload, is properly a 20 rather than a 10 point unit. The External agrees with us on this second point; so from the 1996-97 session the course will be offered, virtually unchanged, at 20 points.

Yes, with the odd adjustment. Take out 'bugger' and 'terrorists,' and add something about the quality of analysis required at this level.

Of course this isn't for Dave, it's for the man on the bus in Stoke Newington. (Yes, through deep research I've discovered the identity of the man on the Clapham omnibus; he's the driver, marooned in Stoke Newington, his skin reflecting his mood.) I disgraced myself that day and had to work my passage back. I was on the bus with Lee, who was thinking of moving house from West Hampstead and had already got rid of the car; and we'd already done the swish end, Church Street, looking at possible houses, popping into the bookshop and across the road at the *Vortex*, refusing to admit that things seemed a bit precious (even the second-hand bookshop downstairs looked a bit precious). So we decided to take a look at the other end of the borough to see if the warnings of friends would impress us: Stoke Newington had a fearsome reputation for its racist police and that sort of thing.

It was certainly lively, a marked middle-eastern (Turkish) and West Indian presence. Young, arrogant-looking over-fed boys screaming round in MGs: black men, blonde girls (bringing to mind a Carrington play). It's the old thing, isn't it. Someone points out something, directs your gaze and you see what they want you to see: I remember being in the South of France, my favourite village in the *Alpes Maritimes*, Cabris, at the Look Out, looking down over the wide valley of Peymeinade, all the way to Cannes in one direction, and the lake in the other. (Actually, I was peering down to see if I could see my little ruin down at Spéracèdes; I couldn't.) But there I was, with two friends, looking down at the mess below me, growing depressed: Peymeinade seemed to have spread to fill the entire valley and had crept halfway up the surrounding hills; a sprawl of yellow tiles and swimming pools, unnaturally blue, violating my memory of the place. But one of the people I was with was a painter, and she pointed out the green-black cypresses breaking up the view; and instantly, the eyesore which was Peymeinade assumed detail, gave the scene new possibilities of shape, colour. (It didn't entirely lift the mood, but it *looked* better.) Anyway, we were in Stoke Newington, Lee and I, on the bus to what would now be Dalston, and what I saw was a film set of Carrington extras – the 'tanklike black women,' the 'white street-walking bitches' of his play. A woman dramatist, or Lee, even, might see something else, assorted menacing threat in trousers.

We were onto the second bus now, Lee and I, and it was hot, summer: this was like going on holiday. Destination Hackney. Hackney had an improved PR image, of having the highest concentration of artists in Europe, cheap and unsafe, contributing to the creative tension. I knew bits of it, only I hadn't identified them as Hackney. My old magazine had moved offices into the area, so I was an occasional visitor. And there was the *Centreprise Bookshop*. Years ago I'd brought my Italians from Summer School to Petticoat Lane. Not far. So now I was 'doing' Hackney in this spirit, Lee figuratively on my arm. She found a seat on the crowded bus, somewhat to the irritation of the woman – one of the Carrington's tankwomen – who was occupying two seats: tankwoman had to remove her shopping and shift slightly and that didn't please her. I was still at the front hovering next to the driver: I'd asked him a question and he hadn't responded so I felt a bit stranded.

So he was taciturn; why not? His close-cropped hair and closed expression signalled a generation-gap between us, so I thought I'd pull rank slightly and ask him again about the cricket scores. (West Indies were playing Australia in the West Indies and we feared that our unbeaten record might be coming to an end.)

I was right about him. It's not that he was sneering, he was dismissive, which was worse. This was something more than signalling bad news for the team, so I quickly apologized for being into cricket.

'So you may as well let us off then, Mister,' this from a woman who had appeared from nowhere. 'Because you not goin' any-where.' She was pressing down on me so I had to shift. And, indeed, we were in a bit of a jam. The driver barely acknowledged her but pressed a button and the doors opened. At that point the bus edged forward and the woman stayed put; but with the invitation of an open door someone from the pavement got on, through the wrong doors, and made no attempt to come forward and pay. Without comment or change of expression the driver closed the doors.

Should I commiserate, show solidarity? I caught Lee's eye – she was suffering, sitting, uncomfortably, on the edge of the seat, trying not to block the aisle; I signalled that I'd soon be with her, that I was just having a word with the driver.

'Must be a bit tedious, eh...' and in case he misunderstood, 'having to put up with all this.' I spoke out of the side of my mouth because the woman was still standing there. I made a gesture vague enough not to offend her. This wasn't explicit enough for the driver, so I gestured towards the traffic. 'All this... standing about in the traffic. Not moving.'

'I'm moving, man.'

'Yeah?'

'What speed you want. 40 miles an hour? 100 miles? Brans Hatch?'

'Ah. A philosopher. I see you're a philosopher.'

'I studied philosophy.'

Lee was smiling but she couldn't hear the conversation; it was her discomfiture that was evident. I signalled that I was suffering, too. The bus was stationary. The driver was relaxed; but I had started something.

'So, I see you're...' I thought of and cancelled half a dozen openings, 'confusing the opposition. The enemy. Sitting here confusing the enemy.'

'That's right.' As if he was waiting for me. This was still on the edge of being amusing rather than irritating. And something clicked to stop me moving back to Lee, as the bus edged forward. Good, smooth, driving, I thought, but you don't congratulate a driver for driving well: in the same movement as he edged the bus forward he admitted to being a graduate. 'Communication Studies.' I wished he hadn't said that. 'University of North London.' This was desperate – a Balham student!

I dismissed the thought as ungenerous. But that's the sort of foolishness that Balham taught. Nothing you could identify as Sociology. Psychology. Watching Television.

The driver volunteered that he had got a 2.ii and had just missed the 2.i by one mark. Definitely a Balham student, but who cared as long as he could drive the bus; I'd better get back to Lee. But the driver suddenly wanted to talk.

He said most students played it safe (I really didn't want to hear about students) – played it safe and got their 2.i's and weren't to be seen now driving buses: Did I see them driving buses?

I didn't see anything wrong with averagely uneducated people driving buses (even though the degree might be in something called Communication Studies) but I didn't want a philosophical discussion.

He was doing it on purpose; he saw me trying to edge away: you couldn't walk away from the driver when he was telling you that he had read linguistics and Gothic as well as philosophy. Oh yes, he'd done all that, and what's more...

I saw Lee get up in defeat because it was more comfortable than trying to hang on to the edge of the seat next to the tankwoman, so I excused myself and went towards her and rang the bell.

'We've paid, haven't we?' Lee asked a bit puzzled. Because the driver was signalling. For a moment I thought he'd remembered the cricket score, and squeezed forward to find out.

But what he said was that he'd done Prose Fiction as well as Gothic and Linguistics. In the Gothic he'd done *The Italian* and *The Monk* and *Dracula*. As well as *Silence of the Lambs*.

We escaped after this, waving goodbye, and I gave him the
thumbs up sign from the pavement, where I swear, he was
mouthing D.E.R.I.D.A. from the driver's seat.

Lee was getting cross; I was indulging myself; I was caught out
trying to imagine what this man would be like as a Communica-
tions Studies student at City, drifting by mistake into one of our
Second Year creative writing seminars. Into Poetry. He was a
competent bus driver, so he might well have applied the tricks of
distinguishing brake from petrol pedal, bringing the skills of
manipulating clutch and avoiding accident to the writing of a
sestina; he had let that man onto the bus and not insisted on the
fare being paid, so that was a hopeful sign, *only just a fail*. (If he
chooses to improve his *writing* credentials by paying for the
passenger out of his own pocket, so that the company doesn't lose
out, then our man was on the right side of the line. *Low 2.ii, even*.
Ah, but now we're marking his *civic* awareness. He'd read some
philosophy. Question of ethics, here. It's not so much that the
company didn't lose out, just a small matter of rightness, justice,
your-place-in-the-queueness to other paying passengers. Unless
this was a revolutionary situation. Surely Dalston was ripe for it.
Though he didn't know the cricket score. Bad sign. And he did
mouth D.E.R.I.D.A. *Very* bad sign.

But we are not brutes at City; we like the man's driving, and it
would be good to communicate this to the Second Marker, call him
Dave, in extenuation: if the student was unspeakable you could
indulge in a modicum of wit. But wit at this man's expense was
already proving strenuous. And he had taken a 'difficult' option.
Creative writing. Not your run of the mill Eng Lit scam of tell me
what to think about Wordsworth, but risking exposure by trying to
write some poetry. Better respect that and play it straight. So here's
his report:

This is an uneven folder. There are poems that strain badly
at emotion (an example) which are barely 2.ii level; though
others (example) are marginally more successful. There is
rhythmic monotony even though some poems are cunningly
shaped to disguise it. [Still in the lower reaches of the 2.ii.] There
are poems that state the obvious and could be rescued with wit,

or an experiment with form, but the student has settled for statement-making; lists (Oh, My Chris Logue and Adrian Henry Long Ago!) The obviousness, the banality, the knowingness (Woolworth rhymes and inversions) all suggest a 2.iii (Sorry. Third.) But he didn't have an accident. 2ii (Tutu)

(52)

PS. *To think that this man might end up with a good woman who wouldn't cuckold him.*

(51)

*

Yes, and I could be bothered: what did he mean, 'Flashers?' The gardeners, stage-handy, were poised, still in mid-gesture, waiting for release: It's half-past ten in the morning. It's cold, the snow has only just melted:

'We've got flashers?'

'We've got flashers hiding in the hedge. So we got to cut them down.'

'In this weather!'

(Apparently, the flashers had been spotted last Spring, but the paperwork had just come through to cut down the trees!)

I'm not with it, I'm thinking of the literary editing note I must get to Dave to explain the structure of the course and justify the high number of firsts – seven out of 24. Two groups. I didn't leave the original note; it seemed a bit inadequate. We must also send a note to the External.

The old man, the plump one in his one-piece overall, a 'worker' dressed for the part, holds up a thick branch, neatly sawn off. The bit of tree seems so... firm next to this man, his soft bulk, soft face, jowls.

'They've got flashers so we've got to cut down the trees,' he says.

'But that's ridiculous.'

He refers to the branch in his hand. 'They don't see this as something living.' (I begin to feel guilty for having seen him, vaguely, as 'other'.) 'They got a problem, they say cut down the trees.' This, in sadness rather than anger.

They. 'So who's, um... Who's doing this, who's saying this? I mean, who...?'

'Just orders.' The man must be 60. Sixties. Of course he looks older.

'So who's telling you to cut down the trees!' (I know him of. course, but not being able to put a name to him seems unfriendly, a tiny betrayal.)

'The same ones as had us out in the snow.' He probably isn't able to say No to *them*, his contract probably doesn't run to it; is he in a union, does he vote in General Elections, is he MI5? I was never really sold on unions till my experience in Germany, in the Language School in Köln in '74 where Frau Halterbush sought to deny us that privilege. But I'm overtired, marking, I can't pursue the simplest thought. What short-circuits my mind is being back at Coderington, at elementary school; spelling test on a rainy day and disgracing myself in not being able to distinguish between 'union' and 'onion': I see this man now, in his smooth one-piece outer skin, as onion. I'm beginning to lose sympathy with onion; I wonder if he could make eyes water; he's still holding up the branch.

'They don't think of this as something living. To them it's just a problem. They don't think of this as putting oxygen back into the atmosphere.'

I like the 'back'; he's working to laws other than ego, he isn't just concerned with fighting *them*; he's an ally. But this shouldn't be a tutorial, this should be a seminar. I think of his fellow students coming to the rescue, coming with their placards SAVE OUR TREES or whatever. I remember being in America, with Lindsay. We had friends at Amherst. It was a lovely spring day when we visited. Students, American and healthy and friendly everywhere. Lovely well-kept lawns. And in front of one of the buildings – lovely, period building – was this girl-student holding up a tree. She couldn't have been more than eighteen. Short and stocky. Powerful legs – wearing shorts. And this massive tree hundreds of years old seemed in no danger from anyone. But there she was on the lawn, legs apart, shoulders hunched, holding up the tree. She was holding it up not pushing it down because the ground fell away gently and she was on the side of the incline, pushing. I felt better about America that day. Ah, but that is over *there*. Our students are anxious about exams, resentful about the cut in grants; depressed about job prospects; furious at those of us who survived from the days when you could screw around with no fear of Aids: they're not (tree-saving) allies. What of the staff? The staff are desperately marking, too traumatised to march. (Must get that *note* to Dave; then go to the dentist, the hygienist.) Do I promise this worker to get in touch with *them*, to identify *them*, to *out* them. Publish their names somewhere and invite passers-by to shoot, or maybe to spit on sight? Or am I drifting into a play? *Flasher despoiling campus. Idea: if something nasty chooses to plonk itself down in our midst – call it FASCIST – we must conclude the thing to do is to vandalise our own environment – shit on your own seat – so we can all be deprived together*. I've got to go; I don't promise to save the trees, but I resolve to call *them*.

Just back from the dentist and Rolls rings my room to ask if I'm coming down to lunch. I hadn't thought of lunch, particularly – messing up the work of the hygienist – but Rolls is an ally: he'll be Canadian one day, and is lining up his literary references. Already he's conversant with the Margaret before Atwood and Irving Layton *and* he knew about Carrington before I made Carrington required lunchtime conversation. Good man, Rolls. But there's always a down side. He teaches Gothic, but you can't have everything. So, why not go to lunch, take a break: I was just reading my e-mail, anyway, putting off more urgent things to do. Rolls will ask about the Carrington book. As Head of Department he's anxious for us to publish, and I've been dragging my heels here a bit. (It's hard to think of editing a book of Carrington's plays as *academic* work, but if the academics take it seriously, why not? The Quality Assessment Exercise is coming up, so there's publishing fever in the Department.) The *Introduction* which I've sketched out, will be benign and informative. And a bugger to do.

Rolls will be five minutes, so I decide to glance at my progress with the book. The thing to do is to write about myself under the guise of writing about Carrington. What I'm actually recalling is the joke I heard on Radio Four first thing this morning, one of those

Humphrey Littleton-type jokes; must remember to tell it over lunch. Probably a bit down-market for Humph. More Ronnie Scott: *Her mother was a titled Lady; she was the light-heavyweight champion of South London*. That's what you're up against, Natalie!

M.B. CARRINGTON: SEVEN PLAYS
(Edited by Pewter Stapleton)

Black Cab
Big Momma & the White, Street-walking Bitches
King Lear
Ibrahim and the Countess. Or *(The Third Gentleman of Verona)*

& then three from
The Rainbow Arts Factory/Meet the Hostages/Payback
Battyman/Her House Without Drawing-Rooms/Daughters/
Voltaire's Negroes/From Charlemagne to the Christians in
Spain/Let Me Have Men About Me (with P.S.)/*Severus of Enga*
    *(*with P.S.*)*
+ typescripts from Kent
+ the translations (Surinamese)?
+ the Irish play

The thing was beginning to shape, and the thrust of the *Introduction*, I suppose, would make the final selection easier. Methuen suggested a balance in favour of the set-in-Britain rather than Canada plays, but they didn't insist on it; and that was fine, because those were among the stronger pieces, anyway: my criterion was that any text I put in had to work effectively on stage; that way I could justify editing Carrington rather than Walcott, say, or maybe Mustapha Matura or Edgar White.

But Carrington took more risks than the others. *Big Momma...* was a play that still sent out minor shock waves, not saying the expected things about race, not being PC; and even a play like *Ibrahim...* (a loose dramatisation of Pushkin's novella) didn't do the obvious, careful, PC things. And of course, *King Lear* was the big one, Lear as stroke victim, and the Daughter-therapists, not believing his story that he was an ex-king of England, prod him with his own speeches and recite an alternative version of England, King James's England, in 1606 when the play was first performed, till the thing works despite itself and the King gets up out of his wheelchair.

In Act Two Lear is entering customs in Montserrat, Carrington's island. The King, dressed like an ordinary middle-aged Englishman, is being politely grilled by customs officers, a uniformed man and woman. Lear claims to have been a king, but long ago and far away. They want to know if he was king during the days of Drake & Raleigh & Hawkins and Columbus & Enoch Powell & Ian Smith & Mrs Thatcher. And when he seems confused they take that as complicity and demand reparations for Montserrat.

Lear then disassociates himself from the excesses of England, describing them without euphemism to show which side he's on. The customs officers relent and agree to let him in on condition that he confesses to the milder sins of hanging on to a diction and idiom resistant to the realities of a multicultural environment (that's one charge) and also, for a body-language conveying an insufficient love of black women.

The play is funnier than *The Third Gentleman of Verona*, which is, really, a dramatisation of some of Catullus' poems (Catullus was born in Verona) and playing games with gay relationships. The play wasn't as strong as *King Lear* but I'd seen it at the *Keskadee* and was impressed to see a substantial number of the black women in the audience laughing at the gay goings-on.

I won't make a decision on *The Gentleman... until* I can get hold of the scripts of Carrington's Irish plays. He'd spent three years in Ulster and it was inconceivable that there wouldn't be plays resulting. He'd done a Joyce sketch which was quite amusing, something about the Dublin ladies and Bloom, but he hadn't, as far as I know, expanded it to fuller length. I'm told that the Irish material was among his stuff in Kent. Failing that I was certainly prepared to go to Maryland, where the superstar was now teaching, having pronounced Black arts in Britain dead. (The attempt to catch up with him on his brief visit to Ulster wasn't going to work out.)

He'd always denied he was writing a political Irish play, but we knew better: rumour was that he'd been researching an historical piece about the ancient rulers of Ulster, the O'Neills, and I'm sure that now he was safely out of the province it would miraculously emerge. Carrington never let an opportunity slip: I admit in this I was thinking less of the plays than the mileage I could get in the *Introduction* presenting Carrington (born in Montserrat, an island colonised by the Irish in the 1630s) as someone returning 'home' to Ulster to meddle in the Province's affairs. In a strange sense I envied him.

Ah. Rolls.

*

At lunch La Gardner, our Renaissance lady, brought in her baby daughter, Chloe, who was clutching a disabled toy; the toy was a child with some sort of muscular problem in a wheelchair. Everyone was duly impressed by this, though when her back was turned to get some water, people started to analyse it in terms of power play. It surprised me because I'd always seen La Gardner as someone who was into silks and frills and Renaissancy things: she had a reputation of being formidably bright and not to be crossed; I liked her, and having read one of her books on Queen Elizabeth, was impressed by her prose style. But we still thought of La Gardner as someone born to sit for a Van Eyck painting, the current favourite being the wonderfully bejewelled and brocaded feast of pattern and colour that is her meeting with the Chancellor of Burgundy, who properly kneels before her.

Here, in the City canteen, it was clear that La Gardner was asserting her presence as a contemporary woman against our image of her as *painting*. Smythe had fallen foul of La Gardner because he'd pushed the work-of-art analogy too far. First, as sonnet: not only did he write sonnets to her (about her?) which earned mock disapproval, but he got his First Year students to have a go. The idea that to empathise with a traditional poetic form it helped to approach it from the point of view of the practitioner wasn't the issue; this was part of the value of creative writing in the academy, but it was a serious lack of tact to set students loose on La Gardner, as subject for a Petrarchan sonnet. Anyway, Smythe wasn't around today, he was probably marking at home (he was on

half-sabbatical, anyway), so we didn't have to suffer one of those
politely-charged, literary-nuanced conversations over lunch.
(When there was no tension in this area Smythe was referred to as
Rupert; when things were a bit suspect he reverted to being
Smythe and when La Gardner felt aggrieved she dismissed him as
Mr. Smith. I actually wanted to see Smythe about a couple of
things, one of which was a new course on the Epic that he was
developing, to which he wanted me to contribute: I still had to
think about that.)

Smythe's name came up of course. Apparently, in his absence
a couple of students (or visitors) had access to his room to breast-
feed their infants. Of course no one had problems with that, but
some felt that Smythe was characteristically being voyeuristic,
even at a distance. I must say I had a room next to Smythe in the
Mews (writers in the Mews?), and I'd never seen any breast-
feeding activity.

What concentrated our minds was Rolls' news that the subject
group meeting scheduled for this afternoon might well be hijacked
by the new school manager to get us to rubber-stamp decisions
already made about our working conditions; and he urged us to
turn up ready to protest. But I was ahead of him there.

I didn't want to talk about meetings, so I brought up the
business of their cutting down our trees, to demonstrate my
concern for our working environment. The outrage, though genuine, lacked passion. Someone – an historian – reminded us there
was a passage in Joyce about cutting down trees; there was a weary
acceptance that they had struck again, that *they* were undefeatable
because they struck at random, and enjoyed their vandalism:
maybe our best posture would be to pretend not to notice! It was
that section in *Ulysses*, he said, the historian said, where they
feared that the trees of Ireland were vanishing. Making Ireland as
treeless as Portugal. And someone, maybe not Bloom – he was off
somewhere down on the beach being given the come-on by the
delectable Gerty – anyway there's this fantasy of this wedding,
where all the women guests at the wedding have the names of trees,
have become trees, y'know: Miss Mahogany and the Lady Maple
and that sort of thing; whole forests of them. And of course, at the
end, the bride and groom – the Conifers, don't you know – go off

to honeymoon in the Black Forest. And what's more. What's more... And I was beginning to see possibilities for a little drama there: Mr Breadfruit and Mrs Breadnut. Grafted Mango (girl), Dasheen (boy), Sugarapple (girl), Yam (boy), Guava and Plum (twins)... By which time some around the table were defending Portugal from the charge of being treeless. Ah, but it was all too strenuous. At some point I stopped listening; I was thinking of my hygienist, guilty that I was messing up her work, eating, puzzled at how she could accommodate herself to that horrible job, making it comfortable for you in the chair by resting your head against her breast (Medical Psychology?) I suppose I would have to justify my thinking about her in this way, justifying myself to Lee, to women, to the ethics of marking? But first a cup of tea.

You don't ask for much; just a cup of tea after lunch and maybe a quick scan of your e-mail, and then home to mark. But there's no tea in the staff common room. Am I being neurotic? There *is* something there labelled SAINSBURY'S Blackcurrant Herbal. SAINSBURY'S Peppermint Herbal, and more of the same. I've got nothing against herbal, but I feel pressured – what am I, a writer, doing here? – and what I want is good, old-fashioned Tetley Tea Bags. PG Tips. Anything normal: I've tried to be fair to Natalie and the rest of them; I have to fight the feeling that what I'm doing matters. And on top of that they're cutting down our goddam trees and there is no chunky American student to intervene. Maybe I should go to that subject group meeting and confront the new school manager as if...

And then there was the incident: Smythe in the car-park embracing a woman. The surprise was perhaps to run into Smythe whom we didn't think was on campus. And he wasn't really embracing her, it was an altercation. This was just in the space between the English Department building and the Mews with the three writers' rooms.

I knew the woman but I just couldn't place her; she certainly wasn't Smythe's partner. This middle-aged woman was seriously agitated, waving her arms about though, it seems, willing to be placated. The scene was too public for comfort. Naturally, I passed straight on, nodded my acknowledgement, and   went straight up to my room. I could have sworn I heard the woman complain of being without light and trees, but this must have been my hang-up from earlier, with the men above the tennis courts. In order not to run into the couple again, I decided to sit in my room and read my e-mail.

A short time later Smythe knocked on the door, agitated.

'Come and see this,' he said. (No 'hello,' no 'Hi Pewter.' Just 'Come and see this.')

I followed him. He was clearly still suffering from the incident with the woman. But she had vanished. He took me up to a spot above the tennis courts where the trees were being cut down and someone had made a fire, sensibly, in the cold. The woman, agitated, was there. She was the university printer who had done a couple of brochures for me, but I couldn't remember her name. But, of course, she knew me, which was embarrassing. Then Smythe introduced her as Jenny.

An odd, little ritual. Instead of our men in overalls, a younger man was keeping the fire going, with paper, old files. He was more casually dressed. ...Oh, but Jenny was crying.

'What's up?'

Smythe made a gesture with his hand, one of those 'You can see it for yourself, what's there to say?' gestures – the gesture that Allen Ginsberg made at the US Democratic Convention in Chicago in '68 when Mayor Daley's men teargassed the protesters and helped to scupper Hubert Humphrey's chances of succeeding LBJ to the White House.

'So?' I asked Smythe.

'Student folders.'

I could see now they were student folders. Why was this upsetting Jenny? Are they clearing them out; have they outlived their shelf life?

'These are this year's folders. Collect them, you bums, or we burn the fuckers. Why should a university devote expensive space to your Special Study on Tennessee Williams and Atwood. You've got the degree, now piss off. Only, some of these are second year folders. You might actually need them to refer to at next year's exam board. So burn the fuckers anyway. And any other shit you find lying around. Again, he moved to comfort the woman, Jenny, whose distress seemed more genuine than his. What prompted this was the arrival of a young man with more files for burning. (I couldn't help thinking of a Christopher Fry play that we had mounted in Lampeter in 1965.)

'Here we go. Books. The book burning. At least that makes a modicum of sense. Why should books take up so much space in an institution hostile to learning?'

His overreaction had the benefit of lifting the spirits of Jenny a little and we urged her off to the pub, the *Aunt Sally* at the top of the road. I had a chat with Jenny now, her independence lost now she was being gobbled up by the new University Press; she had spent weeks moving office to some site in the middle of town (no light, no trees) and having got settled in the new, 'brutal' space, they'd ordered her to move again because one of the Accountants wanted her new office, and she'd had enough; she'd had enough. Coming back to her old place and seeing them burning the students' work made her feel there was nowhere left to go.

Smythe wanted to talk to me about the literary magazine, the university magazine, which he edited. Jenny was the printer. He was trying to make it more professional; and my experience of having edited *Rainbow* in London was something he wanted to draw on. He had just got a new grant for the magazine from Yorkshire and Humberside Arts, and that would transform the publication. But he, too, had had enough, I'd better brace myself to take over sooner rather than later as he just had to get out, to go to America where they took these things seriously. Not that they appreciate writers over there, either, but in America they recognised a writer's ability to do them damage. (*They? Them?*) Did we know there was once an economist, Kissinger by name, who had a job at Harvard. It was at the same time that the writer Robert Penn Warren happened to be in residence at Harvard. And if we looked at the Harvard Prospectus for those years, we'd see that it's the writer not the economist who is featured as the drawing card. That must tell us something. Before we left Smythe said we should add our Salman Rushdie books to the City pyre above the tennis courts, a non-symbolic act, so as not to brainwash ourselves that nothing desperate was taking place on our campus.

Evening in the Mews. Smythe

SMYTHE
- who is subject to office gossip – *think of that wonderful poem by Gavin Ewart*
- who is someone thought to misquote shamelessly – *think of your old Latin master*
- who is a wit and a bore – *Like me? Like me.*
- who has a reputation for practical jokes which misfire – like organising a spoof *Any Questions* and surviving with a reprimand
- whose voice disguises a Northern accent so imperfectly that no one knows if it's deliberate – *Ugh.*
- who is writer-in-residence at Sheffield City University – *poor bastard*
- who as writer-in-residence shouldn't be allowed a sabbatical ahead of full-time academic staff – *quite right*
- whose computer PASSWORD is GOWER – *poet or cricketer?*
- who has published two books of poetry – *full marks for restraint*
- who has published *only* two books of poetry – *that's different*
- who is famous for mangling Hopkins's *Wreck of the Deutschland* in performance – *a fine dub poem, that*
- who was neither included in *The New Generation* poets (too old at 42? Nor in the controversial *The New Poetry*, for which he was eligible, and which featured fifty-five British and Irish poets – so at best he's No. 56 – *good, not to be discredited, not to be compromised*
- who is reputed to have little French and less Greek (though he's fond of quoting, among others the Latin poet Terentius Varro) – *oh dear*

- What else?

SMYTHE

- who will now ease up on academic rivals 'who have nothing to show for their pains but their PhDs', and train his fire on

the Accountants, the new subject of his campus novel in
verse, a full-length work in sprung rhythm which the world
will find awesome.

- *And who is involved in something hush hush with Pewter
  Stapleton.*
- SMYTHE (who likes to debate computer PASSWORD codes
  with Pewter – GOWER versus BOYLE) is in his room tonight.

*

I knocked on his door, next to mine, surprised to find his lights
on; I gave him a few moments to compose himself (would Jenny be
in there breast-feeding?) as he seemed always to be taken by
surprise when you entered his room. Also, he tended not to say
'Come in' when you knocked, a cultivated oddity.

He looked up from a picture-book on his desk. (Often, you'd
catch him in the process of folding away a newspaper and hiding
it in a drawer: he said the academics joked about it because they
didn't realize reading the newspaper might be a form of
research for someone not doing Media Studies or rehashing
Milton. I had no problem with that, but he did the same to me;
he hid away his newspaper when I entered. Tonight, it was a
picture-book, a cookery book, and he didn't hide it away.)

'Pewter!' He looked startled.

What was there to say about today; that was already an old
story; so I mentioned it only obliquely.

'So are you all ready and set for foreign parts!' I thought of
his threat to go to America. If someone wasn't spontaneous
there was little you could do to prepare him to be relaxed in your
company. (Even today hadn't really broken the ice.) I remember giving a reading with Smythe, to the first years, a couple of
years ago, first day of term, and noted how he had scrupulously
written out all of his introductory comments, as well as the 'ad libs'
between poems; a man scripting here-I-am-thinking-on-my-feet –
and then he brought the house down with *Deutschland*. (Well, he
created the right level of perplexity: I read something in prose and
was vaguely despondent that the humour seemed to be not only
dated but restricted to a particular age group: was it worth explain-

ing the Arts Council Show Trial in Kilburn in 1979 to get them to see the joke in a story about your friend Philpot breaking out of his Caribbean stereotype? So why were the academics surprised that they had to explain who Pinero was, or Dr. Johnson, never mind Hermes & Hero? On that occasion in the drama studio, reading to the first years, Smythe, with the text of his own poems heavily scored, sounded totally spontaneous, so I was prepared to respect his deliberateness as a mask for someone who might be spontaneous.)

Now we had a little self-conscious exchange about foreign parts that we did our best to send up – foreign parts being those imagined areas of the lady that you, as yet, had no permit (or is it *remit*?) to visit, sort of thing: (Was he apologising for what had happened in the car-park earlier?) Then he admitted (unnecessarily) that he wasn't going to America; there had been a slight possibility, no more, but he was a two-book man, and he had lost out to a 14-book man last time round, a fellow from the South. American South. Well, even in England a two-book man was likely to lose out to a 14-book man from the South; but, as the ad. says: he was not bitter. He seemed more relaxed now. His half-sabbatical was coming to an end, he said, and with the wholesale disruption on campus, offices being closed down, premises sold off, people being forced into the middle of town into offices without trees, effectively breaking up the team *and – and with a new Thatcherite accounting system coming in*, he feared for the magazine, he feared for *The Review*. He didn't have an Arts Council grant to keep the thing going. But then, what was an editor if he didn't struggle on without an Arts Council grant so that he could publish his friends and punish his enemies! Talking of the magazine, did I see his Questionnaire to the Vice Chancellors?

(Yes, we'd seen it: *What is a university*? sent to a hundred of Britain's universities, the Vice Chancellors, and apparently the answers were coming in, and they were saying that a university was a medium-sized business that had to attract customers and stop losing money. Representative or not, this response surprised no one. But I wasn't in the mood for that sort of argument. I brought up the cutting down of trees (again) and the burning of students' work, and Smythe, with some enthusiasm, said he would photograph the result of the next burning for the cover of the *Review* with a caption *AND ONLY ONE OF THEM IS RUSHDIE'S*.

Amusing. A change.

'So what's with the cookery book?' (I pointed to the book, opened, on his desk.)

'Oh, that!'

'Party?'

'Party? No, oh, no, I'm not having a party; bad enough to have to, you know, engage with people one at a time; never mind having them all together in your space. I'm going deaf, anyway, like Mr Naipaul. Naipaul says it's a *good* thing to be going deaf. When you hate people it makes life so much more tolerable.'

I was going deaf; I didn't think it was such a good thing to be going deaf.

'John Osborne was deaf, you know, towards the end.'

'Yes, the poor fellow couldn't hear what rivals were saying about him round the table at the Garrick.'

So we talked about writers and deafness. Writing and deafness. And whether it was more or less sexy than Writers & Teeth? And then I referred back to his book of recipes.

'Looks good.'

'I'm trying to write a poem.'

'A cake poem.'

'No. Well, yes, in a way. I'm trying to write a sort of... love poem. And I suppose a love poem is sort of bread pretending to be cake. Though I can't be bothered to develop the image.'

'Well...' I hesitated. 'Interesting.' (I was going to suggest he read something of an Italian poet I'd been reading, but I hesitated because it seemed a bit private and obscure.)

He seized something from a pile of paper on the far side of the desk (the newspaper):

'Do you know how many people are murdered by hand guns every year?'

I waited; I was mildly interested. He started to read, and stopped.

'This might be a little bit out of date. But it doesn't matter, the point's made.' He read:

'Britain 33.' He checked that I was attending. 'Britain 33; Sweden 36; Switzerland 97; Canada 128; Australia 13 (13, that's odd. Maybe they didn't count the Aborigines) Australia 13; Japan 60; the United States...' And here he really looked up, and then stressed each syllable evenly. 'The. United. States. *Thirteen Thousand, Two Hundred and Twenty*.' He put away the paper and spread his arms. Then he exploded. 'No wonder these guys can write epics. I mean, just the size of the magazines, have you seen the size of their magazines: *Tri-Quarterly. Parnassus.* And what have we got? *Poetry Review*! Do me a favour. And it's not just the murders.' He grabbed the newspaper again. 'It's not just the murders. Listen to this. 'As a promotional exercise,' he looked up and started again. 'a promotional exercise, McDonald's have given away, free, *free, fifty million dollars worth of burgers*.'

The point made, he seemed despondent. He had tried and failed, he said, to write a love poem for the new school manager.

'Ah.'

'You're writing the 'Additional Dialogue', remember?'

'God, yes. I must…'

He imagined the lady, the subject, as a *Renault 4*, you know, the funny…

I knew the *Renault 4*.

Snug. As economically-shaped as, well, as a sonnet. 'That mightn't sound like much,' he said. 'But if this *Renault* was off-white, with plaid seats – tells you something about the owner, yeah? And of the little man down the side lane who fixes it up for her when it breaks down. Add to that, her touching faith in the little man, who really doesn't know all that much about cars, but manages somehow to keep the *Renault* on the road, you've got something approaching, I wouldn't say innocence, that would be patronizing. You've got, well, something close to *truthfulness*.'

He stopped; it was my turn to say something.

'All this for the new school manager.'

'I can't tell you how many goes I've had at this. I've written *sixty* sonnets and I haven't got it right. I'm wondering if a Renault is a little large for the poem.'

'I like the idea of the Renaultpoem,' I said.

So he was writing a Renaultsonnet informed by cakes; I was writing a Leeplay informed by Lindsay that shifted from country to country – Sweden to Spéracèdes – which had lines from my sister, bits of people on the news, but it didn't have Lee's old car – a *Renault* – in: was this clown, despite himself, telling me something?

'We'll have to describe this campus now,' he said switching tone, 'before we lose it; and they tell us that it's all been an illusion, that we've never been here. Apparently, in Russia...'

*

Next morning in my pigeon hole there was the photocopy of a poem. The note from Smythe simply said 'About cutting down trees.' It was called 'Heroic Smile' by the Californian writer Robert Hass – a poem about logging and I think heroism.

4

Carrington's Flat. Crouch End. 1988

I had to get out of Carrington's flat, a flat I knew too well; and
though welcoming, soon gave you the feeling that you were back
where you started, the last time you stayed here, the *first* time
you stayed here, while the world had moved on. So Lee was
otherwise engaged, and even Balham had switched on his
ansaphone. I recalled, and dismissed, another episode with Balham,
connected with this flat; well, maybe I had moved on, too. I didn't
call my sister; too far away at Upton Park. I had a present for
Florence, for my niece, but I wasn't in the mood for family chit
chat, I didn't want to be pinned down to having to make the trek
to the East End tonight, tomorrow: Florence would quiz me
about Spéracèdes; she had visited me when I returned to the
region, a few years ago – her first real trip abroad, I think – to
improve her French; now her French was better than mine. I
liked the idea, really, of being back in London more or less
anonymously; I'd ring them tomorrow, have a chat with Avril,
with my sister.

I'd be moving back into Finchley in about six weeks, where
most of my stuff was still stored: the landlord was relaxed about
my running it as a house-share again, but I was through with
that, though I hadn't worked out what I would do with the extra
space: I thought vaguely of the huge sitting room as somewhere
where we might do a bit of rehearsal, the old City Lit crowd, the
Theatre 69 crowd improvising the odd play. Someone had taken
over from me at the City Lit, I couldn't muscle in there now. Yet,
I felt like going out tonight.

My old friends Maureen and Philpot, my favourite 'old time
Caribbean Couple', lived on the other side of London, in Queens
Park; they wouldn't be expecting anything, any explanation.
They had a fractured personal life, but when they were back
together they made you feel things were possible for you, too;
and also, you didn't have to sort out where your loyalties lay
between them; you liked them equally. But it was Maureen who

made me feel guilty. We went back a long way; and I *had* helped to name their daughter.

*

Before setting out for Maureen and Philpot's, first another call to Carrington in Ulster. Of course the real reason I was disorientated on coming back to London (why am I so defensive about this?) was the death of my mother while I'd been in Germany that time, the fact that they couldn't get in touch with me, and the mess of the whole thing. My travelling used to be a bit of a running joke in the family, now I wasn't so sure. Trips to the US. Crisscrossing Europe. The Caribbean. And where had it all got me? What did I have to show for it. The plays? A book of stories (*Random Thoughts and Stories*) – and something which, in 1971, passed for a book of poems. Working in foreign countries. Working on building sites in France. It was never spelt out, but these were charges that I had to deal with when I reported back to Upton Park. To my mother. To Avril (though not to my brother-in-law Stewart). Certainly, to my niece, to Florence. All in their different ways would expect an update. My mother's party piece, before the trips abroad, was that she wouldn't be alive when I got back. And, for a few years towards the end, I half-suspected this might be true.

Avril and Stewart were thinking of moving house, another routine disturbed, not that you can expect other people to provide your stability. Though, in a way, I did. You always ate well at Avril's (they were in the hotel trade) and we appreciated it – my brother and I – that they never 'lived in' but always maintained a house for my mother and Florence. Though Florence, naturally, had always wanted to be brought up in a hotel.

I didn't want to talk about the family doings tonight, about the need to repair houses in the West Indies and about my own plans for securing property not in England but in the South of France. About not having a proper job. Philpot and Maureen wouldn't ask these questions; to them my life-style already signified a sort of success.

But first, I was in Carrington's place; I must ring Carrington, talk to the man.

Was everything OK, was the flat all right?

The flat was like home. Splendid. I started telling a joke about West Indian v British hospitality, but lost the point halfway through. The flat looked more trendy, now; not exactly up-market, but...

Carrington was a married man now; a married man had to have a certain... well, let's just say a certain... air of not being transient. Something like that.

It was clear that Madame Thatcher was proving very good for some married men. And what with the boxes, the cartons: was this the big move to Ireland and *root*, to Ulster?

The boxes – he was embarrassed about this – the boxes were destined for Kent. They were his archives that Kent were in the process of buying. Yes yes, he knew: Kent was the fellow for whom he'd written 'additional' dialogue in his *King Lear*, providing him with a woman half his age to meet the future and abandon the King. But no, Kent the University were offering, in their wisdom, to buy Carrington's text of the play. And the other plays. Minap, he said, thought he should go through the manuscripts and correct the spelling mistakes before handing them over: Minap, Cook Islands princess, well-brought up in New Zealand and Canada, was strangely West Indian in some ways. (I knew better than to join in with a man's little jokes against his wife, particularly a newish, young wife.) So we talked about other things, the conference in Paris that we'd recently attended, wondered if anyone had got in touch with Isabel from Zaragoza. Carrington oozed enthusiasm for Ulster; the fact that there was so much interest in 'Writing' at the university both energised and appalled him. He stressed that his job as writer-in-residence wasn't a sinecure: why didn't I come over and do a play with him? In any case, Minap wanted to meet me, and I had to see the daughters before they grew into women and started inviting trouble.

I promised to come over to Ulster, and we talked about work. He was at the moment rehearsing a Walcott play, *Ti Jean*...

Walcott with an Ulster accent! Aren't we oppressed enough?

He reminded me that we had to lash West Indians out of their island complacency, one way of which was to make them sound like other people we didn't like the sound of. Carrington was conducting another conversation on the phone, in babytalk, and somehow I didn't know whether to trust it: could he be lying in bed with Minap, playing a game? I'd been in that situation before when the partner, called to the phone, didn't let on, indeed, the incident adding some piquancy to the situation. It was as if Carrington was sending up my most intimate moments. When he made another wife-joke I was convinced Minap was in on it, so I distanced myself – if only, for nothing else, out of loyalty to Lee, who was telepathic, anyway.

He asked about the mail, whether there was anything for him piling up in the entrance downstairs: the woman downstairs sent on his letters, but sometimes she didn't get round to it.

I offered to hang up and ring him back, save his bill while I went down and had a look. We hadn't worked out the financial arrangements for the flat; I'd obviously pay for the services, and then we'd see. But Carrington scorned such financial niceties, he'd hang on while I went downstairs to take a look at the mail.

There was something for Carrington and, surprisingly, a package addressed to me: From Lee! Sent on from the house in Finchley. It was a book of translations of Leopardi. Some of them done by Lee. Brilliant. I hadn't really read Leopardi. They printed the original alongside the translations. I'd put my O level Italian to the test. Was I already reading too much in Lee's covering note? Back upstairs I warned Carrington that he could expect gas and telephone bills through the post.

*

On my way to Queens Park to Philpot's and Maureen's, walking up Carrington's road towards the station, clutching my Leopardi present, I wriggled my toe in the shoe to see if I could emphasise the hurt, the wound from Lee's cup, but it seemed to be one of those domestic accidents that would heal themselves. *How did Lee know I'd be back in the country. Why did her choice of present make me feel so gross? Did she know what I would do tomorrow? Did she know when I would die? I needed someone like Maureen, like Philpot to reassure me. I didn't need to apologise in their company*). Lee was let off the hook. Waiting for the train I read again the note that accompanied the book. Beautiful handwriting. (Beautiful

Lee.) It was written on Rainbow Arts Factory headed paper (official?). She wrote to me as if I were 'a friend'. She'd done her bit for Black Arts and now it was time for her to give herself a break, and explore other strands of her heritage which had no platform in this country. Maybe she would go off to America or Geneva and bond with her family, who were all in exile. But because she wasn't black, she was made to feel invisible in the presence of the Afro-Caribbean and South Asian privileged among the ethnic minorities: was I serious about wanting to take over the *Rainbow*?

Flattering but devastating, approaching me, addressing me in this way. Yeh, it's always useful to know there's a job out there somewhere, in the background; useful to be able to present yourself to family as not drifting: even I couldn't face the Language School racket any more. Spéracèdes would probably have to remain unrenovated while I tried to buy something here. Another piss-off. Always getting there late, as Lee says, missing the train. There was a possibility of doing the French play at the *Keskadee*, reviving the *Caribbean Theatre Workshop* in London. But who had the stamina! *Keskadee* isn't exactly moving forward, must contact Oscar at some point. Maybe an academic job. Succumb. Teach Wycherley: *could I teach Wycherley*? Too humiliating to follow the likes of Balham into academia. Maybe Lee's offer wasn't so bad after all. But what was behind this, the letter? Of course there'd be fierce competition for the job. And was I committed enough for it?

Standing on the shabby BR platform you had a slight sense of relief in not being a woman. Hornsey. British rail: you didn't quite accept that there was stations called Hornsey. Puts you in mind of those Sherlock Holmes-type stories where the gruesome clue is revealed at the end, skeletons bricked up in one of the original underground stations, disused for 70 years. Anyway, there was I, waiting for the train to take me to Finsbury Park, then change to Oxford Circus, then on to the Bakerloo Line to Queens Park – why was travel in London so ridiculous? But then I've lived in Manchester; no better there.

On my way back from Philpot and Maureen's I was trying to shake off the feeling of having got it wrong. Maureen and Philpot

were together all right, but at the world's expense. Maureen told
a story of a child of, I don't know, age seven, murdering her infant
sister because the sister annoyed her. And Philpot, of course,
topped it with a horror story of his own: the feeling was that the
world had become so alien, that it had made those independent
people suspend their separate lives in order to face it together. I
hated seeing them become just another, elderly couple. This sense
of their settling down seemed to make aspects of their past, that I
treasured, something, if not to apologise for, at least to explain. The
naming of their daughter, for instance. I remember that arctic
winter of '62-'63. Philpot turned up in Lampeter, where I was
studying, to discuss the naming of his daughter. Maureen had
always held it against me that the infant ended up with a boy's
name, Nigel. She didn't mind the other jackarses who were
misleading Philpot, but I was at university and should have more
sense than those who were working in places like J. Lyons and
Brillo and London Transport. Not that she was cowed by this. On
the contrary, she was suspicious of the student crowd – students
and nurses – that Philpot cultivated, as if to compensate for
Maureen's labouring in factories in places like Great Portland
Street and Baker Street making ladies belts and whatnot.

But Maureen remained good-natured, and her protest gradually dwindled, to a point where we got the balance right between
us. We came to England at about the same time. '55-'56. Lived
in Maida Vale for a while, Maureen and others respecting the
family's 'middle class' credentials, which meant a lot to my
mother who, praise God, didn't have to do those jobs.

Now, who had made the better use of their chances –
Maureen was not unlike my sister in one respect, raising an
eyebrow at my lack of 'family': Maureen had a managing role
in the belt factory now – not the same factory as in Great
Portland Street, but the same industry – and the feeling was that
we had, Maureen and I, settled for a draw in some sort of game
that Philpot pretended to recognise or acknowledge. I was
thinking about these sorts of things, making my way back from
Queens Park, taking the train to Waterloo this time and picking
up the Northern Line to Archway when I saw that Balham picture
again on the station.

It was weird; the combination of London and the proximity of Balham, the place; that must be making me neurotic about Balham the man. If I was a racist, that would be my defence; but this black man – American singer? Pop star? – certainly looked like *our* black man. I consciously refused to analyse it further.

On the train, not to be steam-rolled by my own fantasies, I tried to reconnect with thoughts of Maureen and Philpot. And Nigel –Nigella – who hadn't been present. Nigel had left home, set up in her own flat after university and had her own mortgage, only now changing her name to something girlie. I remember Nigel over the years, unexpectedly on the phone, exerting gentle pressure because I was her parents' friend and she knew I couldn't disappoint the parents. I remember her phoning late one night after an incident at a train station (her parents must have been apart, then). It was cold, she said, waiting, and she needed a hot drink; and there was one of those newfangled coffee machines that had taken her money. She had put in her whatever-it-was for hot chocolate, and had pressed the button, and the liquid had dribbled down without the machine releasing a cup. So what did I think – she knew she was being silly, but – was it racism? We both knew that Maureen would not have approved of her drinking (or eating) in public, 'in the street', so losing her money to the drinks machine would not have engendered sympathy at home. Could the machine be programmed in such a way to deny black people a cup?

I told her it was an interesting thought; but unless the machine was very big and had a racist concealed inside – with peep-holes to see who was coming – then it couldn't be sure to know when to withhold the cup.

The machine *was* big enough, she said; it was suspiciously large. Though it had all the stuff in. Not just hot chocolate, but tea and coke and fanta and all sorts of chocolate bars and crisps. So it was possible that you couldn't get all that *and* a racist inside the machine, unless he was a very small racist, or a woman. (Nigel was studying for a Law degree at the time, either at Oxford or at Luton (old joke) – I had high hopes for her.) We thought of other possibilities: someone in another part of the station sitting in a little office with a remote control. I liked the idea: *idea for a play*? Would it be a man looking up from his *Daily*

Sketch? Or a woman from filing her nails. To flick the remote? There were other possibilities. I saw Nigel as a crusading Lawyer, a radical. I remember seeing an American movie where some rich kids somewhere in California lured this nice girl into their flat, drugged her, abused her, raped her and killed her – and of course got off for lack of evidence. 'Insufficient evidence'. The sister of the murdered woman vowed, in court, before she was dragged away, to see the boys dead, the four smirking, well-brought-up, rich kids dead. Then one was shot. Then another. They couldn't hold the sister. Insufficient evidence. And so on. That's how I saw Nigel operating. Either with the gun or through the law. My fantasy.

But I couldn't appropriate Nigel's scene; I wasn't even sure she'd make it to being a lawyer. So I promised her a cup in her next machine, and not a plastic one, either, but china, the kind we used at home – and I mean at home in St. Caesare, not in this cupless province called England. Better still, I promised to take her to tea at one of those places – Harrods, The Dorchester – where you could imbibe your hot chocolate in style and comfort. By now, having talked her through to her approaching train, I'd been thinking less of Nigel than of my own niece, Florence who, unlike Nigel, *had* been taken to tea at such places.

It *was* Balham. *It was Balham.* I stopped at Archway station and observed the picture. Balham, the fare-dodger, caught, warning other people against his fate. There was a series of pictures that I'd seen illustrating this, but Balham was the only black representative. This is the sort of thing people used to call politically illiterate. But this man was a Sociologist, a 'film-maker,' a polytechnic lecturer. What was it with Thatcher's Britain that infantilized people? This is the man from whom I had had (rightly) to protect my young Italians from Bari. Why does history conspire to prove me right?

*

It annoyed me that Balham – clown, buffoon – it annoyed me that his presence on the underground forced from my mind other thoughts, thoughts of Lee; Lee magically whisked to St Caesare, to the drawing-room in Coderington – not as a prize, not as a trophy, dear God, but as a partner, a wife, a Number One Wife, evidence of a world in balance, evidence that luck (the Force, the Force) was with us. Lee had just translated Leopardi from the Italian; that was a drawing-roomy sort of experience. That would reinstate the drawing-room after thirty years of neglect, of abandonment. Lee would revive the old Sunday afternoon crowd, Professeur Croissant, our resident historian, pretending to be sober. And she would make the clergyman gulp. Mr Ryan was our new Methodist Minister from Ireland, and came to lunch on the Sundays he was preaching at Coderington: he had a long nose and an Adam's apple competing for attention. Lee would innocently (and by doing nothing) set the Adam's apple off, till we got a confession. She would come into the drawing-room at strategic points, when the adults were sounding off and threatening to embarrass the children. And there'd be talk in our house about poems in the Italian language.

And that idiotic man, the one who pretended to be Italian; not that he really pretended to be Italian, but he sort of pretended to be Italian – called himself da Firenze (from Florence, get it!) would be dethroned from our myth of leave-taking. da Firenze came round that last Sunday in '56, before we left for England, came round to do sketches of us, of the house. For posterity. When, after all the business of, oh, painting the crack in the dining-room wall, and the little contretemps between the headmaster and the clergyman – when, after all that, my mother asked the painter to say something in the Italian language, Lee's presence would make him fluent, and he would recite Leopardi:

graziosa luma, io mi rammento
Che, or volge l'anno, sovra questo colle
Io venia pien d'angoscia a rimirarti:
E tu pendevi allor su quella selva,
Siccome or fai, che tutta la rischiari.

and the voice would be Lee's. The figure in the rocking-chair in her summer frock would be Lee's. And later, Lee would take the pressure off us children by being induced to play the piano. That

would divert talk from my mother's ankle that had been strained
coming out of church, so we'd be spared my mother's stoicism.
And later, we'd be saved embarrassment as the man of no God (the
Professeur) chopped logic with the vicar, Mr Ryan, about smoking
and drinking and whether the Irish and the English were the same
people.

Balham had a way of buffooning his way into my life. He had
always pretended to be connected to a shadowy sort of world (of
politics? of film? of crime?) that bemused us, alternatively
amused and bemused us. Till we got bored. For much of the time
we remained mainly bored. There was a literal-mindedness to
the fellow which somehow made you think you could always see
beyond him: his writing wasn't writing, his films weren't art, his
lecturing was part of a self-promoting agenda. Whatever you
thought of Carrington's writing you couldn't deny that the man
delivered – it wasn't just the brown, plush carpets and the
archives boxed up for Kent, but plays like *King Lear* were
genuinely innovative. Minap and the baby daughters proved
something.

But what was Balham? Why romanticise those GCE-induced
walks along Kilburn High Road, as if they meant something?
Thinking back again there would be three or four of us – sometimes
a boy from Kenya, an Indian whom the girls thought handsome,
would join us – marching along the High Road, strolling into the
Casino, pretending to be in some place called Europe, and
proceeding to put the world to rights. Subsequently, Balham and
I went on various quests together (he flattered me by insisting that
I was a better writer than Carrington), yet, I did instinctively try to
protect Lee from him. The sense of having treated him shabbily,
perhaps, has led me, on occasion, to overcompensate. The most
bizarre incident was connected, however tenuously, with this very
flat of Carrington's.

*

It was when I was director of the language school. My
Italians from Bari at Southgate. The last night. Big party; all
that. The party was in Finchley, but a couple of girls and one of

their teachers needed to be put up, and Carrington's flat was, as always, empty. Balham was around, of course, and tagged along to Crouch End, and, because I was responsible for the girls, I wasn't about to leave him there with them. So when he suggested a little quest, I agreed. We set out on foot, me following him.

From the clock tower we headed for Crouch Hill and into Shepherds Hill. Destination Highgate. I made a decision not to pump Balham for information, I didn't want to give him that much satisfaction; I gave him enough credit not to land us in gaol or get us killed. I felt if I probed he might be put on the spot, he might take risks and I might suffer for it. (This is the man who had been beaten up, demonstrating, during his student days in Leicester – and then boasted about it.) Had he learnt anything since then?

Balham had this notion about me that because I'd done a little bit of Latin at school, I was unfitted for a 'post-classical' age. I remember those early debates over the election, Macmillan's 1959 election, when Balham accused me of being sympathetic to the Old Fraud's archaic frame of reference, characterising Britain's special relationship with America in terms of Britain playing Greece to America's Rome. I thought it was an elegant analogy, that's all; it had had nothing to do with my political alliances (tending to Liberal then, graduating to Labour, now Greenish) or my struggles to translate a few lines of Caesar for O Level. If Balham was trying to prove something now, would it be at my expense?

This was proving a long walk: was he having second thoughts? We walked up Shepherds Hill and crossed the Archway Road, climbing still, then a left turn; a quiet residential street near Highgate village, on this side of the village. Late at night.

Balham pointed out a house. The house. It looked like any other house in the street. Imposing. Large houses, some with garages, others with driveways; trees. This one had a driveway, a garage at the side, the back. There was a light on in a downstairs room, seen through the glass door: at two o'clock in the morning – an anti-burglar device? All this discovered after we had walked up the side entrance and Balham had opened the wooden gate: there was a car in the double garage. I balked at that.

So the house wasn't empty! Maybe we weren't breaking in. But if Balham had arranged to meet someone – the daughter of the house? the mother of the house? – why would he want me tagging along, except to witness his conquest; even Balham, in his mid-40s, must have outgrown that. But I was determined not to ask him what sort of macho test this was; I was determined not to crack. The path to the back door wasn't paved but gravelly, rutted, and I had the feeling that Balham on his own would have tiptoed up it, but was now forced to walk normally in deference to an accomplice who refused to panic, and would verify every last detail in the subsequent retelling, rewriting.

Walking slowly, deliberately up the path made sense (though it wasn't dark; there was a moon, street lights); but I knew that once inside the house you had to speak quietly rather than whisper, as the sound would carry less far that way: so this flat-footed progress up the path was the housebreakers equivalent. It was like establishing the right rhythm from the start, and I took credit for it by my presence, and panicked. (The panic was like a sudden current moving through me: I saw myself as a woman abused by this man, and knowingly going along with it, and almost beginning to take credit for it; but the charge soon passed, and I could focus again. I thought to myself: thousands of morons do this every day. Listen to the police statistics; listen to the radio, watch the television. The majority get away with it. We must have faith in intelligence, and not panic.)

Balham shut the wooden gate, almost carelessly, without bolting it, but proceeded across the paved yard, where there were sawn-up logs and branches, in a less cavalier fashion; and paused before the all-glass kitchen door. He might almost be giving me time for second thoughts, to develop doubts (and it's true that I was beginning to be obsessed that I had more to lose than Balham: I had a mother, family who would be devastated if something went wrong and we ended up in the papers: Balham probably had a woman somewhere who, in similar circum-stances, would damn the police and the System). For while the – irritatingly tall – housebreaker stood gazing at the kitchen door, we were still exposed; anyone from the adjoining houses or flats up at this hour could see us. I consoled myself with the thought that

this wasn't Germany (where I'd recently been) and if anything
went wrong the police wouldn't gun you down. Later, I was to be
told that I was out of touch, that this *was* Germany, and that the
police here saw you as just another unwelcome *gasterbeiter*, and
were short of target-practice. But I had to rise above this; I had to
tune in to those inner fantasies which would make me think that
I was concerned with something other than breaking and entering.
(To be caught, brutalised by the police, verbally savaged by the
judge, paraded through the streets in the presence of your mother
and family – and finally put in a cell with racists...).

My ex-partner, back in America, would not have allowed this;
it had been a mistake to let her go back; it had been down hill ever
since. I interrupted my thought-processes, embarrassed, as Balham
expertly opened the door and stepped inside the house. He
beckoned me to remain where I was, and I did, seeming to obey
some other Law. (Why hadn't we worked out beforehand how we
would speak, what gestures to use? Was he just an amateur or was
he setting me up?)

Immediately inside (*spacious, a house with servants*) there
was a little whine, and there was Balham making friendly
gestures towards the dog which remained in its basket and
flopped its tail lazily up and down. My back to the door (*where
was the alarm?*), I was hurling abuse at the dog but the dog didn't
know it for no sound escaped my lips. Perhaps I was deliberately
making myself aware of all this to prove that I had some control.
I was winding myself up to spit out a name, culled from
somewhere, something German which would stun the brute
should it turn vicious. But this lunacy was only fleeting, and I
was breathing normally again. Absurdly, everything seemed
less exposed inside – there was order and Englishness, and security.
But I couldn't quite banish the thought – was I beginning to relish
it: had I gone past some barrier of sense? Because even as I thought
it I didn't quite believe in the shotgun or in another, unseen,
animal leaping for the jugular. (Was I doing this to prove something to a trans-Atlantic partner? She had always asked for simple
things, simpler than this. She would not be impressed.)

Balham was keeping his cool. *The dog*. He had turned on a light
which lit up the kitchen and gave a dreamlike, filmic quality to the

larger part of the room, the dining area. Then he reached for
something – why was he so tall? – a tin on the shelf and, with
difficulty, opened it. It was like a battered half-pound toffee tin,
round. But it wasn't the tin that struck me, it was the gesture; the
man using his height at a time like this (he was much taller than
Carrington and myself) – though the shelf was within anyone's
reach. It bothered me that I was paying attention to irrelevancies
like this, as if a process of reviewing a life had begun.

With the open tin Balham brought a bit of newspaper to the table.
(I clutched at the observation that he was being careful not to mark
the highly polished, oak table with the tin. That Gunter Grass play
came to mind, the one about the Plebeians and the Revolution,
where the workers storming the official building are careful to obey
instructions not to walk on the grass. Why was it so hard to
concentrate? Criminal behaviour was a more intelligent activity
than we credit. So this was a political theft? There was a pair of gloves
on the table, not Balham's; rather fine gloves, a woman's... *The gloves.
The opened tin. The bit of newspaper.* Agatha Christie. Balham calmly
emptied the contents of the little tin – peanuts, they had to be
peanuts – onto the newspaper, and then extracting a bag from his
pocket he replaced the nuts with what looked like more nuts,
similar. He clearly knew the house and had come prepared: with this
realisation my panic swiftly thickened into something else – a soft
but enveloping anger: I had nothing but contempt for this clown.

Balham replaced the battered tin on the shelf, and wrapped up
the original nuts. The dog had come to sniff and he silently ordered
it back to the basket; and when he patted it it gave out a little whine
of satisfaction, no noise to worry about. He finally turned out the
lights, having locked the kitchen door, trapping us inside. I didn't
like my passive role: I soon found myself thinking of that night in
Ebertplatz a year ago, outside the Turkish cafe, when Lindsay and
I were attacked – a part of our German experience. If I lived in
America would I carry a gun to protect myself? Gaining something
that wasn't exactly confidence, I was on the point of making a noise:
could this house be empty all along, the people away, Balham
knowing the people to be away? (Maybe he was the 'boy' employed
to feed the dog.) This clown, this idiot, this *sociologist* was full of
bullshit. But the dog was real; this was an English house; no sane

person would trust Balham with a dog; and Balham didn't live in these parts.

I tried to think, not to be carried along; yes, it was best to lock the kitchen door from inside, and for us to make our escape – the danger palpably receding – through the dining-area into the dimly lit, spacious hall and out of the front door. Even though we had to go round the side entrance again – the deed having been done – to lock the side gate.

*

*   Retracing your steps is hazardous.

*   The dog: why was it so tame? Whom would a good bark have roused?

*   Granted that Balham knew the occupants were out, probably abroad, what of the unexpected? What of visitors staying in the house?

*   What if the dog hadn't been fed for a couple of days – some oversight – and was half-crazed?

*   What...?

*

Again I found myself hanging onto the detail of the side gate as if it were a footnote to a text that was corrupt, and that others, later, would come to see it. When I thought it through a bit I was ready to charge Balham with endangering the enterprise – whatever the enterprise was – out of ego. One journey too many. That one unnecessary journey back to lock the side gate could have been our undoing.

'How about the dog, eh?' We were out of the house, clear, about to recross the Archway Road. Balham was high on his success, one telltale sign was the slowness of his step, his long, loping strides, almost in slow motion, falling in with my pace. Why were we crossing the Archway Road? I was going away from home, from Finchley, but I decided to stick with Balham in case he ended up back at Carrington's place to annoy the Italians. I was responsible for them, at least for tonight.

Again he asked about the dog.

I didn't want to talk about the dog. I wanted to talk about the unnecessary trip back to the side gate. Lack of planning was what I was talking about. The people killed on the battlefield not from enemy fire but by accident, from inattention, that's what I was talking about. The fire-brigade coming to rescue a pensioner's cat stuck in a tree, and then running over the rescued cat as they backed out of the drive. Or, maybe I was confusing myself here. But attention to detail was what I was on about: we should have locked the gate on coming in, and cut out the unnecessary journey later to lock the gate. (Unless we were sure there was no one in the house.)

'We should have filmed the dog.'

'Fuck the dog.'

Balham had the trick of some foolish people who deliberately make themselves slightly more foolish, so as to mask the real foolishness. He was irritatingly smug.

'And if the dog barked; really barked?'

I didn't listen to his answer. He knew the house, he knew the dog wouldn't bark. Even when he had got himself beaten up by the police he had been pursuing a soft target. Leicester in the '60s student revolution wasn't Kent State or Atlanta. Or the LSE or Hornsey School of Art for that matter. What I do know is that this is being laid on for my benefit, and I'm not impressed. Let's say I was a woman he was trying to impress: would he have upped the stakes, gone in with all guns blazing?

We walked a little way down Crouch Hill and stopped. (I wouldn't let him go any further down the Hill; I'd offer him a couch in Finchley if I had to.) So I stood and listened to him talk like a man who had accomplished his mission. He talked about the refusal to be cowed by social pressure. He talked about the necessity to give support to Brothers who could *only* burgle and rob. He talked about the necessity to remind people that your real danger to them was that you could out-think them (you didn't want their prized rubbish) and to demonstrate that you had something left in reserve, something that you could use if you needed to; it was necessary to scare them by your *restraint*, etc.

I heard him but I was thinking of that night in Köln, Ebertplatz, when an American woman and a West Indian man tried to break up a fight in the square, a Turkish man repeatedly knocking a woman to the ground, a German woman, hitting her in the face. A difficult one. The ambivalence. The sickening thwack of fist on face. The threat to us. The need to do something. The taxi-driver at the top of the square, fat, German, cigar-smoking, not wanting to get involved in the foreigners' scrap; but under threats from my unamused partner, whose German was improving, having to ring up the police on his carphone. Half an hour later the police bringing the culprit (and half a dozen of his friends) to our front door at Aquinostrasse. Exit Ebertplatz two days later. What did Balham know about taking risks? Oh, I must write to you, New Haven partner, *sorry, sorry, sorry, sorry, sorry*.

I made the offer of a couch and he accepted. He accepted in a way which made it clear that he'd won some sort of point. Neither of us was prepared to reopen the conversation.

Before turning round Balham had calmly pointed out the skeleton of Alexander Palace in the distance. The building looked strangely intact. He had, naturally, seen it go up in flames some time earlier; a man who lived in Wandsworth or in Shepherds Bush, he had just happened to be in the area on the night of the fire. Early evening it was; he was prepared to go into detail over this. Rumour had it, he said, that the fire had been officially sponsored to make it easier for the Government to build an underground military arsenal under cover of rebuilding the Palace. I wondered at his naiveté: since when did the Government need an excuse for these things?

Rumour, I recalled, was a character from an Elizabethan play, dressed in oddments, playing the Chorus.

He accused me of being literary.

Balham was wearing his waistcoat, his peacock suit, and as there was no woman to impress, he had to strut around me, intellectually, so to speak. He explained that if the dog had barked, and we had to get out quick, we wouldn't want to be fiddling with a bolted side-gate.

(Oh that!) But despite myself I asked a question.

'What's with the peanuts?'

He thought about this for a while. He wasn't thinking, he was being smug.

'Confuse the opposition.'

'With peanuts.' It was a statement. We were into our old routine. It was depressing.

He was explaining. He called forth an image of the lady of the house, preparing the evening meal. The radio on. Radio Four. Radio Three. In the middle of sealing the meat for the casserole, or of cutting up the courgettes, she goes to the shelf, takes down the little tin in question, opens it – with a little difficulty: she is middle-class, slightly guilty about prolonging certain childish pleasures into middle age. Pleasures like nuts. So with the slight ache of puritanism, she half-welcomes the stiffness of the lid... She gets the tin open and, without looking, pours a few nuts into a saucer and, still without looking, pops a few into her mouth. After about the third chew, *hello?* – wooden spatula poised in the air – she *looks*. Wrong nuts. These aren't the nuts I bought at Sainsbury's at the weekend... (These I buy only when I can't get the others I like.) Surely, I had some yesterday, the day before. Not these. Then she thinks back to last night: didn't I hear Meredith...? (Meredith's the dog.) Didn't I hear Meredith?

'Literary types.' (I had given the dog a German name.)

Balham went on to describe the devastation wreaked on the lady of the house when she discovers the switch of the nuts. She thinks back to the night before: didn't I hear a little whine? No no, come on; they'll say your mind's wandering: they'll say it's the change. Pull yourself together, girl. Think of something sensible, traffic lights on the Archway Road that work. Think where you'll be in ten years time. No, perhaps not that. Think of supper, calorie-reduced supper. *All this for a few nuts!... And* she realises she has burnt the meat.

This was sophisticated for Balham; what I had planned to say now seemed like carping. I suppressed the thought that the lady of the house might be a vegetarian.

'The thing is,' he wasn't going to let go of this now, 'not to make the nuts too different. Just different enough for her to come back, after she's burnt the meat, and to notice they're not *very* different. Just as the cornflakes packet doesn't look very different from the ones she bought. And that chair in the odd position was so much like their own chair. And Meredith, who doesn't want to answer to his name any more: he's certainly the same dog they've had all these years.... And that slightly strange man in bed last night...?'

As always Balham was in danger of spoiling a good thing through exaggeration, and his next remarks were just the thug sounding tough. 'Maybe they can get into your house without wanting to rape you. They don't want your jewels. They don't even want to poison you.' (The sight of nuts on a piece of newspaper did have a faint suggestion of rat-poison, in the old days.)

Although I could afford a taxi, I insisted on our walking home to Finchley.

*

Thursday. Sheffield.

On my way home – short-cut through the Hallamshire Hospital, no thought of what's going on there, which means that, in spite of what we say, the NHS must be functioning, or the hospital would be the *subject* – I tried to sustain the sense of expectation generated by the post. Nothing spectacular, but an encouraging letter from Jude Kelly about my new play, about my volcano play, and an invitation to give a talk at the ICA on *Black Theatre in Britain.* I probably won't do the talk, but it's nice to be asked. I nip into the hospital to buy a newspaper, and get distracted.

First I'm conscious of the fact that I buy a newspaper in the hospital but would be uncomfortable buying something to eat from the hospital shop, and I'm vaguely ashamed of my... small-islandness. There are two rows of seats next to the paper shop, with people sitting on them, visiting, waiting. There are only eight seats, four in front, four behind, pinned down. Nice, sharp, primary colours which makes me think of experimental theatre. The smokers are outside the hospital, so I'm well-disposed to the people sitting on the seats inside, however 'hospitally' they seem. They deserve more than random conversation or the obligation to stare blankly at the community of the sick and dying. Or sick and caring. A play for the occasion. Small-scale (or maybe huge and episodic) but the right size for an audience of eight, and

the right tone for the hospital. An exercise for the second years.
Avoid the cliché. Nothing hospitally. Any subject to do with
operations and doctors and nurses and Health Service propaganda
and grapes was out. *If I were doing it, I'd attempt a Restoration
Comedy here. Wycherley. Etherege. The bright, brittle parade of
periwigs and fans to set against the uniformed hospital, to lift the
scene out of its sensibleness; to recover the language of elegance
suspended in hospitally matters: the sick could play the Chorus
demanding to have a full, adult, nuanced vocabulary restored to
them. The very sick could dance and sing for their lives.*

The thing is, students are now frightened of overwriting, of
rhetoric. We're making them cautious about the use of language. I remember being in the BM some time, ostensibly to
take a look at some of those people whom Lee was translating,
Rumi and company. And I manoeuvred my way to the North
Library for old time's sake, the place where, in the '60s I read
plays called *The Whirligig* and that sort of thing, plays that
hadn't been performed since sixteen hundred whenever, flun
kies hovering in the doorway. This time, as I waited for Rumi
to be delivered, doing my browsing bit in the Reading Room
(that's another thing, Halterbush (the librarian) has just outlawed browsing at our university library), I chanced on *Elizabethan Men of Letters*: would I have qualified if I'd lived then,
when those bastards were lucky with the language? Interestingly, *Elizabethan Men of Letters* had nothing to do with Shakespeare & Co, but just Elizabethans who had written letters – to
lovers, to patrons and that sort of thing, laying out their
credentials and asking favours. I liked the expansiveness of all
this, people taking possession of their speech, speech not yet
undermined by the shopping list as the norm, nor as something set
up for *deconstruction*. They were all love letters, of course, they
had the feel and tone of love letters. Young Essex to Elizabeth.
Love Letters. We've missed out here, the letter (never mind the
love letter) isn't our idiom any more. I can't think of a single play
composed entirely of letters. (There's a play composed entirely of
questions.) Novels and short stories, yes. *Letters to Lee?* Though
these would have to be defensive, full of justification and explanation. *Letters to Lee* rising above justification and explanation.

Have Lee and Lindsay from New Haven – Lee here in London – at
opposite ends of the stage, a Restoration flunkey in-between,
ferrying the letters. Loveit. Allwit. Wittol. (Sir Wilfull Witwoud.) All
proving to be post-Restoration, post Women's Movement people.

Ah, but the BM had become as tacky as the hospital. If the
hospital was openly down-market, the BM with its glitzy foyer,
busy bookshop – bookstalls catering for the crush of tourists, not
on their way to the Reading Room – had now been given over to
'Heritage'.

THURSDAY
(1) St James Press
(2) MA Write-up. Rolls/Smythe
(3) 'Additional Dialogue'
(4) Laundrette
(5) Soyinka/J. Kelly
(6) Write reference
(7) St Thomas (Plays)
(8) Kent (playscript)
(9) Halterbush Sketch, expand (BBC? Crucible? J.
    Kelly?)
(10) Avril
(11) Bolton

You needed a break from the marking, yet it was hard to change
gear, to concentrate on other things. I'd had a go at writing up
something for a new MA Course we were putting together, and
abandoned it. So I turned to something easier, updating my entry in
Contemporary Dramatists for the St James Press; it depressed me
that the entry seemed embarrassingly flattering, all those dead
plays listed; but this sort of thing impresses the academics. I felt I
had to do more to deserve entry than this. I'd been an advisor way
back, to the 1973 edition, and had written some of the essays which
I really couldn't be bothered to revise for the present edition. The
prospect of going back over what I may have said about Douglas
Archibald and Errol John and Mustapha Matura and Barry Reckord
was one I couldn't with all honesty face. I hadn't done a Carrington
entry for that. Carrington and Edgar White were an oversight,

clearly. I remember one of my co-advisors at the time predicting that I would be in the next edition *as a subject*. Ah, this little house of art was reassuringly small! So both Carrington and I were to be included, so better get on with it.

My brother Eugene had sent me a cutting for an academic job at Lancaster, and it's that which probably had me thinking about Wycherley and those seventeenth-century social comedy days at the BM. I couldn't think of anything more dreary than to go up to Lancaster and pose as an academic; I didn't even teach Restoration here; I hadn't read or seen a Restoration play in fifteen years; but for my brother, the 'academic' was always going to be preferable to the imaginative, to 'creative writing.' And they didn't rate editing as being more than a stopgap; editing was bringing out other people's work, not one's own. I could agree with him, with them, there. So I was dawdling, toying with writing up a new MA proposal (academic), putting off updating my *Contemporary Dramatists* entry, constructing lists:

(12)   *Omeros* (Caribbean MA?)
(13)   Lit Edn. MA?
(14)   Publishing MA? (with Lee?)
(15)   Great Books MA? (Boston)
(16)   English Stage History MA (with Crucible?) (WYP?)
(17)   Caribbean Lit. MA – with Stage History?
(18)   Caribbean Lit. MA + Resource Centre?
(19)   Yorkshire Writers MA? – Priestley Hughes Drabble
         Byatt Hattersley Harrison...
(20)   South York. Writers MA? (Drabble Byatt Barry
         Hines Montgomery, the poet? Lesley Glaister?)
(21)   Open Day
(22)   Bolton (Bradford Central Library)

I was vaguely interested in the Great Books MA. I remember being in Boston in the late-'70s and being invited to a party, one of those literary occasions that seduced you then (and maybe even now). We were sitting out on the lawn, Lindsay, etc.; nice day; civilised, and the host, the man of the house was regaling us with talk about his job at the university. (Actually, the interesting person there was the wife: she circled around the guests with the drinks tray, wearing a little apron, and before she gave you a chance to make a fool of yourself she pounced: 'Yes, I know; you thought I was the maid,' which, of course, I had. I was a friend of her daughter's, a small-press writer and academic, who was living in England.) The Professor's job consisted of teaching a course on the World's Great Books. *Twenty Books*. And he had a free hand to choose whatever he liked. Of course some authors more or less selected themselves. With Homer you just had to decide which text; as with Shakespeare (*Lear*) and which bits of the Bible. Proust was easy; as was Tolstoy (*Anna Karenina*). And then to the standing army of scribblers. I was pleased that it was Solzhenitsyn rather than Dostoevsky: I had problems with the book selected (*Cancer Ward* rather than *The First Circle*), but that was something we could argue. He was game, our professor; he agreed that Solzhenitsyn was politically sexy and that *Cancer Ward* demonstrated the failure of Soviet medicine, of the communist system. There were other 'Great Books' that I was hazy about, particularly the Americans; I hadn't read enough of Emerson and I would have to reread *Moby Dick* to see if I thought it was 'great', and *The Golden Bowl* was a Henry James that I'd started but never finished. Also, I didn't think there was enough drama on his list. But what I regarded as a successful coup that afternoon was getting him to agree to substitute *The First Circle* for *Cancer Ward* as his Solzhenitsyn entry. (Of course, he may have just been trying to indulge me: I suppose I was also posturing a bit, to let him know the sort of person his daughter was associating with in England.) Could we get away with a *Great Books MA* at City? I'd still go for the classic stuff, just make it less Eurocentric (something from *The Egyptian Book of the Dead*, maybe) and put in a bit more drama (Soyinka) and substitute people like Walcott (*Omeros*) for some of the Americans. (The argument I had used in Boston, on the lawn, was the portrait of Stalin in the book, *The First Circle*, the fact that he was not demonised, the fact that his visionary qualities were acknowledged; *that* made the portrait more chilling; *that* convinced us of the human dimension of evil. Ah, well.)

My sister rang from London with the update on the volcano that
was blowing St. Caesare apart. The family were actually building
a house in St Caesare (another house?) when the rumblings, then
the rough stuff started, and it'd been going on for months; so the
British news media had long lost interest in it. I wasn't part of this
house-building arrangement because I was committed in
Spéracèdes, which I couldn't really present as an alternative to St.
Caesare; as my family were quick to point out, in the South of
France my neighbours were likely to belong to political parties that
if you were foolish enough to name you'd have to wash your mouth
out afterwards. No use pointing out that that might be preferable
to hurricane and earthquake; my family had lived in England a
long time, and they tended not to joke about these matters. But
Avril was concerned about the fate of people – distant relatives,
friends on the island – who couldn't be contacted by phone. Avril's
generosity made me conscious of my own meanness in measuring
out my time. People ring up and ask what I'm doing, and I tell
them: I'm writing. Or I'm marking or editing. Then they have no
alternative but to apologise and cut the thing short. The result is
that everyone is very critical of the university, for abusing me.
(They're right, of course, the university owes them an apology.)

But you couldn't just say to Avril: well, I'm just trying to decide
whether I'm up to teaching *Omeros* on Smythe's Epic course. *Is
that what you're thinking?* Well, I'm thinking that I wouldn't mind
having a go at Walcott's plays, at *Ti Jean... Or* even *Six in the Rain*
(murder close to home, strong stuff). But it would have to be the
poems. *Omeros*: where do you start? You'd have to acknowledge
the Greek thing, that frame of reference. That's OK. Then there's
the *terza rima*, the verse form; that was a killer: how close to Dante
was it supposed to be? I sort of like the looseness of the Walcott.
But was that laziness: should he have spent another fifteen years
on the book getting the *terza rima* right? (Why spend fifteen years
on a book if the results of three years are good enough to earn you
the Nobel? Though Walcott wasn't to know that when he was
writing it.) Am I prepared to wade through the *terza rima* in English
to see how Walcott compares with the Americans having a go at the
form? – all this with my ancient O Level in Italian! I remember
reading one of Hemingway's Paris books where he casually let slip

that performance poets (whom he didn't rate) were to be found in one of the cafes reciting their verse in *terza rima*, and I thought: not bad for an American knowing about this sort of thing in the '20s, particularly if you're a *novelist*. Back to Walcott. The diaspora stuff wouldn't be too difficult; but then there's the feminist criticism of the epic, the pretension, the maleness of it. No, you need one of the Daves for this. I'd been looking at the Portuguese thing, *The Lusiads*, comparing epic to epic, sort of thing. The names were great: Egas Monitz, Nuno Alvarez, Concalo Ribeiro, Vasco da Gama (we know him!), Alfonso de Albukuerque, the Sequeiras, da Cunhas, Sampaios, etc. (and that's just the *Introduction*). But the poem: well, in spite of being one-eyed and heroic, Camoens wasn't a patch on Walcott. I couldn't put Avril through all this stuff when she rang up and asked what I was doing?

In my marking she would assume I was doing something for the family. She would approve of my deducting up to five marks for poor spelling, punctuation and grammar. Indeed, she would be horrified at the mess of some of the scripts handed in: she'd been a nurse, now she was a hotelier: if you made a mistake people got sick, or worse, or came down with food-poisoning. She believed in attention to detail; it would be to trivialise her efforts with Florence to confirm that slackness had crept into the universities (in areas other than dress): I was her guarantee that this wouldn't happen at City. Avril was conscious of having deprived her daughter of certain things: it was perhaps less the open spaces and smell of the sea (sight of the sea); the waking up to grafted mango and sugarapple and guava, etc. The sun. It was more a sense of being in a place where your cousins and uncles were in their own place, governing their business, in charge of this and that, maybe even governing their country. This couldn't be compensated for with soft toys and affection, though heaven knows one tried; this couldn't be compensated for in a society showing its benign racism at school by encouraging you to run and jump and play ball games instead of doing your biology and chemistry. The family had to hold the line so that Florence, unlike so many others, wouldn't be diverted into foolishness. *Marking* was my end of the line, which I held, here, in Sheffield: I sometimes felt sorry for the students being held in check by all this marking. But a man's gotta do....

*

Stapleton (Chesterfield) Pewter. St Caesarian. Born Coderington, 30 September, 1942. Educated. Montserrat Secondary; Kilburn Polytechnic, London (1959-61); St. Davids U. College, Lampeter, BA Philosophy & English (1965); UEA, MA in 17 century Social Comedy, 1967; and U of London, Birkbeck. Taught English in London, Kilburn Polytechnic (1968-70); and France and Germany in the 1970s. Member of the *Cooperative Ouvrière du Bâtimant* (1972-74). Member of various theatre groups, including *Theatre 69* (London) and the *Caribbean Theatre Workshop* (1970-72). Fellowships include C. Day Lewis (London, 1979-80) and Hull College of Higher Education (1978-79); Library bursary in Ipswich (1985-86). Address, 80 Long Lane, Finchley, London N3

PUBLICATIONS

Plays

The Masterpiece (produced Lampeter, 1964)
Cheese on Ten (City Lit, 1968)
Tim... (with others) (Theatre 69, 1969)
The Private Life of the Public Man (Caribbean Theatre Workshop, St. Vincent, 1970. (pub. UWI Extra Mural, 1971)
Dropping Out is Violence (St. Caesare & Montserrat, 1971 (pub. UWI Extra Mural, 1971. rev. Keskadee, 1971)
Vertigo (Bush Theatre, 1976. rev. Liverpool Everyman, 1987.)
Good Neighbours (Oval House, 1976; rev. Tricycle, 1981)

Other

Family Matters (Savacou, 1971 (poems))
Hinterland: Stage by Stage with Edgar White & Michael Carrington (Bim, 65, 1979) rep. *Callaloo*, Vol 15. No 6.
Random Talks (Lokamaya Press, London, 1984.)
Random Talks & Stories (Heinemann, 1984)
Directing the Caribbean Theatre Workshop (Linda Lee Books, 1986)

Random Thoughts (Artrage, London, 1986)

Visiting a Fellow's Flat (Contemporary Review, 1989)

Theatrical Activities

Ran the Writer's Rehearsal Group (with John Elsom) at the City Lit, 1968-70. Directed the *Caribbean Theatre Workshop* in the West Indies, 1970-71.

Apart from the publication of *Good Neighbours* there's been definite slippage in the last few (teaching) years.

*

Did I want to get into this, to work more closely with Smythe, our writer-in-residence? Of course he was a fraud, even though I was impressed by his *Deutschland*. Poets had their party-pieces; I remember Michael Smith, the Jamaican, doing his Shelley on television. Not a big deal. I didn't find Smythe's own poetry especially brilliant, though it had a certain, gritty, whatever, unRupertness: the rhythms reminded you of earlier poetry, and a reviewer had famously compared him to the Geoffrey Hill of the *Mercian Hymns*. Smythe, of course, was appalled at the comparison.

So I was half-inclined to go along with La Gardner's assessment of Smythe. They'd done a joint lecture, an introduction to her Renaissance seminar, and Smythe had rambled on and insulted the students for being provincial in time. So he excavated a bit of literary territory with talk of the three Big boys, Chaucer, Langland and Gower whose sites students should visit. Naturally, La Gardner was at pains to point out that there were other big boys (Usk) and Girls (Ethelfreda, Lady of the Mercians, 10th century) etc. worthy of investigation if only the time permitted. What riled La Gardner, also, was the suspicion that Smythe was adopting an Oxbridge pose in all this – modern history starting with the fall of the Roman Empire, don't you know. In fact, she was the Oxbridge person, she was the one who'd been to Cambridge. Smythe went to, well, another place with lots of plate glass to relieve the brick. Yet, he was often heard to murmur *Non placet* when something at a course meeting displeased him.)

*

'Hello. Lee, *Lee*, (*I knew, I had a sense it would be Lee*) Lee, where, I mean, where are you? Yes, yes, of course, I mean... I mean how, how're you, OK?... No I... nothing, nothing. No, nothing's wrong; it's just... good to hear from you. Really no I'm... OK. Odd aches and pains yes, I know, nothing new. And of course the marking. But tell me about you; how've you been? Hang on let me just – I'm just getting a chair. Yes still in this little... must sort myself out. Yes, I've eaten. Well, I haven't, but I've given up all that. Too much effort, too much effort. Right. So tell me about you?... I'm sorry, that's me going on. No, no, your news is bound to be more interesting than mine; except my arm's hurting and that's not even my marking hand: when're you coming up to Sheffield? OK OK, when am I coming down to London?'

How does a simple telephone call go wrong? Either too conciliatory or too rigid. I'd like I say to the students. You come in too light – your point of entry into the text – you're feeble, we don't know you're there. You come in too heavy, it's all self-promotion – the old Tradition & the Individual Talent argument. So I was too conciliatory tonight, saying Yes too often and not meaning it. Better than arguing, surely, particularly when you're tired and there's the marking and your arm's hurting and with one of the secretaries off work, things piling up, and students turning up when they feel like it to see you; making appointments and not turning up, and then just somehow, with barely a hint of apology, just announcing themselves because they've overslept or they forgot. The boys, that is, always the boys; and now that they can be bothered, just calmly sauntering into your room because the world owes them a favour; that's what you have to put up with to get through the day and here's Lee offended because I'm too conciliatory. *Lack of engagement; lack of taking her seriously*. No no, this is all wrong, this isn't Lee; this is my hate-figure substituted for Lee. Must ring back; must ring back and be less conciliatory.

This isn't school. I'm not, after all, being interviewed for a job. I haven't shot anyone; and therefore I will persist in assuming that I'm not on trial.

What was I thinking five minutes ago? What sort of question was that?

What *was* I thinking five minutes ago?

I suppose I was thinking how badly I'd handled the call. And then I was thinking here am I losing all this time with the marking not done; and I was thinking of a bit of text I lost on the computer today – a little revision of the volcano play – and what a slob I am for not being able to stop making a fool of myself on the computer. Not that I spent time thinking about it, it just flicked through my mind and out again; that's not the sort of thing you bring up when someone asks what you were thinking about five minutes ago. I suppose the big thing I was thinking about five minutes ago – apart from the business of how badly I'd handled the call by being too conciliatory – was something someone said at work about the power imbalance in the seminar room with a man lording it over all the women, intimidating them into male-type learning techniques, adversarial, confrontational-type debates rather than doing the woman-thing of thinking out loud, saying something, perhaps, just to find out in the first place what she's thinking.

I was thinking about that but I didn't want to tell Lee I was thinking about that because it would have seemed too pointed, too much my wanting to get on the good side, sort of thing, so I talked a bit about the marbles.

I didn't think the business of the marbles was that interesting; but I thought the story would give her a sense that things were not all roses at this end of the divide. It was a conversation with Rolls – we were having a drink and he was talking of playing marbles when he was a child. And of course I played marbles when I was a child. And then when he described playing marbles, he said casually: that's one way of playing marbles. And I didn't realise there was more than one way of playing marbles. And there were two or three other people there who all knew three ways of playing marbles. And it just seemed to me unfair that I and no one else in St Caesare, who thought we knew about marbles, knew about the other ways of playing marbles, ways that everyone else seemed to know. And I couldn't hold back the sense of being deprived that this brought on. *That's* what I was really thinking of five minutes before she phoned. And why should I be dragged off to Nuremberg because of that? No, this was out of order: I'll ring back and ask what she's wearing.

And I know it's none of my business, I have no rights, I had less rights than the man at the corner-shop or the gigolo who harassed her on the train home; but what was she wearing? I was wearing her scarf. Not now, not this minute, but earlier in the day I had been wearing her scarf. And her coat. Her coat was missing a couple of buttons and I had to hold it in place, and it seemed such an intimate gesture having to hold her coat in place so that I will never never never put buttons on it. No, I'm not sounding happy; I'm only sounding happy because of this moment. Well, I wouldn't call it dishonest, I'd use another word. Maybe it was the hysteria that came from marking and....

No, I'm not talking of marking, I'm just... well I'm listening ...Yes, I'm here.

Why am I so easily thrown off course? OK, so I'm not malleable, I'm inflexible; get used to it. Why am I seen to be so inflexible? Because I don't like being called names? I DON'T LIKE BEING CALLED NAMES. Why am I so precious, so brittle, *Why am I so stupid!... It*'s not pride. I mean it really pisses me off to have that one trotted out again. And what's wrong with pride anyway? My grandmother had pride, my mother had pride. So that's not what's wrong with pride. So I will ring back and be calm. Though that's the sort of calm that irritates, that winds her up. But I'm not calm enough to ring back. Why should a man be calm when he's being called names. Of course it's worse for her. Do I really think it's worse for her? Yes, it's worse for her; what it must cost to pick up the phone. So it's worse for her. So I'll ring back in this spirit. It's worse for her.

But here am I thinking about myself again; maybe she's right, maybe I'm no different from the likes of Balham: if that's the effect you give, that's what you are. She can't be expected to live with something like that. *Dear Lee*, that must be an appalling thing to face. I must ring back. I'll make myself a cup of tea and then I'll ring back.

*

Your Honour, here is the evidence that I am not Balham.

*

Lord Balham. London. 1988. Evening.

It wasn't exactly a hostile audience at the Institute of Education on Bedford Way – about two-thirds black – but it was disapproving in a muted but heavy and unbudging sort of way. Balham seemed about to show us a film, because there was a stand set up with a white screen. I felt a little removed from the buzz, the charge that seemed to run through the room, because I, perhaps having known him as a schoolboy, took him less seriously than most of the people present.

Balham was dressed in a double-breasted jacket, more or less like the underground poster (of course we all knew the poster by heart now): it wasn't actually a suit, but very sharp. Balham was a big man. At the meeting he'd produced a little booklet of what might be verse, with his picture on the cover (not the same picture as on the underground), and a few lines of autobiography which acknowledged his degree in Sociology and his film-making, and lots and lots of other credits. He also included the information that he was 'Six feet and a half-inch' and some weight or other, which I presumed to be the right weight for someone in excellent physical condition, no paunch, who was six feet and a half-inch.

Tonight he was being conciliatory. (Come to think of it Balham's manner was always conciliatory, even in those years when his reputation for radicalism had hardened.) I suspected this conciliatoriness; he was toying with the audience. He was responding to some charge or other, citing his age – almost the same age as Kent – in mitigation.

Same age as Kent!

'Is he for real?' Lee asked. Kent wasn't a new county, Kent was there, well, had been there for ever. What was he on about? I couldn't be bothered to work it out; and Lee's cigarette was beginning to get on my nerves. Balham, in his late-40s was in much better shape than most of his audience at 30. And I, being his age, felt compromised. He was playing, as I suspected, a game: he was of an age, he said, to know better than to sue for peace. He was a fighting man, a man of war. He was at the right fighting age, as one or two unfortunates from a well-known terrorist organisation had reason to discover. But enough, he hadn't come here tonight to talk about Namibia. (Lee glanced at me in puzzlement.) He would talk about Namibia on a more suitable occasion. Then he clenched his fist in a half-hearted way and shouted something in a language we didn't understand; though three or four in the audience responded in kind. Others were getting impatient. Lee was beginning to get blotches on her face, and Balham, surveying all, was well pleased. It was the old thing again of lowering expectations, to the point where you could more than fulfil them.

Balham reiterated his age, *not yet* the age of Kent.

What's this thing about Kent?

A character in *King Lear*. Aged 48 (And) perhaps an oblique reference to Carrington who had written a play about King Lear. This was a literary audience. We knew about these things. (Of course, I remembered now when someone asks his age in the Shakespeare play, Kent did say something or other to that effect. But Balham wasn't through with us. He was of course, as we would expect, referring to the Carrington, specifically the soliloquy of being 48, urging risk. I told Lee not to take it personally.) After this Balham uncovered what we thought was a screen for the film: it revealed the offending London Underground picture of himself. This forced us to look at it again. He wasn't actually beaming, as I'd remembered, he had a slightly quizzical look. Now, the model, *six feet and a half-inch*, of whatever weight, deigned to talk to us through the picture. He pointed to the face, clean-shaven with its modified Grace Jones. It was a mistake to say, as some had said, that the fare-dodger had a proud expression on his face. Because, he would remind us – and here Balham waved a finger at the

doubters – black people were not facile. ('Facile' was his word.)
There was mild assent from the audience.

Nor were they to be fooled. We, in the privileged Arts industry,
he said, riding some dissent, must never lose sight of the fact that
black people were not facile. If one wanted to take on society,
Balham continued, and of course one does want to take on society
– his enunciation getting very crisp – one would do it in a far more
uncomfortable way for society than to confirm in this portrait, one
of its favourite images about us. He'd talk about that alternative
some other time. Now, he said: time to put this, what, rather minor
act of resistance into perspective.

'Bullshit.' That wasn't Lee. It was an Asian woman, and
Balham turned to her with something like a leer. Now, Balham
spoke to her only, level-voiced, as if explaining something difficult to a child. The main thing to note in the face in the picture, he
told the woman, was that it contained neither fear not panic; just
concern. It was, if you like, a detail in the story, though central to
the plot. The expression shows – and here he released the woman
from his concentration, and shared the information with the rest of
us – the expression shows that 'the figure' is likely to have been
aware of the situation he subsequently finds himself in, but is not
'oppressed' by it. It was, in fact, an amusing non-joke in our image.
(A woman in costume shouted something like 'Right on, Brother.'
She was very dark, but with old-fashioned glossy hair, long. She
was American; and it suddenly seemed as if she were with Balham.
Maybe it was she and not the Asian woman standing next to her he
had been focusing on earlier.) Nevertheless, he was losing it a bit,
and this surprised me – I almost wished he'd get back on the rails,
and not make too great a fool of himself. We were of the same
generation, went to the same school. I realised with some guilt that
I didn't want Balham to humiliate himself in front of Lee, as though
it would in some way humiliate me in her eyes. And it was as if this
were instantly communicated to Balham, because he suddenly
dropped the double-talk and came straight. He was educating us
to the picture, like those instructors you saw at the National
Gallery or the Louvre, surrounded by school parties, or groups of
Americans or Japanese with their identikit black hair. So here he
was, in a well-fitting jacket. He carried, not a briefcase but a

modified shoulder-bag, held in the hand: no hint of vagrancy. From this picture neither he nor any civilian black man could be *placed*, could be classed (except that this was Britain, where 'black' itself, was a class; a place; except that this was London, old provincial London town where posters had to do what posters did best, i.e. be tailored to the natives' ability to comprehend). It was in that sense, Balham returned to an earlier point, that his age was important: travelling without a valid ticket on London Transport couldn't then be used to reinforce the national propaganda against *Black youth*; this wasn't South Africa in *every* respect; a black man of two score years and eight couldn't still be called a boy. (*I have years on my back, 48:* that was the phrase.) Balham was continuing: it would equally be absurd to conclude from this poster that black men of a certain age went about London not paying their fare. To start with, a good proportion of them actually worked for London Transport; and it was, unhappily, also true that, as a group, that generation – like TV directors and landladies in university towns – tended to be among the more conservative members in the society. Black women of that age. Now that was a different proposition! (Someone queried his knowledge of Black women but he ignored it.)

What the poster *did*, he glossed rather than stressed, giving up on part of the audience – what the poster did was to present a critical, not a negative image of the black man. Rather *our* negative image of us, than *their* negative image of us. It was vulgar to think that we had to create positive images of ourselves, always, endlessly, merely to match society's negative. One had to refuse, at times, to take on their agenda. Part of the pressure of racism, he said, was to turn you into a goody goody.

Balham's thinking had got more sophisticated than I remembered it, and I wondered if it was I who had grown rusty. But by now the questions were coming thick and fast, and little debates had broken out throughout the hall. Someone was asking Balham (thinking aloud, really) if all this 'rationalisation' had taken place *before* he had perpetrated the London Transport ad.

The whole thing had been his initiative: he wasn't following an LT agenda.

What was he getting out of it?

Work. Money. And the opportunity to define a problem concerning us, before it was defined in a less acceptable way, etc.

The debate went on. Lee was getting bored. It was all very tiring. Balham wanted us all to go out for a meal, but we were tired; we wanted to get home. He was very loving towards the woman I suspected him to have been with, and indeed, towards Lee, but she had long seen through him; and we got a taxi alone to West Hampstead.

*

Recalling this now doesn't help me much. What's left but to go to bed!

*

Unearned income. Friday, early.

If I were to put a label on it I would call it Unearned Income. Don't ask me what *it* is. *It* is something that's not living; it's not even writing. *It* must be a space between living and writing; *it* is therefore nonsense. But it doesn't feel like nonsense. It's 5 o'clock in the morning, and I'm sitting here relieved that what's got to me in the past few hours (minutes, hours?) was a bad dream. How pathetic. But my tongue still feels as if it's been impaled with the needle and I'm dying of Aids. The tongue is swollen, I promise you, and I know the woman who did it. She's not an ex-student but she's someone I know; she worked at the bookshop, Waterstones. But that's not her, really, she's only suggestive of someone I knew much earlier, some earlier school; maybe back to GCE days. Anyway, anyway, *the dream*: after I escaped from her clutches and her needle, I staggered to the hotel lobby which promptly turned into a shop. This is all at home now: St Caesare. So, in this shop I run into a fellow in the late stage of the disease. Do I know him? I don't know him. But he knows the woman with the needle with petals on the end of it (yes, the needle had petals on the end of it) and she had pierced his tongue too. Before me; that's why he's at a more advanced stage of the disease. Appar-

ently the woman has no end of victims, he says this with some
unction. Look at him, his lip is swollen purple; we're in the same
boat, he's my friend. Earlier the girl had said to me, as we
embraced, that she had been gang-raped in Egypt. For hours on
end, she said. She said it without passion, without anger; after
the rape she had got them to own up for, as a white woman, her
compensation would be double that of a local woman. That had
tickled the pride of the Egyptian rapists. So they owned up and
she walked away with the compensation.

There's a hint of pride in her voice. Even then I'm thinking:
she's slept with the world; how could she be safe? Then the
needle, sharp pain straight through the tongue – and a fluent
(prepared?) 'doctor's' explanation – all the words I don't understand
– of what she's doing to me. My eyes are open; no one has forced
me into this. So I scramble back to the hotel where it's safe. The
hotel turns into a shop; my cousin's shop on the island, on St
Caesare; the shop turns into a Chinese supermarket, everything
stacked everywhere. I'm picking my way through this stuff,
through the stacks looking for the bathroom, looking for a sink;
can't find a sink, just stray Chinese women stacking, eating. Then
I run into the appalling man with the swollen lip, done for by my
lover; I reckon I have ten years to live, and try to live with that
thought.

Waking, I'm too appalled to be relieved. One thing, I'm the
same age, waking, as I am in the dream. I'm appalled that my
waking life confirms this detail. But the dream: is that where I
am when the constraints go? And I think: if suddenly I go gagga,
if I suddenly lose my functions, is this what I'm left with? No
Lee, no ruin in the South of France, renovated; no play to eclipse
Carrington, just this. So repair work must start with Lee, with
talking to Lee differently; by relating to Lee differently; by giving
Lee a ring. But it's too early in the morning for that.

Better get on with some marking; not the best frame of mind
to be marking, what with lack of sleep, etc. But who said this
world was perfect.

*

I would do some marking if it weren't for the smoke coming from downstairs. I very nearly picked up the phone to complain to Lee before realising the time, and furthermore feeling that she'd regard it as backhanded criticism of her own smoking. I thought: this is the sort of thing you need to be able to do. Pick up the phone and complain to a friend that the smokers in the building were irritating the hell out of you; more, were driving you mad. They had to be stopped, put down, exiled. There was a whole range of people, like my sister, that you wouldn't bring that sort of concern to, because they'd suspect that there was something more, something worse that you were trying to conceal – maybe racism at the university – and their concern would be suitably weighted. I didn't really have that type of relationship with people at work, so I thought, what the hell. I rang some friends in France. They were an hour ahead in France and they rose early. I rang the friend who'd found me the ruin in Spéracèdes and who was more or less overseeing the 'renovation', and we talked politics, and it was good to know that in France they thought we were as badly governed as we thought ourselves to be in England; and I agreed to go down in the summer and do some building, drink some wine, eat some decent food; and we agreed to write a book, jointly, on our days with the *co-operative*.

That's the problem with telephone calls; once you start making them you can't stop; so I started ringing those people I could ring at this time in the morning; a friend in London who'd become a father for the first time at 50 – he'd be up – so we had a chat about fatherhood at 50, and commiserated with both baby and mother; and I agreed to pop in next time I was in town.

Meanwhile I had to write up a proposal quickly; things didn't stop because of the marking.

INTRODUCTION TO WEST INDIAN LITERATURE?
(Options; Exam + Dissertation) (level?)

WK ONE:	THE CARIBBEAN: HISTORICAL SURVEY
WK TWO:	THE WEST INDIES: INTELLECTUAL, CULTURAL, LITERARY SIGNPOSTS
WK THREE:	THE NOVEL: *In the Castle of my Skin* (George Lamming, 1953)

WK FOUR: THE NOVEL: *The Lonely Londoners (Samuel Selvon, 1956)*
                              Miguel Street (V.S. Naipaul, 1959)
WK FIVE: THE NOVEL: *Palace of the Peacock* (Wilson Harris, 1960)
WK SIX: THE NOVEL: *Wide Sargasso Sea* (Jean Rhys, 1966)
WK SEVEN: SEMINAR ON THE NOVEL
WK EIGHT: INTRODUCTION TO POETRY: *Hinterland*
                              (Ed. E.A. Markham) & *Voiceprint* (Ed. Morris etc.):
WK NINE: WALCOTT
WK TEN: WALCOTT
WK ELEVEN: BRATHWAITE (and the folk tradition)
WK TWELVE: THE BRATHWAITE INFLUENCE
                              (calypso/kaiso/reggae/pop/performance)
WK THIRTEEN: SEMINAR

NO. No No No No No. All too Anglo, too conventional, too *old*. Where's the Black British element? For that matter, where's the short story, where's the drama? And why do a course like this except to challenge the British notion of what is Caribbean? Bring in the French, Dutch, Spanish. Bring in people like Marquez: he shares a Caribbean coast with the rest of us. Maybe tackle the thing through a series of adaptations. Brontë into Rhys. Brontë into Maryse Condé. Folktales from the Surinamese, etc. (Might consult Carrington on this.) Above all, I couldn't accommodate myself to there being no drama. The plays of Walcott, of Matura, of Edgar White, of Carrington deserved better; and, certainly, the 'disaster' literature coming out of St. Caesare and Montserrat would have to be looked at. Maybe we could lose one of the novels. And yet... I was still mapping out a shape for the course: when I got a clearer feel for it, then I could see if it made sense. Introduction or MA? West Indian or Caribbean? An MA in *West Indian* literature, if it's not to be a ghetto thing, would have to be seen in the context of what it's not; it is *not* an MA in *Caribbean Studies*. For that, one would have to bring in the big battalions. Students would have to choose from things like Caribbean Intellectual History and non-Anglophone writing; Linguistics (including studies in patois, nation language, dialect); Anthropology (pre-Columbian and African survivals)

French or Spanish or Dutch, and maybe things like Sport and Dance and Music. And there would have to be a core, which would be something like *20th Century Caribbean History*. Now that would take a small team of expensively educated experts that City would find amusing if you proposed their employment to deliver *one* MA Course. Hence, *MA in West Indian Literature*. Option B. Then I must think of the resources, Library etc. to deliver my course.*

Friday. Late.

I've just come back from Leeds, just seen Soyinka's *The Beatification of Area Boy*. Ah, Soyinka has restored my faith in theatre. So has Jude Kelly, the Director. Rumour is that we might be losing the poor woman to the National. But I'm sure she has the character to resist that. *Must ring her about the volcano play*. The most memorable moment in the Soyinka play was when a boy sitting next to me – couldn't have been more than 14 – was a bit confused at people going out during the interval. So he turned to me and asked if it was half-time. It was a non-theatrical audience; and they were totally entranced. I half-promised to go back tonight, though I'm not so sure I can make it. I must review it for some paper or other.

Going up to Leeds was a form of liberation; it meant that you'd broken the back of the marking and could take a night out, could go to the theatre. There were no scripts accompanying me on the train. (The train, the endless train. 30 miles. Dear God: travel in these parts must have been easier in the Middle Ages. Quicker.) So to pass the time I took a collection of short stories and Hugh Trevor-Roper's *The Last Days of Hitler*, which for some reason I'd never read. And when I got home I was anxious to finish it. I'd got to the point of 'The siege of the Bunker', and was trying to make people I knew in Germany in '74-'76 – Herr Soltec, Herr Zakenfels, Frau Halterbush – change places with Eva Braun, the Goebbels' family (occupying rooms abandoned by Dr Morell), Hauptsturmfuehrer Schwaegermann and all those people with wonderful names – Dr Stumpfegger; Sturmbannfuehrer and all the women. Frau Junge; Fraeulein Manzialy (the vegetarian cook); Fraeulein Krueger (Bormann's Assistant's secretary), etc. Frau Halterbush was the star. As I read on I was beginning to be a bit sorry for the secretaries who seemed to be still secretarying even after all the men they worked for had said their goodbyes and murdered their family or taken flight. The image of cockroaches came to mind. Would these secretary-women live on, endlessly, for ever? Clearly, they have and have moved to take over the world because these are the people who tell us what to do and what not to do at City. Frau Halterbush, our last school manager now made sense; pity she slipped away before I had time to check carefully for any residual traces of German.

The burning began to assault me; the room was full of smoke; it was pouring in under the door, coming up through the floorboards. I knew they would prevent me getting out, though I fancy they neglected the fire escape, in the same way that Hitler's Water Tower was a built-in escape. Somewhere down there, were the human chimneys, puffing me to oblivion, orchestrated by Frau Halterbush, our ex-school manager.

Footnote

SEMESTER TWO: CARIBBEAN WRITING IN BRITAIN.
AN UPDATE

WK ONE:	The Caribbean Artist's Movement (1966-72) The struggle for visibility)
WK TWO:	CAM Fallout: (The Black Bookfair; Savacou; *Artrage*; The Bluefoot Travellers) LKJ
WK THREE:	Bookshops and Publishers
WK FOUR:	Literary criticism
WK FIVE:	Short stories (*The Penguin Book of Caribbean Short Stories*. Ed. E.A. Markham, 1996)
WK SIX:	In transition a) Andrew Salkey, Caryll Phillips, James Berry, Roy Heath

WK SEVEN: Against narrative realism (Canada & the USA)
                       (Jamaica Kincaid & Michelle Cliff)
WK EIGHT: New voices
                       (i) Pauline Melville & Lawrence Scott
WK NINE: Theatre: Wall, BTC, CTW, Temba, Talawa...
                       (Mustapha, Edgar White, Carrington)
WK TEN: The failure of Black British theatre
WK ELEVEN: New Voices
                       (ii) Nichols, D'Aguiar, Dabydeen, Andrea Levy, etc.
WK TWELVE: Seminar on Black British writing
                       (Agard, etc., Mark de Brito)
WK THIRTEEN: Seminar on Caribbean writing

PART TWO

5

It was cold; February, the wrong day for the trip, but they were expecting me, so I was heading for Ulster alone. Christmas hadn't gone as planned. Lee and I had escaped to Paris for a week but the less said about that the better. Difficult to know how to console someone for the loss of a husband when you yourself felt that loss so differently. It wasn't grief, exactly, it wasn't quite the sense of waste that Lee felt, a life, two lives unfulfilled *together*, for who were we to say that his life wasn't fulfilled. He'd gone out and done his thing for humanity, he'd got killed in the attempt; he was – even though the newspapers were meanish in their interest (the television was a bit better, oddly enough) – a hero. He'd left children, not entirely unprovided for, who would have to work out the benefits of a father as hero, fading gradually into myth, as opposed to the benefits of a flesh and blood father who, because he was always elsewhere, in effect had left them fatherless.

Lee's sense of – despair, was that too strong a word? – had to do with something more bleak than the loss of a man, long-detached as a partner. It was her sense of rightness that was mocked. (Those people who grasped things towards them were, it seemed, allowed to keep them; those who gave others latitude, accepted that space didn't necessarily mean loss of intimacy, were being mocked; those who deferred pleasure, pleasures, were being made to pay. And here was I, temperamentally or otherwise, signing up with the deferring party: what did I hope to achieve in the meantime? A great play on the West End stage? Democracy in China? The end of apartheid in South Africa? And humiliatingly, shamefaced, unserious, I had to admit yes, yes, *yes*.)

There was something that was nagging me that was too embarrassing to admit to Lee. Peter's death in the Sudan embarrassed me because men like him were going out to Africa – for whatever reason – to tend to people's need while men like me were sitting around in England doing nothing useful; were drifting into Europe teaching English to the natives as if having a German or a Frenchman speak his second (usually third or fourth) language in my accent was some sort of compensation for having been *colonised*. My life seemed utterly trivial compared to Peter's.

Yes, of course it was self-pity to want to prove something before stepping into this dead man's shoes, before stepping into *any* dead man's shoes. This wasn't the spirit in which to help Lee cope with her own sense of loss, so we decided to lick our wounds separately.

Lee took refuge with family, her mother and sister coming over from Geneva, to speculate, as usual, about the fate of the family who had chosen to remain in Tehran out of sentiment; out of hope, keeping their heads down. It was back to making separate plans. I alternated between a sort of sullen solitariness and spells of frenzy doing the rounds, reacquainting myself with Eugene and Rachael, my brother and sister-in-law down in Battersea. We used to make mild jokes about their names, so solid and unobjectionable, so fitted for travel on the one hand – or, on the other, right-sounding, so left at home; so like their owners. I received a polite, though, I thought, genuine welcome at the house. Rachael was also from St Caesare and my brother was lucky, the saying went, to be able to find someone from the island not related to you. Rachael worked in one of those offices where her status was difficult to define, and it was too late now after all these years, to ask precisely what she did, so in conversation, you gave her the benefit of the doubt. The son, Julian, I knew absolutely nothing about: he was now bigger than me, and was suspiciously polite. I rather enjoyed being with them and wondered why, over the years, we had tended to skirt one another. My excuse was that I was so little in the country. Eugene hinted at some schemes involving property in St Caesare, that he wished to put to me, but later; it was as if he wasn't quite sure of me. And, in that, he was obviously right. (It was embarrassing, for instance, that although they had lived in that house for many years I still managed to get lost finding the place. We had the old conversation about the affectation of people living north of the river. I was always going to be a stranger in this family.)

My visits to my sister's home in the East End were more like home because, apart from anything else, my mother had lived in the house. Yet the business of crossing London to visit family depressed me: Why were we so spread out? Were we trying to colonise London, or to make up for the lack of space in St Caesare? Foolish. People lived where they did because it was convenient, that's all. Nevertheless, this thin sprinkling of family – my mother buried back in St Caesare – makes us all feel newly vulnerable, Avril and Eugene as much as me, in spite of their children, for the children had no real interest in their parents' home.

Anyway, I owed Carrington because I felt that my being in his flat longer than planned had somehow kept him away from London. On the one brief trip he made, to give a lunchtime talk at the ICA, he spent the night on the couch. The couch was, in fact, a single bed, and I was paying rent for the flat; nevertheless, seeing him bunk down there in a room full of books while I occupied the bedroom at the top (the other bedroom was set up as a study) made me think I owed an explanation, not so much to him, perhaps, but to Minap, as she would certainly have asked my intentions about the flat: was I, in fact, preventing her and the children coming to town? So I was visiting Ulster in a mood of mild contrition. I had bought an Indian scarf on the Charing Cross Road as a present for Minap and planned to pick up some sweets on the way for the children. For Carrington, I staggered under a massive case of books, things he wanted from the flat.

It's amazing how the propaganda gets to you. At Heathrow, I wheeled the trolley towards the Ulster check-in, acutely conscious that everyone knew I was going to Ulster and had their eyes on me. They must be speculating about what's inside Carrington's suit-case. They don't know I'm going to a university; they don't know what I've got is books. I'm pleased at the heaviness of the suitcase: it can't be anything but books. I've also got my shoulder-bag: does that make me look too much the traveller? (Balham's picture on the underground?) At the barrier, people X-raying the luggage conduct the body-search with a degree of tolerant inefficiency that isn't altogether reassuring. I bleep coming through the scan. There are metal and other objects in my pockets, and the searcher pauses in his quest – a vaguely sexual act, this: does it attract a certain

sort of person? In a more decadent society would they have men
searching the women and vice versa? If there had been a revolution in my absence on the continent, a quiet one, a hush-hush
affair, would this be one sign of it: the men at customs feeling up
the women? Mild paranoia now: which of these women would you
want... And suddenly, the thought of women pursued by unattrac-
tive, unwanted men makes me think of women being oppressed in
a way I hadn't realised.

At the other side of the X-ray, a man decides to take a look at
my case of books, and although he doesn't search thoroughly, I'm
pleased at this degree of caution because I am, after all, about to
fly. Then, after a long winding route pushing, then chasing my
trolley, struggling to keep control because we're careering down-
hill, I'm at the real Ulster check-in. No problem. But into the
waiting area, past the uniformed men at Security Control, I have
a feeling that a couple of the people waiting to board, solitary
middle-aged types hidden behind their newspaper – one woman,
a Le Carré-type – aren't passengers. This is too transparent, so I
no longer feel like a suspect, but I'm vaguely worried that security
is so primitive: if they are that amateurish, is any of us safe? In
order to seem nonchalant, I defer going into the little bookshop to
browse (and to buy some sweets for the children) and saunter to the
other end of the lounge, to the counter, and buy some cashew nuts
and a huge coke in a plastic cup that makes me feel stupid: why
am I drinking this huge coke instead of a cup of tea, a hot
chocolate? The lounge is divided into smoking and non-smoking,
and the little business of noting that, and finding a table in non-
smoking, takes my mind off me as suspect. Other people around
seem pretty relaxed; lots of Irish voices. This, too, is reassuring.
(Like going into an Indian restaurant and finding real Indians
eating there.) I open my newspaper, an ordinary passenger.

The flight takes an hour, and outside Aldergrove Airport,
Carrington is waiting. How odd, I think, to find him in this
context. It's cold, it's drizzling, it's misty, it's miserable; but there
is Carrington, looking tamed in the environment. Nevertheless, he
is effusive; he says it's an hour's drive to Portrush, and apologises;
he says he's got a university car (I don't know the significance of
this) and we cross to the car-park, work our way out and are soon

heading north to what I'm told is the Antrim coast. Beautiful, apparently, when it stops raining; the gloom, though it is mid-afternoon, the fogged, streaked window, making this seem like an adventure.

There is a roundabout which slows us down getting out of the airport, yellow signs announcing VEHICLE CONTROL STOP, and ramps. With the best will in the world you couldn't get past the guards, bulky with bullet-proof vests coming tentatively (tentative because of the rain, because of the danger, because it's The Irish Way, the way of guards?) peering in and waving us on. We're not important enough to be stopped. Carrington, clearly, isn't the man he thought he was, university car or no university car. The field, adjacent to the road is floodlit, though the lights don't yet make an impact. It must cost something having all these lights burn in mid-afternoon. Soon after this we're heading north.

The landscape seems curiously normal; flat, rolling farm country. I'd expected broken-down farmhouses, instead, there are tidy substantial buildings, villas, set back from the road: you could be travelling in Mittleuropa.

For company Carrington provides music. Old rock'n'roll cassettes. Little Richard. Elvis. Real '60s stuff. '50s. He says his daughter is into Little Richard, that Little Richard is about to make yet another comeback. That they're all making a comeback. Those who are not dead or working for the CIA. Reminiscing about rock'n'roll gives us both a rest from our various obsessions. Then Carrington talks about a new play that he's been *commissioned* to write. He likes commissions; it helps him to get on with the job. I, naturally, refuse to reveal that I'd had a go at a play in France. Nothing will come of it: to reveal that would only invite Carrington, the professional, to give me advice. So we talk about other things; about Carrington doing something for the radio, about *my* doing something for the radio: about Carrington doing great things at the university; about *my* house-building France, and the great book that will come out of *that*; about the Paris conference, about Carrington editing a new university magazine and finding the right title for it; we talk about Lee and *Rainbow* (with Carrington saying that Lee should get out of that business and let black and white racists fight it out amongst themselves). We were talking of Carrington's getting a mention in a French reference-book, something called *Desfammes*, when we went round what seemed the third roundabout in quick succession: was this a design fault or a security trap? Carrington said that though we were going to Portrush, we'd pop into the university for a few minutes. I'd meant to talk about Balham, but that could wait.

*

Minap was a surprise because she was so much not foreign. I couldn't understand why her accent had seemed a bit exaggerated over the phone, because now she sounded like any other middle-class English woman, though without the more loaded hints of class. It turned out that she had been brought up in New Zealand, which, apparently, is where lots of Cook Islanders end up, and had also been to school in England, where her sister had been something of a beauty queen, and Canada, where she met Carrington at York university, when he had been writer-in-residence there.

Minap was still under thirty, and seemed effortlessly welcoming. I apologised for not bringing a present for the children and she reassured me that it didn't matter, and I presented her with some wine because Carrington had called in at the off-licence on the way. (I wouldn't unpack the scarf until later.) We were allowed to take a sleeping child up to bed, with orders not to excite her, while Carrington apologised for having been delayed at the university.

'That comes from being so important,' Minap said, pleasantly.

'I know,' Carrington clowned. 'Good thing I turned down the job as president of, where was it? Costa Rica.'

I liked Minap. She decided to put the child to bed herself, and let Carrington (whom I now had to call Michael) show me my room. He did this by way of their own room at the top of the house – all three bedrooms were at the top of the house – to show off their 'Canaletto Scene' from the window. All I could see were a few lights, peeping through the black and wet.

Downstairs, Carrington insisted on whisky, the 'Irish' drink, while we waited for Minap. The house, I thought, was not well-heated.

*

Minap on your mind. It's the middle of the night. Night,
anyway. I'm in the room next to the children, the parents on the
other side. A good place for the children. Enclosed. Womblike.
Do parents think like this? It's cold but I have enough bedding,
damp rather than cold, the mustiness of an unused room. The
extra bedding makes it uncomfortable, though I suspect that's
not why I can't sleep. I want to go to the loo, but not badly
enough, maybe flushing will wake up someone, the tank might
be next to the children's bedroom, in a cupboard in the
children's bedroom. Though that would be the hot-water tank,
for extra warmth, not the other. Go to the loo now and I'll be
known forever as the man who woke the children. This in child-
terms might make me a sort of child-molester. Though, parents,
rather than children are the ones who suffer when the children
wake up in the middle of the night. I feel that a man the age of
Kent shouldn't have these anxieties. (Maybe that's what brought
on the dream: how to be a guest in a family at my age.) Having
these anxieties means you're not keeping abreast of what's
going on in Uganda, in South Yemen (is that still the hardship
posting for British diplomats who fall out of line – as was the
case during the Wilson Governments? No, that was North
Yemen. George Brown, as Foreign Secretary, would send you
to North Yemen, till you toed the line, or defected.) Enough of
Yemen: what's the state of play between Reagan and Gorbachev?
Old Reagan and Young Gorbachev... Is New Guinea coping
without me? Why hasn't my French improved?

On the way across I was reading a book by Margaret Drabble,
just a novel taken almost at random from Carrington's shelves.
Back in England, I recovered my taste for English fiction, part of
a debriefing process, so to speak. In this very English book, the
woman at the centre is all the right things: ordinary – from the East
End – full of doubts, getting by in her chaotic way, without
husband – though she borrows someone else's (my women friends
wouldn't like that, Lee wouldn't). She has a lot of hangers-on in the
house, in her life, including an ex-husband. I can't be bothered to
think of the point of the story – was it the twin brother who sent her

hate mail? No. What comes to the fore is a parallel thought that I
no longer like staying in other people's homes, too confirmed a
bachelor, too set. I'm wondering: am I inhibiting their lovemak-
ing? Would I, the stranger, be alert to sounds that the children, if
awake, would simply associate with the life of the house, the fact
that doors and cupboards and carpets come to life at night and
make human – animal – noises? Or are they this minute thinking:
he's tired out by the journey, let's risk it. Or – Minap would seem
to be past all that – he's a big boy, he's been around, he's not
English, he won't come rushing in to rescue me as if I were a
wounded cat...

...And I'm oppressed by this: this is no way to think of people
who've offered you hospitality. (Of course there was that French
play – play or novel? Existentialist – where the husband extends
hospitality to the traveller by inviting him to share the wife's
bed, while he, the husband, bunks down on the couch. Is this
nearer to the French experience or to the Drabble book?... I have
no particular feelings for Carrington (Michael), but I'm sensitive
on Minap's behalf. I like her, but wonder why in all the men she
must have met, *of all the men in the world,* she chose him. They're
both attractive people, a good match. This is grandfatherly talk. I
remind myself that Carrington is my age and I don't envy them,
except, perhaps for the children. (Maybe that's what brought on
the dream which woke me up. All the women were in it. Lee, of
course, but also Lindsay and my mother. And Balham's first
French partner, Pauline. Pauline with the funny accent. Pauline
who developed that into an anti-British crusade. But in the dream
Pauline soon faded into somebody else, and I was in my mother's
room in Upton Park, being interrogated. These sessions usually
took place before I went abroad, or when I got back. And they
always had to do with the woman in my life. Though she knew
better than to ask directly.

'And when you goin' see her?' (She had given a nightgown to
Lindsay, many sizes too large for her. But Lindsay had kept it,
touched by the gesture. If the woman in my life had been Lee,
my mother clearly wouldn't have registered that. And I wouldn't
have assisted her.)

'You see her?'

'Eh?... Oh, you know.'

'You going see her soon?'

'Yes. Of course.'

'You not getting any younger.'

'Oh, I don't know.'

'None of us getting any younger... You have to see her soon.'

And I played the game.

'She asked about you, you know.'

'Yes?' she laughed. 'I don't believe so.'

'Oh yes, no question.'

'I don't believe she even remember me.'

'Oh, she asks about you all the time.' *Overdoing it?*

'You tell her I going down?... You must...'

'No, you not going down.'

'Going right down. But, is life.'

'And she's still got the nightgown.'

A flash of panic from her.

'You remember, your nightgown?'

Panic subsiding: 'I don't believe that.' She was laughing now. 'It must be old now. Out of fashion... She take it in?'

...If Minap were to come into my room now it would embarrass us both... Yes, I remember what brought that Drabble book to mind. The woman, Kate, is having an affair with the husband of one of her friends, and this woman, a middle-class, up-market social worker, accepts the condition of her life without apparent rancour and, reviewing things, calmly acknowledges that her husband is not a nice man. Nevertheless, she has no urge to change her life. I remember travelling in Guyana with the *Caribbean Theatre Workshop* in 1971 and being put up briefly in Georgetown by a family where the father, good, liberal man, agonised over the fact that he didn't much like his younger son. Maybe this sort of thing is different with couples: how does a husband live with the knowledge – because, surely, he must know – that the wife thinks he's not a nice man? I suspect Lee's beginning to feel this about me. Enough. If, as in the play, the man says: I have done the state some service, and all these other people – including people in the Drabble book – with their children who are not obviously deformed or evil, could

say: I have done the state some service, I also, having been abroad
and back and managed... over half a lifetime, not to break into
people's cars (though I did once break into a house, courtesy of
Balham), not to beat up women... I could say that, too – having
passed some exams, and been uncle to a few people. I've
managed so far not to be crippled, senile, a burden to the neighbours, and importantly, not to be old.

I fancied this line of speculation kept me awake all night, but
when Minap entered the room, stealthily, with a cup of tea, I
woke up. Shortly afterwards, I was being challenged by Minap
II (I'd forgotten her name), night-gowned (which put me in mind
of Lindsay in my mother's nightgown), big-eyed, finger in her
mouth. She stood in the doorway not blinking, and I opened my
eyes wide to play the game. Then she said something in a
foreign language and disappeared.

*

We visited the countryside, mainly the coast, and drank a lot
of whisky (you could order hot whisky in the pub!). You learnt new
terms, like walking along the 'Strand', the sea-front, gritting your
teeth with the cold, fine spray and grit from the sea peppering your
face. What was odd was the absence of any beach, any sand; it was
all boulders, decorated with seaweed, and the steel-grey water
churning, both patient and relentless, suggestive of something old,
prehistoric. But on land, things looked normal, a surprise, driving
through the little village-town of Portrush with its abandoned-
looking railway station. The one filmic thing, the one media image
was the police station which had a high, messy, barbed-wire fence
surrounding it. The thing looked so theatrical that I wondered if it
was done for effect. But later, in Derry, in Belfast, the iron grilles
in the road, the reinforced-steel army vehicles made one less
smug. Yet, it was disorientating to find that Belfast (apart from the
military presence) looked like an old-fashioned English provincial town, a Victorian centre, and the newer bits full of identikit
Marks & Spencers, Boots, etc.

Carrington wanted me to meet people. A man wasn't going to let
a young family interfere with his responsibilities as host. Of

course, what that meant was that I couldn't prolong the visit, couldn't become a strain.

Baby-sitter acquired, we went to dinner in Portstewart the following night. Portstewart was only three or four miles away and was, in Carrington's words, an academic ghetto, full of senior staff. At least, in Portrush, where he lived, the students were more in evidence, largely because of the railway. Dinner was at Bernard and Tessa's. Bernard was the Professor of English, head of Carrington's Department. He was from the real Ireland, the south, and so Carrington promised me a relaxed evening, West Indian-style.

At the Professor's at Portstewart, I was to have some of my prejudices challenged, the sorts of prejudices about things and people far from London you'd deny having, so much that I wondered if Bernard wasn't a secret propaganda weapon to turn us on to Ireland, Irishness, the North, though, he, himself, was from the South. He sounded like any other Irish builder, or those characters in Irish drama on the radio. And, in truth, Bernard did come out with Irishisms, though they were mainly anecdotes about Yeats, about what Yeats really said at the Playhouse riots in 1912, and, later in the evening, in quoting Swift. I was irritated with myself in not expecting a subtle intelligence being filtered through that voice. But if the English had been success-ful in their 'class' indoctrination in the West Indies they had done an even better job at home, because, I learnt later, the junior members of the Professor's Department, the English contingent, vied with one another to mimic his speech. Carrington – Michael – to my relief, had an amused tolerance for this kind of fourth form childishness.

There were other guests at table in Portstewart, a couple of psychologists and someone from the South, visiting, involved in theatre, friend of the family. So quite a bit of talk was about theatre. Carrington was in great form, anxious to demonstrate, it seemed, that he was at home in Ulster, in this house, hugging and kissing other people's wives and dominating the early conversation. This was before we sat down to dinner: Carrington was allowed to tell jokes – as if stored up for the occasion – then drink in hand, we were ushered out of the narrow, chaotic kitchen; a little bit like the

house in the Drabble book I was reading, and the sort of kitchen
– a cat, a dog, evidence of children – that my mother would have
warned us against. Bernard welcomed us standing around watching him prepare dinner, politely offering to help. Tessa left her
husband to it. She was an anthropologist but didn't teach in the
department. She thought we'd be more comfortable in the sitting-
room at the front of the house.

At dinner the psychologists allowed me to keep one prejudice
in place: they regaled us with more talk, this time about shit.
Scientists, they were citing shit as one way of monitoring our
health, the consistency of shit: on inspection, it must prove to have
the consistency of toothpaste and the colour of the back of
Carrington's hand. I was secretly pleased I was slightly darker
than Carrington, a small thing, but it added a little 'tone' to my
evening. As the psychologists talked about tapeworms, the rest of
the party thought that we needed something a little stronger than
wine to settle our stomachs. In the light of all this scatology, a
repeat of Carrington's 'Irish' jokes (for half the party who hadn't
been there earlier) proved almost welcoming.

Carrington reminded us that he was a Montserratian (not a
man of dubious provenance, like me, or someone traumatised
by New Zealand gentility, like his wife). And that Montserrat
had had the rare experience to have been colonised, not by the
French or the English or the Spanish or whatever, but by the
Irish. Their only colony. Their dissidents had landed in the
1630s and named it for Ireland. Not the island itself, which had,
of course been misnamed by Columbus on his Second Voyage in
1493. But all the place-names were Irish. It was that fact of history
that licensed him (as no Englishman was licensed) to tell an Irish
joke.

He told jokes; he mentioned a play he was writing set in Dublin
where all those respectable, in quotes, ladies in *Ulysses* get
together to read out Bloom's improper letters to them. This
engaged the gathering, most of whom remembered the original
scene where the fellow is threatened with horse-whipping by the
woman in boots with a riding-crop. 'The Honourable Mrs. Mervyn
Talboys.' 'The Amazon.' 'With jackboots, cockspurs and a sort of
scarlet-woman vest, waistcoat. And a riding crop.' And as she lays

into Bloom, Bernard has her foreplay word-perfect. 'Oh, did you, my fine fellow...' Remember Bloom says he meant only to ask for a refined birching. To stimulate the circulation. 'Oh, did you, my fine fellow? Well, by the living God, you'll get the surprise of your life now, believe me, the most unmerciful hiding a man ever bargained for. You have lashed the dormant tigress in my nature into fury.' *Lash, lash, lash, lash!*

And everyone round the table is lost in admiration for the man-beating, the Honourable Mrs. Mervyn Talboys. Later, Carrington told an Irish joke where he couldn't be upstaged. This one was local; it was *now*: so they're standing on the platform, early evening, waiting for a train to the university in Coleraine. But there's no train. (Not that there's never a train, there's no train tonight.) So the relief bus pulls up and the conductor invites everyone on the platform to get on the bus. So far so good. The bus heads up the road to the next station, Dhu Varren. Same thing. The few people there get on, all except one woman, Chinese, who still hovers, waiting for the no-train. (The Noh train! Wrong country) She doesn't respond to the conductors' (or fellow passengers') urgings to get on the bus. She makes as if to get on, then she decides not to. Obviously, there's a bomb threat, there's going to be no train; maybe she's new to the province, a first year student. Eventually, in exasperation, the conductor points to the bus and says: *This is the train*. The woman looks at the 'train' in the shape of an Ulsterbus and panics. And, of course, Carrington, on the 'train' panics: if people are so *reckless* with language, how can anyone be safe? Eventually, the 'train' drives off in the middle of the street, without the Chinese lady. An Irish joke?

There was much comment round the table about jokes, 'The Joke', 'Jokes & Sanity'; 'Jokes, Sanity & Pedantry'; 'Englishness, Jokes, Sanity & Pederasty' – essay papers? Research topics? How about Inscrutable-Chinese-at-Portrush-Station-Waiting-for-Noh-Train? We needed some cognac as well as whisky to get over that and then Minap was probed a bit about changing cultures and the naming of the children. After that Tessa endeared herself to me by asking about my time in France.

It was clear how people's perceptions of you were formed by your friends, which, when you thought about it, was obvious,

really. Everyone related to me as a friend and colleague of
Carrington's, someone who had worked in his touring theatre in
the Caribbean in the '70s, and then gone back to my profession
as language teacher, only to return to *theatre* in a community
sort of way. So I played down my teaching and odd-jobbing and
emphasised my role in theatre both in London and the Caribbean. (Though that degenerated into an anecdote about living
in a haunted house in St Vincent in 1970.)

Before we left Bernard and Tessa's, Carrington got second
wind, and this time the joke *was* very good. It was a stray remark
of Gore Vidal's that he had picked up (I wasn't irritated, oddly
enough, by this literary-academic in-world). Vidal, apparently,
wakes up some days (he lives in Italy writing his books, pontifi-
cating) thinking that he had once been Governor of Alaska. Not
only was he Governor of Alaska for at least one term, but he
remembers them as good years – The Good Years. And he's not
in any sense disappointed that the history books have failed to
record anything of the event. So much so that when he ran into old
George McGovern recently (remember McGovern who was
humiliated by Nixon in the Presidential race in whenever?) –
when Vidal ran into the ex-Presidential hopeful, McGovern com-
plained that he couldn't make a living on the American academic
talk circuit because the new generation in the universities had
forgotten who he was; and Vidal promptly told him how to solve the
problem. Quite simply he should announce that he had *beaten* Nixon
in the race in 1972, and had been President of the US for at least one
term. As an ex-president, he would in consequence clean up on the
talk circuit. Vidal reminded McGovern that with the collective
American amnesia, no one at the Lecture Bureau would remember
that he had won only one State and the District of Columbia in the
election, and the few old-timers, like Vidal, who had something of
a memory left, could quickly be bought off. McGovern, of course,
was a puritan, and consequently didn't find Vidal's suggestion
remotely amusing. But Carrington promised us all a play on doing
a Vidal, using characters near and dear to us. Minap said he needed
only to make it autobiographical, to be convincing.

The evening ended with 'deconstructing' Woody Allen. Only
fitfully in academic life, I'd never quite got to grips with these new

terms that clever critics used to put us off reading novels, making them seem not as stories that people wrote down to relieve their own frustrations, stories, hopefully, to impress and excite and to make money, but as texts for students to be silly about. We were waiting for our taxi back to Portrush and the theatre woman, whose name I forget, who had been talking to us about African and Caribbean drama – about the Walcott play that Carrington had done at the university – now said that she'd been reading a piece on Ethiopian theatre and was struck by the fact, which had nothing, particularly, to do with theatre, that Ethiopian names seemed to be reversible, the playwright Makonnen Endalkachew, for instance, naming his son Endalkachew Makonnen – both of whom, incidentally, had ended up as prime minister of their country. Carrington's initial fascination (as was mine) was in making a connection between the naming and being made Prime Minister. Then we became fascinated by the class implications – Pewter Stapleton: Stapleton Pewter? – of the reversal of Christian and Surname. The party somehow battened onto Woody Allen, or rather Allen Woody, and the sorts of films this new back-to-front creature might create. Then there was the Thatcher Margaret phenomenon, the Pope the III, Julian and Joyce James discoveries, (Joyce James writing a slim novel, plot-driven, and with narrative drive) when the taxi rescued us.

Back at the house, a little routine which impressed me in its caution, its commonsense, its being fair to everybody: they held the taxi for the baby-sitter, who was local, lived only a few streets away, and went into the house. By the time the baby-sitter came out – only a couple of minutes – Minap had been up to look in on the children and Carrington had found enough change (from Minap's handbag) to pay both baby-sitter and taxi. It was smiles and thanks all round. Over a drink – I didn't want to bring up what was on my mind, coming home to find the children mutilated, the baby-sitter crazed, bloodstained; kitchen-knife, scissors... – I raised the subject in a more general way, and yes, they did have momentary visions of the house burning down. Carrington had memories of paraffin heaters in the '60s going up in flames; Minap was anxious, if the baby-sitter was new, that she might invite a boyfriend in who was unreliable, or drunk. But you had to live in the world; they no longer phoned the house when they were out for the evening. Though, of course, they left the phone number where they were going. (Was my habit, I thought, of sometimes living in houses without phones, a sign of independence or selfishness?)

It was Minap now who made me an appendage of Carrington, wanting to know more of the *Caribbean Theatre Workshop* days, back in the '70s, in St Vincent, Montserrat, St Caesare, Trinidad, Guyana. I didn't mind this, coming from Minap; what slightly surprised me was that people had drunk so much at Bernard's and Tessa's, and we were drinking again, and some of them at dinner had to teach next morning, and these two had young children; and I was the one who seemed to be wilting: this was, really, frontier country. This was an old breed.

I pointed out to Minap that my experience at the *Workshop* was much less varied and exciting than Michael's had been. After being conned in St Vincent, and accused of bad language in Montserrat and threatened with being an agent of revolution in Trinidad, I had abandoned the theatre and come back to England, with St Caesare the only real success under my belt. Since then, I'd virtually given up theatre. Left it to Carrington, to Michael. Except for a new play I was writing.

Nonsense, said Carrington, he expected me to explode on the scene again. Saying I'd given up was only like old Lance Gibbs in – did I remember that Test at the Oval, in, when was it, '66, '69? when the English bowlers couldn't get the ball to rise above waist height and the papers were saying the pitch was dead, and Lance took a look at the end of the day, and when they asked him if the pitch was dead he said: not dead, man, but sleeping? And Lance proved true to his word next day when he went on to bowl, West Indies winning the match! But Minap had had enough of cricket, a game she didn't understand: fortunately, in the days when she grew up in New Zealand, New Zealand always lost at cricket, so the people she knew there affected not to be interested in the game. Not quite the same now, she understood. So tell her about St Vincent, Guyana.

As it was, as I had said to the woman at Bernard and Tessa's, the theatre woman, after Trinidad that I got down to Guyana, though I didn't do anything at the Playhouse, but I did put in a spell on building that road in the interior that Michael and I wrote the play about.

'*Down Mahdia Way.*'
'*Down Mahdia Way.*'
That's it.
'Still not produced in this country.'

But Minap shut him up. She didn't want to hear again about building a road in the interior of Guyana, of hundreds of people under canvas, of raining for days on end, not the soft Irish variety, but the real Caribbean tropical deluge, of digging culverts in the rain, of panning for gold in the rain, knee-deep in brown water, of meeting the Amerindians: Minap had heard it all; and she didn't believe any of it. What was *my* story.

I'd gone to the Caribbean on holiday, 1970, after a spell in London of drudgery and teaching at the old Kilburn Polytechnic, English & Liberal Studies. Remember Liberal Studies?

Michael remembered Liberal Studies well. (He didn't, he was in Canada during those years; just as he had been when Lance Gibbs had made his remark about the pitch sleeping.)

Yes, yes, but as I was saying, I was exploring the islands for the first time, my first time back since leaving as a schoolboy in '56. And I thought why not start with the Windward Islands; hence St Vincent. There, to bump into Michael who I knew was around, before he left for better things. Michael was heroically teaching in a school during the day and rehearsing his theatre at night, and getting frustrated.

Carrington pointed out that he had only been doing my job in the Caribbean. In London this guy from Jamaica, Noel Vaz, had come up to him, and said he was in charge of the Creative Arts Institute in Jamaica. This was at the Theatre Royal, Stratford: *Black Cab*. Vaz comes up to him after the play and says it'd be good to have someone making this kind of 'non-naturalistic' theatre, back in the West Indies, (though maybe Dennis Scott was doing that). The university might help to fund a small touring company, what with all these new University Centres being opened up in the islands, with a bit of money from the Canadians, he was sure that some sort of theatre-in-Education package could be negotiated. And Carrington had said to Vaz: Stapleton is the man you should be talking to: he's the academic-minded one. So, in a sense, though he had taken the *Workshop* idea out he had half-expected me to follow. Naturally, there was no money to take the company out from London so he had had to create one in each island. And, of course, write the plays as well.

Minap was solicitous. It was too cruel: she understood he even had to govern the islands in his spare time. And what was worse his spelling mistakes had even been bought for good money by a university in England.

Carrington took the point, thanked me again for bringing over the case of books and retired to his daughters, and I promised Minap the true uninterrupted story of the haunted hotel in St Vincent. But first, I wanted to hear about her.

*

There was, however, one thing that got in the way of all the diversions (and oddities) of Ulster, and it was Carrington's and Minap's elder daughter, Susu. I'd already made up my mind not to play up the media-type images, armoured cars and security-vans in Belfast and Derry, soldiers with guns, guards in bullet-proof vests, almost presenting themselves as targets, with their greater bulk giving the impression of being less mobile than ordinary people. Though you found yourself employing little tests with people on the street, sidling up to them and asking directions, just to see, with all that going on, whether they'd respond to you *differently* – with a bark, or a bit of Monty Python gibberish – but no, everyone seemed courteous and anxious to help, though sometimes you couldn't understand the accents.

What continued to disturb me was Susu (which must have been short for Susan or maybe something in Minap's culture. Carrington curiously called her something like *Pschu-pschuface*. And she called him *NO*). The more I tried to put it out of my mind, as being silly, one step nearer to madness, sort of thing, to *oldness*, the more I couldn't help seeing her as the child (no name yet agreed on; why not Susu?) that Lee and I fantasized over. She stood the same way, knowing, but willing to be trusting; open face challenging you to be at your most resourceful to keep it so. It's not that one wanted this child (indeed, it reassured me that one didn't, and the psychology of child-kidnappers was one

I found hard to fathom. Maybe there was a gender thing here, as child-kidnappers, if the papers were to be believed, tended to be women, though sometimes they operated as a couple, as it made more sense). What bothered me was the way Susu called my bluff. Exposed me for all to see. Time and again you found yourself upstaged: there you are walking along the road thinking something or other. You cross the street, go round the corner, and all of a sudden there it is hitting you in the face. Time and again. As if you were *inventing* the world. Lee and I had long *imagined* Susu. Long before Susu turned up at Carrington's door. And however hard I tried to insist that our Susu was better than this Susu, I couldn't find anything wrong with Susu. Do you pity the world for living out your fantasies: God, no, you had to celebrate these people!

Such thoughts contributed to my not wanting to outstay my welcome in Ulster.

At the University in Coleraine, Carrington strove hard to impress that his job as writer-in-residence was no sinecure. He ran creative writing 'workshops', he helped to line up speakers for public events; he had directed the Walcott play and he was preparing to edit the university magazine. It hadn't come out yet, the first issue, and they were still arguing over the name, Carrington's latest preference being *Michael Holding*, not that it had anything to do with cricket in a sense of carrying cricket commentary and scores, but he wanted it to contain the spirit of Michael Holding – speed, grace, control. Grace under pressure, he said; that's what the Kennedys, back in the '60s, used to be on about, and it had eluded them, and the world had paid a terrible price. Now, Carrington's image was simple. Think of Socrates. A fraud, but one who didn't devalue thinking, as the planting of so many stooges in the dialogues was clearly the work of totalitarian Plato, not Socrates. Think, also, of football. The circus in modern times, patriarchal and racist. How to protest the debasement of thinking, and of sport! Think of Socrates playing football. That was how he had come by his image of *Michael Holding*; but naturally, people just thought he proposed Michael Holding because he, like Holding, was West Indian. And, of course, they didn't understand cricket in this country. (Did I remember Michael Holding at the

Oval in 1976: 8 for 92 in the first innings, 14 wickets in the match, 14 for 149?) One of his colleagues at Coleraine had had the temerity to suggest that as there had been a little poetry magazine in England, in the '70s, called *Joe Dimaggio*, after the American baseball star, *Michael Holding* might seem derivative. Carrington couldn't find words to express his contempt.

He involved me in a couple of his seminars at the university, and I have to say I found them a little bit daunting. One, in particular, had me wondering whether he wasn't taking sophistication too far. We were in his room on the third floor of the tower, Department of English, Media & Theatre Studies. The brutality of the glass & concrete building put me in mind of Köln University, to which at least the students had applied political graffiti, in mitigation. Carrington's room was a concrete oblong, unpainted, raw, with a sort of National Theatre roughness Writ Small. We sat there with eight students wedged between us, Carrington at his desk behind the window, me at the door, the students, mostly women, trapped. Meanwhile a big girl with a Northern Irish accent read out a story about two women who had been at school together, running into each other in the street many years later. One had done well for herself, as her middle-class dress and shoes indicated. The other, the handle of her shopping-bag broken, her shopping all over the wet pavement, down at heel, looks up to find the person helping her is an old school-friend.

Over coffee they swap stories. The woman who's done well doesn't want to crow as she can't help noticing the bruise on the other woman's face. Finally, over to the victim who reveals, with embarrassment and apology, that her man knocks her about. The man is black. The student reads out the scene of domestic violence. There is an attack on the wife, we are told, on account of the husband's jealousy. There is no reason to be jealous, but he is jealous, and it makes him violent. He used not to be violent and now he is violent. The two children, as well as the wife, are suffering from this violence.

The reader stops. A pause. Difficult to know what to say. The attacker, the black man is so generalised, so lightly sketched, that we have no idea what's driving him, all we have is a fairly mechanical fist colliding with his wife's unprotected face, her body; we have not been let into the mind of the attacker. There is no dialogue.

Carrington's job as tutor to this third year writing seminar, is to help the writer make it *credible*. And this, he proceeds to do. He takes the assaults as given; doesn't question the bruising, or the fact that the neighbours don't come to help. (That must be made credible, too.) What he wants the student to do is to put it in context, to provide psychological motivation, to let us into the man's need to punish this woman who had been bright at school and represented a class to which he aspired; or represented a whiteness that had always oppressed him, and as he couldn't get at the Prime Minister of Great Britain or the President of the United States, he took it out on their representative, his Irish wife. Or, was this just misogyny; and should we find something also, in the woman's conduct which made him, a man, insecure, etc. All the time the writer was scribbling notes.

Later in the refectory, Carrington explained to me that his job wasn't to turn these people into writers, as most of them weren't even aiming at publication, but to use writing to point out the clichés they held in real life. It seemed to me that what he had been doing in the seminar was to legitimise one such cliché, and we argued about that.

Carrington was, not surprisingly, a workaholic. Even when he was baby-sitting, he was devising new plays, sometimes with Susu. (He did this sometimes in the day because Minap went to a language class, Japanese, at the university.) And we discussed his writing projects. New plays, old plays. Old projects, like a series on the Philpot-character that he'd been planning since the *Caribbean Theatre Workshop* days and hadn't done justice to. Then about the Allen Woody idea. He'd contributed the odd line from time to time to the radio show, *Week Ending* (one of the 'Additional Material' people) and he was always on the lookout for jokes for that. He was working on one at the moment, an Italian whom he had glimpsed outside the Senior Common Room at Queens University in Belfast, talking to his car.

What's so unusual about an Italian talking to his car?

First of all it may not have been his car. (Then he told me an Italian joke about mistaken identity, Pirandello-type.) But this conversation with the car in Belfast had to mean something out of the ordinary because it had been so *reasonable*. Carrington was trying to conjure up witty answers that the car might make, mildly racist in the style that would appeal to *Week Ending*.

And more. And more.

What to make of this: Carrington presenting himself, at home, as a bit of a character, his *tsutsuutsutsuutsutsu tsutsuutsutsuutsutsu tsutsuutsutsuutsutsu pschu-pschuface No! tsutsuutsutsuutsutsu* with Susu being a feature of father-daughter play in the house. She hadn't, in fact, that first morning, greeted me in a foreign language but with her version of *tsutsuutsutsuutsutsu*. Though, according to Carrington, who wasn't there, it may well have been Little Richard's *Awopbob-laoobopalopbamboom* that she was adapting. All of that reassured me in my view of Carrington as the fake-Dad, the Dad overdoing it a bit; but I felt I owed Minap an apology. I had, unthinkingly, thought of her somewhat in Cook Island TV terms, islanders marooned out there in the Pacific, first brought to our notice in the '60s, because they provided the odd beauty-Queen, like Guam, to the Miss World and Miss Universe contests. What I hadn't known was their New Zealand connection, and the fact that people of Minap's status had all been educated in New Zealand and had their closest family there. And so, her very precise English that I had detected on the phone was just middle-class New Zealandspeak. She didn't, of course, reject the Cook Islands, but I felt to engage her exclusively on that matter would be to make her into an 'ethnic' – the new creature, sanctioned by British racism.

Whereas Carrington was all frenzy, Minap brought a sort of balance to the proceedings. (I had met the South African playwright Athol Fugard, socially, when his play *Demetos* was being staged in the West End, and he was like that, bristling while his wife, calm, in meditation-mode, provided 'balance' at the table.) One day Carrington bought a card for a colleague who was having a baby: what to put on the card? No, it wasn't a question of how well he knew the person, it was something else. That very morning he'd seen a funeral, a fleet of cars in the rain, and they were special cars, apart from the hearse, brought out for the occasion, old-fashioned Daimlers that one didn't see on the streets of Ulster everyday. The cars were so spacious that the mourners could sit four abreast, in two rows, without in any sense of being crushed, the fleet almost driving itself along the dead, flat road, the only resistance, the rain. So… what was he to write on this card where someone had given birth? Minap and I weren't devoid of sensibility; we told him what to write on the card.

She didn't seem to do things for effect. Yet, it wasn't because of a lack of knowingness. One afternoon, for instance, when we were talking about this and that, languages, language, racism; giving examples of 'otherness,' Minap upstaged ours, without appearing to try. Once she had been shopping in Marks & Spencer's, the food store. Just for some light shopping. This was in England not in Ulster. She bought a cake, some rather interesting-looking Italian bread, parbaked, and some fresh salmon in a packet, chunks, quite a lot of it, for nearly £10. At the check-out counter the woman, very polite, looked up, looked at her, paused, and enquired if the salmon was also for her, although the only other person in her queue was an old man, a pensioner with a penny-pinching, collapsed face. Minap was clearly foreign-looking enough for the middle-aged woman on the till to suspect that her few items of shopping might not include the fairly expensive packet of fresh salmon. Minap seemed amused by the whole thing.

The question of Balham came up, of course, and Lee in her role as editor of *Rainbow*. Balham was said to be making a film for TV on *The Underclass*, a term that sounded vaguely American. Balham had developed a reputation for getting grants for his projects. He had been funded by the GLC and would, as we both hoped, have to get a proper job now the GLC was no more. Carrington's tolerant contempt of Balham was such that when I told him about the Underground ad, Carrington admitted to be already turning it into a musical. Carrington said Balham put in mind of the judge in the Wesker play, a play about the judge prosecuting himself on the Bench. I didn't know the play. I began seriously to worry about being out of touch. So many shared references seemed to be passing me by. I hoped it was the academic context that had sharpened this lot, and not me becoming uninformed, already on the road to ending up tentative, *socially gauche*. Maybe I should, after all, take over the magazine from Lee: Black Arts would give me an excuse, a structure, a context in which to reinform myself about things. The magazine published poetry and fiction and artwork, as well as critical essays. And it ran interviews with artists. (I could interview Carrington.) It would make me visit art galleries more determinedly, and give me a reason to suffer through poetry readings. Did I want to get into all this: BLACK ARTISTS: WHITE INSTITUTIONS debate? That was a point of entry if I needed one. Carrington's institution was a white institution; was he being neutralised here? Was the fact that he was telling a white student how best to make a black man credibly violent the price one had to pay? Was this the institution or was it Carrington? I would think on't.

6

I must write to Lee I must write to Lee...

Dear Lee,

It's always just out of reach, isn't it? Just like some old...
myth. But then *sense* or lack of pride or *time* – give it a couple
of years, give it a few seconds – will suddenly make it gel. Then
we'll grow into it; then our time will come; will come into it. No,
no, the time's now...

Suddenly, we're the right *size*; the home is the right *style*; all
things in life assuming the right *age*. The age of Lee. So there.
Easier than we thought. Don't laugh, don't scoff. Bet you're
doing one or the other. Ah, if I knew you better I'd know which.
You're smiling. You're doing the opposite of smiling, one of the
opposites of smiling. That's it. You've asked for it. Today I will
go out and cry for your benefit in front of my friends, in front
of my enemies. Tonight I will appear on television picking my
nose.....

Dear Lee,

(What's so dear about Lee. Dear Lee.)

I took up your suggestion, some while back, and wrote down
some of the words alien to me in our script. Not 'Sorry' that's
not alien to me, that's my partner, my verbal crutch. Not
'Kindness.' All my names are kindness, not just the middle
one. No, things like 'Gentleness'. I heard someone in the
supermarket the other day, a woman, say to her partner: 'Be
gentle', after the man had made a slightly mild remark about
someone in the news. And I thought, yes, with a few more like
her around, we might civilize this country yet. So now I write
out in my schoolboy hand. I must be gentle. No, first: I MUST
NOT BE ABRASIVE: I MUST NOT BE ABRASIVE: I MUST... a hundred
times, then I'll write I MUST BE GENTLE a hundred times. Why

a hundred? Write it for as long as gentleness eludes me. Ah, the start of literacy. From this, other missing words; words into phrases; into sentences. But I'm losing it, now I'm writing down words like 'guffaw' and 'lorsque.' So now I'm good for a guffaw, so much better than hysterical laughter, so much better than (fill in the blanks). Oh, tell the world to be generous and compassionate and to die of strange accidents.

Dear Lee. (Lee Lee...Lee)

*

Some time after I got back to London Carrington phoned with a new proposal. He was sick of being seen as a dramatist and nothing else. He was planning to put together a group novel, and had meant to talk to me about it. No, this wasn't something that had come out of his creative writing class, it had older, more respectable antecedents: there was this group novel put together in America early in the century, twelve authors contributing, including Henry James, each person writing a separate chapter, like *The Grandmother*, *The Daughter-in-Law*, *The Friend of the Family*, etc. I could be the uncle in France renovating my house or in Germany teaching English to the natives. There were lots of things to commend a group project as I knew, having done group plays at the City Lit. Everyone had material lying about, to start with; and also, it would be seen as an anti-ego thing, something to impress the women (to convince Lee of the possibility of change?). I said I would think about it, intrigued about who my prospective writing companions might be. But we didn't pursue it; I didn't think even to ask the name of the original American book. Instead we reminisced a bit about my Ulster visit, recalling the last night out in Portrush (and, by way of association, the night in Paris after the conference – when we'd gone out on the town). I put down the phone feeling I'd been upstaged again. I'd been thinking vaguely about Lee, about whether I should make a new, big effort, absorbed in this rather than in the visit to Ulster, and I hadn't really thanked them properly. I'd been thinking of a decent present for Minap – Minap breast-feeding without embarrassment, Minap opening the fridge and drinking straight from the flagon of orange juice, Minap being tolerant as Carrington played the Dad upstairs tsutsuutsutsuutsutsu tsutsuutsutsuutsutsu tsutsuutsutsuutsutsu pschu-pschuface. No: tsutsuutsutsuutsutsu: Carrington and Susu threatening to bring the ceiling down while we two, adults, downstairs, smiled at each other, tolerantly. Susu's sister, whose name I never did get, looked on noiselessly, her eyes open. So I lost myself thinking of a suitable present, and thinking of Lee; and now felt like an ill-mannered heel.

So Carrington wanted me to recognize how much he'd put himself out for me in Ulster. Fair enough; I was happy to recognize that. In fact I was, no doubt about it, impressed overall with Carrington, the fertility of his imagination. For the first time I saw him as being more than someone who'd had the necessary luck, and ridden it. It's not just that everything for him signified a play – that was probably the same for me – it was his professionalism to push the task through to completion that impressed me. (I would have to look to my own fragments.)

One afternoon in his concrete bunker at the university he'd been talking about the current play, something he'd had to put aside because of the deadlines. He was trying to determine his own shape, he said, his size, which made him look at the fragments *differently*: he'd stopped handing over unfinished work to the university at Kent, to the archives: through haste he had been pressured into creating spaces of the wrong size: some were so much smaller than your own life that they were embarrassing. It was brutish to live in a space that was smaller than it needed to be – *if it was of your own making*. Of course you can also make a fool of yourself by going the other way, creating from fragments something larger than your skill permitted. He'd been there, too. But you couldn't accept defeat in this war, you had to try to raise your talent to try to match even the falsest of false starts. There was mention of Pushkin and we had this image of fragments being released on your death, half-finished monsters claiming you as parent. I'd seen a programme on Russia where on a certain day of the year the people of St. Petersburg took to the streets not just quoting but enacting Pushkin. Butchers. Bakers. Pushkin in the parks, etc. And Pushkin came over as being pretty human.

Not that Carrington was talking about perfectionism. No, it was better to press on and produce something merely flawed, a *Hamlet*-thing, say – rather than to go to your grave waiting for perfection. And perfection was his children, anyway, his daughters, not in scribbling. He quoted Paul Valery to the effect that a work of art is never finished, just abandoned.

But take some of those plays from the *Caribbean Theatre Workshop* days, 1970, 1971. They were just sketches, of course. Mike Leighish, the Philpot character sketches. *The Philpot Murders*, most of them set in England: Philpot at the supermarket in Manchester explaining why he had to take action against the assistant who refused to wrap his cheese. Imagine the effect if you made Cheese a beautiful woman (or an ugly woman, for that matter) and gave her dialogue? Then you'd get past this dreary, naturalistic nonsense of whether the assistant didn't wrap the cheese because the customer was *black*. Even the Brothers and Sisters at home made vulgar assumptions about us, in these respects. *Play Two*: Philpot on a bus in the heart of the country, mittle-England, Leicester, Sheffield, somewhere like that. He witnesses a schoolboy beating up a schoolgirl. Not on. Here's Philpot explaining his action against the schoolboy. What action? Too crude to say that Philpot takes his gun and shoots the boy dead, this isn't America. Not yet. Philpot has *imagination*! And again. And again. (Carrington has a script and he's turning the pages.) *Play Seventeen*. Philpot defending himself against boys. No no. These aren't *English* plays. No rubbish about buggery. None of your childish English bumboy rubbish. It isn't even particularly feminist, Philpot's a dinosaur with the rest of them. But he's *different*. Here he is defending himself against a higher court, not the Old Bailey and that stuff. Maybe something like the, you know, those old Caves that the Indians used to worship at in St Caesare. Worship or sacrifice, whatever.

Carrington reads from his script.

'And now as you ask about the boy, let me tell you 'bout boys. You want me tell you about boys?...Boys are rude, man. You have to stamp on that kinda rudeness.'

I knew the script; I'd heard the speech. For 'boys' I'd substituted 'dogs'. Racist dogs; I'd been bitten by a couple of them in my time.

'Why, you might ask, must they be killed?'

'Because they get someone who looks like you to beat up the dog, then someone who looks like them to feed it. Grow up.

'...No, I'm not pleading for extenuating circumstances like war, marriage...I'm a simple man using simple language. Boys are a menace and must be killed...'

Sometimes they put it in a sack, torture it with a stick, and let it out when your face is the first one the dog will see.

'*Boys*, as you know, is a four-letter word. We're allowed them, of course; but such are the ways of temptation...Just think of the sound of it, Boys. Pronounced with a devilish lisp. *Boys*. Pronounced like a second language. *Boys*. Coming like a fart from a racist's armpit. *Boys*. Would you really want, would you really want your space to be contaminated by boys...?

It's not the boys, of course, that you take out at that moment, it's the *dogs*.

'Even I, a man of *war*, etc etc...Boys is known to have brought on the rash, blushing for those of a blushing tendency. Scholarly studies abound. Eminent professors from Leipzig, Wyoming & Padua...'

He looks up as if to say: how am I doing?

I like Padua.

'Yes, I like Padua,' I say.

Carrington is contrite. 'Well, *Week Ending* didn't go for it.'

Minap hadn't come out to dinner in Portrush, she was baby-sitting. It was my last night and Carrington wanted to take me out. We avoided the Chinese restaurant across the road, convenient, he said, in the rain, but tonight it was only the ice-cutting wind to distract us. Lots of Irish poets had written poems to the Chinese restaurant on Lower Main Street, which said something either about the Irish poets or about the cuisine in Northern Ireland. And Irish poets weren't the worst. Though the Chinese prawn and ginger thing was OK. But tonight we would eat Greek, Portrush's culinary high-spot.

Having eaten Greek and spent a lot of money we both ended up feeling like guilty schoolboys, Carrington, I suspect for slightly abandoning his family and I, for instinctively comparing the meal with meals I'd had in France and Germany, whatever, and finding it somewhat modest. Was I overdoing the thing of ignoring Ulster's 'troubles'?

Walking home to Lower Main Street we recalled our last night in Paris, the Commonwealth conference, promenading after hours with the two Spanish girls from Zaragosa, Isabella and whatever, and the fellow from the hotel: *The Paris Five*, doing our thing, serenading the good people of St Paul. Along the Rue de Rivoli. But as we walked along the strand in Portrush, frozen, self-protection led us to recall the old days of Empire, sports day in St Caesare, in Montserrat. Free coca cola and a bun – how we tried to carry out our mothers' instructions *not* to eat the bun, but at the same time not to let ourselves in for comment for refusing the bun. The bun and cake were intended to put you in good voice for the Kipling which had to be sung; the bun and coca cola were also said to protect you from the fierceness of the sun. Kipling's 'Recessional' is what we remembered from those times. Carrington still claimed to know the words, but he didn't particularly want to sing it on the streets of Portrush. OK, he would confine his singing these days, now, to his daughters.

*

That's why I felt, in a strange way, closer to Minap. She put you at your ease; with her there was no competition; I felt she was actually interested in the old stories – about the haunted house in St Vincent, for instance. (I didn't want to talk about the house in Spéracèdes, courtesy to Lee.)

The haunted house in St Vincent. 1970.
It was on the waterfront, and owned by someone who lived way up on the hill in Cane Gardens, in what in England would be one of the leafy suburbs. And Michael had been the only guest at the hotel – local people spurning it and scaring off visitors because it was haunted; and the fact of Michael sleeping there for six weeks without harm still didn't encourage anyone else to have a go. No one had any problems with the hotel during the day. When Michael took me to lunch there, to make his proposal about my taking over the theatre company from him, they were doing brisk

business. And the same for evening meals. What seemed funny I
remember, was the way everyone referred to him as 'teacher.' Even
the young Manager of the hotel, when he came up to say hello,
addressed Michael as 'teacher', a sign of status. 'Of course, you
were teaching at Timmy's.'

'Timmy's was the worst grammar school in town.' (It was
Carrington's story, too. Here, in Portrush, he was 'bonding' with a
child who was having a disturbed sleep, not fully attending.)
'Timmy in his cork hat.'

I confirmed that tiny Kingstown had *four* Grammar Schools.
Michael reminded us that 'Timmy's favourite author was H.G. De
Lisser,' a point lost on Minap. Michael was trapped till the end of
term, till Christmas, even though, theatre-wise, he should be
moving on to another island. Though there was still unfinished
business with the play. The idea was to take it, or bits of it round
the schools, etc. Or to bring children from some of the outlying
areas in to Kingstown to see it. Naturally it was less a Theatre in
Education job than the dare of the haunted house that made me
decide to take it on, and release Michael to go down to Montserrat
and Trinidad, whatever. If Michael had spent x weeks in the
haunted hotel...

(Six weeks)

Six weeks in the haunted, pink hotel without mishap...

(Without Minap, too, but without mishap)

...Within a week of my moving in, a week of his moving out, the
place decided to live up to its reputation. As I, in Portrush, in
telling the story, was living up to mine.

So he goes to the dentist

(Michael and I are upstairs. I, in a state between anger and
contrition, Michael relaxed, half-pacing, gently jiggling an
unsleeping child when he thinks of it. Minap has tactfully let me
go to the bathroom, but I'm in the bedroom with Michael.)

So he goes to the dentist. Big man, bruises on the, y'know...
knuckles

And that's only the dentist

(Downstairs, I'd told the story of the haunted house in St.
Vincent. Haunted hotel. And even though I heard myself doing it,

I couldn't prevent myself, subtly, turning it into a story against Michael. Minap, of course, laughed it off, and conspired to agree, even. But it was tacky, it was Balham-type behaviour. It was what depressed Lee about us, about all of us. But you can't ask for another chance to tell the story. Though, I suppose you do, really. So I spent quite some time that night pointlessly retelling the story, without the Carrington edge.)

But this was after our little interlude upstairs, undoing something, undoing a little act of betrayal maybe.

So the dentist sits him in this chair and the assistant straps him in – nice girl, slim but strong – belts him into the chair and yanks his mouth open

Been there, been there

And the dentist, who of course isn't a dentist

Of course

Got a PhD in Jane Austen or something. Never been near dental school

'Course not

Slaps him about, punches him in the face, you know, and manages not to snarl, but gets rid of, whatever

A few teeth

Yeah

So he gets up and calmly shakes the dentist's hand and smiles and says... you know, with difficulty because

Of course

And says, Thank you very much, Doctor, you're a... y'know, white man, and all that sort of business

And he goes downstairs to pay. And the dollybird behind the counter consults her computer, and extracts a bill

And this strong man, huge man, knuckles bare to the bone, gazes at the bill and

Clutches the bill in pain, pain

And cries

And cries and cries

And cries

"And what's all this crying?" Minap comes in to rescue her child.

*

So later, when it didn't matter, I replayed the hotel scene, out of deference to Minap, out of deference to Lee. I had gone out to dinner that night, to the owners of the hotel, who lived up the hill, of course, one of those exclusive suburbs, called Cane Gardens, and after a pleasant evening, decided to forego a lift back to town. I was walking down the hill, a bit light-headed, looking up at the clear sky, the stars, breathing in what seemed unpolluted air, hoping I wasn't turning into a foreigner to be so conscious of these things, when I was nearly knocked down by a car free-wheeling down the hill without lights. When I got to the hotel, already shaken, I found my confusion mirrored in the street: I'd run into a rowdy crowd, gathered outside the hotel, and a policeman.

'Is the crazy man,' someone shouted, I thought, at me. 'Gaol is the safest place for you tonight.' And he *was* talking to me – a rough-looking fellow, with his chest exposed. He turned to the policeman. 'Ain't I right, officer?' The policeman seemed slightly embarrassed, and approached me with an air of near dignity.

'I think you're the man we want.'

'Yes?'

'It's Mr…Carrington, yes?'

I had to put him right, and it embarrassed me, because I didn't want to correct his mistake in front of the crowd. I remember making it worse by calling him 'Superintendent', though he wasn't so elevated.

'There's nothing to worry about,' he near-whispered. And as if this wasn't enough, 'Take my word for it.' There was someone from the crowd creeping up behind us, the same young man, with his shirt just flung over his shoulders, and the policeman and I instinctively formed a barrier of understanding against him.

'You goin' let that boy get dead.' A prediction, delivered with force, because that 'boy' seemed to be me.

'All this talk of a gun…' the policeman started and stopped. He must have seen my instinctive 'freezing' and didn't want to unsettle me further.

'He already kill one woman wid it.' That man again with the shirt. 'That's why he playin' crazy. He goin' use it again. Lock up the man.'

The 'man' being referred to now was revealed as the young manager of the hotel, the one in the habit of calling Michael *Teacher*. He had taken courage from the fact that Michael had moved in and out of the hotel without harm, and that I had moved in; and had now decided to start sleeping there himself. He had moved into the bridal suite, and after a night's grace, had suddenly gone mad. At the moment, apparently, he was being restrained upstairs in his quarters. The policeman tried to reassure me about the gun. 'Just a lot of damned nonsense. Gossip,' he said.

'I don't understand.'

'You are a man who has travelled,' he explained, but talking more to the crowd than to me, now. 'You have travelled. Like me.' Then he dropped his voice. 'We are expected to see things in perspective. But why deny people their kicks, eh? Don't let them see you flustered by the situation. Good luck.' With that he pounded me on the shoulder and stepped into his mini-moke scattering a couple of onlookers in his exit. His departure was a sort of signal that maybe I wouldn't face the worst, because even the onlookers seemed to be losing interest, a couple of them cursing the departing officer because he had nearly run them over; or perhaps it was because of his failure to arrest someone. But they weren't going away; they were hanging around to see if something would happen, and that prompted me to make my way, more resolutely than I felt, to the side door and up the stairs to the first floor of the hotel, where the bedrooms were.

That's where it was all happening. At the top of the stairs, on the other side from my own room, there was a woman standing in a silk-dressing-gown, oozing perfume. Young woman. Pretty. Cleavage, all that stuff. She grabbed me and shoved me inside the room. Of course, by the time I unscrambled my brain I realised that she had hustled me inside the room while she remained on the outside, on the landing. From the outside she was whispering through a slit in the door.

'You must help me.' And the dressing-gown *did* slip off one shoulder, a bit. 'I'll be here when you want me.' And the door slammed, she on the outside, the lock turned between us. My back was to the room, exposed – you can sense it, can't you? – the needles in the back of my neck made me hesitate to turn round.

There were two people on the bed behind me, who took absolutely no notice of what was going on. A Still Life. The woman was fully clothed, facing my direction, but not seeing, an open book in her hand; then I realised she wasn't sitting on the bed she was sitting on him, on the man lying on his back, strangely elegant in striped pyjamas. The woman's bulk made me think of a mountain but I recognised her; she was the cook in the hotel and the man she was sitting on was the young manager; and he was offering no resistance. Without acknowledging my presence the woman, the mountain, began to sway. (She turned away from the man: was he dead? He was silent, I couldn't see his eyes.) Then the mountain began to hum. Not a hum, exactly, not a groan, either, just a noise which brought the man gently to life – and brought some relief to me. But then the key in the lock rattled through the room, and the perfumed woman outside appeared again through the slit. She just wanted to know if the man was quiet, if he had asked for her, and if we had found the gun. He should be in hospital, she said, the ambulance had been called twice, but he was stubborn; he wanted to kill her. We'd be all right inside, she said; we were safe, *she* was the one in danger. We must try to find the gun; and try to get the man to the hospital.

By now the man had managed to free himself of the mountain resting on him, and had crossed the room, unsteadily, in bare feet, and was clawing ineffectually at the door, invisibly pulling the mountain along with him, a gentle woman soothing him, urging him to rest, not to shame her, to forget everything; and as the door snapped shut from the outside, the man tried to climb up the wall of the room. In the end we manoeuvred him back to bed and trapped him in the sheets, and the mountain prepared to give him a tablet.

The gun. The awkwardness of my position made me prickily aware of the room, of the smallest things: the jar of water on the bedside table, the jar covered by a small, white napkin, round, with tiny tassels, two glasses on a little tray; tablets (in a packet), tablets (in vials), paper napkins; the book which the woman had put down – a Bible. The pictures on the walls of this surprisingly spacious room, which led to another, possibly two, through an arch opposite the bed (twin beds: a bridal suite?) were all places to hide a gun. What if he were reading my mind (people in certain, damaged states are said to be exceptionally cunning) and had the gun under the pillow, biding his time? My eyes settled on a picture, a popular print at the time, of the Kennedy brothers and Martin Luther King, the two assassinated brothers in profile flanking King. Three dead men. Too obvious. I made an excuse to go to the bathroom – a mistake: no one was paying any notice to me – drawing attention to myself.

But the couple on the bed completely ignored me. The mountain was aware of me, but nothing more. There was another print outside the bathroom. Woman & Child. Nothing. Inside the bathroom, too stupid to look behind the cistern, or inside it – this wasn't a cheap film – but I did look. Nothing. Looking behind the picture outside the bathroom had sent a chill down my spine; the last time I'd looked behind a picture in these parts, I'd found a lizard nesting there, one of those repulsive things you can see right through. I dreaded what I might find behind the Kennedy-King-Kennedy frame; but back in the main room I had to sit it out till the couple on the bed could be diverted. Despite their apparent lack of interest I couldn't make things too obvious. The Kennedys seemed to be squeezing King, one brother ruthless, the other determined. But King was fat. He refused to be squeezed. It relieved me slightly that I'd located the site of the gun; now I felt I could be coherent about getting the young manager to hospital. We got him dressed and I promised that he could drive himself there while the mountain said, Yes, Teacher would drive, which I eventually did, in his mini-moke, the main thought in my head being not to have an accident on the way. As he was slowly being got down the stairs – with the woman in the dressing-gown, now wearing a dress, eagerly assisting – I raced back inside to look behind the Kennedy-King-Kennedy picture. No gun. No lizard.

As it happened the young manager discharged himself from the hospital that night – which he had every right to do – and was taken off somewhere, to one of the islands, I think, the little private islands surrounding Kingstown; and then off to Miami next day. But, for some reason, the whole episode was regarded as a success for me, the mountain saying he wouldn't have been got to the hospital but for me, the woman in the dressing-gown thanking me for saving her life, and people, generally, wondering what sort of obeah I was working to enable me to sleep on, unconcerned, in a hotel which had just driven a strong young man mad.

Taking it seriously, Minap had wanted to know what had driven the man mad.

A woman. A Carib woman from the hills. There was a little Carib settlement in the hills on the other side of Kingstown – not the Cane Gardens side. And they kept themselves to themselves. And it just so happened that one adventurous young woman, seeing this hotel empty at night, somehow managed to get in when no one was looking, slept the night, and made her escape before people were up. Of course, she must have been glimpsed from time to time – hence the conviction that there was a jumbie about. And, inevitably, I ran into her. You can imagine my sense of alert, after the incident with the manager. I actually put my mattress on the floor, behind the bedroom door, and put extra pillows on the bed to make it look as if it were being slept in. I had the door to protect me should anyone attempt to come in. And, inevitably, I heard something moving about the hotel in the middle of the night; and when I crept out to investigate – in the dark – I came across her.

'Don't tell them you saw me.' She was even more frightened than I was. But I blew it. I wanted to know who she was. When I realised what she was about I urged her not to let me disturb her, to pretend I wasn't here, but she panicked. 'Don't tell them you saw me,' was all she kept saying. I tried to reassure her, asked her to come back during the day, or to meet me elsewhere, at the Public Library, or out of town. But by then, like a ghost, she had vanished. I never saw her again. (Discrete enquiries over the next few days, revealed the existence of some 'Maroons' in the hills nearby.)

Minap, I thought, had heard other versions of the story, but she was very kind: she praised my bravery. I liked Minap. I missed Lee.

7

Dear Lee...

*So let us look on the bright side... And here you are, with me,
in Spéracèdes...I will insert you into this bracket: I will release
you from this bracket... Was ist los in West Hampstead. Achtung!...
This might have been a lucky house for us... And we played hide
& seek as children do... And Rosemary and Sage are not man
& wife today but things that grow in our garden... Let us agree
that it's still early in the day... She kicked me in the chest, the
bellydancer, that night in Oledenez, you were there, you should
have been there; you were there... And, really, this might have
been a lucky house for us. (Ah, bitterness and boredom are all
life is; and all the world is mind.) But you're good at Canasta,
I'm good at Mah Jongg. Or I'm good at Canasta, you're good
at Mah Jongg, etc... Autumn of our lives, this is not... In spite of
talk of brutality, beatings, arrogance, he was our friend, he
supped at our table. Strike that... Frau Halterbush was not old,
that was a rumour, a tumour... And we were, after all, going in
the same direction, pssssh, pass it on, pass it on...*

He's got a phallic underlip the shape of a cigarette.

I've got a phallic underlip the shape of a cigarette.

She he or it has got a phallic underlip the shape of a cigarette
(a poem?)

....

I have been reading the endings of novels...

a poem for Lee

This might have been a lucky house for us
If tempting failure once again
Wasn't another main road dangerous to cross;

So I come alone buttressed by loss
And dull relief – the old refrain
That this might have been a lucky house for us:

A new place to recapture that touch
Unweighed by a lover's mission to tame;
Like another main road dangerous to cross.

A new place to be dispossessed in, a doss
Without you; yet, knowing too much to claim
That this might have been a lucky house for us.

I think of cricket and losing the toss
Forced to bat on a pitch damaged by rain –
Like another main road dangerous to cross.

I wanted to pull over and follow the bus;
You voted to stay in the fast lane.
This might have been a lucky house for us,
Not another main road dangerous to cross.

*

There was no music that day, no golden oldies around the piano.
It was spring; you could see, from the sitting-room right through
to the back, where Lee's garden was well on the way to recovery.
Lee is here, her back to it all, smoking, pretending not to
acknowledge the presence of Malcolm, here in his capacity as old
friend, not psychiatrist. He sits with a newspaper at his side, on the
settee, not reading it, but glancing down from time to time, turning
the page once or twice. I'm on the chair next to the little table, on
which there are biscuits, pretzels, soft drinks. Despite promising
to be open, I vow privately not to talk about Susu, our Susu. (I'm
thinking, vaguely, about architecture, the Pyramids, the ancient
Zimbabwe monument, my ruin in Spéracèdes. Then for some
reason, I find myself thinking of my brother-in-law, Stewart who
was doing things with plastic grass. I think of Elizabethan formal
gardens, of the English Garden. A way of life. Becoming plastic.
And I'm fighting down the laughter. I panic in case Lee and (to a
lesser extent) Malcolm think I'm making fun of the process.
Instead, I force myself to think – of Lee, of us, of continuity. This
is too pat, too obvious. I recall the trip to Ulster, Carrington's

difficulty in writing a card to a colleague who'd had a baby because
he'd seen a funeral in the street that day – a wet day; and I begin
to wonder if it had rained on the day my mother was buried. I resent
slipping into this way of thinking because that's what Malcolm
wants, that's what Lee wants: Malcolm pretending to read the
newspaper, Lee smoking. It would be out of character, I know, to
ask someone, my sister, if it had rained in St Caesare on the day
of the funeral.

So what was I thinking?

Oh, nothing much, the garden's recovering, looks nice. Everything here so tidy, clean, wholesome... Nice. In the end I say I was
thinking about my own... maleness. This sounds false as I knew it
would; they expect it and I resent it. Lee gives a small signal of
defeat. With the slightest change in body-language she gives up
the effort to pursue this, she decides to release me, to relieve
Malcolm. From now on I am something which must be 'understood'. She goes off to make tea, coffee, which Malcolm declines,
and then leaves.

Lee is tolerant because I told her a secret about my mother. This
is something I've concealed even from my sister. When at Christmas I had visited the house in Upton Park, I hadn't claimed
anything from my mother's room as my sister had urged, but when
I got back from Ulster I thought better of it. There was really
nothing that I wanted as a keepsake, but I remembered an occasion
at the language school in Köln where I had taught in the '70s when
one of the lecturers had died, an older man, English, marooned in
Germany; and when his locker was turned out it contained, among
the papers, some ancient books on Law and Education and things
like the British Constitution; and there was nothing there that
anybody really wanted, but if we didn't take them they would be
disposed of, thrown away; and it had seemed such an unkind way
to deal with the effects of a colleague, so in the end everyone present
took something, because it had seemed right. I had this in mind and
was determined to take something from my mother's room.

The television was still in place, the clutter of the dressing-
table, suitcases on top of the cupboard, clothes, no doubt, inside.
And, already, encroachments from the rest of the house, the
beginnings of what would soon be a storeroom – some of Stewart's

plastic samples. In the end I took three things: a radio which I knew didn't work, her Bible and her walking-stick. (I hovered over another book: my *Random Thoughts*... that we had argued over, had mock-fights over: I couldn't very well take it back.)

I hadn't seriously taken on the Bible since growing up in St Caesare where, as children, you were supposed to start it each year on the First of January and work through it to completion in December. Of course you never even got through Genesis that way. But you knew much of it pretty well, what with Sermons and Sunday School and, of course, at Grammar School where they took you through the Acts of the Apostles. I thought maybe if I were to read it through now, as I was supposed to have done then, this would be some act of homage. It was covered in brown paper (my mother's girlish habits had never deserted her) as children's books are, as ours were, with the title THE HOLY BIBLE printed in large letters, now fading. When I flicked through it, it wasn't a Bible. Curiosity made me open the dressing-table drawer, the top one, and there was the Bible, large and familiar, and uncovered. I took that, too (I took four things) and said nothing about it to my sister. Her attention had been captured by the walking-stick; she had thought the decision to take it strange.

The Bible was a book of Reader's Digest stories of romance. There was nothing outrageous here, just a vein of fantasy, but it left you with a sense of helplessness that this had to be concealed and covered up in brown paper, and called THE HOLY BIBLE: clearly she had feared ridicule. Yes, there would be jokes, but benign ones, this wasn't a cruel family (or was it?). There were always the little jokes: when I was doing GCEs back in the '50s and pretending to be writing a novel, and walked around with a big loose-leaf file, they all referred to it as my 'Dictionary', my mother joining in. That was the level of ragging you got in the house. We'd called her all the right names when it had seemed appropriate: we'd called her Madame Mao and Mrs Gandhi and, yes, Mrs Thatcher; and she was proud of the names even as she rejected them. To the end, as far as I know, she listened to the Sunday morning service on the radio, watched it on television: she wasn't a reader of novels. I'd never seen her read a biography. Certainly not poetry. But the Bible was a constant. My brother-in-law,

Stewart, even had to rig up a special shelf for her bedroom light so that she could read her Bible in bed without having to get up to turn off the lights. And the Bible now turned out to be women wanting romance. Why didn't she ever let on? Didn't she realise that she had an ally in me? I felt shunned, slighted, snubbed.

We talked, Lee and I, of the sorts of signals that my mother had no doubt sent out over the years, that the family had missed. Was the business of wanting to learn to drive a car when she must have been pushing seventy, serious? Certainly not. She used to go to the park to feed the pigeons with bits of stale bread: could you make something of that?

Alone in the house, she once called a man, passing in the street, to fix a radiator which had sprung a leak. She was cautioned for that, for inviting a stranger into the house. No, I couldn't get my mind around it.

*

Malcolm had gone, but I found it no easier to relax, to begin to talk to Lee about those nebulous things which had tended to elude us. There was a feeling that there was an imbalance in the relationship, Lee being much more forthcoming about personal matters than I was, and that I owed it to her (to myself?) to open up. I was, of course, aware that a way out of this, a way to skirt it, was simply to dredge up all my past relationships, to prove they had all been like this, uncommunicative, unpassionate, even; and that this was the nature of the animal. But that was a cop out. It is true I didn't feel *close* to people, had never been close, particularly, to my family; and even the death of my mother had left me feeling, not so much emotional pain, as a sense of frustration and anger; loss, yes, but anger that a life close to us hadn't been more valued, that one hadn't contributed more to its enrichment. And Lee, though she blamed me, felt I was also a victim. It was that business of being a victim that I found hard to bear.

We now accepted analogy, metaphor as a way of proceeding. We talked of the embrace. Of who did the embracing. Of whether it was important who did the embracing. Of whether the power resided in the embrace or the embracing. Of letting go of control.

Of releasing one body so that it was at the mercy of another, so that it mattered when it wasn't touched: we talked of the transference of power from one to the other; of the gift of sex.

So Lee poured the wine, while we sat on the bed, fully clothed, and talked. Talked of other things, other relationships; speculated why certain things worked out, others didn't. I recalled life with Lindsay in Germany, things I hadn't done, said, which was probably a good thing in the end, because she had been released and had rebuilt her life in America. I recalled the time in Köln, mid-'70s when we were baby-sitting a dog, Lindsay and I, for France and Otto, our friends. She was French and he was German, and they were into the business of collecting art and being fashionable, and saw themselves as trailing the footsteps of Gertrude Stein in Paris in the '20s and dreamt of creating something of the ambience of the rue des Fleurs, in Köln. But we liked them, this German-French couple, and liked their acquisitiveness, which naturally made us feel a little superior. So we decided to move into their flat across town from Ebertplatz to baby-sit the dog, while they went off to France. (Otto's parents objected to France, the person, on two counts, her nationality and her name. We never found out what *her* parents thought of him.)

They entertained us in the flat the night before they went off. Lichtensteins hung on the walls. There was a table-tennis table in the lounge. Nat King Cole was singing *Embraceable You*, and Otto brought out the family album. There was another guest, a young Portuguese woman who was very excited about their revolution (it was 1974 or '75) and was hoping it would spread to the rest of Europe. She was also teaching at the language school, where we taught, with France. Otto brought out his album of Hitler memorabilia, S/M porn, racist, sexist abuse; humiliation. At some point the women, including France, decided they'd had enough, and drifted off to look at the pictures on the walls, to drink, browse, drifting towards the tennis-table. It was up to me. Otto hesitated: should he continue to turn the pages? Yes? No? He waited for my decision. He was rather pleased the women were squeamish – I knew Lindsay wasn't squeamish, *I* was, but now it was up to us, Otto and me. He clearly made the point of distancing himself from his past, from what was not his past; though in the book people who looked like him were humiliating people who looked like me: who would force whom to assume embarrassment, responsibility? I looked across at my American, at France, at the Portuguese woman, and I thought: I have, in Lindsay, a better specimen than you, mate. Turn the pages. I gave him the nod. He turned the page, and Nat King Cole went on to another song.

As so often happens in these cases, I forgot the point of the story; I had set out, vaguely, to prove something against myself, but I'd forgotten what it was. Lee thought it was obvious but we didn't want to have an argument so we left it at that.

In contrition one tried to open up another little storeroom of fear: the partner sees in you something you're not. You embrace her vowing to become the thing she sees. You deny what makes you suspect, unworthy. Then she reveals, having seen all, that she wants to connect with what you're determined to deny, to hide: the knowingness of this destablises you, your balance is disturbed; there is an impertinence in all this. So you adjust; you lengthen your arms, and embrace more than you thought constituted a partner. Gone were the little accommodations of, oh, bloodsmeared jeans and partners, partners slept with. Squeamish as ever, you embrace abortions, the bruise administered by this unknown man, the fetish induced by that one which now commits you to performing in a way that embarrasses you both: but if one lost partner depended on it, why not, why not, so you embrace the distant partner who brought Hollywood to your present partner and left you to foot the bill. If she won't eat whelks and cockles you embrace that too and insist they are only fruits of the sea.

By this time Lee, wined and comfortable, is struggling to keep her eyes open.

*

A new obsession: I sit in the British Museum not reading Rumi, the Persian poet. Is Lee a *friend*? Why is life more comfortable with those who are not friends? In a heroic society she would be a dead woman; I would draw my sword, and honour would be served. Even in a modern, fighting society, I would deny her *vocabulary* but grant her speech. Honour served. She would not be burned as a witch, not because the times are against it; they are not, but the *ideology* is against it. And yet what she says to me outweighs what that woman in the Drabble book says of her husband, that he is not a nice man: she has accused me of the withdrawal of intimacy to a brutal and evil end.

So what is this? (So wha' happenin', bwoy?) Are you punishing yourself to punish the partner? I'll upstage you in ways you can't match, sort of thing. I'll deny myself, what, salt – can you deny yourself salt? – cigarettes. I'll deny myself, yes, pets in the home, bank holidays, *togetherness* if ...*And I challenge anyone to ridicule it*. But that's not what I mean, my darling.

As I say, in another society, Lee would be a dead woman. So I sit in the British Museum not reading Rumi, whom Lee has translated; not working on my talk for Radio Four. I'm writing something about my mother's Bible for the radio. Naturally, I will protect her against ridicule. In fact, there is a possibility of doing a whole series of talks about my mother – someone of her class and generation coping with England. For some reason people like her have gone out of fashion – have never been in fashion – with Caribbean writers in this country. We've always been irritated by the host country's assumption that life before migrating here was inevitably less comfortable and civilized than the life of the immigrant. And that's assuming that there was a way of life before England.

I've written some dialogue about those last days in St Caesare in '56. Easy to convert bits of it to Radio Four. The last Sunday on the island, for instance. She had a sprained ankle, coming out of church... She had to walk the last hundred yards or so to the house because the car couldn't make it up the hill, and she was hanging on to whatisname, the fellow who drove the car, who was always drunk, Selwyn. I had to walk the whole way because there was no room in the car; they had to give Professeur Croissant's wife a lift, as she was very fat; and they must have gone into Professeur Croissant's for a drink of water or coconut juice because I caught them up before they reached the house; and I wasn't thinking of her pain, I was thinking that it was a bad thing to catch them up even though I had walked from church, because that would make them think it was all right to make me walk in future. Then I realized we wouldn't be here to do this again, because we'd be in

England. Not nice, though, to be going to England with a sprained ankle. Anyway, Kitty, who would have been cooking lunch, came out and started to fuss over my mother.

Kitty:	So Miss Christine, what happen to your shoes?
Mother:	I'm nothing but a laughing-stock. (*And then to Mady, the young maid, who had been on the veranda a minute ago, but had disappeared when she saw us coming up the hill.*) Child? Ask that child to bring me a glass of water.
Kitty:	(*shouts*) Mady, bring a glass of water for Miss Christine. (*pause*) Mady?
Mady:	(*off*) Comin'.
Kitty:	(*to mother*) So the heel break off? So how the heel come to break off? (*She examines the shoe which Avril is carrying.*)
Mother:	(*thinking of the fact that someone had laughed at her broken off heel outside church*) Some people have no manners, that's what I say.
Kitty:	So what happen when your heel break off? You fall down, Miss Christine?
Mother:	Where the child with the water?
Kitty:	She comin'.
Mother:	They think I don't have shoes in my house! There's hardly a month go by that I don't get new shoes.
Kitty:	Everybody know how much pair of shoes you have upstairs in the house, no bodder with them.
Mother:	They pretending they don't know. They're pretending not to know. I have to get the child to bring out my shoes that people can see how many pairs of shoes I have in this house. Never mind those I give away (*to Kitty*). Don't I give away shoes here to all kind of people who come and ask?
Kitty:	Miss Christine, don't upset yourself.
Mother:	...Sometimes I don't even know their names... Let her lay them out here and clean them and left them for people to see.
Kitty:	Miss Christine, nobody doubting you have shoes come all the way from America and Canada.

Mother: And France.
Kitty: And France itself.
Avril: And Antigua.
Mother: We not counting Antigua.

Mady brings the glass of water covered, as is the custom, with a saucer, and mother orders her to put the shoes out, right there on the step, the broad step at the bottom, for passers-by to see. (Our house was pretty secluded!) Later, when the guests have arrived – the boy Francis who used to draw and studied in Italy so I'll call him da Firenze and the clergyman, Mr Ryan and our headmaster (Professeur Croissant) – and we're all upstairs in the drawing room, and my mother looks distant, and someone refers to the pain in her ankle, bathed and strapped by Kitty, she informs us, calmly, that she is accustomed to pain: someone whose whole body shakes violently just at the thought of going to the dentist, is accustomed to pain; someone later, in England travelling on the train, who feels the train is going too fast and will crash; someone who shuts her eyes at violent scenes on the television – the way some of us do in the cinema – is accustomed to pain! I mustn't sentimentalize her.

But it was a disorientating time when the new family, the new home, the new life stubbornly refused to take shape. I moved back into the old house in Long Lane, in Finchley and there was a sensation of moving back: it felt wrong now that I had no interest in running it as a house-share, though Lee and I were talking about pooling resources, buying something together. I had a plan to renovate the place in France and write about it; but Lee had gone off the idea. Well, I wasn't about to go in search of a new someone to do it with. I didn't want to take over Lee's magazine. I'd just landed a C Day Lewis Fellowship based on a school in Kingsbury and I was going to use the year getting some writing done. Also *Rainbow* provided a focus, a sort of distraction (and an income) for Lee; and that was important to me.

*

Avril and I had always had a good relationship. At least that's what I remember, though Avril claims otherwise, as did my mother: we used to fight, apparently, when we were children. Avril was two years older than me, and clearly had the upper hand when we were little and, both mother and daughter claimed, it was her dominance over me in those early years that made me now conveniently forget we had ever fought. I remember it differently: I remember us playing doctor and nurse in our house in Coderington, and being surprised, then, that my sister, older, bigger, played the nurse and I, the doctor, even though she had to tell me what to do when I examined the patient. No wonder she had to fight. Ah, but we are middle-aged people now, surviving thirty years in this country (for me 'this country' is France, is Germany, is Sweden). We worried, in a similar way, about the cost of that survival: did we have enough to show for it? This was a vulgar a way of looking at things, though neither of us could quite decide whether we had 'survived'. We suspected, in a vague way, that the young people were losing out. The niece, the nephew born in this country, who didn't share our dreams, had to be missing out.

So what was to be done, to coin a phrase? Was this the end of the line? How can you have lived in a place for so long and not be rooted, settled? At the back of our minds (and not always at the back) was the promise, the temptation of one last move which would make final sense (sense, finally) of the journey. My mother's journey had made no sense, no sense. Avril had worked in a factory, had been a nurse, a hotel-manager, and now taught for a few hours to prove a point. (We used to think, coming from St Caesare, that we had the best of both worlds, two languages. But England and France did their best to deny us those languages. You had to insist, said Avril. And she had. She helped out in a kindergarten, where parents wanted their children exposed to French, as well as English. (Actually, they wanted a trained nurse.) Despite ourselves, despite denying it to others, we were still looking for salvation in that final move. Me, to somewhere Mediterranean, with Lee now; Avril, back to St Caesare, or, at a pinch, Montserrat, which is where Stewart came from, though he had family in St Kitts, which he also called home.

But Avril and I got on well together: weren't we still the original
pioneers we were in 1956, determined to counter the vulgar
assumption *they* made about us? Others had made decisions for us
in the old days (even Eugene, though he wasn't much older, made
decisions for us). The old days. Sutherland Avenue days, Ladbroke
Grove days. When Philpot opened his grocery in Sutherland
Avenue, the Harrow Road end of Sutherland Avenue, he had
wanted Avril to help out behind the counter. 'To count the money',
as he needed someone he could trust. We had come from a small
island where the daughter of the house didn't serve behind the
counter of a shop that sold Carnation milk and salt-fish. Even
Philpot's Maureen had refused to serve behind the counter. To the
end of her days my mother 'pitied' the Indians who had to put their
wives and daughters behind the till in their cornershops, thus
proving they were common people. (Our talk of Marks & Spencer,
etc. starting from stalls in the East End, never shifted the argument.) At Upton Park, Avril felt that her home had become her
mother's house. Not that she minded so much, because although
she could have had a flat in this or that place she had managed, or
where Stewart had worked, she didn't fancy it. She liked the idea
of a house, a home. But now, with mother gone and Florence on the
verge of college, what was she to do with her new freedom? I,
according to her, had had freedom all my life and hadn't, it
seemed, done very much with it. No family, no house, no home
(again). My sister had taken over my mother's role, and I understood it; I didn't resent it; we had to get through this phase, work
further back before we could be the brother and sister again,
against the world. Those last days in Coderington in 1956.
Remember that last Sunday? The boy da Firenze who offered to
paint Mother's portrait?

That wasn't his name.

That's what we called him because he'd been to Italy. The same
way we called Teacher Richards, Professeur Croissant.

I don't remember that, you know.

I hadn't known da Firenze before then but I'd heard of him, he
was one of the boys studying abroad, like my brother. He was older
than us, in his twenties. And then one Sunday after church he
promised to paint my mother's 'portrait'. That was important,

portrait was a new word in the family and though I didn't quite
understand his distinction between picture and portrait, I appreciated that there was a difference and that we were probably the
only people in Coderington (with the possible exception of
Professeur Croissant) who knew that there was a distinction to be
made between picture and portrait. All of these things put us in
good stead, I felt, for life in England.

St Anns (where our church was) was hot and airless that Sunday
afternoon so we were aching for snow in England, in Paddington,
in a few weeks' time, disappointed that it was only June when it was
said that the sun came up for long enough to hold off the snow. Old
hands – including my brother Eugene, who was already there –
said we might have to wait till Christmas for that treat. Friends
from Coderington had gone off to Canada the week before, getting
a head-start on us. We joined others in making much of their
departure; and now there was a general feeling in the house that
when it was our turn to leave, Tuesday after next, there wouldn't
be enough people left – you know, the sort of people who came
to our house – to see us off and make an event of it. (It was good
to see friends off to Canada – Canada was Fourth Choice –
because we, at least, were going to England – England had pulled
away from America as Second Choice. But it was clear that France
had given up on us, and anyway, our French wasn't good enough
any more to make it in France. So, going to England was OK.)

We had been unlucky, also, in the new vicar from Ireland; a
young fellow called Mr Ryan, and his wife, Mrs Ryan. Some
members of the church hinted that they might be common,
particularly her, the way you could see through her thin dress when
she was walking ahead of you. Although Mr Ryan himself had
impressed, the way he had avoided running over a cat on his way
to preach at the little church near Look Out one night the previous
week. He was a funny-looking man with an Adam's apple and a
long nose competing for attention.

What really rankled with us that Sunday – although no one said
it; you didn't have to – was that there was no mention from the
pulpit of our impending departure to England. Old Reverend
MacPherson, Mr Ryan's predecessor, would certainly have made
something of this; and would have used the opportunity to praise

my late grandmother at whose table he'd had numerous meals. He would have stressed our close connections with the church, from way back, all the members of our family who had been lay-preachers, including my father, who would have gone on to college if the War hadn't taken him. The preacher in Montserrat next week where we were going would be Mr Jacobs, a lay-preacher. Then again, we were sailing on a Tuesday; that left two days only, after Sunday, to bask in people's envy, after the crucial pulpit send-off.

On top of this, coming out of church, my mother twisted her ankle and broke off the heel of her shoe. It was then that da Firenze came up to us saying something in a foreign language which wasn't French, and threatened to paint my mother's picture. Portrait.

My mother regarded this as an additional slight, the boy wanting to take advantage, to embarrass her without her shoe – and she continued to ignore him while he apologised. In the end we got to Coderington reasonably intact; my mother and sister by car, the rest of us walking up the hill.

It was less close and sticky at the altitude of Coderington; but we were bored, just spinning out the days. My mother insisted that the house which we were about to abandon still had to be kept spotless – maybe because of visitors – and the two women who normally cleaned it, Kitty and Mady (Mady was just a child, my age) had long been rebelling, with sly threats which, if she heard, my mother ignored. That meant that my sister and I were enrolled in the battle to keep the dust off things that were going to be left behind anyway. And it was a big house, twelve rooms! – a house that was famous for having survived both the '24 and '28 hurricanes.

da Firenze had walked up the hill afterwards to apologise to my mother for having embarrassed her after church, and was in the end invited to stay to lunch. (I noted his persistence: I had thought he would have been sent packing.) There were only four of us that day, a bit self-conscious in the dining-room downstairs, particularly now that I was expected to talk at table, with no adults about, no big brother, no visitors from Montserrat. So I told one of the house-stories, the story about the crack the length of the wall facing the yard, surviving both the '24 and '28 hurricanes. I was surprised that my mother and sister, in their subdued mood, didn't challenge my embellishments of the prayers said *then*, before our time, of the food cooked *on that particular occasion*, that night in 1924. Or was it 1928?

'That would make a good subject,' da Firenze said. 'For a painting.'

'What would be a good subject?' my mother asked, surprised.

'The crack. That crack right there, Mrs Stapleton.'

'But we have to repair it.' She said it in a matter-of-fact way, and then switched to complaining about a woman who had laughed outside the church when she had broken off the heel of her shoe.

But it startled me. It was an article of faith, held by my grandmother for as long as she lived, that the crack in the wall shouldn't be tampered with; it had saved the house in two hurricanes (though it was the first hurricane that had put it there) and was an act of God: was my mother now challenging the will of the dead Queen Victoria? – my grandmother's nickname. Was she going to tamper with 'Government House'? And again, it seemed so 'adult' of my mother to want to repair something just before you abandoned it! (But then, really, there was no time to do it before we left for England a week on Tuesday, so maybe my mother was indulging in a bit of theory, as our neighbour, 'that arse' Professeur Croissant would say.)

'What I mean to say, Mrs Stapleton,' da Firenze continued. 'That crack has meaning, real meaning. If you're an artist you have to get into that sort of meaning. Man, you have to crack that sort of meaning.' He paused for appreciation but there wasn't any.

'What meaning you talking about?' My mother wasn't to be trifled with. Like Avril, I waited. We just wanted to know how an artist thought about these things, someone who had been abroad and come back still so young, and whose name was now da Firenze. I couldn't make up my mind whether to trust him. I couldn't read his look. He was tallish and somewhat angular with an awkwardness about him which we associated with boys destined to win scholarships abroad (which he had done, apparently, but then had chosen to study Art instead of Medicine or Law, or Dentistry like my brother). Yet, he spoke of himself as a worker and a sportsman. He surprised you slightly for being somewhat darker than expected, without the dash of Carib, which you would call Portuguese or French or whatever, that one associated with names beginning with de. So we might have to change his nickname.

'Just thinking aloud, Mrs Stapleton.' (Thinking aloud: I liked that!) 'That crack in the wall could be God's wrath, you know.'

'We all have to suffer God's wrath.' This was Sunday; these phrases were traditionally served up with lunch.

'Or, we could make it something else,' the painter continued. 'Put another way, it could be God's smile. Gone a little wrong.'

I sensed danger: I would never have thought of God's smile going wrong. Professeur Croissant was the only one around who talked like this to adults, and he used to have terrible arguments with my grandmother over it and, since my grandmother's death, with my mother.

'What you mean, God's smile?' My mother wasn't impressed. My sister kicked me under the table, but I was good at not laughing in these situations.

da Firenze was explaining himself. 'You know if God was a man and he had occasion to smile.'

'What ignorance you talking about God's smile?'

It was hard now to control the giggling, but we didn't want to bring this to a stop, we wanted more; I concentrated hard to think of a joke that God would smile at. My sister concentrated on her roast chicken.

da Firenze told a story about a friend, an artist who had come from Guadeloupe, and hence was more French than we were (my mother was indignant at being called French and da Firenze had to apologize). Anyway, this friend of his had studied at Montpiller and had been everywhere, and finally ended up in Montreal where he got a job illustrating the Bible. 'Now, this was a good, solid job because the Bible was a big book...'

'It's more than a big book.' My mother took this personally.

'Of course, Mrs Stapleton.'

'Much more than a big book.'

'So right.' Yet, his attitude wasn't one of apology. And he went on to explain that though the Bible was more than a big book, his friend had had to give up the job in Canada illustrating it, because nowhere in the Bible did Christ laugh; and he had found it too depressing. I wondered if da Firenze knew what he was getting himself into.

But he must have judged the mood correctly, because all my mother said was: 'The Church is not a laughing matter.' She even seemed to be shifting ground a little. The fellow couldn't be let off that lightly; but it turned out that my mother was in pain from her twisted ankle, and she called to Kitty to prepare her some hot water and Dettol, in a basin. Before winding up lunch she said simply: 'Christ don't have a call to laugh,' and routine things about Christ and prayer; and we all agreed that grace said at this table over the years had contributed to the crack in the wall not getting any wider, and to the house not falling down. (I began to develop an image of 'prayer' as something performed by muscular people in an effort to hold our house together in a storm. And I thought: this is an example of *theory* of which Professeur Croissant would approve.)

da Firenze had got permission to spend the afternoon doing sketches of the house, 'for posterity', he said. My sister and I spent some time doing our own sketches not for but of Monsieur Posterity – he looked better in French – to whom the pictures would be presented. Avril was much better at it than I was (of course, she was older) so I had to think up the witty things that we would say to M. Posterity as we handed over the pictures – and then the pompous things that he would say to us as he accepted them. Mr Ryan and Professeur Croissant were coming to tea so we had to give up our Posterity game and help dust the house (again) while da Firenze was allowed to wander at will, inside and out, doing his sketches.

Here, thirty years later in Upton Park, our idyll is interrupted by Florence, a dark, beautiful girl in gold earrings and bracelets and rings, an aspect which makes me feel I have to work harder to earn the right to be the uncle. She is very gracious, offers to make me tea – I haven't finished my first cup – wants to know about me. Or, at least, asks about me. A well-brought-up member of the family, I say to myself. Florence is eighteen and about to go to university, which she persists in calling college. She wants to know what college was like in my day, over twenty years ago. I tell her, to annoy Avril, that we did no work whatever, got drunk most nights, and slept it off during the day. She reassures her mother that I am joking. Florence is more adult than I remember; we have to get to know each other again. At the moment we greet each other as interested and interesting specimens. Looking at Florence I think: if I had had doubts in this area, I now come down a little more firmly in favour of evolution: this is a good thing in the family.

Of course, to her, my life is unreal, a series of postcards from places she can't quite imagine. She doesn't believe that 'real' people live in places with unpronounceable names, even though she's travelled. Sometimes she perks up for the evening news, looks for her uncle among the people rushing out of some disaster – being carried out of the disaster – victims being hovered over by someone from the BBC or CNN, whatever. When she doesn't see him she settles back, somewhat disappointed. She's not close enough to him to be relieved. She begins to doubt him, uncertain of the stories she will tell about him.

But here is Florence asserting her own reality. In a few nights she is going to sleep in the park. It is their protest, schoolchildren, young people, against the growing number of homeless in the city, in the country: our family has joined the contemporary world. But, of course, both stepfather and mother are opposed to it. One uncle is opposed to it: where do I stand?

Why is every decision in life a moral one? Florence is the next generation, she has to break rank; she has to extend the area of risk beyond that of her parents, the first generation, even though they were the pioneers. She has learnt from them; she has observed her parents' culture of watchfulness, of taking nothing for granted; of being prepared for the friend turning hostile. She is prepared, too – for this was the nature of living with fear – to see others, black, but from a different island, or from the sub-Continent, as containing something of a threat. But Florence's progress has been normal, we all agree, perhaps to reassure ourselves: she has learnt to deflect racist jabs, deflect them onto the group, the race, away from herself. She is less nervy than her parents, than the adults, when pockets of hate are occasionally revealed in the newspaper, on the television. Listening to her parents' overreaction, she wonders if all those ancient stories are true, those battles fought-before-her-time – battles for housing, battles on the buses, battles in employment. These adults seem less tough than pioneers needed to be: why did they think sleeping out one night, in the company of friends, guarded (though the additional police guard might be a problem) – why did they think this was greater than the risk she encountered most days? They were the people who thought that the danger in attending a pop concert had to do with drugs and sex and not with the racists who gathered under the banner of the music. She is amused, nevertheless, by this visiting uncle, who is trying, as usual, to play it both ways, to please both sides; she likes him.

For me it was a curiously sobering experience to have to engage with the real-life niece rather than with, say, Philpot's daughter Nigel. At times like these one realised the truth of what Lee had been saying, with special force – that there was something unreal, something theatrical about my attachment to Nigel. The name, itself, worried her. It wasn't as crude as wanting to make her an honorary man. No, it was that 'Nigel' encouraged us to relate to her not as a woman, but as a construct, as a *challenge*. It's true that part of our involvement in Nigel's affairs had been to give a brotherly sort of support to her father, to Philpot. Nigel's problems were comfortable for us. There had been, at school, the usual battles with teachers who had made assumptions. Once, in a bit of writing that Nigel had done, she had described her father as an architect, and had talked about his converting houses into flats. And the teacher had queried the word, 'architect;' and Philpot had pursued the matter, visited the school in a hired car, and caused the teacher sleepless nights. (Philpot, who had no formal training, ran his corner shop for a while, but also had spells working on London Transport and, yes, did carpentry and plumbing and general odd-jobbing.) For Philpot it was important for the teacher to know where the child was coming from: this wasn't any ordinary deprived 'black youth' they were looking at, but a child who had had read to her at nights not any foolishness about Hansel and Gretel but this or that LAND ORDINANCE FOR ASCERTAINING THE MODE OF DISPOSING OF LANDS IN THE WESTERN TERRITORIES in the American Land Frauds of 1785, 1787, 1800 and following: this, read to her by a concerned parent who knew that one day soon his daughter would become a campaigning lawyer *to give the English licks*. Fortunately, I wasn't involved in this dispute at any stage, I didn't come to hear about it till it was settled (not settled).

The one that I remember, and this was more recent, was the business of the college gravy. Nigel was at Sixth Form college somewhere in Hertfordshire, just outside London. And the dinner-lady, this time, was the culprit. The woman had wanted to know if Nigel wanted gravy instead of custard, on her sweet, the sweet being something like apple-pie or gooey cake.

On investigation – Philpot was unflagging in overprotecting his daughter, to make up for past neglect, the women say – it turned out that there was an African student, from Ghana (GOD HAS A NEW AFRICA, remember) at the college, and one day he had asked for gravy on his sweet. So next time round the serving-woman, seeing Nigel, wanted to know if she, too, wanted gravy on her sweet.

'She doesn't look to me like a man from Ghana,' was Philpot's line.

Maureen, though not wanting to support Philpot, was unhappy that the school she was paying good money to put her daughter through, took in the sorts of people who were accustomed to having gravy on their sweet. As you can imagine the debate got bogged down with the question of people and their customs, people's right to follow their customs; on the question of whether the serving woman was being malicious or naive or simply trying to be kind. And there were the further considerations, which no one much warmed to when I raised them: the lad from Ghana might not be representative of people in Ghana in his preference for gravy on sweet. Again, this action might not be representative of him. He may have just felt like it on that particular day, and then reverted to his normal custard. Maybe it was a dare, he had bet money on it, and was a couple of pounds richer for it at the end of the day, etc.

Now, in the face of Florence and her concerns – racism at pop concerts, no easy fix as with Nigel – I did the gauche thing and offered to accompany them sleeping in the park. Naturally, the offer was rejected, though not unkindly (her stepfather was going to look in, anyway); and Avril's faint hopes that I might do something to avert the madness, were disappointed. I had to work my way back into favour; but this was nothing new to me.

And Florence helped. She had interrupted our talk about St
Caesare and paid us the compliment of being interested in our
reminiscence. She had been to St Caesare and hadn't liked it
much, to the disappointment of Avril: after that, what of the past
could she usefully hand on to her daughter? It's not that she didn't
like the place, Florence stressed; it's just that she couldn't
understand why a place as small as that called itself a country. She
couldn't work out what you did there. It was embarrassing, meeting
the same people a dozen times a day and having to find something
new to say each time. And then meeting them again next day. And
then going over to Montserrat on the ferry and meeting them again
over there. After two weeks she just wanted to scream, to hide. So
now Florence relented, and faked an interest in her great-grandmother's old house in Codrington, even in that last Sunday (or the
Sunday before the last) on the island of family myth which meant
so much to mother and uncle. She liked the way talk of the old
house animated these two who were usually so serious.

The business of people coming to lunch or tea or dinner on a
Sunday was normal. Over there we were the hosts, always the
hosts. It was the highlight of our week when my grandmother was
alive (that would be Florence's great-grandmother: it was important for her to know she had a history of which she could be proud),
with much of Saturday given over to baking, of bread and cakes,
and to preparing the roast for Sunday. (On very special occasions,
a pig had to be killed, or a goat.)

Things weren't quite the same by 1956, but in the old days, in
the days of Queen Victoria and Rev MacPherson (why did he call
her Queen Victoria? Oh, my grandmother was Lord of the Manor;
she ruled the household. She was lame in one leg but her presence
was everywhere. She controlled what we spent, including my
mother; from her room she overseered the weighing of the cotton
on the 'estate' at the other end of the island, everything). In those
days the Sunday-afternoon *drama*, played out in our drawing
room, was conducted by real actors. But we – Avril and I – were
just *understudies*. These were new words – words like understudy,
learnt from my brother, or perhaps from Professeur Croissant (who
was just a schoolteacher, and British not French, and black). My

brother, who was, of course, already in England, after a year studying in Trinidad, had claimed that in 'dialogues' abroad, important actors all had their understudies, who were a bit like servants, a bit like Kitty and Mady (Mady was short for Madeline); but unlike servants, would step in and play the part when the main actors got a cold or broke a leg, etc. What that meant to me was having Kitty step in and play the part of my mother after my mother had twisted her ankle outside church, though my mother had managed to keep playing herself, even with a limp. And Kitty would never have been able to manage the pout – she had her own pout but it was different from my mother's pout: in fact, Florence had inherited a little of the pout. It was the pout that had silenced the woman outside church who had laughed when my mother had twisted her ankle. And Kitty went to a different church, anyway, so my mother would never have consented to her as understudy. I had already decided, after Eugene had left for England, for Paddington, where he was doing a job which didn't require him to use his Latin (though we weren't allowed to say this) to be his understudy – criticising the sermon sometimes and standing up to my grandmother. (I was looking forward to giving up Latin, too, when I got to Paddington.)

Of the other understudies no one could replace Queen Victoria. Even after she had started taking her meals in her room, her presence was felt throughout the house. One thing that fascinated me about her, towards the end, was her new set of teeth, which didn't quite fit. But she wore them when there were visitors. I liked her wearing them because they changed the shape of her face, and altered her voice – bringing a new sound into the family. No one could understudy her. Mr Ryan, too, the new clergyman, seemed a comedown after Rev MacPherson, but at least they said the same sorts of things at table. And, like Rev MacPherson, he didn't seem to want to bring his wife over to St Caesare when he preached there: the manse was in Montserrat; they left St Caesare open to the French Catholics and the Hallelujah people.

This was enough for Florence. For those of her generation a little family history went a long way. She had other things on her mind; she was going out with her friends; she'd done her bit, she had indulged us.

8

If I were to take over this magazine of Lee's I would do it differently. I, too, was increasingly depressed by the sorts of people who were muscling in on Black Arts and by the stuff that tended to get printed. So I was prepared to have a go. Getting appointed editor was a bit more difficult than I'd anticipated. But that's another story.

*

Lee had been determined to give it up. She had found a new publisher for her translations and wanted to give more time to that – and even if she had to do more teaching, that would be less hassle than editing a Black Arts magazine.

It was during this period of drift, of trying to edit a magazine, of trying to sort out where I lived; or trying to determine whether I was destined to live with this person, that person or alone, that I came to appreciate something of the selfishness of my position. So many accidents seem to be befalling friends or acquaintances that I began to wonder if my lack of root, of grounding, of commitment wasn't indeed, as Lee said, something of a self-protective device. This came home to me one day in court when I saw a man about to lose his house. Part of my plan for the magazine was to keep the Black Artists, White Institutions slot but to change the frame a bit to show how the non-artist (black or white) was being treated by the *Institution* (the country). So I paid a visit to the courts.

It was a hard-to-find place in Camden, discreet, and I wondered if this was intended to respect the susceptibilities of those who were called upon to defend themselves there, but a couple of hours witnessing the proceedings soon disabused me of this. I knew very little about courts except courtroom drama on television; I always assumed them to be fairly accurate, because their forte wasn't imagination, so you more or less accepted the way they portrayed things in the court, except, of course, you didn't expect the real drama to be as well-shaped, as unmessy, as the fiction. I had visited the Old Bailey a couple of times, once with my

Italians from Bari. And I seem to remember the trip to the Old Bailey was pretty dull and the judge surprisingly human. But this was different.

This man in Camden, – Clerkenwell Court in Islington, to be exact – sitting up there in his wig, in his element, terrorised us. There was a menace here completely absent in those kindly or buffoony judges that crop up in John Mortimer. I decided not to be put off by the menace of this fellow; it was like a Rumpole session written by someone, not Mortimer, in complicity with the system, but by someone who really believed it to be evil. First of all, the judge was fat and bored, and condescending. He was a youngish man, fresh-faced, yet he had folds of fat under his chin, and he sat – lounged, really – middle of the afternoon, in gown and wig, looking bored, being supercilious. He was clearly a young Roman Emperor who hadn't seen battle, but who'd been to Cambridge. His voice was silky, soft. I sat through at least a dozen cases, and the awfulness of it made one disbelieve, despair, angry and, in the end, apologetic to people – like Balham – who came up with a different reading of *Daily Life in Britain* from me. But there was one consistently hopeful sign: there was a vein of resistance; it was not coordinated but it was sustained, and it was carried forward by a succession of women, black women. None of these women had my mother's sense of... pride in family, and yet, here they were taking on this man who owned England.

Most of the cases had to do with non-payment of rent. Private landlords or the council pursuing single men – nearly all Irish or black – to pay an extra £2.00 or £1.90 or £3.30 a week to make up the arrears for their rooms: they were nearly all desperate people living in rooms costing between £40 and £50 a week. And the men were all compliant; they were polite, some of them confused (though this may have been a tactic); they were respectful to their accusers. The private landlords seemed to be Greek (Cypriot?) men and West Indian women – one West Indian woman was a young lawyer working on behalf of the Council, and the judge treated her, like everyone else, dismissively. In his bored way he was patient with them all, explaining clearly (is that what I was like, teaching English to foreigners?) what they needed to do, and in the end they thanked him. Thanked him.

The judge played the judge to perfection. It was so filmic that I began to speculate on what he did for a living in real life. But this was Camden High Court. He had no difficulty with accents. The foreign-sounding, the Rastaman (whose voice was quiet, whose manner was respectful) posed no problems for this judge. I wondered if the Rastaman had thrown in a sentence of gibberish, whether the judge would still have understood him.

But two things remained in my mind: the man who was about to lose his flat because he had borrowed money from a loan shark to pay for his daughter's wedding and he couldn't repay the money; and the woman who threatened the judge with exposure in the press. The wedding had cost £10,000 and the loan worked out at £17,000 altogether. The borrower had a bit of a foreign accent, which I thought might hurt his case. Nevertheless, he had managed, over the past three years, to repay nearly £14,000, just over £3,000 remaining. He had a plan for repayment, clearing the debt over two years, including a down-payment of £200 in cash. But the prosecuting lawyers rejected the offer and the judge, at his most supercilious, thought it preposterous that the man should use the loan shark as his bank (even though he was paying interest on the loan): he demanded the money be repaid in two months, or the flat be sold. The flat would be sold for £60,000 or the nearest offer.

The defendant tried to explain that his flat was worth £80,000, but it transpired that the loan shark's solicitors had had it valued at £60,000 (apparently, the valuer had driven up, had stood on the pavement opposite, and made a guess. His report, as the owner struggled to point out, said that if the flat had a new kitchen, central heating and was modernised; it would be worth something more than £60,000. And the flat did, in fact, have all those features. But the judge was not to be diverted. The flat would be sold for £60,000, or nearest offer).

'And now Mr Salamis, you know what you need to do.'

Our man was ready for him. 'I think I will have to jump out of the window.'

And the judge didn't flicker either. 'In that case they will be able to repossess in two months.' At that point I knew where my alliances lay. At that point with a gun in my hand, I would use it. I wished we were in America or in some country where we believed in Direct Action. I resolved to be less harsh on the likes of Balham in future.

What followed seemed to the few remaining people in the courtroom as a bit of comic-opera. A woman, a black woman, took the stand. She was housed by the council in a short-stay flat, and refused now to be moved into new accommodation. The council's lawyer – another young woman – explained that a short-stay flat was for people in transit and that the defendant had been in the flat for two years; and that perfectly good alternative accommodation had been found for her at affordable rent, but she had refused to go because she didn't want to be moved to a new postal district. The judge tried to confirm the woman's particulars but she refused to divulge them, saying they were all on the record, and what wasn't written down wasn't people's business to know. When the judge – in a characteristically patient way – persisted, she threatened him with exposure in the newspapers.

She didn't even seem particularly angry; she was rambling, talking across him, interrupting the lawyer, making the point over and over again that she was in a flat, that she was happy in the flat, that she didn't wish to be removed from the flat; that it didn't make sense to move her from one council flat in which she was happy to another council flat where she didn't know whether she'd be happy; and that the council should leave her where she was and give the new, empty flat to someone else. Long-stay, short-stay: that wasn't her business; and when she finished what she had to say, she walked off the witness stand, and out of the court, even while they were deciding her fate; walked out threatening them with exposure in the newspapers.

I didn't know this was possible, I thought they'd have her for contempt of court – that's what would have happened on television – but the judge let her walk right out of the courtroom. The young prosecuting lawyer, a Welsh woman, very fat and bedraggled in a gown which refused to hang, asked for costs, but the Judge dissuaded her with a lazy wave of the hand.

If the black woman were more educated, if her challenge to the judge was less easily deflected, would she have got away with it? It was people like myself and my sister who were really at risk in this society. I think that's why we stuck together so much during these months.

*

The sensation was one of being caught out doing something you shouldn't, but you found so irresistible that you knew you'd return to it at the first opportunity; like nibbling away at my grandmother's sweetbread, knowing that she'd find out sooner or later, and then you'd pay the price. Or something less serious, perhaps, just the recognition of a failing; like someone trying to slim but wolfing the slice of cake when no one was looking. My sister and I have often been accused of refusing to let go (the whole family, really, have had to live with this), an irritating thing to be charged with; it had to be demonstrated that Day One in our scheme of things, wasn't the day in '56, when we landed in this country. Anyway, we tried not to burden Florence with it.

Stewart tended to be at home during my visits to the house. Stewart was always good fun. He was a man with great prospects who felt that it was not in the least embarrassing to be called a 'short-order cook' (Avril's endearment) or the Brisket who didn't quite make it. He was from one of those large Montserrat families who owned businesses all over the place, but had never in fact cashed in on the family fortune. Apparently, there'd been no family row: he'd been sent off somewhere – to Canada – to study business administration, and had somehow ended up as a cook in a hotel. In England he'd continued in that line, spurning all attempts to own his own business. When Avril realised he was never going to 'improve himself', she left her job as a nurse and did a course in Hotel Management; and together they had done extremely well, sometimes working in the same establishment. But, of course their progress was always going to be limited, because of their disinclination to travel (Florence's schooling, my mother) and wanting to be together more of the time. At the moment neither of them was in the hotel business: Avril embarking on a new career that she wasn't saying much about, and Stewart selling plastic grass. This was a new one to me. It seemed a bit of a joke, like bringing back the plastic flowers of the '50s and '60s. He didn't mind our ridicule. Apparently this was the in thing, the growth industry in Thatcher's Britain – an extension of the plastic Christmas-tree boom. There was money to be made selling plastic grass and hedges, not only to the middle-classes in those areas where they used to pave over gardens, but to some of the stately homes who had gone in for it in a big way: this was protection from the public who were trampling on the grass and vandalising hedges; so the ruling classes were hitting back with plastic. Stewart wasn't, as Avril mocked, going to become a door-to-door salesman, like those old men who still came around selling pools coupons, or the Indians in the '50s selling nicknacks out of suitcases; it was done on another level altogether. The process of selling was apparently called 'Networking', which was like a commercial chain letter: you recruited a certain number of people to do the selling and you got 'royalties' from what they sold, and when they recruited more people in their turn, you got royalties from that as well. It wasn't an American thing, it was a Swedish thing using American methods. And the beauty of it was you could do your selling by video. It was what they called 'Cocooning.' When a man got to be a certain age, Stewart said, what better than just to sit at home in front of his video and cocoon. Avril was tolerant of this; she gave all this cocooning nonsense six months and then Stewart would be back in some hotel cooking again. Stewart pointed out that through his contacts he had been offered a job at the Novotel in Oslo but that Avril was frightened of his going because she knew he would send the Norwegian women crazy.

Avril thought the remark not worthy of comment; so Stewart went off to play with his video, and Avril and I were left to put the world to rights. Neither of us liked the idea of plastic grass much. This wasn't how it was intended to end – plastic grass after thirty years. It reassured you, it depressed you to remember – to remember.

*

England hadn't yet deprived us of memory, of Coderington, our frozen bits of *then*. Pre-England. At tea, upstairs in the drawing-room, on the Sunday we liked to remember, Professeur Croissant left us in no doubt that whatever changes had taken place in our house, he was still an original actor and no understudy. He had lots of sharp things to say about da Firenze's sketches; he talked about da Firenze's 'artistic licence'. There was a sketch of my grandfather and grandmother on the front veranda looking out, with Mady at the trough below washing clothes by hand. Mady wasn't really recognisable but...

'First of all,' Professeur Croissant said, 'I have to look at these things as a historian, I can't help it, as Harry Truman followed Roosevelt.'

'This is just an impression, PC,' da Firenze tried to make light of it.

'Granted, it's an impression. But impression of what, man? First of all, it looks here as if you have a lame woman standing bolt upright. With a husband that's actually taller than her in this picture. Mass Nattie was never taller than Miss Dovie. No way, man, that's to make nonsense of the facts of history. I don't mind you fellas rewriting history; that doesn't bother me, as long as you do it intelligently. No use just putting Harry S Truman before Franklin D Roosevelt as if the world was different than it is. And look how you have that girl, virtually naked? They wouldn't allow that. No way, man. With all her business showing and thing. You're giving a false impression, man, of these people. I don't go for that at all, at all.'

I wanted to hear da Firenze defend himself, but he seemed less bold than at lunch when he'd been talking about the crack in the dining-room wall and God's smile. He told Professeur Croissant that these were just studies for paintings he'd do later, and that he'd correct any false impressions in the paintings; an answer that was a great disappointment to me.

Then Mr Ryan, the clergyman-understudy, came and my mother emerged from her room with her ankle bandaged, and she asked Mady (who was wearing a smart dress which didn't show any of her 'business') to tell Kitty to send the tea things up to the drawing-room.

So, what had I been doing today?

What do you say – that I'd been to church? You didn't want to bring that up, in case they asked about the sermon. We were understudies, not the real actors – my mother for my grandmother who had died, my sister and I for my brother, who was in England.

If I were a real actor and not just an understudy, I would dare to answer truthfully. I would say that earlier that day, in the dining-room I'd been sizing up the table which was promised to a cousin; I had looked at the sideboard, which was going to a neighbour who had such a small house that I couldn't see how it could be fitted in, and I had spent a lot of time trying to imagine how they would fit the sideboard into the little house. I knew that my grandmother would have asked the same question, and got an answer to it; but I wasn't up to that yet. And my brother, too, who had a reputation for wit and sharpness (or rudeness and mannishness) would somehow have raised the issue, even to be slapped down; but I wasn't up to it yet.

I wasn't going to tell them at tea that, between lunch and doing sketches for what my sister and I called M. Posterity and dusting the drawing-room, what I was doing was wondering how good an understudy for my brother I'd become; and whether I'd make a fool of myself when I opened my mouth in company. Like now. And the visiting clergyman would say, helpfully, that the prospect of spending three weeks on a boat must be exciting to me. Instead of excitement, there would be anxiety, but I wasn't going to tell them that. 'It's an Italian boat,' I heard myself saying. 'We're a land people,' Professeur Croissant would warn. 'We're not a sea people. No sir. Even though we've had longer boat journeys than that, I say no more. Maybe that's why we never took to the sea. Italian boat or no Italian boat'; and the painter da Firenze would say that Italian paintings were very good. And my mother would say that a boat wasn't a painting. And I would be thinking, if I were a real understudy, I would somehow find a way of proving that a boat was a painting; before my mother started (again) to worry that we had packed all the wrong things and had left the valuables behind, and Professeur Croissant would irritate us all by saying that was a good thing, because if England didn't work out, then the trip back would be easier.

Lee, not being family, tired of these stories, stories of all the suitcases, carefully labelled, full; my mother's famous trunk, full, though not locked because some of the crockery inside would be exchanged, as we had to entertain to the end, with the best china. We'd been over it dozens of times: most of what was left out had to be left out, had to be left behind. No more cases. The radio in the

*drawing-room was too big to carry: I would soon be hearing John
Arlot's cricket commentaries in England, no need to take a radio so
heavily associated in my mind with cricket. I resented – admired
and resented in near-equal measure – that the books in the
drawing-room bookcase, were earmarked for various people, including Professeur Croissant. He would inherit my John Bunyan,
my* Robinson Crusoe, *my Booker T Washington. He would inherit*
Gibbon's Decline and Fall of the Roman Empire, *passed on to me,
even before I got round to looking at it. The sermons and religious
stuff would go to other people. (Interestingly, PC had asked for
these, but my mother said it would be a mockery to put religious
books in the hands of a heathen.) But why couldn't we take some
of this with us instead of all that cassava-bread and tisane for
people living in places like Leeds and Manor House?*

Then, there was the piano...

In these meandering moments in Upton Park, my sister and I
might fix on any detail, picking it up at the point, say, when Mr
Ryan, the clergyman, enquired about my mother's ankle. Remember? My mother explained (no longer astonishing us) that she was
accustomed to pain, that it was God's will. Then the vicar turned
to Professeur Croissant and asked if he was a Methodist, if we all
belonged to the same church.

This time it was my mother who tried to prevent herself giggling.

PC – the older boys called the Professeur, PC – said that
although everyone knew slavery hadn't been abolished – despite
the lies the history-books told you...

But he had to stop there because my mother made him take
back the offensive word, 'lie', in the drawing-room. He must have
had known he would have to take something back. In my grandmother's time, it would be the word 'slavery' that he'd have to take
back. But he took it back in good spirit, and said that though
slavery hadn't been abolished, we had, nevertheless, to preserve
the few gains we'd made and...

My mother had difficulty containing herself.

...he preferred to sit in his own house on a Sunday to catch up
on his reading; to try and understand the forces of History.

'Rum shop,' was what my mother blurted out, trying to control
her giggling. 'Rum shop is your history.'

'Ah, Mrs Stapleton. Yes, you got me there, I can't deny it. The spirit is strong but the flesh is weak.' And he turned back to the clergyman to assure him that no offence was meant, that he and his kind were welcome on the island, for the people of St Caesare didn't bear grudges.

I looked at my sister, we were panicking a bit, because we didn't want my mother to cover her confusion by asking one of us to play the piano. But PC saved the day by conceding to Mr Ryan that as his accent was Irish not English, he was not to be blamed. My mother recovered enough to pick up on that, and said that we had Irish potatoes in the garden and would miss them in England; then Mady came in with a new coconut tart and fresh drinks, and everyone but my mother took second helpings. During this, both the Professeur and the clergyman assured my mother that we would get Irish potatoes in England, though they would be called English there.

The Professeur was near the bookcase now checking up on his inheritance. He claimed that English and French were, to him, second languages, but history and politics had condemned us to struggle along with them; his real language, the language of these islands, was his wife's language, which nobody spoke, not even his wife. Mr Ryan wanted to know where Professeur's wife was from, and PC said she was an 'Ancestor', meaning that she was descended from one of the original inhabitants of these islands; but everyone knew that PC's wife was just another St Caesare woman like everyone else; but no one bothered to pick him up on that nowadays. In spite of all this talk of English and French not being his languages, PC had a store of very long words in both languages that he used to roll out on occasions like this, and the boys – my brother and the older boys from the sixth form – would show due appreciation by shouting, 'Word Words', to everyone's delight.

But he was talking to us again; a ginger-beer in hand:

'You know, we must be the healthiest people in the world. On this island.' The couple of pimples on his narrow face seemed to contradict this, though looking closer, I could see that one was just congealed blood from shaving.

'We not so healthy,' my mother said, amused.

'Well, let's all give thanks,' Mr Ryan said, holding up his glass and gulping alarmingly, even before he had drunk, 'for the great journey you are about the embark on.' Everyone drank to that, but PC hadn't finished the point he had been making. He cleared his throat to indicate as much.

'We're healthy, they say, because of this.' And he held up his glass of ginger beer. 'I hand it to Mrs Stapleton. This is far better than alcohol.' This made everyone slightly uneasy because we didn't know if he was building up to making a point that would embarrass someone. But all he added was, 'In a warm climate.' Then, very pleasantly he turned to the clergyman. 'I believe you say, "better far?"'

'I beg your pardon, Headmaster.'

'Rather than, "far better", the English say, "better far". Am I not right? Or should I say, the Irish?'

'Well, I... I think they're both...'

'I haven't studied English, but I've studied the English. A little.'

Now we were getting back to the old times. The Professeur made a show of including the rest of us in the conversation. da Firenze said something about having difficulty with German-type languages like English, but in the end we all agreed, if a little uncertainly, that there was a difference between 'better far' and 'far better'; and that the juice we were drinking – whether coconut water or ginger beer – was 'better far' for you than alcohol.

'That's the rum talking,' was the look my mother wore, and I fancy she was trying to share that, silently, with us.

'We're not a drinking family,' she said, simply; and the vicar nodded and swallowed.

'Never drink or smoke.'

'It's healthier just to chew the tobacco,' da Firenze told us, but the company weren't having that, even if he *had* seen it in Italy.

'Of course, the Caribs used to do that kind of thing,' PC, the historian, reminded us. 'In the time of Columbus.' And to Mr Ryan. 'You were involved in that little episode, I believe. Your ancestors.'

Mr Ryan swallowed hard.

'Sir Walter Raleigh and all that. Jamestown...' PC was beginning to pressure the vicar with facts. After a puzzled moment Mr Ryan suddenly seemed relieved. He reminded us, gently, that the Irish weren't to be confused with the English – though even pirates weren't outside the scope of Christ's love.

I was framing something in my mind about pirates ambushing one of Caesar's cohorts somewhere in Hither Gaul, when the Professeur boomed.

'In spite of the *Counterblast against Tobacco...*' (I liked the word *Counterblast*) 'by the King,' PC went on, losing us 'many in London still smoke and drink.' As none of us knew what to say, he helped us out. 'I refer, of course, to James the First. 1604.'

'They should set a better example,' my mother uncomfortably assured us, bringing the conversation back to our reach. But Mr Ryan seemed to take this personally. Then, he confessed.

'My wife, I'm afraid, is a smoker.'

We didn't know that; maybe that's why he hid her away from company. Did he know that Jules, the lay preacher from Look Out who came in on his horse, had preached a sermon against smoking, from the same pulpit; and had convinced us that as cats and dogs didn't smoke, we shouldn't fall below those dumb animals by smoking ourselves. Now we were embarrassed for Mr Ryan. Gradually, I had an image of the vicar's wife smoking next to a dog, not smoking. Mr Ryan's Adam's apple was working furiously, up and down, the movement so sharp, that I felt the pain. What with that and the thinness and length of his nose, I started to see his face as an axe, a hatchet coming down, coming down upon Mrs Ryan, something biblical in its awfulness; and she, poor woman, defending herself by blowing smoke, pouring smoke up into his face. And when the smoke cleared I saw that she was wounded: how would she explain that in church next Sunday?

My reverie was interrupted sharply, as I sensed everyone looking at me. It turned out that someone had asked my feelings (again) on going to England; and all I could think of in the confusion was whether it was proper to admit my fear that the Latin there would be harder than the Latin at the grammar school over in Montserrat, and that was hard enough. I was stuck, but when Professeur Croissant came to my aid with 'Master Pewter doesn't have an inkling. And fair enough, fair enough.' I resented it enough to answer for myself.

'I prefer Montpellier,' I said, in a voice which didn't sound like me; and with that my sister collapsed laughing.

But having drawn the attention to herself, *she* now had to answer the question; and I got my own back as I listened to her saying that she, too, wanted to go to Montpellier, to study Botany.

The Professeur said that was very good; Montpellier was very good for Medicine, my brother's area of study. (This was dangerous territory as we weren't allowed to refer to Eugene's interrupted studies, to the fact that he was now in Paddington, doing a job that didn't require him to use his Latin.) But Professeur Croissant saved the day, and went on to remind us that Montpellier was in France not in England, and that the different tribes of Europe mustn't be confused. My mother and the Professeur then had a little exchange on whether Europe had tribes, because she didn't think she wanted to go to any place that had tribes. In the end PC, confident that he had won the argument, conceded, saying he'd let that pass, he'd let that pass; and the conversation flowed back to da Firenze and painting and Italy. To Venice where there were no roads (which made it less developed than Coderington?) and people living there had to travel by boat to do their shopping, etc. My mother said that that was dangerous because what if they fell into the water and couldn't swim. None of us could swim; it was good we weren't going to Venice.

The Professeur was relaxed about that. We were land people, he said again; as sure as Harry Truman followed Roosevelt, we were land people; and then my mother perked up and prevailed on da Firenze to give us some examples of the Italian language.

Avril, in Upton Park, challenged my memory of this. She suspected that I was writing something more about those times, and she didn't want to encourage me. I hadn't yet, managed to earn her trust, either.

*

I saw a bit of Balham during that time. Balham was like a joke that wasn't funny first time, so you had to repeat it. He was now a polytechnic lecturer, delivering courses on things like postcolonial literature (he claims to have invented the term) and on arts administration. Since we were both in the Arts now we tended to run into each other at 'events' – at the ICA, the Whitechapel Arts Gallery, Keskadee, The Tricycle in Kilburn. I'm thinking now of

the meeting at the Commonwealth Institute's 1987 Literature
Conference featuring Lamming and Wilson Harris and Selvon –
the full line-up. Good to see Martin Carter. A foppish Austin
Clarke in from Canada. A dapper, beautifully formally dressed
A.J. Seymour from Guyana. Brilliant. And the women, younger.
Olive Senior, Lorna Goodison... And Balham.

'Old Man!' he loomed up like a giraffe.

'Lord Balham.'

This is how we greeted each other. Balham had always made
much of the fact that I was older than he was – if not by quite a year,
at least by having been born in a different year: I seemed always
to be twenty to his nineteen, thirty to his twenty-nine and now, a
little more mid-fortyish than he. I pretended it didn't matter.
When we were doing GCEs, or even at university, to be called 'Old
Man' was a sort of badge of pride that could be worn; somehow it
gave you a little bit of authority that seemed to confirm that if you
hadn't really lived, you had at least *read*. (I used to read plays
furiously in those days, one a day on average, particularly in the
year between school and university, and that had amused Balham,
though he was always gracious about it.) 'Old Man' at that time,
those times, pulled together stray things that were perhaps in
themselves forgettable – the fact that I had *driven* to Italy the
summer after my first year at university. 'Old Man' of... was it
Tuscany or Venice? – gave one *gravitas*.

So I retaliated by calling him Lord Balham. This should be
death to a man striving so hard for street credibility. I seem to
remember it started out as just plain Balham. (He'd never, as far
as I know, lived in Balham, but in the times when he had tried to
distance himself from me, he would characterise me as just
another North Londoner (in the days when I was probably living
in Nacka in Sweden or in Buckforst or Ebertplatz in Köln or in
Spéracèdes in the Alpes Maritimes and his family lived in
Cricklewood). If I was the perennial North Londoner he was from
the unsung south of the river. And Balham, because – we didn't
quite know anyone who lived in Balham – it seemed just right; we
agreed on this: it was as if Balham and I had become his own
parents, christening him. He used the name, writing letters to the
press (again, who else wrote letters to the press?) and on his
'Sociological' bits and pieces that were published. And, of course,

on his poetry pamphlet – he'd published a poetry pamphlet! I had helped to create Balham.)

Of course, we weighed the name differently. 'Lord Balham' was intended to compromise him slightly, to suggest a place in the 'Establishment' – if not quite as a retired functionary at the Ministry of Ag & Fish, say, at least as a pretend calypsonian. There was something of the Geoffrey Boycott syndrome here (I hated Boycott for the boring way in which he held up West Indies advance time after time when he opened the innings for England. Boycott's supporters in the media used constantly to refer to him as Sir Geoffrey, not only out of affection, but to nudge the pen, supposedly, of the person who writes out the Queen's New Years's Honours Lists). I liked this analogy because Balham claimed not to be interested in cricket, as it drained vital energy away from West Indians, as it made West Indian crowds forget their real problems when they saw their man hit a bit of leather with a stick. He claimed that English teams deliberately lost to West Indies, on orders from the government or the police, to prevent the crowds expressing real dissent, to protest their condition in England. So, as a sociologist, he was interested in cricket (just as, for research purposes, he had once been interested in the Bible and the Koran, whatever his private reservations). But now as an arts administrator and lecturer, he was interested in our giving our dissent shape, and in finding the right form to display that shape, and in making the enemy fund it.

'And how's his Lordship?'

'Struggling, Old Man, struggling.'

(The idiot doesn't change.)

(What a tiresome little man.)

We were in the refectory, in-between sessions, and the crush of people happily prevented us doing more than shout slogans at each other.

'Where're you hanging out these days?' he asked. (He knew.)

'Oh, you know.'

'Lee tells me you're house-hunting.'

'Ah!'

'Thought you were going to settle in Frogland.'

'Might come to it.'

'Because your Frog's pretty good, isn't it?'

'Well...'

'We must get together, I want to practice my Frog. This is a little thing that might amuse you.' And he slipped his poetry pamphlet into my hand. Before I could respond, to say I'd already got it – it had come in to *Rainbow* for review and Lee had passed it on to me, in disbelief – he had gone, squeezing his way through the crowd.

I'm glad Lee wasn't here: we had had a session gloating over the pamphlet, the awfulness of it. (Actually it depressed her and made her even more determined to get out of the game.) But I rather enjoyed seeing Balham make a fool of himself. The pamphlet was called *The Provoked Muse* and was very earnest. Lee and I had flicked through titles like 'Re-Appropriating The Wealth of Nations' and 'Eat Your Own Shit'. Who could be bothered with this stuff?

When, eventually, I looked closely at Balham's book, *The Provoked Muse* was as bad as I'd hoped. Not ordinarily bad, it seemed even worse than most of the stuff we'd been subjected to under the guise of poetry, it was pretentiously bad. 'Eat Your Own Shit', for instance, was a poem about dumping nuclear waste in Africa and a demand that the Western offenders take it back. There were titles in other languages. (Nothing wrong with that, but Balham had a way of unconsciously sending up things you might otherwise support: I remember his claiming to have been in Paris in '68 and to have got his, what was it? *Lasser Passer* at the *Odeon*. I *knew* he wasn't in Paris in '68; he was in Leicester. His French partner had left him by then, and was bringing up their child on her own, in France.) Now, in *The Provoked Muse*, there was a huge poem called, 'Que Idade Tem¿ (How Old Are You)': the *note* said this was Portuguese.

Two things struck me about that. The fact that I misunderstood it (as your average reader would), and the glee with which this was anticipated in the 'notes' at the back of the book. This was clearly to divert attention from the poem's ordinariness. I had an unpleasant sensation of Balham at his polytechnic podium lecturing, and we, his students, being enlightened. On first reading, he seemed to be making large claims for his mother, who was immensely old and ubiquitous. But when I turned back to the 'notes', it transpired that the poem had nothing to do with the poet's mother (was I becoming mother- fixated?). It was about what the Jamaican poet, Louise Bennett called, in another context, 'Colonization in Reverse'. The 'note' said there was a lot of sociological evidence about the 'age profile' of people living in Britain, the percentage of over-30s, over-60s, etc; and that the form of English arrogance represented by the question: *How long have you been here?* was merely sustained by the literal answer – 15 years, 30 years, 40 years. Balham's poem:

Housing-estate, Borstal & Public School
Will fight to override
The 35-year rule:
But this immigrant has remeasured his stride,

was a 'strategy' for dealing with that question. And the nearly two pages of *notes* explained it. It's not simply that anyone who asked you the question should have lived in the country at least as long as you, but – more interestingly – just as the 'bigots' were sustained by something outside their person – a grandfather in the war, an Elizabethan pirate circumnavigating the globe – the immigrant had to do the same. Say, the West Indian family had arrived here thirty-five years ago: say, there were four members in the family – small, because *broken* by circumstances. These four people together added up to *one-hundred and forty years experience in this country*. Now, say this was 1986. That took you back to 1846 (before the European revolutions in '48, but never mind). This was the context, said Balham's *note* of his references in 'Que Idade Temé', to Lord John Russell and Peel and Corn Laws and annexations of the Orange Free State and the Punjab. He challenged his readers, his listeners to be literate.

I was ashamed to admit that I was less 'literate' than the poem, I let Balham inform me of this version of 'Black History'. If this was only half the family, for reasons already given, what did you get when you reunited the family? Let's say you had an average family of six (because our families weren't as big as the racists said). With four members, we're already at 1846. Add another two; two at 35

years, gains us another 70 years experience in this country.
Remember we're working *backwards*. This took us back to 1776.
Or thereabouts. And what's happening in the 1770s? *We're* there,
veterans of the anti-slavery campaign. Equiano and all that. That's
all behind us. Lord North and all that. Forget that rubbish. The
Malvinos. Remember the Malvinos. We might live to hear of them
again. But this is the 1770s. Peoples' uprisings all over the place.
Blackburn, London, wherever; alas, not filmed. Remember the
Jonathan Strong Movement? Granville Sharp and all that? There
we are, people who look like us, picketing the *Daily Advertiser*.
And what's that great cheer? What's that howl of triumph which no
one there saw fit to record? That's *us*, celebrating when our friend
Cetewayo gave the fellow *licks*, the man from Chelmsford. These
are a few pointers, Balham said, to decoding his poem 'Que Idade
Temè'. (Ok, I'm paraphrasing; but I'm not sending it up.)

True, the 'notes', all 17 pages of them, intrigued me. But I had
to ask myself, if the 'notes' were so diverting, and the poems so
dull, how were we to deal with the pamphlet if we reviewed it in the
magazine. When, later, I expressed my dilemma to Lee she was
appalled that I found Balham's *notes* interesting. She wondered,
perhaps, if I hadn't gone native.

Balham was later to say that our puzzlement over the poems
amused him. He said he expected me to ignore the poems and to
review the notes. He said his ideological attitude to the poems he
wrote was similar to Robert Mitchum's attitude to the films he
made. He quoted Mitchum, who when called up to testify before
the Committee for Un-American Activities, 'in America's most
characteristic phase', denied being an actor, and said he had made
nineteen films to prove it. According to Balham, his own tactics
with the Arts were similar. Of course, he wasn't a poet. Or a film-
maker. Or even a sociologist, any more. He only pursued these
things to provide structures and to preserve the evidence. And to
raise money. It was well known that a black person couldn't raise
money for business in this country – unless you were maybe an
Indian and sexy with curry, and had a willing extended family. But
they'd always toss you something if you were on the fringes of Art,
because (a) they had no interest in Art and (b) Art had become a

sort of cut-price religion of our time; unlike sport which was an expensive circus. And by indulging the 'Artist' you diverted people's creative attention from real matters; you divided them by making them compete for the crumbs, and you prevented them joining the real circus of corporate crime and political nepotism – which might cause serious threat to the state. No, Balham was concerned with Arts administration and with decolonization. No one had ever accused him of being interested in Art. OK, so he'd written a novel very quickly (we didn't know that) and made a few films: he had to keep his hand in, to secure the credibility of the artist without the hassle of having to make art. He sent his love to Lee.

*

Balham was to get a literary award for his pamphlet.

PART THREE

9

Friday. Evening.

I couldn't believe it, the stuff was in my pigeon hole, stuff stacked on the floor. How could Dave have second-marked all this material in a day? (This wasn't the Dave of the literary editing, this was another Dave.) Last week when a couple of my scripts had come back suspiciously quickly, I knew that someone marking this quickly had to be commenting on my slowness. I phoned Rolls to check on how fast he was marking. He could deliver his second marking at the same pace as Dave. Oh, so the problem was with me. I would accept defeat. I decided to opt out of the race, I came home and sat down and made myself comfortable and read some very long sentences, very slowly. I knew I was a slow reader; I'd always been a slow reader, and it bothered me when I was younger, particularly at university having to get through a fair bit of Dickens; but over the years I've come to treasure my slow reading, almost as a protest against the haste and frenzied skating across words which now passes for reading. Everyone skims. Teachers. People researching television programmes and most of all, students. When they get fed up with skimming they ask you to make a precis: reading has now become a chore employed in the service of other things, one of which is passing exams. So, I'm one of those dedicated to restoring reading to its rightful pace – a walking pace, a sitting-down-in-the-armchair-for-hours pace. I want to experience it as a sensual encounter, the pleasure of black print on white page; of books beautifully bound, of the gift of narrative and poetry attractively packaged. Of course I made an exception for theatre: theatre was out there to be experienced with others, the complete experience, from foreplay to orgasm with consenting strangers – something like that. Yet, when I received the shock of the second marker marking all those short story scripts in a day I did come home and read some Proust. I chose something that I knew quite well; and I read 4,500 words of Proust (the size of the second year folder) and it took me three-quarters of an hour. Now, none of my second yearers was Proust, granted, but it still worked out that if

Dave had five hours sleep last night, and let's say ten minutes for lunch and that sort of thing, he would still have managed each script in twenty-five minutes: Was this possible? How could you keep it up? Did being an academic give you training to deal with *creative writing* in this manner? OK. Forget Proust. I searched the shelves for something that a middling second year student might produce and how I as a reviewer (reviewer, editor, not marker) might deal with it. I went down-market, down *down* market. I took out Balham's old pamphlet that had, depressingly, picked up an award. I also dug out a copy of the *Rainbow* in which I'd reviewed it.

I'd been to the library, I remember, the Church End library, (I expect no less of you, Dave): I had come to terms with some of these titles; foreign names. Not just 'Que Idade Temὲ' but *Mauvaise Pierre* (Bad Stone) and *Nuit Blanche* (White Night) and *Toute Eaux* (All the Waters: a brand of septic tank). Upstairs in the Reference Room I'd taken down all the dictionaries and set to work. *Mauvais gout* I knew and understood, but *mauvaise pierre*? The opposite of *mauvaise* must be something like *precieuse*. So, *pierre precieuses*? But he wasn't talking about jewellery, he was talking about building a house, literally a stone house: who was going to use *bad* stones in his house? Unless it was something quaint and biblical. (I knew what the phrase meant on the building site when, having selected the best stones for your facade, and the bricks on the inside to define the thickness of the wall, the resulting gap – if any – was filled with *mauvaises pierres*. I knew about this because I had restored houses in the South of France, but Balham, despite having been partnered, two decades ago, by a French woman, wouldn't know this. If he did it would be in the *notes*.)

Now the *Notes* proved more confusing than I remembered. When I looked at what seemed to be the right place in the *notes* I read: *Who's to say that after the Civil Wars of 84, and the Flavians and their slaves built a road from Chester to London, that the first Miss Na and Uncle Mike and Tan Tan didn't settle along that road on a 200 acre farm called Balaams, and put down root?* This was maybe a misprint, a *note* belonging somewhere else – this was a small-press publication after all.

But I had, crucially, given Balham the full scholarly treatment and even now was impelled to take the phrase-book off the shelf.

First of all under *pierre*. *Poser la premiere pierre* (to lay the
foundation stone). OK. Then, *un coeur de pierre* (a heart of stone).
Too close for comfort, that. Better look under *mauvaise*. What
about... avois *mauvais jours* (hard times?) Or even – if, for once, he
was into imagery – ...*une mauvaise langue* (a sharp tongue)? Like
stone. The lady of the *Toutes Eaux* having a sharp tongue? Or having
to suffer a sharp tongue? Sharp fists. No, too sophisticated for
Balham. Maybe he meant something really depressing like this
one... *une femme de mauvaise vie* (a prostitute).

I remember playing with this for hours and coming away with
two rather possible poems in French – of French phrases – to do
with *mauvaise pierre* and *Toutes Eaux*; and each, I'm still convinced, had more to do with the expectation generated by Balham's
titles than the traditional slavery and chain gang verses which he
had yoked to them. The banality of it was more amusing than
depressing. I had ended the review: 'This pamphlet presents
writing of sociological interest, but the verse lacks resonance'.
OK, this revisiting took me only forty minutes. But I knew this
stuff, I'd done it before. So maybe it was possible, after all, to
second mark at twice my pace.

I will force myself to mark faster in future, that way maybe
there'll be a bit of time left over for the life. The Life.

Had to get away. The body was rebelling from the marking. I
hadn't marked the scripts, yet; the scriptwriting, but I had only one
script-writing group. A doddle. The mind had long packed up. The
whole flat seemed used, used. After all this marking, I felt the
place should be redecorated. No wonder Lee didn't want to come
here. How could she be expected to come here and eat supper on
this table polluted by scripts with poor spelling and attitudes to
people so immature that they couldn't possibly stand their own
against some passing racist or demagogue. Yet this is what's
absorbing me; the whole body feels tormented, bruised; the arm
hurts. We should demand danger money. No, had to get away.
There'll be some moderating of scripts later; and stuff to be
selected for the External. And the scriptwriting. But, must get
out of here, out of the country, just for a few days. I got on the
phone to my friend Ralph in the Alpes Maritimes, and he agreed
to pick me up at the Nice airport. In a day or two. I hadn't booked

but there'd be a flight. I'd ring back with the time when I managed to book.

Going away (like marking) has always been a productive time for me. I hope I don't mean that; I hope Lee, (who's she with?) isn't picking up bad vibes from this kind of thinking. But the whole thing galvanizes me into tidying up things whenever there's a necessity to be away from my desk even for a weekend; and the prospect of escaping to France in a few days has got me going. So, to my Friday night list:

Saturday
(1) *CARRINGTON: SEVEN PLAYS*
    Black Cab
    Big Momma & The White Street-Walking Bitches
    King Lear
    Ibrahim and the Countess
    Payback
    *Severus of Enga (*or the Dutch connection, one of the
    Surinamese plays – Doelwitt or De Rooy?*)*
    The O'Neill play?

(2) St James Press
(3) MA West Indian Literature
(4) Laundrette
(5) Reference
(6) Lee's Party
(7) Volcano play
(8) <u>Book flight.</u>

Tired. Must get away from it. Bad time to go away. Tidying up helps you to be ruthless. So it was easy to eliminate most of the Smythe-type things. (Incidentally, he called me half an hour ago to propose a run-through of the sketch we were planning to do at the University, a surprise thing: were my 'Additional Dialogues' ready. He'd booked space for Monday. I didn't have the heart to tell him that Monday I'll be out of here.) Equally the MA Epic with Smythe wasn't on, as I would hone up a West Indian Literature MA instead. The short story would have to be reinstated. That's where the energy seemed to be at the moment. Jamaica Kincaid. Olive Senior. Pauline Melville. Those wonderful lesbian women in Canada. Makeda Silvera, etc. That young girl in wherever, Belgium, Alecia McKenzie. Endless. Some men too, Lawrence Scott. Endless. And I was having fun thinking through the reading list, with all the old favourites trotted out: CLR James, not just *Beyond a Boundary* and *The Black Jacobins*, but his assorted essays. Essays by Wilson Harris, Lamming, Brathwaite; Ramchand, Rohlehr etc. But also people I should have read but haven't much. Ivan Van Sertima and the African presence in America and Europe. Van Sertima for the early presence; and Dabydeen concentrating on Britain. Then I must pick the brains of various people in London for stuff on the music and religion and all that business. Also, something by Edward Said, got to have him. This will occupy me fully; so I'll disclaim interest in the other MAs. Apart from the Writing one.

One problematic thing was Lee's party. Anvil Press in London had brought out her new book and there was to be a party. These occasions always threatened to be what politicians call defining moments. For Lee would bring someone to the party and I would be humiliated. Or I would bring someone to the party and Lee would be humiliated. The latest was that Lee was threatening not to come to her own party: did she think I'd bring someone to humiliate her? Did she think I'd turn up with Natalie?

But at least I'd sorted out the *Carrington Seven* – a Carrington Seven; it wasn't definitive. A couple of playscripts had come in from St. Croix of something he'd done there. Translations/ adaptations. Dutch/ Surinamese stuff. But I haven't had time to look at them. I still had to get down to Kent to wade through the archives. I still hadn't got a handle on the *Introduction*. Carrington had sabotaged my chances with the group novel. He had been too busy to pursue it himself and had talked of my taking it on with Lee; and after we had done quite a bit of work on it, the publishers suddenly went cool on the idea. I didn't believe that Carrington didn't have anything to do with that. But I won't let *that* affect my introduction to his plays.

Better just go to the laundrette.

*

I wake with a mouth full of blood, bits of teeth. (Time to get out of here, head south.) I wake with a mouth full of blood, bits of teeth. I rush out of the classroom trying to minimise the embarrassment. I'd been late for the class, Literary Editing, and the students, one woman in particular, were a little restive. The woman looked at her watch as I entered, a hint of value for money; so this latest mishap of mine was met with something less than sympathy. It seemed as if more than a cap lifted off the tooth as I tried to assess the damage.

What was unsettling me was that I was now dreaming of work. The bloody mouth was bad enough but – going off to France without Lee – why was I dreaming about literary editing? My life had become narrow. I don't recall dreaming about building when I was restoring houses in the South of France. Why, my life was richer, then. Even when I was teaching, even when I taught in language schools in Germany, I dreamt, I'm sure, of dallying in the arms of a Lindsay or of some Karen or Bettina or at the very least sailing down an unpolluted Rhine in a superior barge with the girl I went to grammar school with in Montserrat. And this business of dreaming about teeth was depressing. Every writer I know seemed to be having Martin Amis-type problems with teeth: is this how they will characterise writers of our time? People obsessed with teeth? The Elizabethans had the language; the Restoration boys had wit – and the girls, too: Mrs Aphra Behn, Mrs Centlivre (sort of wit, anyway; sparkle); the Theatre of the Absurd had absurdity; Kitchen Sinkery had anger (or the Angry Young Men had women to do their ironing); but for us, it's teeth. The Teeth. Naturally, I will write something and call the main character Teeth. Or Tooth. (Like the Welsh joke, the man with one tooth in the middle of his mouth. Who he? Dai Central Eating. But more sophisticated.) I needed a break from all this, I had to get away from City, from dreams which didn't include Lee or Lindsay; even the ruin in Spéracèdes brought on more natural dreams, was better than this.

As I went to make a cup of tea I realised that what must have woken me was the smoke coming up from below. This was the middle of the night, it was an attack; this was intolerable; the old prunes downstairs must be doing it on purpose. Then I remembered the Hitler book; and the play which was screaming to come out of it: I map something out in my head. Too tired to write it down. Have a cognac, have two cognacs, have three cognacs, fall asleep again in the chair. Get up and write the 'Additional Dialogues' for Smythe.

The weekend is frantic. Waves of energy; frenzy, maybe. I've booked for Thursday. South of France; too late, but time to clean up odds and ends of marking before then; sort out what's going to the External. On Monday I find time to look in on a couple of meetings at the university. One was forgettable; the other, maybe, wasn't.

Any Other Business
(A Stapleton/Smythe play)

An English (and other) Course Committee Meeting at Collegegate. Assorted Daves and Phils and Keifs, Julies, Emmas and Allans troop into the room, a basement room without ventilation. Grumble, grumbling; they apologise when they see the room occupied, and start to withdraw.

A DAVE: Even they couldn't put us in that...

A JULIE: ...cellar, that...

A KEIF: Bunker, that's what I call it. And who were they, anyway, those women?

A DAVE: Talk of the weird sisters. Weren't they speaking German?

A DAVE: Nicely dressed, though.

A DAVE: As if they were in costume.

A DAVE: Something creepy about them.

A JULIE: Now now.

A DAVE: Sorry, not politically correct.
           (*fade*)

(*Lights UP on same room.* SCHOOL MANAGER *and* FOUR WOMEN *talking amongst themselves*)

Sc. MANAGER: ...like that Raymond Carver story where the
                    couple end up playing tug-of-war with the
                    baby. (*She shudders; the* WOMEN *shudder*
                    with delight.)
WOMAN: Horrible, horrible.
WOMAN: And that horrible last line:
                    (*They all say it together*)
                    'And in this manner, the issue was decided.'
                    (*They shudder.*)

(*Enter* A DAVE *and* A JULIE)

A DAVE: It's in here; the meeting's taking place in here!
A JULIE: I don't believe it.
A DAVE: I tell you we're in the bunker and we don't
                    even play golf.
A DAVE: And we don't even play golf.
A JULIE: It's the photocopying room all over again.
WOMAN: (*to* A DAVE *and* A JULIE) Would you like a
                    cigarette?
A DAVE & A JULIE: No, thank you.

(*The* WOMAN *lights a cigarette and offers the rest of the packet*
round; all except the SCHOOL MANAGER *accept and light up*)

Sc. MANAGER: (*welcoming*) I know you're busy with your
                    marking, so I won't keep you; it's just that I
                    know you're anxious about the sort of...
                    flow of Information from the Centre; and I'm
                    just here to, y'know – to listen, really but –
                    to clarify one or two things that...
A DAVE: It's a bad time for a meeting.
A JULIE: It's always a bad time for a meeting, but...
Sc. MANAGER: I know, I wish they'd just go away, meetings,
                    but... And I know you're tired and...
A DAVE: Emotional.
Sc. MANAGER: upset by the tree they've cut down and every
                    thing. Like some one said: How can you own

a farm if you don't know anything about
geography.

(THE WOMEN *nod;* A DAVE *and* A JULIE *look at each other*)

Sc. MANAGER:	So... Well let me tell you about the arrangements for the skips. The skips on this Campus are now locked. If anyone requires rubbish to be moved from the area please ring the help desk on Extension 4222.

(A DAVE *puts up his hand*)

A DAVE:	'Scuse me.
Sc. MANAGER:	(*sweetly*) Let me finish. The help desk will arrange for the porters to remove the rubbish. Please note that porters will only remove normal everyday waste...
A DAVE:	That's nice to know.
A JULIE:	At least it beats the marking.
A DAVE:	I suppose so.
Sc. MANAGER:	...and will not give access to the skips for complete room clearances, surplus furniture...
A DAVE:	I'll have some of that.
A JULIE:	What's that?
A DAVE:	Surplus furniture.
A JULIE:	You all right, A Dave?
Sc. MANAGER:	If you require surplus furniture to be removed please ring the help desk, state what the item is and where it is located.
A DAVE:	(*to* A JULIE) Shall we go?

(*They shift, waiting for an opportunity to go*)

Sc. MANAGER:	They will make arrangements for its removal. The help desk can also arrange for skips to be hired for a department when there is a large amount of rubbish or a complete room

clearance. This will be recharged to the
department concerned.

(*Signalling to each other,* A DAVE *and* A JULIE *start creeping out.
Enter, in a rush,* A DAVE DAVE, A JULIE 2, FIONA, SMYTHE *and*
PEWTER. A DAVE *and* A JULIE *decide to stay after all.*)

A DAVE DAVE:	But it's a bunker.
A JULIE 2:	It's like the photocopying room with all the fumes.
A DAVE DAVE:	And passive smoking.
A JULIE 2:	And in America they wouldn't allow it. It's carcinogenic, breathing in the fumes from the photocopier.
Sc. MANAGER:	Yes, we need a window in the photocopying room. Only there's no outer wall. Of course, meanwhile, to keep the fumes down, it would be a good idea to cut down on the photocopying we do in the department.
A DAVE DAVE:	Is this meeting about the photocopying machine?
A JULIE 2:	The photocopying room is important.
Sc. MANAGER:	The meeting is about what you want it to be; I'm here to listen and to let you know your voice is being heard.
A DAVE:	That's very…interesting.
Sc. MANAGER:	Patronising, you were going to say.
A KEIF:	Listen I've got things to say that've got nothing to do with the photocopier.

(*He leaps up with a scroll of paper.*)

A DAVE DAVE:	Like Peter Lilly at the annual Tory Conference.
A JULIE 2:	Is he going to sing, then?
A KEIF:	(*looks up*) We really do object to this meeting being held here, by the way, under the squash courts, in the basement, in a bunker.

A DAVE: (*Interrupting. To* A JULIE) I know who they put me in mind of, now. (*Points to* WOMEN) Those women in the bunker. You know, the last days of our friend   SIX LETTERS. Hang on. I'm sure Roi will know their names. (*He leans over and speaks to someone sitting next to him on the left; a tall fair-haired man with a little smile. The man languidly takes out his pen and writes on a sheet of paper.* A DAVE *speaks to someone on his right.*) *Trust* the historian to show us up.

A KEIF: (*continuing*) ...and to be called out in the middle of the day, on a Monday, when we'd be better occupied at home recovering from the marking; I mean I only came because I wanted to know whether you were serious about offering additional secretarial help, with the secretaries in the office...

A DAVE DAVE: Secretaries!

A FIONA: Admin. support.

A KEIF: OK, I apologise... with the Admin staff snowed under; and what with the amount of Admin we're saddled with...

Sc. MANAGER: I know in the old days...

(*The historian passes the paper back to* A DAVE *who reads it, nods and passes it on. The recipient reaches over and asks* A DAVE *for clarification.*)

A DAVE: (*in a stage whisper*) The women in the bunker, loyal to the end: Frau Gerda Christian, Frau Gertrud Junge, Fräulein Else Kreuger and Baroness Von Varo.
(*and pointing to the* Sc. MANAGER)
In the service of Frau Halterbush.

A KEIF: ...and there's the business of the ... female admin staff having to lift all those crates, heavy crates.

THE WOMEN: Kinder, kirche, küche; kinder, kirche,
                    küche; kinder, kirche, küche.

Sc. MANAGER: How heavy are these crates?
                    (*No one knows*)
                    No one should be asked to lift crates over 15
                    kilogrammes in weight (*to* WOMEN) Better
                    make a note of that.

A KEIF: (*stops dead*) Wait a minute. (*He points at*
                    SMYTHE, *at* PEWTER) You're having us on,
                    aren't you? Happy Demob Hour and all that
                    stuff. This is your *Any Questions* trick all over
                    again. OK, OK. (*to the* WOMEN) Great costume,
                    by the way (*and to the* Sc. MANAGER) I'll tell
                    you what, Frau, Frau...

SMYTHE: Halterbush.

A KEIF: Frau Halterbush, I grant you this: your pred-
                    ecessor could never have pulled this off: no
                    sense of humour. So (*looks round*) we're here,
                    the show's on. Let's enjoy the show. (S*its back*
                    with his arms folded.)

A FIONA: I have to make a pee-pee.

A DAVE: What, is this meeting being held in French,
                    then?

A DAVE DAVE: A translation meeting.

A FIONA: You're all so beastly and male. (*She sulks.*)
                    You just don't want me to make a pee-pee.

                    (*An uneasy pause; then the* HISTORIAN, *with a*
                    little smile on his face, comes to the rescue.)

HISTORIAN: Now tell me... what, what in your opinion,
                    were the factors, that led to the decay of the
                    Carolingian Empire?

Sc. MANAGER: Ah, if only they had a fax machine that
                    worked.

HISTORIAN: D'you want to hear the follow-up questions
                    first?

Sc. MANAGER:	No, no, I expect they'll only get more challenging. Of course Charles, Charles the Great, was always going to be a hard act to follow. 'Iron' Charles, as we call him. You might remember the bloodbath at Verdun. I forget the details. Poor Louis, Louis the Pious, succeeding, lacked bottle, really. That was among the factors that led to the decay of the Empire.
HISTORIAN:	Is that…?
Sc. MANAGER:	…Charles himself had suffered great personal tragedy towards the end. In 810 Pipin, his son, died. In 811 Charles his eldest son died. In 810 Charles' eldest daughter died.
HISTORIAN:	And his white elephant…
A DAVE:	What?
HISTORIAN:	Had a white elephant. Sent to him by Harun al-Rashid, Caliph of Bagdad, fellow in the Arabian Nights. It died. The elephant.
Sc. MANAGER:	…Daughters never married, did they. Wouldn't want to be treasured so much by the old man that you weren't allowed to marry, would you? … By then civil disobedience…
A DAVE:	This is too depressing, let's have something cheerful.
Sc. MANAGER:	I'm sorry, I know, we're all a bit tired and pathetic after the marking. What we need now is a performance poet to remind us of the '60s.

(*Everyone groans, screams*) Oh No No No…….

Later, having a drink at the *Aunt Sally* up the road, the mood was flat. Smythe and I were joined by Rolls, his wife Liz and Julie; and over drinks the school manager revealed how she felt about what we had put her through.

'Terrified, actually.' (She was very gracious about it). 'You know, how do I pull this off: it's like being interviewed all over again. I mean, you know, you can't help knowing what the entire staff felt about the last school manager. Poor cow. I mean, do you want someone to manage the school or do you want a surrogate academic? Bit of both, I suppose.'

(We said the usual things about wanting someone who was sensitive to what the academy is; someone who respects what we deliver; and who respects those who deliver it; and who respects, you know, the students.) But we thought she was brilliant!.

'I'm not complaining because from what I hear all I need to do is to drink a cup of coffee without slurping and as school manager, if I pull that off, I'll be OK in your eyes. So yes, why not have a go at Rupert's *Demob Hour* sketch for the subject group? If you're all so close to mental collapse anything would be a relief. That's the least I could do to help. I mean, I did think you were a bit obsessive about, you know, I thought, why don't they give it a rest? But then you academics tend to be a bit relentless. Or am I talking out of turn? But I'm just gullible, I suppose. I can still believe that when you get some sharp minds together, there must be a sort of excitement, that tiny rousing tingle on the back of the neck... and I like the notion that you're always being challenged, kept up to the mark because of the young blood coming through each year. But that's not how it is, is it?'

The image of young blood coming up embarrassed us a little. There was something predatory about it. The Dracula image was too close for comfort. I had images of men – the man in charge, the tutor, tin god, sitting there surrounded by young woman flesh, feeding off it. Though half the staff was female: were *they* in a more healthy relationship with their (largely female) students than we were?

Rolls said something and Smythe answered and a little heated exchange ensued. But Liz soon called them to order.

I had complicated matters, according to the school manager, by coming to warn her that Smythe was writing a campus novel and that she would certainly be in it. So we could imagine her panic preparing for this little sketch of ours. It would have been better if all the staff were in on it; not just three or four because then you wouldn't have to prepare for the unexpected. Would someone embarrass her, hurl something about Wittgenstein at her, that everyone else in the room knew how to answer? (Smythe started telling a Wittgenstein joke, but got stuck.) So, yes, the simplest things threw her into a panic: what should she wear? Should she appear knowing about literature or talk about holidays in Umbria? Was she part of the academic pack or was she just glorified support staff? When in academic company should she permit herself to say 'fuck'?

Oh, you can't say fuck.

Oh no, couldn't say fuck.

Fuckin' hell.

Or should she just keep her knees together and refer discretely to Virginia Woolf's *A Room of One's Own*?

So we apologised to the school manager for putting her through this shit just for a possible few pages in Smythe's as-yet-unwritten novel where she would appear not as herself, but as the *genus* New University School Manager.

Actually I was thinking of the abandoned project, the group novel, the Sister-in-law, Mother-in-law thing. Why not the school manager? She had mentioned Virginia Woolf, she had mentioned Wittgenstein, she mentioned holidaying in Umbria: I began to have a sense of what her private library might be like: we could take this further.

I asked how she had prepared herself for the sketch.

She went shopping at Debenham's, wasn't that pathetic?

Oh, no, no, no. You *have* to go shopping in Debenham's. Didn't someone in *Ulysses* go shopping in Debenham's? Or was that in Proust. Or Homer?

Then the school manager relaxed and said she had read last year's Booker Prize winner and hadn't liked it much, so she knew she'd better steer clear of contemporary fiction. She suspected we might be into poetry, the way we criticised everybody. She'd been to a poetry event recently, not a reading exactly, though someone read a couple of poems which seemed hardly worth the effort. But the poetry crowd was so intimidating; ill-dressed for the most part and self-important.

We agreed enthusiastically. O, poetry readings! Poetry events were the pits. Obscene affairs. Pathetic. Shouldn't be allowed. They should be shut down by the police. They insulted your intelligence and were bad for your health anyway. Better stick to the old *News at Ten*.

That's why she thought she might like this place; we brought all these poor dysfunctional creatures, the writers, in from the cold and were said to humiliate them in the gentlest possible way. And it seemed such a mad, caring thing to do. But already she was hearing the sound of her own voice and that was a warning sign. They said that sort of thing led you on to asking academic-type questions, questions like what's the university for anyway? And surely that wasn't allowed. She was only a school manager, after all.

At which point, Smythe proposed marriage to the school manager.

'You're such a fuck artist,' the school manager said.

*

At the end of all this, I felt too fuzzy to summon up the energy for France. But I did get to Germany, to Berlin. That's because someone else took the initiative, and it sounded mad. Balham called from Berlin asking my advice. He was in Berlin and he wanted to know what I remembered of the city because he had to do business with the natives. I reminded the fraud that the last time I was in Berlin was when we were there together after the Wall had come down. *My* Germany was Köln, where I'd done the language school circuit, and that was twenty years ago. But he reminded me that for men of our provenance, one German city was much like another.

Was he really in Berlin?

He had come to follow up some business opportunities. Did I remember 1990?

1990 was great. What with Inge and…

Frau Halterbush. Halterbush had cleaned up. Was a multimillionaire. Was running for Parliament. He might even marry her.

So what was Berlin like?

Oh, crazy. Building, building, a city of cranes, money everywhere, naked and shameless. I wouldn't recognise it from 1990. And there was a killing to be made in the arts. The city had gone on an arts spree. Including Black arts. The guilt-trip thing. This was the time to shame the Germans into coughing up more. Surely, a man would rather be doing this than mucking about in a place where the natives could no longer make their own knives and forks.

Sounds good, I said.
So, would I come?
Why not?

*

I wouldn't go to Germany, of course, but I had to find a way of
not letting Balham have Berlin to himself. So I had a think while
I tidied up. Tidying up I left notes to myself about things to do
about the MA West Indian Literature option when I got back. An
idea for a Caribbean Resource Centre; that's really the framework
that would save an Anglophone course from being ghettoised.
Acquisitions of magazines and journals in all the Caribbean
languages. Audio material; tape deck in the library; collection of
loose stuff. Manifestos (art, literary, political, religious): conference papers; interviews with writers & artists. Start of a contemporary MS collection. Stuff on Cuba. Harlem. Exchange with other
institutions. New staff. *The school would love this*.

Maybe I was wrong about Dave; he'd altered quite a few of my
marks; the movement was generally up, only one was brought
down, though there was never more than a three mark gap between
us, but a couple were important because they threatened to change
class, one of whom was Natalie: she was one of two who had gone
up to 2.i. Natalie to 61. The other 60 I could confirm without
rereading. Natalie, I would have to look at again (What are you
wearing!). Maybe Dave was just clever, to be able to mark work at
this speed: if you could work at this speed and be accurate, why
weren't you in another city making millions or in Columbia or
wherever, doing the drugs thing?
   I wasn't going to be oppressed or beleaguered. I was OK. Even
though I wasn't going to France.

*

Berlin would be better than Spéracèdes, without a partner,
obsessed with what might have been. I wouldn't have to succumb
again to the depression brought on by that man's book – *A Year in*

Provence ← which made it impossible for the rest of us, who had known the region for years, to renovate our ruins and write about it. It was bad enough to have got to France *after* Hemingway and Fitzgerald and that lot; but to be *post* Peter Mayle was ridiculous. Now, my own copious notes on building with the *Cooperative* will never see the light of day: unlike Carrington, no one has collected *my* archives.

And yes, there was a little voice asking: *what's the ruin for*? A ruin in Spéracèdes was something to be shared; it was to be our private gesture to all those people whose houses we'd built or ⌐restored in the '70s – German bankers, American industrialists, the lot. I was, don't you see, using their properties to hone my skills for ours.

The ruin could have been rescued; Lee and the boys, now. Lee wasn't madly keen on France, but yet...Lee had no faith in our future, which was more to the point. So what was it for? Why not a flat in Finchley? Or Crouch End. Or Sheffield. Spéracèdes wasn't a place to retire to, your life over; it's to be enjoyed at a time when you and your friends are young and vigorous and riding motorbikes into the pool with Passolini flying over from Italy to film it; the women walking round topless wouldn't feel the need to go down to the beach, to Cannes, to slum it with the film festival lot. None of which fits my ruin. It stands down there like an awkward statement. A symbol. A ruin in Spéracèdes; a ruin in St Caesare. Two ruins. But at least St Caesare had once been a family home. With Spéracèdes, it's the wrong way round. No, it was good to miss out on all that, and head for Berlin.

So hard to lie to yourself because even here, even now I can hear Lee asking: Now what's the real reason? And I would deny that there was a real reason; and in the end I would admit a reason, which Lee would accept as real, because it was the last volunteered. And, yes, I had hoped to take my mother to the house in France.

Once, before going off on my travels, I had popped in, as usual, to the house in Upton Park for our little chat. I was sitting in her room upstairs on the easy chair; she on the bed, the television on, blinking, the sound turned down. And we played our usual game of friendly banter, she chiding me for not liking cakes with fruit in, me thanking her for saving me some of the plain cake that Florence had made: it was then that she dryly remarked that she hadn't had a holiday in thirty years. I actually stopped in mid-chew.

My first impulse had been to deny it, not because it wasn't true, but because it had seemed such an odd thing to say; it seemed so much the sentiment of someone at the far edge of privation, the sort of thing that, in another context, would make you want to protest, to rush out and defend the victim. And yet it wasn't like that (had she been *working* these thirty years? An ungenerous thought). It was true, yes, that she hadn't been back home to St Caesare (to West Indies), but that was largely of her doing; she had never, to my knowledge, expressed a wish to go back to see what things were like. It was true that she hadn't left the country, hadn't left London, even, in these years: would a view of Manchester, of Milan have eased the sense of... being in the wrong place? Or being constrained? The English took their sorrows to the seaside, to Blackpool, to Benidorm: these were, we like to think, the small dreams rejected by the family. Some of our own people from the Caribbean went back to show off – new clothes, new accents, foreign partners – their new status: we, having spent decades recouping our original position, getting back to where we had been when we left, felt we had to prove more before going back. It seemed so obvious we didn't discuss it openly: you took it for granted that this was why 'Miss Christine', 'Mother Stapleton', 'Princess of Coderington Hill', had never expressed a wish to go back. That's what I was thinking as I praised the non-currant cake.

I was on her territory, in her room. I had learnt, over the years, that coming here was to submit myself to a process of cross-examination, however gentle, at the end of which I would plead guilty before leaving. She had observed, earlier, *apropros* a news item on television, that the Governor of Hong Kong was only three years older than I was, and had children old enough to be at university. This was an old charge from a new angle. I had apologised, routinely, for the children. I apologised, more feelingly, for not having got myself 'with all my advantages'; at my age – nearly 50 – installed as Governor of Hong Kong, and thus restoring to the Mother of the Governor, a role commensurate with her inner status – that of keeping an eye on the morality and hygiene of the colony, and spending her afternoons, in summer-dresses, opening new supermarkets and banks. This had amused her enough to call me ignorant. Maybe this would be regarded as a large enough input by me so that I wouldn't have to read to her – not from the Bible (I now know why) but from one of her religious tracts, before leaving.

But still, in these meetings, I had to account for lost time, obscurely, to demonstrate competence; to show that my store of knowledge – though wasted – was nevertheless secure: one was expected to outguess people on TV quiz programmes, people 'who don't have your education'. I sometimes tried to send it up by reciting random facts – anything I happened to be browsing through for a *Talk*, or whatever, like a list of rivers and towns in Yugoslavia, or African writers or politicians that other people couldn't pronounce. This would bring forth a dubious look, which made her girlish, and a reprimand for talking nonsense. I could then get away to Finchley, or wherever, on the grounds that travel in London at night was dangerous, and leave the letter-writing and other chores – she suffered from rheumatism or arthritis in her fingers – to the niece.

And I *had* thought, over the years, of taking her abroad, somewhere. Florence had come over to France, 'to improve her French' when I returned there briefly in the early '80s. I'd spent time, over the years, trying to pacify little patches of territory in this or that country. Friends had assisted in this pioneering work. When that had been achieved – so the theory went – then the 'family' would come, would come in style: a version of my mother, summery and gloved, cutting the ribbons to a Manhattan-style structure in Kowloon, declaring it open. But, yes, I saw myself picking her up at Nice Airport, one day, and driving off to summer in the Alpes Maritimes.

Sometimes – dredging up an old memory – I would call her La Contessa, even though that fraud da Firenze, had never completed those portraits of her. But he had promised to paint her in the 'Italian Style', so that was part of our reality. I didn't give it weight at the time but one of the images of her that da Firenze had wanted to capture was La Contessa on her horse. We had a big horse, Ruby, which was very docile, and La Contessa was

dressed up and put upon the horse for the portrait, because the
Queens of France and maybe of England were sometimes painted
sitting on a horse. And the horse would soon be given away,
anyway, and with the horse would go the 'groom', and all those
parts of the house that we couldn't take with us to England; so,
at the very least, this portrait would be part of the record of the
house. So here was La Contessa on her horse. She was got up
there not without difficulty (she couldn't ride). Ruby stood high,
even against the front steps, and La Contessa's dress (gown?) was
freshly ironed. The groom and the painter had to be careful where
they put their hands as they lifted her on. Eventually, she was in
the saddle and Ruby, not knowing what this was all about, took
a leisurely step forward, then another... and a third: was the
portrait laughing? My mother's screams seemed so out of proportion to the danger that for a moment no one knew what to do. In
the end she was hustled down, somewhat indelicately. My
punishment, I remember, was to have witnessed this. She had
regarded such unseemly behaviour on horseback as an acknowledgement of sexuality, a display, in public, of a wanton nature.
(An Australian cricketer, and Lee's probing, made me more
curious about these incidents.)

I was in her room, some time later – on much the same sort of
errand – and we were watching the television: it didn't matter that
the sound wasn't on, it was cricket, a game she didn't understand.
I didn't, of course, bring up the business of holidays, but it had
been on my mind: I realised the crudity of somehow defining
holiday as in some sense the reverse of *work*; holiday as a reward
for *work*, or as a relief from *work*; and of course, we still had the
conventional notion of work as paid employment, and therefore
little to do with what La Contessa did. Though – this too was true
– holidays at first had to be deferred, even by those who had
'earned' them in a conventional way, those who had endured the
attritions of the workplace, an environment which, if not always
hostile, was demeaning. It was there where people pretended not
to understand your accent, where they expected your face to be
stretched into a permanent smile, etc. And then, some of these
workers had spurned the holiday and had decided instead to cede
that privilege to young nieces and nephews who needed to learn

something of a world outside the one into which they had, accidentally, been born.

So we were watching this cricket match. It was early summer. Not warm. The understanding, unstated, was that we'd watch the cricket until it was time for her Australian soap opera, and then switch channels. Though I was preparing to leave before then. But it seemed mildly appropriate, preparing to turn from one Australian *play* to another. At that moment a bowler, Australian, whose modern haircut had already puzzled La Contessa, now deprived himself of the benefit of her doubt. Walking back to his mark, facing us in close-up, this big man with the strange hairstyle brought the shiny, red ball to his lips, looked at it, and then licked it, copiously. Even I couldn't defend him after that. I had to agree that he was 'nasty', and volunteered for good measure – to steer the conversation to safer territory – that poisonous chemicals had been sprayed on the ground in its preparation. But this didn't work. The image that stuck was of a man so uncontrollable in his sexuality, so lascivious, that he couldn't resist licking the red ball in public: La Contessa warned me about visiting so dangerous a country, in my travels.

No wonder, said Lee sympathetically, that she had to hide her real reading-matter between brown paper covers.

It was good that the stars also had their difficulty. Carrington had lost the battle at the university over the naming of his magazine, which was eventually called *Writing Ulster*. His colleagues had rejected *Michael Holding* and also fun titles like *Page Four* and *Caesar's Wife* – and even compromises like *Gestation Period*. True, he had worked up a very good Hesseltine Michael sketch for *Week Ending* – a joke based on Little Richard's becoming Prime Minister of Britain and opening Prime Minister's Question Time each week with Awopbobaloopopalopbamboom. Apart from anything else, Hesseltine Michael was much funnier than Richard Little. But he didn't have it all his own way; the National Theatre insisted on putting on Shakespeare's *King Lear* at the Barbican rather than Carrington's. And our man was forced to deny being in the middle of writing a controversial play set in Northern Ireland.

10

It's the diminishing returns thing: clearing your desk and stopping in the middle, not remembering why you're doing this. There was a time when to drop everything and to set out, to go off, gave instant value to what was left behind. And, in the same way, propelled you forward. Even if it was just to prove that not having the money wouldn't deny you the right to travel. That's how we saw Europe, Lindsay and I. We took the train, yes, and the coach, the ferry; but we hitched – from Paris to Spéracèdes; from Stockholm to Oslo, North to Lillihammur, a place that was in the news about a year ago courtesy of the Winter Olympics: and Lindsay had rung from Boston to ask if I remembered our going to Lillihammur. I remembered going to Lillihammur, being offered a lift there by a man who didn't speak English or French, and him offering us a bed for the night, in a barn; and our deciding that the open road was safer, and continuing to hitch after dark, with all our luggage, rather than be murdered in the night, some place far from Shepherds Bush, from Holland Park. And we gave a lecture at a school in Lillihammur and read some poems, and had enough money for pizza back in Oslo. Packing, in Manchester, in the late '70s for Köln: there was a point to that, a sense of living in two places, *working* in two places; teaching our version of English in two places, writing naturalistic sketches about those places then changing the scene, one for the other, our surrealist phase, impressing one critic enough to call us 'ironists'. So I tore up my ticket for France, not minding the waste. It wasn't refundable, anyway.

I tore up my ticket in the sense of putting it in a drawer, the bottom drawer where unmountable plays are supposed to lodge. Like burning £130. Lee sent £8.00 a month to a family in, I forget where, somewhere like Indonesia or Nepal in support of a granny. I remember the picture of the granny, the recipient, which had appeared in *The Guardian* (the paper). Another thing we were supposed to do together, but Lee had continued with it. (£130 for the granny? That granny is probably dead, so it would be another granny: and then after that another granny. Even if it's gone up to £10 now that's still a lot of granny. I couldn't leave a note to myself to ask Lee about the granny. But that didn't stop me imagining what £130, given away to British Airways, would buy a granny.

Are there allies out there in the world – in unsuspecting Bolton? Sorry Bolton. I'm the External at the Institute there, their creative writing course and three packets of stuff have just been delivered which won't fit into my pigeon hole. That won't prevent me going *away*. Other people's marking is never as traumatic as yours. Having sorted out your own you can treat the other place with a sort of benign neglect. I'll deal with them after Germany. Maybe I'll go down to Kent instead. Kent were giving me trouble over Carrington's typescripts; they weren't prepared to photocopy them, of course, so I would have to go down, spend a couple of days: I had friends in the department, though. Kent is so understated, don't you think? Spend a few days there, claiming the benefit of not being in France. Or Berlin.

What emerged during the week were odd characters that I would have written for the group novel that Lee and I might have edited. I would call this one *Mad Horace*, or... *Why Not? The Years When I Wasn't in Portugal*. Or *Uncles & Aunts Partoutes*. If I couldn't be at home keeping the partner happy and setting an example to the children, I might as well acknowledge my wandering tendency: Wandering Jew. Vagrant. Refugee. Like all the errant uncles of history. I may not have worked on the Panama Canal, like Great-uncle George, who then went on to Cuba and *just* missed winning the *bourlette*; I may not have found myself, to paraphrase the poet, at the hot gates, fighting in warm rain, knee deep in salt marsh, heaving my cutlass, bitten by flies. (Where in God's name was he, our hero?) But...

But in my Chapter, I would be the travelled Uncle Horace who missed being mentioned in the dispatches, who, through malice, has been airbrushed out of the photographs. *And now Uncle Horace is himself again...*

*

One day a book came through the post from Lee (she'd already sent me the new book of translations, which was glorious, glorious). But this little green-covered book with illustrations; woodcuts balancing the text, really suggested all those things about love that Smythe's Renaultsonnet had failed to capture; one of those lovely books that you had to fondle and sniff, the sort that reminds you of the sensory privations that accompany the computer screen, the web. The colour of the book was green, like Lee's politics. It was a treat, unexpected, and I sat down to read: *The Man Who Planted Trees*, by Jean Giono.

*

Berlin. January 1990.

THE YEARS WHEN I WASN'T IN PORTUGAL
(a novel by several hands, 'edited' by Pewter Stapleton)
Chapter One: The Uncle

I'm walking down Otto-Grotewohl-Strasse in the fading light. I'm going again in the direction of the station but I'm not going towards the station, particularly: Köln's my patch, not Berlin, East Berlin. I'm trying not to look at the blocks of flats, sorry to see them as ugly as visiting journalists had always claimed them to be. On my one brief visit to East Berlin, what, ten years ago – it was only for a weekend – I wasn't shown all this, the famous workers' flats: the attempt at colour, blue bordering, patches of blue tile – tiles? Yes, they're falling off – making a bad thing worse. Anyway, the people are housed, not sleeping under bridges as in London. Do these flats really lack heat, water? People in the street look fairly relaxed, altogether more normal than on the other side; smaller, less-bloated: they're wheeling babies in prams, the young couples. Clearly, they think it worthwhile having babies. The old don't seem to fare too well. Maybe they're just being honest. Ah, well... I'm wandering down the street, dwarfed, everything so large, so few people, so little traffic: *where's the revolution, for Christ sake, this is 1990!* I'm walking away from the restaurant to give Balham and the lady from the Pergamum space to do their business.

I've already made a fool of myself by calling her Frau Halterbush – my own joke from an earlier age. Balham had hinted that we were going to meet Frau Halterbush from the Pergamum Museum, in the East. But the woman he brought to the restaurant was called something else, Inge, who, it turned out, wasn't from the Museum but a tourist guide, a friend of Frau

Halterbush's who was too busy to see Balham. I didn't know what to think
of the Pergamum Museum. I'd visited it briefly, on that tour back then,
in the '70s. Monumental, was what came to mind, the towering Greek and
Roman temples, etc. But somehow, in recent years, the image had become
corrupted in my mind with similarly-named Robert Maxwell publishing
enterprise, the string of ludicrous biographies compiled to his heroes in
the East: Honecker, General Jaruzelski, Ceausescu and that crowd;
Brezhnev. So when Balham said that the revolution had spread to the
Pergamum and that Frau Halterbush had come out on top and planned
to put on an exhibition of Black Arts to teach the racists in her department
a lesson, I was inclined to give it credence.

Balham had come on ahead of me. We weren't really travelling
together; my destination was France, the South, but I was also curious
about Berlin, and Balham seemed to have contacts there. I was considered
an expert in Black Arts now and it seemed ungracious to spurn Balham's
offer of a trip, his determination to play host. Though, of course, I was
paying my own way. Anyway, I let him book me into his hotel, the Plaza
(I was on the 5th floor, he was on the 3rd, we weren't together). We'd met
last night and, decided more or less not to travel together. Although this
wasn't my part of Germany, I had to show Balham that I could get by in
Germany. He had spent most of today in the East and I, to be honest,
wanted to take a look at the Western side of the wall which, for some reason
that I forget now, I'd managed not to have seen on my previous brief visit.
So we had agreed to meet at the restaurant in the evening, on Balham's
patch – the East – just a few yards from Checkpoint Charlie, the
Vietnamese restaurant all the world knew of, because of its location.

Inge, I have to admit, proved a bit of a disappointment. I was expecting
Frau Halterbush. I had images of Frau Halterbush, as her name implies,
formidable in size and confidence, having shouldered her way to the top.
(I remembered those German women back in Köln in the '70s, fighting
their way on and off the trams: if there was no room to swing shoulders
and umbrellas, breasts would be brought into play, like reinforced pillows,
to cushion all resistance. Also, Halterbush was the name of a formidable
cleaner at the language school where I once taught, in the Hohestrasse.)
So I saw Balham's Frau Halterbush sweeping aside the Assyrian fossils at
the Pergamum to make way for vital black images from Shepherds Bush
and Manchester's Moss Side and Whalley Range. And to demonstrate the
extent of her victory, she would cross Berlin to go to the Vietnamese

restaurant in sight of what was still called Checkpoint Charlie, to dine with a black man in a track suit. (Balham wore his track suit in East Berlin – the track suit was in ANC colours; in the West I should imagine he'd wear his smart blazer. That's what he had on last night, anyway, at the hotel.) Tonight, Frau Halterbush would be dining with not one, but two black men – to prove the triumph of the revolution.

But Inge was different. She was tired and seemed a bit distant. Of the present situation she thought, yes, things were going this way, and then again they were going that way. Sometimes too much this way, sometimes...? But it was good the people were still showing spirit. She, for one, was tired. The people down in Leipzig seemed not to get tired. That was a little frightening, too. She didn't quite sigh when she said: it will all turn into hamburgers and going to shop on Bismarckstrasse. Some even want to go to London to shop at the Harrods. Then, to humour us, I think (this was a child, a woman of the revolution), she said crisply: 'It's very confusing.' Balham failed to pick up her tone, and his easy scorn for 'American' hamburgers and shopping at 'The Harrods', brought a tight little smile to Inge's lips. I felt our man was being had.

But Inge was all right. Mid-30s, slim, neat, altogether more manageable than Frau Halterbush; she never quite dropped her guard, except when she said something about Honecker pollution making Germany dirty. She loved her place, she wasn't going West, like the rest of them; but she was confused about why the whole world seemed to be getting excited about their struggle, which was, in reality, quite a small thing. Maybe it wasn't small, but they were a small country. (She used the DDR & Germany interchangeably.) Her English was excellent, so you had a suspicion that by saying DDR rather than the more usual GDR, she was somehow preventing some aspect of her Germanness being translated. Or maybe I was just on the wrong track. The presence of Balham had made me ultra-sensitive.

But it was clear that Inge wasn't interested in an exhibition of Black Art at the Pergamum; or in the aspects of the revolution that excited Balham and, yes, myself. For when I asked her, stupidly, whether it wasn't, nevertheless, 'exciting' living through it all, her 'of course', came with a little shrug, a knowingness. Then: 'I do not go to sit on the Wall.' She continued guardedly. 'So maybe you go there, and it is exciting. It's still November 9 [this was January 1990] and everyone is celebrating.' That's when I excused myself and left them to discuss their business. I was in the way. Earlier, Inge had taken a couple of small, white tablets, with a couple of mouthfuls of water. And I couldn't prevent myself, sitting there, seeing behind that small, commonplace gesture, something to interpret, something which had to do with East German people, dentists, gynaecologists, whatever, trying to get on with their work, as best they could, in the circumstances. I silently apologised to Inge as I left.

Balham had accompanied me to the Wall that afternoon, as an act of indulgence. For Checkpoint Charlie was the tourist's crossing point, and he preferred to take other routes. To upstage him I admitted to being a tourist. We took a bus from the bottom of the road from the Plaza – opposite the post office, the young woman at the desk had given directions – which went to the Brandenburg Gate. The walk to the Gate itself through woods, in the wet – a straggly army of tourists churning up the mud – put me in mind of those old black and white films about World War II. And when we joined people queuing up to cross over to the East, this reinforced the Pathe Newsreel quality further.

The first thing that struck you at the Wall was the noise. All the banging and chipping; and yes, they were using coal chisels and hammers, and crowbars and sledgehammers; and there was one man with a pneumatic drill, though I couldn't see for the life of me how it was powered. The soldiers 'guarding it,' dressed in slack-green, as if their shapes were affected, drifted round as if they'd lost a war, trying to mind their own business, if only they could detect what that was, going through the motions to keep warm, on this strangely cold day. All along the Western side, people, some with stalls, more just with little squares of cloth on the ground, were selling bits of Wall for DM 1.50 and upwards. It was the graffiti that was valued; no one was buying bits of prestressed stone without daubs of paint on them. The hamburger and hotdog stands, the wurst stalls, were doing brisk business, too, and we both felt a little superior in not being tempted by this vision of what would unite the two worlds.

What raised my spirits was the fact that after queuing for twenty minutes, we discovered that only Germans were allowed to cross at the Brandenburg Gate, and that we'd have to walk down to Checkpoint Charlie – twenty minutes away – to get our visa. Now, how did this, almost Berliner, Herr Balham, not know something so basic? Later, when I tackled him – savouring not taking it up immediately – he said he knew lots of ways of crossing into the East without help of the Americans; he wasn't, after all, a Le Carré spy. For his meeting at Humboldt University later today, he wouldn't need the help of these rascals: and did I know that both Marx and Engels had studied at the Humboldt?

The wall-beetles were strung out along the whole length of Honecker's monument. They put me in mind of a Jan Carew story about Guyanese pork-knockers, early explorers in the interior, reducing whole mountains to rubble, in their quest for gold. Here, at the Wall, they'd gone right through to the other side in many places, with people peeping through as if into a mysterious garden. Iron reinforcements were hanging in the air which made the thing unsafe, and soldiers had put up barriers, iron trellises; but everyone ignored them, simply walking between them and the Wall. Most of the monument, the bottom 6 to 8 feet which could be reached from the ground, had been skinned, the outer surface of graffiti gone; and although the more adventurous beetles clambered to the top, still with its pre-revolution virtue, ignoring and ignored by the soldiers, the workers down below were using aerosol cans to repaint their capitalist and racist slogans, before chipping.

It's gratifying that thoughts that come to you at a time like this are not *solely* to do with aesthetics: there are the problems of falsifying history. Even the most greedy must give a momentary thought to what to spray on the booty, that sort of thing. The top strip of Wall was like a '60s cartoon. (It put me in mind of those dark, cavernous, crazy-angled passages and corridors down at the Free University (CIA Re-education Center?) at Dahlem-Dorf, where a friend of ours used to teach.) Every possible combination of letters, of symbol, assaulted you, in colour. Some we could understand. There were cries of freedom jostling anti-Russian, anti-Polish, anti-Jewish, anti-Black propaganda. But most needed an army of PhD students to decipher: what did FMO '89 mean? English-speakers were ill-served. 'HI FUCKING WALL', or 'HELLO SWEETIES NORBERT' made you feel you could do better. I don't recall being driven to daub slogans on walls before: could I be provoked into it? Here, at the Wall, the world was to be made aware of RAY THOMAS, AUSTRALIA, 23.9.85 (or was it 88?). Does it matter to anyone, to Ray Thomas, even, if we got the date wrong? What if the fellow had died in '86, and we have him down here (and tourists taking pictures of his bit of Wall) as writing his name in '88? Is that more than a sub-aesthetic conceit? A friend, of course, could have written Ray Thomas' name, which wouldn't make it false. Anyway, there it was; the '86 or '88 needn't be turned into a problem.

It was cold, drizzling; and if it wasn't too demeaning (or if Balham wasn't with me, which, in this case, amounted to the same thing) I might have succumbed to a warm wurst to sustain me through the mud to Checkpoint Charlie. The guards at the Gate had said it was a twenty-minute walk. We had already been walking for more than twenty minutes and still we weren't there: was this another way of pulling rank? – *We Germans can do it in twenty minutes, sort of thing: you foreigners need three hours, Ja!* Sometimes travel does, indeed, coarsen the mind. Balham accompanied me to Checkpoint Charlie, saw me to the queue, and then swung back; he had an appointment. He had impressed on me the need to get in there now, before the revolution became middle-aged – he gave it three months – and reverted to type with hamburgers and Woolworths and exclusion zones against tinkers and black people. And I promised, without fail, to open the first West Indian-run language school on Unter den Linden.

*

I really had to do some marking for Bolton; Bolton was a new university, so new it wouldn't even be a university till next year (I really must stop thinking of UEA and Sussex and that lot as new universities, they've had thirty-odd years at it; we can't go on endlessly asking if they will make it. I must go down to Kent, another new-old, old-new institution, dear God; I had to start answering the phone (I might even reconnect the ansaphone). And it's true, with no one knowing you're around you can really get on with things. For reasons best known to myself I phoned Bolton and volunteered to attend the Exam Board. Maybe I just wanted to stop off in Manchester and buy some books.

*

Just now she asked, an unsuspecting partner on the phone asks, what I am thinking. Well now, what *am* I thinking? I'm thinking about you, my love – and wondering, also, if there are elections coming up in Burkina Faso. What am I thinking? I'm thinking about you and me, about me and my place at City, my place in the world, my time in the world – in relation to what? To Sylvia Plath, to the island of Mauritius. Plath I'll leave to the iconists but Mauritius I'll visit. Mauritius as an offshore Caribbean island forcing us to reclaim all the land (and sea) in-between (for I'm a man you know, more travelled than Columbus, the Italian). But that's not what I'm thinking, was thinking; that's cheating.

I'm thinking of the Soyinka play, of his getting away with a title like *The Beatification of Area Boy* (he deserved the Nobel for that sort of risk); I'm thinking Fukuyama and the end of history: would love to meet the man and say: *Hi Fuku*. Puts me in mind of that meeting between De Gaulle and Galbraith who was Kennedy's Ambassador to India at the time, two seriously tall men, at Kennedy's funeral in 1963. There's a crowd of people at the reception and De Gaulle, somewhat at a loss and near-sighted, is standing at the end of the room bemused that everyone seems to be talking English. He sees Galbraith at the other end of the room talking to the Emperor Haile Selassie, who is a very short man. De Gaulle strides across the room to Galbraith, nods to Haile Selassie, and says to Galbraith in French: *why are you talking to such a short man?* (Is there a play there?)

I'm thinking Aung San Suu Kyi and I'm thinking of a scene in Tuscany where my mother, dressed in 14th century costume, is looking down from a balcony on the Piazza Signoria while a game of Florentine football is in progress. There is jousting before the game (which will be a match between the blues and the greens) and Balham and I are doing our thing with the lances. On horseback, of course. In the course of this, before Balham or I hit the sand, a line of verse 'The sharks, not knowing about cliché, fin our beach,' comes to me, and I think of a career change and slim volumes.

I'm thinking Lee and the singing voice of Louis Armstrong and Rumi the poet (must read the *Masnavi*), and green days at UEA and my book, *The Concept of Plain Dealing in Restoration Comedy with Special Reference to Wycherley* awaiting a publisher since 1966 and that job at Warwick going to someone else, and that scene in the Shadwell play – was it Shadwell? – where the main character, a man, is learning to swim, and he rigs up a swimming contraption in his study or somewhere – and tries to swim without benefit of water, and I think it would be worth staging it at the *Keskadee* just for the pleasure of hearing someone in the audience say: *What foolishness he doin'; man pretendin' he swimmin' out a de water*. I'm thinking I must tell my students about Jean Giono's book, sent to me by Lee, but now I'm lying again, so I'd better stop.

*

I'm thinking of Lee's extraordinary book of translations which I've just been reading; and of course, they're not translations but wonderfully inventive, modest, rhythmically assured original poems which manage to hint at other, older poems behind them, which deflect attention from themselves and affirm a tradition of loving and living far back in time. This puts my little hysterical need to assert, to appropriate, in some sort of perspective. How pathetic, to be competing with Balham. How crude to be tempted by his good luck in the new Germany. When I reclaim my bit of Germany, of Berlin, I will relegate Balham to his rightful place, as I remember it.

*

You're impressed by the efficiency and dedication at these institutions and yet, on the train back from Bolton, via Manchester, you can't banish a fantasy: if you were a scholar you weren't meant for this. You should be travelling, as at some earlier time, to those centres of learning that the world knows about. From somewhere to Alexandria. (Athens was too clichéic.) When I got back to Sheffield (Bolton accomplished), I went to the library and looked up some famous names:

Padua, University of, Italian UNIVERSITA DEGLI STUDI DI PADOVA, autonomous co-educational state institution of higher learning in Padua, Italy. The university was founded in 1222 by a secession of about a thousand students from the University of Bologna, by additional migrations from Bologna in 1306 and 1322. Like Bologna, it was a student-controlled university, with students electing the professors and fixing their salaries. In 1228 a number of students seceded from Padua to Vercelli, but the university survived the secession and the vicissitudes of local despotism to achieve its greatest distinction in the 16th and 17th centuries, becoming one of the two or three leading universities of Europe. Among its professors were famous philosophers, humanists and scientists, including Galileo.

At first mainly a school of civil and canon law, the university was originally organised into four national groups, and in 1260 the four were merged into two, transalpine and cisalpine. A separate university for arts and medicine developed in the 14th century, divorcing itself completely from the law university. In 1517 the Venetian republic created a magistracy of three "Reformers of the Studium" who gradually took over the governance of the university from the students, until in 1815 it was under the rule of a single "magnificent rector." The university's botanical garden founded in 1545, is the oldest in Europe. Its astronomical observatory was founded in 1761. Modern faculties include law, political science, arts and literature, philosophy, education, mathematics, physics and natural sciences, economics and commerce, statistics, pharmacy, agriculture, engineering, and medicine. The Geologic Institute contains a geological museum.

Ah, well, can't have everything at City. Though I couldn't help thinking that it was my niece who should be doing this sort of academic labour; she was the one named, as the Americans say, for the Italian. But maybe she left this type of foolishness to me, to uncles – the sort of people who consort with Balhams, the sort of people who, instead of getting on with their life, were measuring out their living in Sheffields and Boltons, marking time.

I did try, in my reclusive week, to write a poem, to pick up on Smythe's idea of a sonnet to the lady with car, or to the lady who was a car; but it was impossible. It was either impossible or it was too easy. All I ended up doing was writing out a lot of lines, the sort of stuff you see published in the poetry magazines, and that was too humiliating; but something formal, something that had a shape, a rhyme-scheme, the right stresses – that was the sort of thing that came, I suppose, from a lifetime's dedication, like with the ballet, or playing the violin. It amazed me that people who produced the stuff you saw published in the poetry magazines were prepared to put their names to it. Ah well.

Still demob-happy, eschewing Berlin, I went to a party at Rolls'. Though some of the light-headedness that signalled the end of marking had passed, there were still things to do, a few scripts to moderate, and the attrition of Exam Boards to come. Also, the MA marking, of which I was only a Second Marker, was still to come. But we had broken the back of the beast and even those in the Department who weren't particularly imaginative had vague notions of the shape and dimensions of the monster that had been seen off. For some it was a sea creature, prehistoric, communicating by sonar, for some it was winged and literary, for others, Stephen Kingish. But we all had a sense of evolutionary rightness, having defeated the monster.

And we always looked forward to a civilised evening at Rolls, not just that you ate and drank well there, but Liz, his wife, successful short story writer and unapologetic Canadian, maintained her independence by refusing to be press-ganged into teaching on the MA Writing course: she thought to lose one member of the family to City was enough. She was growing ever more successful in making Rolls into a credible Canadian; already his pronunciation was hinting at open spaces west of Ontario.

Subjects outlawed chez Rolls were Sheffield City University and all its doings, more specifically, our reduced living space, our rumoured move from Collegegate Campus to some factory site in the middle of town, the burning of student scripts, old-Halterbush's sense of dress, the projected sharing of office space, the turning of academic staff into bureaucrats, the anti-browsing rule in the library, the laying waste of our public spaces, like the drama studio, the threat to our extracurricular budget, the squeezing of our named degrees by offering students more choice (you, too, may swap 19c poetry for elementary German and get an English degree), the reluctance to purchase contemporary manuscripts for the library, etc. Anyone initiating conversation along these lines would be denied wine and forced to read something from one of Smythe's two books of poems. (Smythe was doing a gig that night and would be very early or very late.)

Football: *Euro 96* enabled us to display our knowledge of foreign names, and there was a feeling that neither England nor Scotland should win. And then there was a question of whether a new news magazine *INNER PIGS EYE* was fascist or green: yes, it was a sort of local *PRIVATE EYE*, hence *fascist*. No, they stocked it at the local whole-food shop. So green. But there was a poem by Smythe in it, hence fascist. Ah, the picture of the man on the first page in fascist regalia was maybe a send-up, but the Smythe poem clinched it. Fascist.

I looked round the table and wondered how many of these people had been abused in childhood, and imagined their ways of disguising it: I half-wished, in a way, that I was a poet, licensed to record these things quickly rather than to have to create a whole world on stage. But then there were always stories and... but this was indulgent. I raised the question of cricket; we had India and Pakistan coming over this summer. India were less interesting, despite Tendulker, thought by some to be the best batsman in the world; the excitement was going to be with Pakistan: I hoped that Pakistan's expected victory over England would encourage the less fascist of the population to give their children names like Waqar and Inzaman and Ijaz. (Was it a bit of racism that made good protestants in England who supported the UN neglect to call their sons Boutros Boutros after the UN Secretary General!) People thought we might legislate for the Windsor and other leading families and members of the Cabinet to call their children – whether sons or daughters – Waqar, Inzaman, Ijaz and Boutros if they were going to be taken seriously. Shadab Moin Hesseltine seemed vaguely credible. Someone told a Michael Portillo joke, pronouncing the name in the Spanish way, and we were all satisfied to be racist in this particular (and peculiar) case. Now, talking of Canada...

But there was the usual dinner party bore, the partner of one of the Katies or Fionnas, who was researching something at the other university, fish, and pulling rank. As we were having nibbles he proceeded to pontificate about a worm that grew in cod; it was harmless, of course, but unaesthetic, and occasionally it came to life when you unfroze the fish and put quite a few housewives off their dinner. The question: should the public be warned to expect, occasionally, something wriggly but harmless when they unfroze their cod?

If the worm was harmless was his job scientific or aesthetic, part of the beauty industry? We were rescued when Smythe arrived, looking like a poet, wearing a cape; and proceeded to read us a *kenning*. And another. And then a prose *Edda*.

We were indoors, but looked out on the beautiful courtyard, perfect for summer barbecues; but still pleasant looking out on it. Smythe read his kennings (He called them epic love poems) and then dismissed them as being derivative, and to me, as if I were in on the joke, he mentioned 'The Thorkslls'. This was a reference to a 'kenning' story by my man, T. Coraghessan Boyle, the BOYLE of my computer PASSWORD, the American 'epic realist'. We didn't explain the joke. Then, with a couple of quick drinks Smythe had to take himself off to his gig.

The feeling was that Smythe was being Smythe, saved from being a sad figure because of the affectation, because he was partially in on the joke. OK, said someone, so Smythe had read up a bit on skaldic verse, but did he really know his *kenning* from his *Edda*? The Daves and Julies surprised me by the range of their interest: *I* didn't know about this stuff. So I was slightly relieved when the conversation switched to condoms.

Apparently, Dave (Steve) had been in the chemist's earlier in
the week, in Boots, and at the till stood next to a man, a really old
guy, who was buying a pack of twelve condoms. *Twelve*! So how old
was this old man? Initially, the old man was, maybe seventy, but
by the time we returned to the story later in the meal, he was well
into his nineties. Someone at table (I was later to think of her as
the Germaine Greer woman) thought a man in his nineties with an
eight-pack of condoms was likely to do less harm to women than
a younger man who would be travelling without condoms, so they
wished him the best of luck. (The men thought the ninety-year-
old man would be better advised to do an Open University course
in something like the archaeology of the female form instead of
buying condoms at Boots, and started speculating about which
department he would be likely to find himself teaching in at
City.)

For light relief I was indulged to ramble on about my ruin in
Spéracèdes: could we all go down to the South of France and re-
establish the English section there and say no to the move to the
middle of town in Sheffield. And we might even do a little building
between seminars.

Then there was the IT talk which you couldn't escape these
days. The Internet. Electronic Education – caught up somehow
with talk about the country's public spaces. I got drawn in to the
public squalor debate; the fact that we should be nostalgic for the
time when the public clocks had merely stopped; for now they were
being removed from the public squares. At least, before, you could
put your hand on your heart and say that the time in England was
right twice a day. And there were the parks: they might well be
cleaner than they were, but they were less safe. This was my cue
to tell a story of a couple of women I knew in London, one a
headmistress, the other not, who were determined to keep the
parks near their homes open at night, and would set out to walk
through the local park, sometimes without the dog, in the evenings,
to prevent no-go areas developing. Naturally, when we were
around we accompanied them, but that wasn't very often. Though
knowing that they were doing this, wherever we were in the world,
we had our sensors out; that, too, was a sort of 'net'. Then there was
the tube, the underground, as public space...

The mention of *net* reconnected us to the other conversation. Apparently, there was a university in the Highlands (I think they said it was called The University of the Highlands and Islands) where it was all done on the internet; best thing for a scattered population. Distance learning, and all that. Everything on the web. (This, strangely, put me in mind of my brother-in-law, Stewart, his cocooning.) Yes, but should *all* universities go this way? Pretending to be catering for little scattered groups! No organic life on campus? Everything on line. Teaching materials on line. Web sites. All that. Were we not disbanding, unbonding society? (And who pray, would be bonking whom in that department?)

But to return to open spaces. Clocks. Parks. The tube. It was Julie's theory: how about universities as open space? Not the Open University. Not the internet thing, but all universities, our university. Now that we were aiming to educate a third of the population to university level, universities will now be the public spaces that most people in the country would have visited, would have spent time in, that and the supermarkets; that and the supermarkets and *Spain*. They weren't the private oases of privilege they once were; and we, the teachers (and maybe the administrators) were custodians of these open spaces: we were the guards and bus-conductors and park-keepers of the nation out of the house. Or perhaps, if we preferred a different vocabulary, we were the curators of the national heritage. OK, we were the nurses of a Health Service deprived of doctors and other resources; but people thought my metaphor a bit poetic.

I was fascinated by the idea of university as public space, though I was yet to be convinced. I had the (old fashioned) notion that universities were special places, that they were different in tone from other places. Yes, perhaps they should be made, marginally, more efficient, *and they have been*, but the habit of managing and measuring and accounting by accountants had degraded the enterprise. You could not move from the position of a lecturer teaching eight hours a week – which was what it was when *we* were at university – to doing *fourteen* hours not just without loss of efficiency (who's measuring efficiency, and how?) not just without lowering of standards, but without serious damage to a tutor's health. (And what about the life, the partner, spending quality time with the family?

Even clapped-out politicians used that one to death.) We were all ill, *ill*; would that we knew it.

There were no accountants at dinner; they were, we supposed, accounting in their accounting houses elsewhere, but we knew their arguments: critical mass (classes of 150 or over); transferable skills (elementary word processing instead of Chaucer); scientific approach to the Humanities (teaching traditional verse by counting syllables and stress, never mind rhythm and sense); innovative course delivery (watching a play on video instead of rehearsing it in the studio). Oh, and there were other things like not hankering after leafy campuses, of not being neurotic about space, light, air, etc.

I was an elitist or exhibitionist in seeing the campus as an Olympic Stadium devoted to the games of intellect and imagination. Shouldn't we make a public apology to the nation for not having produced Booker and Nobel prizewinners at City? Though one of our MA writing novelists had won a national competition last year. And here, like a character in my play, I stamp my foot and say in a high-pitched voice: why can't we have real books and contemporary manuscripts (not just an expansion of the *net*), and be able to browse in the new library; to sniff the paper (the glue?) and to pursue our extra curricula activities of literary societies, literary magazines and literature festivals without having to define them in terms of improving students' grades!

When I got home I continued to develop the idea of university as public space, if nothing else to challenge my own prejudices: maybe I should even do it as a talk for Radio Three. Radio Four.

I know what made me uneasy about all this – a feeling I got with my colleagues: of being out of sync. They were professionals dedicated to making the thing work, because whatever the present situation, it was better than where *they* had been a generation ago, two generations ago. This posed a problem for me: there was a dead mother, grandmother demanding explanation for having let the team down. On the team were Grand-uncle Ned, Doctor (in Boston)... Next to him Grand-uncle Bird, Lawyer (New York) and you, Sir, Justice of the Peace, who came to England twice (in the days before *Empire Windrush*; for him 1948 would be but yesterday) and protested at its lawlessness. Come in Aunt Dulcie, recognition for playing your church organ at nine years old, or fourteen years old. And me, in line, just back from Padua. Come in, Grandmother, with your house in Coderington, organising the planting, the harvesting, the grinding of the cassava, the weighing of the cotton, the animals to be impounded in the animal pound; the baking of bread and cakes at weekends, the Sunday roast, the drawing-room visitors after church; the stories of the family outdoing Anancy. Proud? My problem was I wasn't proud enough.

*

One night I dreamt I'd put my name forward, or allowed my name to be put forward for the UN. I must have read somewhere that Boutros Boutros Ghali was retiring. And it was one of those things. You were embarrassed if the news got out in case they thought you ill-qualified. I should imagine this is how American presidential hopefuls feel, when the possibility of running first strikes them. When the germ of the idea first came to Abe Lincoln it must have been as ludicrous as when it first came to Ronald Reagan. I've got Gore Vidal's book on Lincoln somewhere; another one I didn't get through. (I remember checking up on Lincoln and realising he was the *sixteenth* president of the US; and thinking that I needed to investigate the space between Washington (No. 1) and Lincoln (No. 16) before even attempting to talk seriously to Americans: maybe I should devote a summer ('Life is very short, and Mailer is very long', Vidal says elsewhere) to those books of Vidal's.) But, to the UN.

I was in a hotel with the delegates; we were all writers; the names of the high fliers were all there, printed on an envelope, all writers, most of them known to me, some of whom were contributing to my group novel – extending its life into dream. (A couple of these friends have recently died but they were alive then – another way of extending your life: having your friends dream about you when you're dead!) Anyway, there was this man, this poet, I felt very close to (he was 79 when he died). We were checking out of the hotel and presumably heading for New York. So we must have had one of those writers' meetings at the hotel (like the jamboree in Paris but much, much plusher than Paris), and I was going back to my room to pack when my friend (of 79) went past in the other direction, already packed. He didn't have a trolley, but one of those platforms-on-wheels things that you get on train stations, piled as high as I've ever seen them. The size of the luggage convinced me that this man was serious, the UN job was his. Of course when I woke and lingered over the dream with the dead poet, I saw all his stuff on the trolley, inevitably, as a sort of warning to me, wanting to take it with you when you go, sort of thing. Maleness. The inability to let go. The patheticness of possessions. Me, surrounded by books here in Sheffield, dying an Ionesco-ish death on stage. Lee in London. Lindsay in Boston. (Let go of Lindsay; must write to her.) The ruin in Spéracèdes. Ruin in St Caesare. The suitcases of my friend, the poet, had been suspiciously new; smart. (Must reread Dante.)

On a more, perhaps, practical note, thinking back on papers I'd recently marked, I was struck by how few dream-sequences there'd been in the work. True, we'd all cautioned against the mildly interesting story which ended – *and then I woke up*. Sub-GCE stuff. But at the same time we drew attention to how you could profitably use the dream. Or to the fact that some works (Adamov's *Professor Taranne*) were dreams written down. (In a rather unworthy spoof of Smythe I was thinking of writing, I had him complaining that none of the poems in this batch had grouse-shooting themes, say; 'The Glorious 12th' having no resonance for students at City.) Later – sleeping becoming a problem – I wondered if it was the wasted £130, the trying to envisage what it would buy in the Third World, that had brought on this dream: who's doing serious work on the dream literature of Bangladesh and Somalia? I'm sure the post-colonial brigade are into this; some I've come across are very active, determined to take literature to those outposts which even the Bible missed. (*O, for a reflective Edward Said as neighbour, as colleague.*) Maybe I'm doing the lumpenlecturers an injustice but when I hear them talk, I think: come on: would you get past the interview to serve at my grandmother's table in Coderington? Don't be mean; they've let us write ourselves into the literary Bible, and here are our signatures all over the text: Achebe. Rushdie. Narayan. Walcott. Naipaul. Soyinka. Atwood. Mailer. All of that stuff reassures me as long as

I don't hate that lot as much as Carrington does, I'm still in a game
not yet run; I can still think how to account for my wasted £130.
But there's a problem: what to say to the guy in New Guinea, in
Tobago who dreams of becoming President of the US one day – and
sleeping with the women in *Baywatch*? But I suppose if you're poor
there are worse fantasies to have.

11

Balham called again. (Balham, a man who refused to be killed, refused to be put down, refused to stay found out.) I was feeling positive; I'd cleared a lot of space, the space I usually clear when I'm going abroad, paying the bills, gas, water, telephone. The Bradford address on the Yorkshire Water bill got me thinking again about the lecture I'd have to give at the Central Library there. Initially, it was supposed to be part of the Writer-on-Writer series though they were promoting it nationally, and I thought I'd do something on Walcott, or even Carrington. But the library people were pretty relaxed so I was thinking of maybe doing something about the university as public space.

That was a detail, but the flexibility of not making up my mind on this pleased me, made me think I was extending my own mental space, and hopefully expanding my work to fill it. I'd gone through all my old playscripts (if I was going to do this for Carrington, might as well do it for myself) and realized that the problem in the past was in trying to revise them. They were what they were; some of them worked well enough; they could go to the archives, if anybody wanted them. But I was still attached to the material, which I'd consistently underdeveloped, evidence of self-censorship everywhere. (I'd promised to do something about this after my mother's death, and hadn't.) What all this stuff needed was *narrative*: that's what I'd do, turn these bit plays into a massive novel. That'd take care of the half-sabbatical coming up. That and the volcano play. And coming in still to do the special studies. And the admin...

The novel could rescue all those sorts of things that were lumpy and sketchy on the stage. In the novel I could accommodate meeting someone, a woman, at a party and saying: why not pop in sometime for a cup of tea, and then coming home one day to find the woman on my doorstep about to ring my doorbell. Well, the enormity of that; a casual remark materializing into a woman of substance, young, maybe beautiful, cared for – for years and years cared for, dressed, the clothes casually (or carefully) worn today enough to feed someone from Burkina Faso for a year – *on your doorstep*. Well, that isn't the *start* of it: this thing I'd casually

summoned up had a doctor and a dentist, neither of whom would
confuse her with anyone else; she had or had had parents and
relatives; boyfriends; girlfriends (girlfriends?). She'd visited countries and had encountered the problems of waking up somewhere
else (*Another Part of the Wood*? A little play within the novel? Or an
attempt at a love poem, the love sequence that Smythe couldn't
write). My *novel* would accommodate this. When my optician
casually says: *You're shortsighted*, the *novel* could cope with the
resonances of that.

And then Balham (the fool) rang; what I'd been doing, though
I hadn't thought of it in that way, was rejecting Balham and all
his works. I've got a friend who used to complain about the
telephone; the fact that it was a breach of her space; anyone
could ring up, catch her off-guard, bring unwanted narrative into
her life. She wasn't interested in going ex-directory, that was
another form of exclusion she didn't need. Not that I felt like this
about Balham; I was amazed at how easily I could accommodate him now and still have space for myself.

I did have one thought, then – recalling something that Lee had
said about dreams – that I had a sort of responsibility in protecting
people I knew through what I thought about them. So my earlier
reminiscences had brought on a stage-Balham. Did I do this to other
people: Lee. Lindsay. My mother? Once, two or three years ago when
I was having some very uncharitable thoughts about the ruin in
Spéracèdes, I got a letter from Lindsay, out of the blue, the first one
in about two years. Where were the thoughts to bring forth the book
on my grandmother, dead since 1953, same year as Stalin: I hadn't
done for her what Solzhenitsyn, a victim and critic, had done for
Stalin in *The First Circle*. I hadn't rescued my own father from his
mysterious fate (Unknown Soldier?), not spoken about much in the
family. My *novel*.

I can now look at all that Balham Berlin stuff as a detail, a
fragment of the past, as something that has merely happened in my
life.

*

Berlin. January, 1990

When I got back to the Vietnamese restaurant on Otto-Grotewohl-Strasse Balham and Inge had gone and there was a note for me, regretting, etc. I was actually relieved. My hands were frozen and I decided instead of hanging about and eating on my own, to go back to the *Plaza* over the border. There was no queue the other way (German pedestrians, as I discovered earlier, crossed elsewhere). The main difficulty of this international border (a little house you had to go through) was whether you went through the wrong 'unmarked' door into a sitting-room and remained in the East, or through that corridor, turn right, show your papers and have someone press a button under his desk to open a door into the West. (That put me in mind of a game we used to play in St Caesare, when we were children. We lived in the British sector, but we had family, like my Aunt Augusta, in the North, the French half of the island. I remember my cousin Horace and I setting out for Aunt Augusta's, using the back way, the bush road, and stumbling into the French village, Dumaville, before we realised that we had crossed into France. There was nothing to distinguish the acacia trees on this side from the acacia trees on the other side. I remember Horace and I, observing them closely – we were about eleven at the time – determined that there must be a difference between Britain and France.)

Just across the street was an underground station: Potsdamer Platz. (I began not just to observe these names, but to write them down: they might end up in a talk for Radio Four): one change to Uhlandstrasse, and home. Balham and I had supper in the hotel. I was tired and wanted to relax, and I suspected Balham's invitation to go East again to sample night life on Karl Marx Plaza wasn't meant to be taken seriously. The Plaza dining-room was a bit grim, ill-lit either for lovers or pensioners and, indeed, made me wonder if Balham and I weren't doing a passable imitation of men, sad, lonely farts approaching 50. Balham, though, seemed ahead of the game: I caught the girl who served us glancing at him in that calculating way which made me suspect – and Balham's nonchalance, his smugness which made me *know* – that something was afoot. The random nature of his conversation confirmed this. He said something about his meeting with Inge; then about Frau Halterbush whom he described in rather racist terms. He also talked about Lee as if they were old friends, and made some point or other about Islamic art in Berlin. At some point Balham was wondering if, instead of mucking about with art, we shouldn't be selling condoms, safe and reliable ones, to the East Germans. He was sure that the UN or some international Agency would fund it. He seemed rather put out that Inge had a husband. 'She's curious about you,' he said, finally.

I didn't want to pursue that. So I turned to our reason for coming to Berlin.

'So, the exhibition's on?'

'Art exhibition. Poetry reading at the Humboldt, the whole thing. I've pencilled you in.'

'Me? What for?'

'Oh, to talk about colour-blindness in your plays. Your characters could be German!'

I had never liked this man. I finished my drink, and I took myself up to the fifth floor, to watch television, wondering vaguely whether we'd missed out in not going East.

*

The phone rang in Sheffield.

'I'm off to Berlin,' I said, 'call you when I get back.' When the caller hung up I was ashamed at the lie.

*

1990

Breakfast was not at the *Plaza*, for which we had paid in advance, but at the *Kopenhagen*. The *Kopenhagen* was just a cafe round the corner from the Plaza, on the main street. It was virtually empty as we sat in what seemed vaguely like a greenhouse, all glass and plants, facing the street, working through our bits and pieces – cheese, sausages, etc, with Balham burbling on about the political differences between *Die Welt* and the *Leipziger*

Volkszietung. I couldn't read German after all *my* time in Germany, never mind Balham. This was Balham's delayed adolescence, his Paris '68 outing which we had both missed, though he lied about it. We were having our German breakfast, looking out on Kurfurstendamstrasse on a Sunday morning pretending that this was not just a cafe round the corner from the Mercedes Benz showrooms on Knesebeckstrasse (a name no TV pundit would have cause to remember) – here we are pretending that this was Paris of the '20s, the Boulevard St Germain: here we are (where is the woman, where is Lee? *Helas*!) sitting in the *Deux Magots* with its Americans and Surrealists, reordering, restructuring. Or again: we might be on Montparnasse – *La Coupole* and Josephine Baker, or at the *Dôme* – long after Lenin and then Trotsky hid here – denying that we're American scribblers. Ah.

But reality breaks in. January 1990. Berlin. Balham and I are conscious of so many single, black men drifting through the city, looking lost, making *deracinated* seem more than a faded, slightly pseudish abstract term: we were, partnerless, contributing to that image. Though it could be worse: all those jabbering idiots crossing the street, one jabbering idiot, it seemed, at each set of traffic-lights. Pressure. Pressure of the flesh. There was so much *flesh* on these people. These were solid, well-fed, well-dressed German gentlemen, openly wearing animal skins like everyone else. That image helped reassure me. If I were Balham, I would train my video camera on all this 'ammunition' and use it for home consumption back in England. But I was wrong in supposing that Balham was thinking along these lines. He had lapsed into his own world which he revealed by talking about 'strategic openings' in the East. I wasn't listening. I was back in my world in more congenial company, an old partner – a partnership to be renewed? Thinking not to miss another Prague Spring of the feelings, another May '68 in Paris, to renew that touch, now beginning to fade, the sound of the voice, the taste of salt on skin after tennis. Or a mannerism that made me pause at strangers in the street – all this cloud, mist, clearing, till with rising anger I apprehend Balham: he is like something mechanised, like a drill, going through something soft.

'And what's the strategy for today?'

We agreed to meet at the Pergamum at 2 o'clock; there I'd be shown the space in the basement they had earmarked for the Black Arts exhibition; there I would meet the formidable Frau Halterbush. Of the exhibition, Balham thought they might take a selection from what he referred to as *The Other Story*, a current London exhibition of Black Art at the Heywood Gallery. Or again, they might concentrate on those who had boycotted *The Other Story*: those who had objected to being ghettoised in London but wouldn't mind being black in Berlin.

At some point over breakfast we agreed to open a bookshop in Berlin (it seems as if we meant East Berlin) and we recalled the history of such ventures in London, the assaults made on them by fascists (and, some say, by the police) in the '70s, the '80s. In this connection, I had no objection to Balham using military imagery. We were nineties men, Balham assured me: our decade would involve not just publishing lots of books and making films, and establishing our presence in this or that unlikely place; not just being in Azania at the right time to hear Mandela's presidential speech and to dance with young Winnie after the proceedings, not just being there to vote in other people's elections in order to discredit them (a thing he'd done early and often in the West) *but* to provide an arts framework for cover. This must be the decade of the black man as arts administrator, etc.

I didn't get to the Pergamum at two because I took the official tour to the East and that caused problems. I took the tour because, with my BBC talk in mind, I wanted to hear how the Germans were talking about themselves, to see how they presented themselves to foreigners. The bus left the top of the road, on Kurfurstendamstrasse, twice a day, at 11 am and 2 pm. It was cheap. DM43: DM30 for transport and DM13 for the Guided Tour. We sorted out our visa formalities on the bus. Very relaxed. No one was turned back or held up. Americans. British. A Japanese family. Me. A few Germans, too.

We crossed further north than I'd expected, along Invalidenstrasse. The name suggested the usual ironies that would pass for wit on the BBC. At the border there was a short hold-up, entry formalities, change of driver and guide. The East German official who boarded actually looked everyone in the face to see that we matched the picture on the passport: would he have spotted it if I had been carrying Balham's? Or would he know the difference between our Japanese family and the one staying at the Plaza? Crude thoughts kept surfacing as we crossed the Spree river, but the commentary of the guide prevailed. We learnt that there were 50 checkpoints between East and West, etc. We went past a theatre where *My Fair Lady* was playing; past the new sleek Japanese-built International Trade Center (like a single-towered World Trade Center in New York?): I jotted down the name of the street: Friedrichstrasse. The guide pointed out the *Grand Hotel*, 'the newest in Berlin,' but I didn't see it; I was on the wrong side of the coach. All in all he was even-tempered, not boastful.

I thought of Inge: would she, as guide, be pointing up the women's role in all this? In this attempt to build socialism. Or better, to dismantle socialism? Instead of statues to heroic doctors outside the hospital, men who had discovered cures for things that we in the West also claimed to have discovered, would she be lamenting the lack of women among them? Was her headache at the restaurant sporadic or a constant feature of her life? But the guide droned on, broke through, telling us about the National Library with its seven million volumes. There's Humboldt University looking very impressive, like a grander and more distinguished version of University College, London. Unter den Linden (future site of our bookshop: *Balham & Stapleton*?): I took in the grand sweep of the university steps, half-expecting to see Balham.

Two o'clock at the Pergamum was going to be difficult because our tour ended at two, back in the West; and although we were going to visit the Pergamum, I doubt whether they'd appreciate my doing a bunk. And now for the Changing of the Guard.

We were outside the building with the eternal flame, honouring the War dead (my father had died during the War, we never knew how, where: which side had disposed of him?); the bus stopped to give us a good view. This was going to be the famous goose-step. First, three soldiers came out of an adjacent building on the right, as we looked at it, about twenty yards away, marching more or less normally, if a little flamboyantly, towards the building with the flame. After about ten yards they stopped, changed arms, and then

did the goose-step for a few impressive yards, which brought them
up to the steps of the building. Right turn, then up to relieve their
fellows, who then reversed the process. The unflattering comments on the bus (by an American to her grown-up son) counter-
pointed the guide who explained that the goose-step had nothing
to do with Hitler, but was an ancient German rite (reich?) And that
it was ceremonial.

We didn't stop at Brecht's theatre, but talked a lot about
Meyerhold, who had a street named after him. (Is there a
Mandela Allee?) The rest was the tourist picture we know,
uninviting apartment buildings on Karl Marx Allee. Pollution.
Though we saw a Christmas tree stuck high up on an upper
floor: it was tied to the window, on its side, breaking the
monotony. The Soviet Memorial Park was as expected, its
symbolism obvious; the stone entrance (brown, Swedish gran-
ite) sloping away on both sides representing flags at half-mast.
At the high points, monumental figures symbolising Youth &
Age. Lots of panels with stories to tell. At the far end on a
mound (there were bodies, they said, buried here) another
monumental figure with a broken swastika under foot and a
child held aloft. It was, of course, vandalised, which we knew,
and I'm sure that the guide, lying to us about why it was
cordoned off, knew we knew.

We got to the Pergamum about a quarter past one, so I made
only a halfhearted attempt to locate Balham and Halterbush. I asked
a couple of women attendants if they were Frau Halterbush and
they said no. Actually, the first one said no, and the other (who,
I obviously knew wasn't the successful revolutionary) clearly misunderstood, thought I was asking for the exit, and showed me out.
Too early, as it happened. I was one of the first back on the coach.
But I'd taken a look at the place. The Greek and Roman temples I
remembered. The huge Babylonian street (detail) seemed newer
and bigger than before. These would survive the revolution. The
space I would have liked for Black Arts, on the top floor, was
occupied by an Iranian display, very detailed, including contemporary novels and books of verse. (I took down a few titles to see what
Lee would make of them.) *Our* projected space was in the basement
(symbolism?) and roped off.

Inside (it was only half-past one, then) I scrawled a note to Balham, being careful to refer to him as Lord Balham, and left it with an attendant. I thought maybe that, too, would become a document of the revolution.

The bus pulled out well before two; no Balham, no Halterbush.

I was leaving for France next day. I wanted to spend the day in the West, visit some bookshops in the Tiergarten area, drift down to the Free University at Dahlem-Dorf. The girl at reception seemed to expect something of me. She was the one who'd served us at dinner the night before, and seemed to have entered Balham's harem. She seemed young, frail. (She was one of three people there, in the foyer, two young women and a man. They were pleasant, giving us the wrong information about the city. The man was uniformed, plump, already fading into the background. The girls didn't seem to wear uniforms. Maybe they wore them so well you didn't notice. Balham's woman had strong hands. The virus of fat hadn't yet got to her. She was tall, and had peasant's hands.)

Yet it seemed boorish not to wait for Balham to do the bookshop together. So I hung about... She didn't really have peasant's hands, they hadn't done peasant's work, particularly: the largeness and strength played up the slimness of her figure. The face was strong (impossible not to dwell on this after her encounter with Balham); the mouth was strong, erotic. You imagined the hands doing what hands do. Yet, no bulk at all. It wasn't entirely to please her that I twice used the shoeshine machine round the corner next to the lift. Using the shoe-polisher put me in mind of early years in Köln, encountering my first bread-slicer at the local bakery in Buckfrost, and having my bread sliced. Anyway, why am I thinking so much about Balham's woman; mine – whom I can no longer call mine – is so much more engaging.

Later, another woman: I didn't notice her hands. I'd popped back, without Balham, from the bookshop, to warm up. Berlin was stupidly cold. (I understood now what it must have been like that year of the airlift. Or was that supposed to be the mild winter? I forget.) I'd bought a wurst on the pavement, mildly surprised that the stall-holder was Indian: I'd expected the Turks to have moved into this area by now. (We used to buy Turkish pizzas, in

Ebertplatz, in the old days.) So I was fired by idle curiosity to see who was doing what in Germany these days. That's what I was churning over when I went back up to my room. The door was open and inside was a young Asian woman cleaning. She seemed to panic slightly at my approach. Was it *me*? I indicated she could continue, ignore me. Before I withdrew I did the usual sort of thing – tidied a few papers on the desk, put empty bottles from the minibar onto the tray on top of the fridge, etc – to indicate that I didn't really think of her as a maid. And to put her at ease, I asked where she came from.

'Thai.'

'Thailand!'

She nodded, but speeded up her work as if she were under sentence not to pause.

'What's your name?'

She was about to answer when a very large lady, young and slow-moving, strode majestically along the corridor past us. She glanced in and smiled, giving me a little nod, and continued down the corridor without breaking her stride. I turned again to the young woman from Thailand.

'So, what's your name?'

This time the panic was unmistakable. Without stopping her hoovering, she indicated in dumb show the woman who had just gone past. I knew who she was; she was in charge of the cleaners: I'd seen her at the stores cupboard next to the lift on this floor sorting out towels and toiletry; but the panic of the young Thai seemed out of all proportion to being simply an oppressed employee. So, she was illegal. She would now face competition from Germans coming over from the East. Nevertheless, this was 1990. I had to show that I didn't collude in this: how to do it without getting the poor woman sacked? It was in this mild confusion that I picked up the first thing my hands fell on – a pair of shoes – and walked out of the room with them. What do you do with a pair of shoes, except to go to the shoe-cleaning machine, at the bottom of the lift!

There was a note for me from Balham, at the desk.

*

Ah, why romanticise the past! Later that night, I rang Lee to tell her about the nightmare. Guilt, surely, for thinking of going to Berlin after the marking rather than coming down to London to her launch party. But confessing this sort of dream had to be more healthy than ignoring it. So this is the dream.

I'm on to the autoroute with Balham. He is driving. After about half an hour, we turn off at a sign saying 'Les Adrets' (this is in the South of France; I know it well). The supply road is narrow and winding. It's night; why is it always night with Balham? We cross the bridge over the lake, which I imagine to be the one that we could see from our vantage point at Cabris, Lac de St Cassian. Then we cross the main road and head up the hill to Montauroux. (Trust Balham to choose a French-sounding village for his rendezvous. My villages, in the other Departement, are Spéracèdes (which, to most people sounds Greek) and Cabris, which no one can pronounce with confidence because, knowing it to be French, they hesitate to pronounce the 's', and so people think they're talking about Capri. But no, Balham must head towards Montauroux.)

This is still the dream. The village had gone to bed. I have a sensation of Balham as a night person. My other friends are day-people, like me. Lee, well you're an afternoon person, an evening person, a something-promising-to-happen person while Balham is a looking-for-evidence person. If I were a normal sort of person, a woman, I would be a bit frightened of Balham. But I was Balham's equal at Balham's game, he had to know that. The large square with its stopped clock on the Hotel de Ville is larger than I expected – an act of will to produce this perfectly flat space on the top of the mountain village – space for the boule-players, bowls, the hangers-on. Tunisians, etc. These Var villages are more spacious than those in the Alpes Maritimes. I somehow prefer the cosiness of the Alpes Maritimes. Though, as I'm thinking this, I have to admit that the road out of the village, with its awkward bends, its narrowness, the houses and shops jutting out at odd angles – that this is *very* Alpes Maritimes. Balham negotiates his way out of the village like a native. Though this is meant for my benefit, it's still impressive. About a quarter of a mile along a road with plane trees saving us from the precipice on the left, we come to a whole panel of street signs, and Balham just hesitates, before taking a turn. And we're climbing again.

At the top of the winding road, at another junction, he hesitates – longer pause now, to make it look good – and decides on a dirt road. It's evening. We drive down the lane, villas on both sides at irregular intervals, but little sign of life; the odd light on. (Balham is telling the story about how easy it is to register to vote in New York, and how he has voted in two presidential elections just to show how corrupt the system is; and that to emphasise the corruption of the system, it is important to vote Republican, or even something further right, if anything further right could be found; so that when you reveal all, it's not the long-suffering Democrats who would have egg on their face; not that he was an apologist for the Democrats, who were indistinguishable, in ways that mattered, from the rest.)

Maybe a quarter of a mile on, the road worsens, not gravel now but dirt, and rutted. South of France. Fortunately, it hasn't been raining. It's hard, maybe frost-hard. It's cold at this altitude.

A dog barking. Balham, ignoring it, manages not to run it over. The house on the left, to which it belongs, is set back from the road, 30 yards, 40 yards. No one looks out. No lights. No more villas now, trees on both sides, forest. A ruin. Then a tight curve to the left, and we stop.

In the distance, on a rise, a large house, two storeys, partly hidden behind trees. A large evergreen shields it. This is a rather grand structure, like some of those renovations we used to do in the Alpes Maritimes, old mills, etc for American industrialists and Parisian and German bankers.

But this one is square, severe – why so high? Not your ordinary villa. Elaborately landscaped, lots of terraces leading up to it, with fruit-trees, etc. Oliviers. And at the very bottom, tennis-courts. Balham doesn't attempt to drive up to the villa; the road goes along the length of the tennis courts, which takes it left of the house, and presumably then does a loop and right again at what is obviously the pool – we could see the pool-house – right under an upstairs terrace.

'We won't go in,' Balham says, clearly knowing what I'm thinking. 'Security lights. They come on, automatically.'

I am neither surprised nor impressed. This is the Highgate experience all over again, the man is disturbed.

'See that window?'

There is no light in any of the windows.

'The middle one.'

I can see it. There are three windows on the upper floor, which can be seen, despite the evergreen. Two on the right are close together, which suggests they are in the same room; then one on its own. On the left is a door, framed in its private terrace. Windows and door are shuttered, occupants away. He's clearly referring to the window in the middle, on its own.

'The fat judge jumped from that window,' he says, and then starts to turn the car around.

And then I woke up. Lee's suggestion of therapy for these bad dreams depressed me. Didn't she realise I was telling her how the world looked at night in her absence? The irritating thing, the really irritating thing, is that we never got around to talking about her book.

*

Lee suggested I was suppressing something more profound than distrust of Balham. But we'd talked about that before; I'd written about it; I'd even made money out of that Berlin experience with Balham last time round. It was my sort of party-piece, encountering the dead man in the street as I tried to get out of Berlin and head for France.

At the top of the road from the Plaza, before crossing over, I ran into a little knot of people. Something going on, as we weren't exactly at the lights. Big, well-dressed Germans, lots of animal skins. I edged my way round the source of attraction – a dead man on the ground. I saw the man's face turn purple and the crowd looking on. I saw the body abused by officials while we (yes, me too) looked on... and at some point I picked up my case and started walking. When I stopped I was back at the hotel, the Plaza and, with a minimum of formality, was back up to my recently vacated room on the fifth floor. I sat on the bed in my coat, fingers frozen; then got up and washed my hands in warm water to get the circulation back, and then moved to the – ridiculously narrow – desk. Pen and paper were provided. What to make of this little scene outside the Cafe

Kopenhagen. A little crowd. Middle of the day. 12.30. Man lying on the pavement. Heart-attack. Crowd looking on, well-dressed, well-fed. Animal-skins. The ambulance crew, two young men, both muscular and fat – strange combination: you expect them to have high-pitched, singing voices. They are the attendants. One pulls the dead man's shirt free of the trousers in one swift movement and with the scissors, – large new-looking scissors – cuts the shirt open and swiftly puts the oxygen mask on the man; starts pumping the man, the flesh, the dead. This can't be right. It's freezing. He's crushing the man's chest. (Shouldn't he be kissing him instead?) The dead man is middle-aged, not rich, mouth open, stained teeth (upright, he could be at the dentist's). He's going purple. A muscular man is pumping the dead man's chest. Sexual rite? People looking on, impenitent. (Must try harder.) Police half-heartedly shooing us away. You note the name of the street when there's a dead man on it. Knesebeckstrasse.

Is it moral to make money out of these dreams? Discuss. In this one they're torturing my mother; I'm not going to dwell on how: what is it? Is this what late-night TV brings on? Is it the *news*, the pornography of news? Do they think I'm someone who could be endlessly abused, trifled with: *do they think I'm a nice man? They.*

The first dream (they come like buses, in quick succession after a long wait) – the first one about Lee, pleasantly about Lee, is interrupted as the second, unwanted, bus rolls up. The second one was about squatters, young people, sort of thuggish-looking, slightly overweight and polite, white-skinned, short-cropped hair: they've taken possession of our house, my house, my mother's house. They lie around, languid, on soiled sheets, lots of them; I have to dislodge them without violence (the family have asked little of me so far, but to dislodge young thugs from their house, without violence), and I don't manage that; there is violence, against my mother; and now I'm in fighting mood. Oh Natalie, I have been generous with you; I have been *gentle* with you. I have, criminally, shielded you from your failure to *imagine*. Hopefully, you have a sister, a friend who's doing her physics, her chemistry; easier to assess her worth. Sorry, my love, sorry. Get out of my life and let me get on with my Art; fulfil my destiny as a little-know figure.

In bullish, writing mood, I sit down at my desk and think of nothing much and tap something out. If it's a play I'll give it to my tormentors, my co-authors (anyone's welcome). It seems to be called:

Was Ist Los in Huddersfield?
Characters (to include):

WIDOW FROM LIMAVADY
WHITE RACIST (woman) MARRIED TO BLACK RACIST (man)
MAN IN WHEELCHAIR FOR 30 YEARS (known to be able to walk)
SHEIKH HASINA WAZED, PRIME MINISTER OF BANGLADESH
STAPLETON'S GRANDMOTHER, BALHAM'S AUNT FROM LUTON,
CARRINGTON'S FATHER (The Bishop of Toronto?)
THE SOUND OF A CREAKING DOOR (a male character)
THE FILTER OF LIGHT FROM A DOOR, AJAR (a female character)
BEARDED MAN IN KINGSTOWN, ST VINCENT, RECITING THE LETTERS
OF HELOISE & ABELARD (maybe word-perfect, in French) TO
PASSERS-BY
TWO-BATTY HAYNES
FRAU HALTERBUSH
LEE

After a little tussle of who had the right to the Tuscan scene (my grandmother or Balham's aunt from Luton) we agreed to let them share it: I had a stake in Italy because of fond memories of my Italians from Bari and further back, of my sister's first husband, the 'artist' da Firenze, Florence's father. I even had O level Italian, for Christ's sake, and drove as a first year student, to Italy that summer. I would take not only my grandmother but all the women in the family, for their photo-call from *the palazzo de Signora* in Florence. OK, that's me. Balham, on the other hand, would come armed with statistics on Italy to prove something or other that we couldn't be bothered to work out. I suppose that gave him the right to take his Luton aunt to Florence.

This was going to be Lee's play heavily disguised. The gullible would be distracted by the grotesquerie. The man, 30 years in the wheelchair, who could walk all the time, was too Pinterish, they'd say; the Widow from Limavady too Irish, too sexist; the Grandmother (done it, done it) and the white racist/black racist couple too ahead of its time (the English audience can't be expected to face that sort of reality; not a white English audience, not a black English audience); TWO-BATTY HAYNES and the BANGLADESH PRIME MINISTER had possibilities. Haynes was a rough man from St Caesare, from the islands, cane-cutter sort of thing; comes over in the '50s; goes to America, maybe, makes a lot of money and isn't into all this rubbish of passing on wealth to the next generation who are lay-abouts, on the dole anyway, pimps and teenage mothers, that sort of thing – Herr Michael Howard's people. So this man Haynes, goes to a special clinic in Switzerland (or maybe St John's Wood) and has an extra arse grafted on to the side of the present one so that he can take up two seats on the aeroplane (he can afford it) or in the cinema, and further, to show what he thinks of those who find him crude, to be able to shit *twice* on the world whereas those without the operation could shit only once. I saw possibilities in Two-Batty Haynes.

With Sheikh Hasina Wazed, it would be nice if she could pull off her coup to bring those fellows to justice – fellows who killed her father, old Mujib, so messily, twenty-odd years ago and got away with it, with cushy postings to China and Argentina and Denmark. (Puts me in mind of that Ingrid Bergman-Anthony Quinn film where the lady – in a white dress? – steps off the train and demands *justice*.)

I'll include Rolls as well, in the *Dramatis Personae*. I'd got him to the point where he was virtually Canadian – missing hockey and maple-syrup like mad. And I had him pursuing his *Gothic* thing from – what was it? – *The Italian & The Monk & Dracula & Silence of the Lambs* to discovering a cache of stuff in some forbidden German castle (I read about this in the *TLS*) called the *Corvey Collection*, and bringing it all to City and putting the place on the scholarly map and then being head-hunted to McGill, having rejected Cambridge and Anglia University-Polytechnic – all done with a private Canadian gesture that I could imagine

Margaret Trudeau to have employed that night she spent with the Stones. I made Rolls a tall, handsome man (he was slightly tall and slightly handsome but I made him really tall and handsome like a Mountie, hoping this would undermine his confidence, slightly) to see what problems he'd have as he gradually turned into a woman in the play: would he have the imagination to embrace it? Would he resist his luck? A modern gothic tale. (Would Liz, the wife-writer, write it up with me?) *Is this a better way of occupying my time then just going ahead and dramatizing the Symposium of Mr Plato?*

Carrington's plays are about colonizing territory, gaining hinterland. O God, O God, I'm turning into an academic. Sweet Allah, show me another path. Prerogative/curse of the small-islander. Plays set in all five continents. A man more travelled than Columbus. Brathwaite's Tom? No. *Carrington is a dramatist without a theme.* But what's a dramatist without a theme? We would have to call him a playwright (ugh) not a dramatist? He makes plays out of lists of names, cricket scores, lists of garrison commanders in Mauritius, the flight details at the airport; his e-mail... Actually I don't recall a Carrington play about e-mail. (A gap in the Carrington *oeuvre*?) Got you. Bastard.

Private folders	*From*	*Subject*	*Received*
Inbox	A+ Bettige, T	Urgent: RAE - PREPARATION	1/18/96 2:09 PM
Sent Mail	A+ Baxter, J	FW: hefce	1/26/96 4:53 PM
Wastebasket	A Treefell, J	FW: Urgent message	2/13/96 4:55 PM
	A Miller, A	Prizewinning Writers	2/13/96 5:03 PM
	A Worgirl, M	BA/Humanities Research Board: N	2/30/96 12:35 PM
	A+ Bettrid, T	FW: Research funding , questionnaire	3/11/96 12:21 AM
	A Earnsh, P	Research seminars	3/17/96 4:34 PM
	A Casey, J	Level 2 'Little' Book Entries	3/18/96 3:21 PM
	A Slater, P	RE: English office printer	3/23/96 3:03 PM
		15 messages. 8 unread. 7:13 PM	

No, not even Carrington could make anything of this – unless
you changed the setting to a village somewhere in whatever distant
country was fighting its civil war. And even then... But going back
to our group play: the one about the racists might be interesting.
Funnily enough I thought Carrington had done that. I'm sure we
talked of it back then, in St Vincent – each one giving the other a
year to do it, sort of thing. But I don't remember the play. Must get
down to Kent, to the archives. Must ring the man in Maryland.

But first, why not map out those talks for Radio Four.

SIX Talks (Proposal)

1:   *Pride or Race or Class?* (What makes you unable to settle
     for second best. A privileged state? An oppressed state?)

2:   *Defence of Poetry* (not Philip Sidney, – 'Fool... look in they
     heart and write' – but my sister's refusal to allow her daughter
     to run and jump at school – 'So who's she running and jumping
     from?')

3:   *Racism on Campus* ('accountants' treating you as intellectual
     equals; imaginative equals. My first computer PASSWORD, was
     SUNSHINE – selected by the technician – a minor 'accountant')

4:   *A Place to Hide: An Immigrant's Diary Exposed.*

5:   *Reparations* (people recovering their public spaces: clocks,
     parks at night, transport systems, universities, etc. ('Opti-
     mism' as public space?)

6:   Natalie confronted by a 'no coloured' sign – 1950s? 2010?
     Natalie erecting a 'whites only' sign – 2020?

A Place to Hide is something I'm trying to think through before
it resurfaces as dream; as Gothic nightmare. I'd just written up a
new address book; and yet again when it came to 'S' I couldn't
bring myself to put Stapleton on the first page. Instead, I filled up

three pages with all sorts of junk; with other people's names, with institutions beginning with 'S' – South Bank Centre. St Caesare Associations in England, etc. And only then did I slip in my own name: was this the lack of preening which was female? Was it the sense of not wanting to be exposed, to be on the frontline in an alien space? Were the Balhams of this world less clownish than they seemed – more courageous – for going the other way, for appearing to go the other way. That was the talk. That was the BBC talk. That was all six talks.

*

I spoke to Carrington. An Irish play, yes, but not O'Neill.

*

Carrington's idea of a play, a work of art, as a big thing that doesn't scar the landscape or make permanent noise, certainly will modify the way I write about him. In one sense he's all splash. Lope. And yet the idea of playwright as great architect works for him. He manages not to despoil the skyline, except at those times when the play is performed – and the space taken up isn't vertical. The play is invisible to those who don't want it. As to the question of erecting a structure: almost any other construct, apart from music, colonises more space, permanently. But what of the ego thing: could it be that someone like Carrington, with all these plays, isn't as *male* as we think? Because imaginative art doesn't force you off the pavement, apartheid-like; will always vacate its space when you need it! Will disappear when you get bored with its presence. Ah, this is getting complicated.

*

I'm at the airport, I'm at Heathrow; why not ring the university; the Department. Where am I? I'm at the airport. No, I'm not coming from anywhere, I'm going somewhere. Any messages? OK. And the scripts for marking (must get on with my volcano play); the scriptwriting. That's fine, that's fine. I'll get on to that when I get back. Not sure, yet, where I'm heading. Not sure of that, either. Keep you posted. But, hang on. There's one second year script. Short stories. Just want to have someone moderate. Her name....

So, where are we? What's on offer?

AF 819	1900	DELAYED	2000
05956	+1930	VIENNA	
A2209	+1930	ROME	
184189	+1930	ROME	
IB4189	+1930	BARCELONA	
LH4051	+1930	COLOGNE - BONN	
LH4077	1955	MUNICH	
SR837	+1955	GENEVA	
AF821	+2000	PARIS - GDG	

There's the fat Camden judge (unkilled; unhung) and a child-molester hurrying to their plane. Here are a couple of lads who might be the types to hurl abuse at Florence coming back from the corner shop. These lads are leaving the country; good. But I don't like the feel of some of these people coming in, coming home. I'm at the airport. In a Chekhov play, I'd have to get on the plane. So many people who seem to *know* where they're going.

AZ2247	+2000	MILAN
LH4065	+2000	BERLIN-TEGEL
TP459	+2000	LISBON
LH4127	+2005	STUTTGART
IT4447	2010	LYON
LP41111	2030	HAMBURG
IT4499	2030	STRASBOURG
LH4023	2030	NUREMBERG
IT4465	2045	TOULOUSE
OU491	2100	ZAGREB

Is there a decent airport play? Can't think of one. I'm heading for the British Airways ticket desk. That'll narrow the choice. I'm thinking of the postcard I'll send to my colleagues at City.

*

I can think straight here. I'm thinking: a new start. I'm awake; yes. Certain things behind me; behind us. So, it is early; certain things haven't happened. I haven't yet met Lee; but I know now what I didn't know then, before I met Lee. I have a knowledge of Rumi, pre-Lee, and Leopardi in my luggage. I have an awareness of my own too-flexible, too-rigid self. I am passionate about things, the leaves in autumn, sort of thing, the drop of water straining (not straining) to fall from that leaf. I am less intolerant; I will make space in the world for that evil man (but not too much space). I will divest my mind of the pride of knowing (though not completely). I am pre-Socratic. I am ignorant. A little smug in my ignorance (for it would be arrogant to strive for perfection). So, as I say: This is the first day of the rest of our lives. I will ring Lee. I will invent the telephone and ring Lee. She is telepathic; she will know her number. I will call her The Princess.

Born in Montserrat, West Indies in 1939, E.A. Markham completed his education in Britain, which has been his home since 1956. He has worked in the theatre as playwright and director, in the media and as a literary editor. His previous publications include six collections of poems, two of short stories and a travel book.

He has been writer-in-residence at the Universities of Humberside and Ulster, has taught at the University of Newcastle and is now Professor of Creative Writing at Sheffield Hallam University. He is director of the biennial Hallam Literature Festival.

In 1997, E.A. Markham was awarded the Certificate of Honour by the Government of Montserrat.